Lee County Elegy

Courtney Allen

ISBN: 1979932913
ISBN 13: 9781979932912

Part One

Prologue

FOR MYRA, AS travel weary as she had become, the last hours of her journey proved most difficult. Her trip had taken its own time with the arduous train ride steaming north through the flat rural countryside as she read a newspaper and watched the world coast by in a place as serene as the morning sky. For all she had anticipated, going back home after so many years was at best a new beginning, and she held high hopes this would be so. Yet in the worst event she feared what could become of her story, and if that were the case, she certainly wouldn't care but to leave it behind.

She thought through these effects as she watched the day roll by although she didn't know what the outcome might be. From her window in the passenger car, the outreaches of South Georgia up from Americus were the colors of rural solitude: a palate of gold and field-green, the land furrowed earthen-brown, and sparse dwellings set in white against the vast horizon. The distant tree line was a jagged edge black under a sky of blue; birds flying far afield, their angular wings small specs above the land and hills. The train clattered along its track, and she bided her time with memories so washed out they seemed an illusion faraway. The thoughts of yesteryear as if seen through fragile sheets of rice paper held to a window in the morning light, beyond where the veil of faces had become faded and their voices lost to time.

It wasn't her fault the way things had come to pass. This long trip had taken a while in its planning, but the further she came, the more her uncertainty grew. Could family be waiting, ones misplaced while the instances had been sorted through in the last moments of indecision? She supposed they would have done what they could and moved ahead as she had in her own life, not wanting to suffer because of events least understood. Even in the last minutes before leaving for her trip, Myra had wrestled with her thoughts, not knowing what to think.

The day became warm and she lowered the glass window to allow in the breeze. From below she could feel the vibration of the steel wheels and hear the squeaking of the chassis as the train moved over the track and earth. The scent of the loam came in from the farmland, wafting like the taste of minerals, potash and zinc and lime. Sunlight glinted from the glass of the windows and was cast into her squinting eyes.

The conductor of the rail company made his rounds and checked on the passengers from time to time. Yet she paid little attention as she drifted off elsewhere to wonder what could have been if it had transpired in a different way. She looked back reluctantly to the days of her childhood when life had been less certain and assurances harder to find. In a past she hadn't forgotten but had buried long ago with other misgivings to possibly pull from a shelf and dust off in the later years of her life.

The hours stretched on and she had to be patient. To pass the time, she thumbed through an old journal she had in her coat, but she'd read it so many times she knew almost every word. She slipped it away and consulted her watch. By this time, however, she had been waiting so long, what was the hurry now?

Nonetheless, she was prepared. She stowed a suitcase of well-tailored clothing and good leather shoes, light rouge, and perfume she'd bought from a boutique in Albany; also her ivory encased compact, fitted gloves and silk ribbons for her hair. Her wallet contained photographs and information she could share, also an old war medal and cash she'd saved for the trip. In a sense, these effects mollified her apprehension and put her at ease, yet material possessions were only skin-deep. She realized life could be fragile and the value of such so much more when one comes from a hard land of furrowed dirt and lashes from a moldboard plow.

Hours had stretched into days and days into weeks. The days had moved on as slowly as a cold winter night, and she'd counted each off on the calendar over her woodstove box. She'd planned well in advance knowing this time might come, and finally it had. Yet this eventual journey had taken its toll in more ways than one. Not just in the distance from Lee County, but in the heartbreak that bound her to it.

The day was waning into a sky of thick cloud when the landscape began to change. As the track rounded a bend through a draping of oaks and tall pines, the large city of Atlanta came into view and she tensed. It took her breath away and she was stilled by the size of it, the vast structures and all that stood across the gray skyline. Brick buildings and commercial warehouses lined the tracks; industrial plants smoked in the distance; houses and fields of corn interspersed paved roads and churches on the street corners. In one hand she grasped the necklace with a cross on it. In the other she anxiously held her purse. In a last breath, she knew life had a way of holding its own secrets, the kind that when revealed in the closing hours were far from being anticipated ahead of time. So, the thought of returning to the place where her life had begun had become daunting enough. Yet not understanding the circumstances under which she had departed in the first place had brought her this far.

As the landscape transformed and the train entered its last station, she couldn't allow her heart to slow much less predict what might be ahead. The sky was dark and ominous. The crowd was thickening too which certainly didn't calm her nerves. She stood from her padded leather seat and took up her coat to look out the glass windows of the passenger car. From as far back as she could remember, her origins were as unclear as seeing through the storm front gathering over the city she'd come to visit. It had been so long ago, yet she thought she surely might recall the scale of this place: the cars and people, buildings and factories, the smell of petrol exhaust and the acrid scent of burning coal—yet she hardly could. When she stepped off the train into a lingering fog of steam vapor, she was almost rushed away by the crowd on the platform, but she had to turn to retrieve her luggage. A porter assisted her and she walked out to the busy street.

In the streets, the many people moving along the sidewalks were such as the blood quickening through her veins, her cheeks reddening as daylight streamed onto her pretty face. What could be worse? Guessing only left her with further questions, yet not knowing was more difficult. The previous night, she admitted she had planned this trip to find herself here in the city. This meant looking through remembrances of city dwellers and dark backstreets which had run through the recesses of her mind since early childhood. And this, in and of itself was likely the greatest challenge she had faced so far.

She held a set of directions she withdrew from her purse, and she looked one way then the next. She was if anything overwhelmed. However in a country marked by ruin and strife, the world had changed in ways she couldn't understand. The dispossessed stood in their ragged clothes and walked the city's streets. Vagrants mulled about looking for work. They stood in large gatherings in dark alleys between the buildings, circled around paper sacks holding a few loaves of bread. The abandoned that filled the cities of the nation had been presented on the front pages of newspapers across the nation's breast and this frightened her. Talk, too, of another war in Europe was unsettling enough, and all of this seemed to compound her trepidation. But considering she had lost parts of herself along the way, she realized she was not exactly blessed in ways that fairytales were written. After all, none of it had come easily by any means.

The traffic was thick and big cars moved along the street. People were crossing in all directions. Where could she start? She was looking for a tall spire to the north, one atop the Methodist Church of Atlanta, and also for the woman that had written the letters she had received. That was her first step, she knew. Just then rain began to spatter on the pavement and thunder broke. She had to hurry. Hope was placed upon hope, and she took up her suitcase then tipped the porter as she turned to leave.

She made her way through the people and along the sidewalk. As she neared the church, she could see an old woman standing by the front door. She was wrapped in a shawl and she seemed to be watching. Was this her, she thought? Was this the woman she had come to meet? A rushing sensation ran through her mind, and she paused at the street corner, remembering back.

If this return trip could heal her, this was uncertain and yet to be revealed. To be more precise, if the woman might know and Myra could find herself here, an endearing light would forever shine and so many questions could be answered. With her she carried more than her luggage but the old journal and her own daughter's crucifix, even her past, and her life as well. The journal, however, was not yet completed, and to do so she would have to remember back to when her story first began.

Chapter I

THE FLINT RIVER basin that fell away from Americus in Sumter County lay in the bosom of Lee fifty miles to the south where the verdant fields rested like a patchwork quilt on the bed of the earth. In the good years, they made claim the fields were christened by the hands of their Savior, sun-ripened and sweetened by the first breath of autumn in the fertile land north of Albany, Georgia. However, *in the good years,* before most was lost to misfortune and the roof caved in, the days were as prosperous as they were long. Well enough, although the land was difficult and labor sometimes endless. Yet, the farmlands and mortgaged land grants worked by the parched and back-broken men of Lee County were soon taken by regional banks as the country's strife was made painfully clear in America's economic collapse following the fall of 1929.

Their hardships became unimaginable as seen on their faces of grief. Breadlines of wretchedness were drawn out along the windblown streets in the south and beyond. Crime grew rampantly as desperation overcame many. Hope was gathered but unprecedented destitution prevailed in the waning hours of sunset. In remote cases, some children were abandoned and had no place to live. In South Georgia, many sharecroppers and land tenants took up the rails to Atlanta and were never heard from again. Word was that the railway stations along Albany up to Macon running from Savannah and further south were overrun with the indigent and lost, hungered and decrepit. In the deep south, the tracks were long with sorrow of agrarian poverty that had followed generations from as far back as the sailing ships of Ireland and Scotland. A few wayward landowners who had lost their farms while measuring their imminent despair, took their own godforsaken lives when the roads of abjection became impassable and the burdens of life exceedingly cumbersome. At best, gathered firewood was honest and warmed the souls of many, and for a short while the hens that laid their eggs subsisted on meager crumbs and grit in the barnyard. Yet time ran its course, and the disease of hunger took some of the very best, one by one, as the sun rose on the dawn of the depression era.

The bank man arrived in a Model A Ford, his leather boot hitting the dirt-clod road as he stepped out, wielding papers of foreclosure such as a flag of defeat in front of them huddled on their porches of rotten wood and rusted tin roofs. Butter churns aside frayed-backed cane chairs; doors sagging after decades of neglect; broken lives and broken glass windowpanes against an edifice of clapboard dreams. As if the bank had come with a writ to take their first born. They all pined and said, *Our Savior, God bless, what good are You now?* Although the banker's solemn face was road-weary and dejected as anyone. He had had no other choice, he would summons them. "The bank ain't no charity organization, don't you understand?" And he stepped back with a curt nod when he walked away and drove off in a trailing line of dust to the highway. Many had lost all they had, not to save all they ever *wished* to have.

Years before these tragedies, Myra was a little girl of three with tattered clothing and little to call her own, tears smeared down her chapped face and hands smudged with chocolate the old man had given her in the Atlanta train station. Having seldom traveled much further than a few blocks from her own house, she was naturally frightened to be leaving the city all together. Yet nonetheless, the countryside coasted by with the clatter of rail tracks underneath her wooden seat and the yellow sun high in the morning sky. Years later after she had grown to be a woman, she would hardly recall that day until she had a daughter of her own and finally returned to look for her past in the backstreets of Atlanta. Even with this, she wandered back to the beginnings of her life to help move away from the hardships and misgivings she couldn't resolve, ones that became permanently branded into her heart.

That morning south toward Americus, the rural landscape seemed to run forever with endless fields and no fence lines, a thinly scattered inhabitance scarce of roads, people, or signs of life. A few barns were seen in the vastness with cows dotting the horizon, yet little more than a flat land stretching to the crest of the earth with a wide sky in the distance. Other than a small suitcase, her possessions were few. Yet good fortune was with her as the dawn of a new day awaited at the end of the rail line—this journey she hadn't planned for, yet, nevertheless had undertaken just on the notions of other people, whom incidentally she hardly knew. Mr. Grayson was, after all, a man of his word they promised Myra while helping her onboard through a blur of tears and understandable reticence. She couldn't have known better when the elderly pastor sat her on the train with a sack lunch, southward to Americus, her final destination. Gladly they paid the conductor a gratuity to watch out for her on the long trip, and he had checked on her periodically, faithfully on the way south. Although the church group lacked the money for an accompanying ticket as their charity had limited funds, the conductor fortunately offered charity enough.

Along the ride, few travelers were aboard and although some had smiling faces, several were of austere demeanor, the ones she avoided when she could. She rather preferred to watch out of the glass windows from her assigned seat and eat her lunch from the paper sack. Through several station stops, the ride took the entire day. Yet she eventually arrived, sleepy, yet still alone and bewildered by her circumstances. However, there, she met the kind and gentle Mr. Grayson. She soon learned he was far from being a wealthy man, only one of modest means with a bay jenny, a john mule, and a plot of farmland. Yet, he eventually proved to be a good one having been raised himself they said under the premise of honesty and goodwill, with a heart cast of the purest gold.

She wasn't but three and stood to his knees. He took her down to the water of the Flint and set her out to dog paddle in the light current as he waded closely by. He was such a big man that she sat in the cleft of his elbow like a sack of peaches. But she would smile as they walked up the path from the river's edge because he would sing to her out of key and bounce her in his arm. He had two sons and they all lived in a small house. She had come from such gray surroundings, but as time went she learned to love the tall trees and wildflowers, the deer and birds of the river, the fresh air and the white fields of cotton. Life was good on the farm, and she soon began trips to the schoolhouse and made friends there, too.

Many years following these events, Myra grew to be a teen and the grip of the depression took the country by storm, leaving many in the region homeless or without a means by which to live. In the small towns of South Georgia, the banks were shuttering down, and the dollar was ever more difficult to come by as the days stretched into weeks then months. At the time, Myra was still young. And her family was inevitably so limited with resources that they hardly knew any difference either way.

However, though hard times were to come, a glimmer of good providence arose at the inception of these inclement misfortunes.

In December of 1929, in Leesburg of Lee County, Georgia, the two-room courthouse and annex building burned to the ground, and Mr. Grayson's lien and security deed burned up in the fire along with them. As the story was conveyed, a coal fire escaped the boiler's chest and lighted a pile of workmen's clothing then the wooden beams that supported the government structure. A young black boy by the name of

Mariah Moses had fallen asleep while tending the coal pile just as a trial was being gaveled underway concerning the town's mayor and some elusive funds absent from the city's coffers.

According to what Mariah later told the townsfolk, he was jolted awake when the intense heat roared and the building was suddenly on fire. He had run to the basement door looking for help, but no one was there in back of the building, nothing but standing pines, wild dogwood, and a dumping bin.

After he ran hollering through the streets, the volunteers came from near and far. Yet what little remained of the courthouse was as futile as the paper and parchment floating in the black flames set against the overcast sky. Two sides of the courthouse heaved forward and fell inward as the townsfolk gasped. With that, the lives of many and their records went up in orange-red tendrils and coal soot, such as a stroke of good luck in the winds of great fortune. As the circumstances had evolved, the Great Depression was well underway, and the banks were hungry to reclaim their land deeds, as it stood.

What remained of the roofless courthouse was a partial shell of smoldering and blackened brick. The following years proved that sorting out the details became too arduous. The boundaries of land parcels and property surveys that had been consumed in the fire indefinably weighed in the balance. Yet how can a bank foreclose on a mortgaged plot of land when there-in lies *no governmental records, deeds, tax plats, land titles, or survey maps* with which to conclude a legal case for foreclosure?

Maclin Grayson's length of inherited land was a good ways from Americus when traveling the backroads through Flintside. His property was set on an undulating swell of low-slung hills in Lee County, resting against a long stretch of Lake Blackshear which ran to the north and south. However, fertile and beautiful, their parcel was remote. And the value, regrettably, had become discounted as the outer field wouldn't drain properly after the Corp of Engineers constructed the dam on the

Flint in order to create Lake Blackshear. Just a few inches of rainwater and the lake overflowed its bank, turning their outer stretch of ground sodden. As far as distance, the winding road through Flintside and up to Americus took nearly two or three full days by wagon in the most cooperative of weather, beginning on a road of deep gullies and low marsh rendered by the construction process. From their farm, Flintside was small, and also a difficult trudge around the bend, with not much to look at except a lumberyard, feed store, a few merchants, the school-house, and the church.

"No man was 'ere so poor in his misfortunes as we-uns after that dam was built," Mac Grayson said. He spat chaw into the shadows of the church steps, and quickly added as to the ruinous news of the country's economy, "But I didn't know all was such, cause we are so lacking ourselves."

Mac emphasized this point to his brethren outside of Mount Olive Church after Thomas Burch read the outdated *Albany Herald* article to the congregation. It was a frost-bitten December morning. *Black Tuesday* was the headline; the paper dated October 30, 1929. Most couldn't have read the piece; none were as educated as Burch who was the local schoolmaster. Most of them hadn't reached the third grade as reading and writing couldn't fill a bucket of sweet utter milk or plow a field of earth with the first day of spring.

"Well, Mac," Burch replied. "No one much did either. Like the article says, however, our country has hit the skids. Now everybody knows that the banks may be in trouble, too. But for many, at least there have been no records replaced in the county so far. And there probably won't be for a long while."

"At least, so far," Mac replied

Burch creased the paper and slipped it under his arm. Ten or fifteen locals stood in a circle around him. One man tilted a tin to his lip and

13

tapped in a bump of snuff. Another drew out a pipe and tamped the tobacco just so. As he took a match to the rim, Burch went on. "They'll never get the parcels surveyed off and all the boundaries in place. Not at the rate they're carrying on."

One man, a neighbor of Grayson by the name of Wilton Meyer said, "Hell, it don't matter none. Everyone's broke as a rusted plowshare, anyway. Getting money out of the bank is like trying to shake a drop of shine out of an empty mason jug."

The collection of men grumbled at large and traded thoughts. One man, Daniel Bray, said, "Hell no, don't matter. You're right. Sounds that some of the damned banks might be coming out to collect, but on the other hand, some may be closing down. Now, if that ain't a blatant contradiction, I don't know what is. But, it's all no damned good, no matter which way you look at it."

Another man, Chesley Kutner, remarked, "No never mind the documents burned up in the courthouse fire. The banks couldn't do anything with our land, as is. What are they going to do with it? How are they going to carry it, too? They don't have enough to eat and support themselves with, either. The land would just lay idle, anyway. With no cotton and no corn. There's nobody to buy it anyway. Nobody."

"The best is that we ain't yet been put out on the side of the road like some," Mac conceded.

The preacher, a man they called Jasper John, stepped down the steps of the small church and faced the men in the circle. He was as sturdy as a tall hickory, with wide hands, lamb chop sideburns, and lines crossing his forehead as fine as worn marble. He studied their torn faces and said, "The Lord is with us in all of our seasons. Even in the winter season of our discontentment. Be a-sure He is with us in all of our trials. Today's challenges will create tomorrow's opportunities."

"Hell on earth, then Jasper John. Damned, 'cause the country's done fallen to hell anyway," Mac Grayson replied to that.

That Sunday afternoon, Mac returned to his cabin on the hillside to attend his failing cotton. The boll weevil was a voracious beetle that had consumed the cotton crop from Arkansas, to Texas, from North Carolina down to Southern Georgia with little left but the stalks and deadening roots. He had worked his fingers to the bone, had driven a plow from dawn until dusk. He had diligently worked his land with the bend of his back and the strength in his arms since he was a boy. Although life was not done with him yet as the ever evolving difficulties had only begun.

Just weeks following this conversation with the townsfolk at Mt. Olive— in the month of February 1930, months following the great collapse— Mac Grayson suffered yet another devastating event that challenged his life for the remainder of his days. An event far more reaching than the circumstances of his land being partially flooded. Not that the flooding and national economic disaster weren't enough—they most certainly were.

An accident occurred on a merchant's property at the local lumberyard.

Several bystanders witnessed the event which crippled Grayson severely. With tender care, they laid him out in the back of his wagon and ran to retrieve his teenage daughter, Myra, the only one on his farm that afternoon. His two sons, her older brothers, were returning empty handed from a livestock auction in Leesburg, carrying only the goat back with them which they had failed to sell.

They laid him out quivering, his eyes flashing with tension. His face grew crimson as the immense pain stiffened him from head to toe and ran through him such as a bolt of lightning coursing through his body. One witness stated: "Then he went completely limp, like a sack o' taters. Drool running from his mouth and his head bleeding pretty badly." The proprietor of the lumberyard ran out when he heard the commotion.

15

Was he somehow responsible? This was his first line of thinking, not being as concerned with Grayson as with his own liability at that moment. The doctor from Leesburg came quickly with his medical kit, but he soon determined Mr. Grayson might be paralyzed for good—from the neck downward. However, he remarked that given enough time and a good amount of praying, the sensation of touch might return to his legs. But, if, or when, was unknown. Only God could know that he later proclaimed.

His daughter ran to his side. "Papa! What happened? Are you gonna be alright?"

"Listen little Myra, a tall stack of lumber fell on top of me," he had whispered almost inaudibly as she put her ear to his lips. Blood was streaming from the side of his head, saturating his shirt. On his back lying in his wagon, he seemed to look up to the blue sky, not into the present but into a time much further toward the future. "This has hurt me damned good. You may have to care for me for a good long while, now. Do you understand what I'm telling you?"

Myra sobbed and rested her head on his shoulder. "You took me in Papa! You made the best for me, and I could never let you down."

After the doctor left they took him to his farm, but he was so large, this required seven men to set him in his bed. Myra cried and couldn't cease as she held his arm and wouldn't release him. He strained to raise his head and look about but he was unable to move his body. His eyes peered from side to side, yet all he could put forth was a loud moaning. By midnight his bed was soaked red. She dressed the wound on the back of his head and wrapped torn cloth to slow the bleeding. She took her Bible and they prayed but to no avail; his condition wouldn't improve. The days became difficult and stretched into weeks. Taking into account all he had done, what was left would remain with his children. Life can't always be a bed of roses Maclin once told her. As a matter of fact, very rarely it is.

As the long days went, she cared for her father, sat on his bedside, and warmed him during the cold nights with hot water bottles she filled from a pan on the woodstove. She fed him, though he wasn't very hungry, and she gave him water when he thirsted. She rubbed his legs and back with oil and the feeling slowly returned to his toes, little by little, thank God. Mac's boys, Arden and Cade did what they could on the farm to help support them with their required duties and chores. In this time of reflection, she realized how fragile life had become, and she inquired with him about his family and the history of their land in Lee County, a record she knew little of as she had never been informed. One late night after an evening meal, he told her of his family, his father and his father's father, and their family's story of decades past as she listened intently:

Mac explained to her that many years prior in the summer of 1838 (as it had been recorded in the family's old journal), his grandfather, Samuel Grayson, retired from the naval branch of the U.S. armed services. With the war having been well-fought, his grandfather took his leave to a life of deserved rest and solitude back to his native home there in South Georgia. In lieu of a cash pension, Mac told Myra, Samuel acquired their farmland in Flintside (close enough to his hometown of Americus) as an even exchange in the form of a military grant of sixty acres instated by the U.S. Treasury. Two wholesome acres they awarded him; two for each year contracted in the military service of his beloved country.

Mac informed Myra that his grandfather's honored career had, in fact, covered the War of 1812 as a navy ensign, stationed at the mouth of the Potomac River where his vessel shelled incoming British merchant ships attempting to off load goods in the port of Springfield. During his time of service, Mac explained, Samuel's rank was elevated to LCDR, Lieutenant Commander, and he had sailed in a defensive position up the eastern coastline from Jacksonville to Portland until the age of forty-eight.

Mac went on to say that his grandfather's awarded acreage where they now lived ran along the western flank of the Flint River. He explained to Myra that, as it had been recorded in the family journal, a ceremony of allegiance had taken place, and Samuel received the land deed in confidence on the front steps of the U.S. Legislature in Washington D.C. Then he made the nine hundred mile trek south, back home where he planned to live out the remainder of his days.

However, the journal recorded that when he arrived in the weeks following, he gathered that there had been a mistake. The land and the view were far more than he had expected. The acreage ranged by the banks of the Flint and reached into the surrounding hills with the serene beauty of a Thomas Hill painting (these exact words as recorded in the journal's contents). The journal further stated that he held the deed in his hand and used it to wipe the tears away from his weather-wrinkled face, now that he'd finally returned home to Lee County after so many years away with his military service.

The open fields, as seen from his vantage point way up on the road, were flush with wild berry, tall yarrow, and wire grass. The river held the land in the turn of the shoreline where willows lined the sandy banks and shadows danced against river rock. Before the turn of Samuel's fiftieth birthday, the fields had been plowed by numerous slave hands and were white with cotton. Maclin told her that Samuel took a bank loan against the harvest and built the cabin from where he could look on the waters of the Flint glinting in the afternoon sunlight.

As Mac told their story, Myra listened intently. She had set him up on a stack of pillows and he took his pipe and smoked. She sat in a cane chair and watched his eyes glistening, his old hands motioning in silent gestures with his storytelling. He took a short break when she brought him water to drink, and he wiped his face with a cotton cloth in the coolness of the night.

He settled back and continued. He went on to explain that within a year Samuel Grayson had married Lauren McFarland, a young daughter of a textile merchant in nearby Dawson, and she bore their son, Earl Grayson (Mac's father). Earl learned to fish the river, and he hand-made a canoe from frame and hide alongside a local, left-behind Indian elder named Chebona Bula. When the old Indian died, the young Grayson took the corpse, wrapped in canvas with rope, and buried him on his family land as there was nowhere else to lay the old man's body.

Many years on, Earl fought with the Confederate Army as a volunteer against the advancing General Sherman in the Battle of Chickamauga. Yet, he was severely injured and returned to Lee County for retirement, thankful to be alive as he had left to war with two legs, but had only returned with one. Regardless of his ailment, his family grew and his only son, Maclin, was bore by his wife Nancy Shelton on a Christmas Eve whilst a mantle of snow fell on their farmland near Flintside. Earl proposed this to be a sign of good will that the Lord had given this favored gift on the eve of their dear Savior's birth. With the worn family journal left behind by Mac's mother, Nancy (this journal known as Nancy's Journal), the story of the Grayson family was passed down after her death in the years that followed.

After the gray old man had articulated his story that evening, he fell asleep, exhausted. Myra tucked his bedsheet up under his chin and slipped out but left the candle to burn on his bedside table. She was ever thankful he had taken her in to be with his family as she had arrived from a wretched confluence of circumstances as a little girl. And she greatly desired, regardless of her youth, to care for him and to fill a serviceable void in his life as he had lost his wife to mental illness not long before.

Chapter 2

ARDEN WAS LONG on stride as he came over the rise with a young fawn laid over his shoulder. From the house Myra could see Cade coming up behind, but he was head high over his brother although he was years younger with a fair complexion and ice-blue eyes. Arden took the low path by the lake and negotiated the craggy rocks then stooped to rest his 30/30 in the sand. He spread out the small deer and cleaned the drying blood from its hide in the shallow water. The devastating drought of the previous years had drained the narrow lake to nothing more than a small river, and the fields were parched dry from what little rain had fallen since '27.

Overhead on the embankment, Cade stood waiting. He turned to see their cabin just beyond the cotton field, made of heavy logs, squatted low, bright in the July sun with a bent-up, single ridge roof of tin and moss chinking falling out in places. It sat by their small barn a ways back from the lake, flat brown against the late day sky of thickening clouds and a dark storm front on the horizon. The cotton house having collapsed aside the barn had fallen into the shape of a converted lean-to, the walls insistently tilting against the faded barn board, its weakness made obvious with age and broken framework.

Their younger sister, Myra, stood on the front stoop of the house like a waiting rabbit, hand over her forehead shading the light, looking for them to return home.

"Finally looking like rain, Arden." Cade turned back, shifting his weight from foot to foot while holding his rifle by the forestock. "I can carry the fawn for you, there."

"I got her, Cade. No need. I ran her down, but you did your part and dressed her good enough." He glanced up. Arden was older than his brother, into his twenties and mostly agreeable, but usually the one in charge. His chestnut hair curled behind his ears and ran down his back past his shoulders. His brown eyes were dark in the waning daylight and when he stood, sunlight shot over the embankment and shone against the side of his strong face.

"I got it. I'm on my way," he said.

"Let's git," Cade said. "Myra's waving for us to come on." He glanced back, and his sister, all thin legs and arms, was now urgently waving both hands in the air.

"What, she's hungry I guess." Arden brushed the dirt from his knees, took up the deer in one swift motion and lifted his gun. "Gonna take a while to get this skinned back and on the stove. I believe we'll do a quarter-roast tonight."

He climbed up the trail and stood by Cade. Smoke wisped out of the cabin's stovepipe up through the red oaks into the sky. It appeared Myra had lit the fire early as they had asked her to. This indicated she had pulled the water, had washed the beans and had put them on, had prepared the biscuits and had brought in more kindling, too. While they were out, she had been busy quilting a winter blanket on the kitchen table.

She was also becoming more proficient at duties such as sharpening knives and the ax blade, even shoeing the mules, fitting their tack, and harnessing them to the wagon. She was growing up and her responsibilities had begun to increase with maturity. While their father had become disabled and was now in a daybed, she had begun to carry more weight on the farm. And they were glad of it; they needed all they could get.

They came up from the lake, and they could see her waiting at their home on the rise. The two wide shutters of the house were opened on the front glassless window and were latched back to its rough log exterior. In the side yard, bed covers and clothing hung on the numerous clotheslines which was a construction of cross-cording strung between four pine saplings. Out beyond the barn on the hill, a few broad magnolias remained that their mother had planted years ago. Wild Texas rose grew on the fence. A water trough honed out of a hollowed log was scotched-up between two thick pine stumps around the end of the house, this just steps away from the well their Great-Grandpa had dug many years before their time.

Their few remaining chickens scattered across the yard when Myra came out to hurry them home.

"She's in need of something, I can see that," Arden said as they headed up the path. "I hope Papa's alright."

The path was straight as an arrow from the river bank up to the house, well-worn and brick-hard by mid-summer after decades of use. Regrettably, the remaining cotton was sparse. What was left ranged a long distance over the horizon with just a few scantlings of white seen here and there. The boll weevil had taken its share not to suggest the horrid drought hadn't taken its toll as well. The thin cotton edged the path that ran up from the lakeshore to the barnyard, and the boys couldn't help but simper as they strode up the hill. Due to the recent collapse of the nation's economy, the cotton that remained wouldn't be worth the sweat to haul it in, considering Ches Kutner's cost for pulling his team of mules and mechanical combine down the road from his land. Money was tight. There was scarcely enough to be had as the financial banks in Americus and Albany were indefinitely restricting withdrawal amounts. The cotton fields and rail stations, come fall, would be lined with stakebody trailers filled with un-sellable cotton. "Why waste all your hard work in order to take it in, if that is going to be the case," their disabled father had suggested.

"Fallowed and all of our hard work," Cade remarked as he rounded the path into their yard of strewn woodchips.

"Don't forget the cost of seed we spent added to that."

"And now almost thirty acres of nothing."

"The seed was so damned high, but now seed ain't worth diddle."

"Nothing's going to be left out there anyway but maybe three pound a cotton per acre, you think?"

"If that," Arden said. "I bet there won't be fifty pounds in the whole damned field."

"I'd shat if I had to pick the whole thirty for near nothing. But maybe we could get a little something if we tried."

When they approached, Myra was there on the steps, holding out a fold of paper in her hand.

Arden stopped, facing Myra on the stoop. Arden was built like a short brick house, olive complexion, sinew wrapped forearms like ropes, thick legs resembling tree logs, his head the size of a river rock, much like his father. His stoic disposition belied a disgruntled temper that he carried within which could suddenly erupt once on a blue moon if circumstances warranted.

He said, "Myra, what is it? What's with your arm waving up here?" He rested the fawn on the chopping stump and his gun against the house.

"Jasper John brought out a letter this morning. Rode out on his mule." She handed it to him and bit her fingernails with a frail determination. She was nearly seventeen. She'd read the letter through twice, and other than her brothers, she was likely the only one within a mile that could read at all, except for Jasper John, a few of the merchants in Flintside, and Mr. Burch, the schoolmaster.

Cade came and stood by Arden, Cade tall and thin as a rail with wedge-shaped shoulders. An angular face with sharp features, he appeared different from his brother and father. His controlled manner was stable yet edgy at times. The pitch of his voice, strong and baritone could be easily heard far afield.

The neatly typed letter was addressed to their father, Maclin Grayson:

From:
St. Frances Hospital
15 Ware Street
Americus, Georgia
Staff Dr. Walter Roberts

To:
Maclin Grayson
Bent River Road
Flintside, Georgia

Mr. Grayson,
*   Please excuse me for baring such short notice regarding your wife, Ila Mae, and her position at our beloved hospital of care. As much as I would prefer to inform you of good news, I am afraid the situation at St. Francis has become dire. With the current economic climate in the State of Georgia, we are unable to continue our care for your wife as the funds have run out and no additional financial support from the state will be available in the foreseeable future. We are short on all supplies including food, and we have hardly enough to feed ourselves. In the same breath, I must covey to you that her physical condition remains well but her mental state has only worsened and the medications that are required have also been depleted. Our only option is to let her out, or have you retrieve her as soon as possible. Of*

course, there is the third option of payment, however, in the total of $720.00 dollars for another year's residency to further your wife's care. I'm assured as anyone else that in this time of our banks' financial conditions, it is unlikely you or your family could raise this sum in any event. Nonetheless, $20.00 will be required to release her as her expenses have mounted in this time of inadequate funding. In closing, our prayers are with you and your family, and we wish you Godspeed with your decision and your hopeful trip to Americus to retrieve her.

Sincerely, Dr. Walter Roberts

Arden chose his words carefully and spoke in his gravelly voice to the other two. "This is not good news we have." He quickly gleaned the letter again while shaking his head in dismay. "We have no other choice. We're going to Americus, or I'll be damned. We'll have to get her and bring her home. We don't have much time, and the wagon's rear crossbeam is still broken, too."

"Lord, how can we handle her? Now with Papa down, too? I know we have to. I'm determined as you, Arden." Myra frowned. "But, we should tell Papa right away," she said. "I waited for you two to return from your hunting." She pulled a lock of dark auburn out of her face as she looked up from the letter which Arden held. Her eyes were deep as green jasper with flecks of brown, and the dimming daylight pooled in them, but Arden glanced up to study the darkening clouds in the sky.

Cade replied sharply, "Ain't any use. He can't do much about it. He can hardly sit up in bed anymore."

"Well, he can still think, can't he?" she said. She took the letter from Arden, but Cade held her thin wrist tightly.

"Let him be for now." Cade drew her arm up closer. "He's probably asleep anyway."

"Cade, let her go tell him. Better sooner than later. He still has a say so."

Myra said, "But the thought of her returning here is unimaginable. It's been so long now. With her condition the way she left, she couldn't have improved any since. She's probably worse off. How are we going to cope with her?"

Arden looked down, his expression growing anxious. "Myra, damned if I know, but we can't leave her up there. The letter says they'll put her out on the street. As this stands, I'll have to see about repairing the wagon as soon as possible."

"How long you think it'll take to fix it?" Cade asked his brother.

At that moment, thunder broke from the accumulation of clouds overhead, and rain began to splatter on the ground and cabin's roof. The red oaks that stood as tall as church spires above their cabin swayed in the sky and creaked in protest as the strengthening wind drew up. The cat claw briars that had taken around the smokehouse bristled as the wind began whistling through the trees.

"Get on in!" Arden motioned toward Myra with his hand.

She ran up the steps into the house, followed by Cade. Arden slammed the shutters tightly against the window frame while Myra fastened them from inside. When he ran up the steps, lightning streaked over the river followed by a roar of thunder. He shut the door and pulled his long hair aside, out of his jacket collar and let it fall.

"Rain," Cade said.

"Finally," Arden replied.

"Too little, too late," Myra concluded.

They stood in stunned silence for a moment, Myra still holding the letter. They looked at one another, their faces weary.

Arden asked, "Where are we going to put her?"

Myra said, "Where? I guess in with Papa. How are we going to manage her and Papa too though?" She wiped a tear from her eye with the thought of their worsening predicament.

They listened to the rain tapping on the metal roof.

"It'll slack off for long. I'll get a haunch on the stove in a bit." Arden slipped off his jacket, set it on the heavy plank table in the center of the room, and stepped into the storage closet for the last of the roasted peanuts. Myra tended the fire with a few pokes then added a branch of cherry.

Cade ran his hand over his head of short hair. "Arden, we should rethink our cotton, seeing how we might need the extra income now," he said as his older brother walked away. "Can't we do *something* with what little cotton is out there?"

"Let it go," he said from the storage closet.

They heard bags sliding around, a box being moved on the wooden floor, empty tin cans clanging on the shelves.

"Might as well leave it be," Myra said, dejected. "They say it isn't going to be but five cents a pound, and there's hardly anything left out in the field. We've been over this a few times," she explained.

"Five cents is five cents, though. Better than nothin'."

"But Kutner's combine would cost us three," she put in.

"We could pick for a ways up here by the cabin where it's still thick enough then take what little we have over to Hansen in Warwick."

"It's a waste, Cade, don't you see? Besides, Warwick is so far."

"Then we better keep the smokehouse full up this fall. We ain't got much left in Papa's box. Then what are we going to do?"

"We'll have to think, use our heads for once. Improvise and adapt. Overcome what we must!" she said, turning and crossing her arms with a surprising burst of gumption. She was quickly growing up, her brothers well-knew. Given to harsh consequences, she could be valuable in the most testing of times they were growing to recognize.

"Damned if we don't have the availability of a modern combine but can't use it, now. What I wish we had though," he said while changing the subject, "was modern electricity and one on those electric box radios. You know, like the one we heard up in Americus inside that Rexall Drug store? I wish I had one of those." He smiled, dreaming of one in the future. "Guess I'll have to go into the big city for that. And make a million bucks to afford it."

Myra added, "Are you crazy? We'll never have electricity unless they ever finish the hydro dam on Blackshear. But a phone? You can't get one of those down here. Have you ever seen those thin wires they connect to them? They'll never run little wires like that way out here. Maybe over in Albany you could. But we probably never will."

Several weeks prior to this, the three had ridden their two mules into Flintside to buy a few necessities—this exercise requiring them to vote on every purchase as their savings were running low, although with Arden being the oldest he usually had the final say. Molasses, lard, salt, biscuit flour, coffee, lamp oil, candles, even long strips of smoked jerky which Cade requested, were on their shopping list.

The Graysons were traditionally cotton growers not produce farmers like many in the south. Generally, they grew and sold their cotton, but in turn bought their vegetables from local farmers such as Wilton Meyer or Mel Parrish. However in the year of 1930, the southern cotton crop completely failed which left many cotton growers high and dry. Now the season was coming to an end. And with little money left and little cotton to harvest, only a few necessities could be afforded.

In town at the small general store, when they took their goods up to the counter, the owner Mr. Jenkins pulled out a big can he used as a cash bin. He said, "You boys gettin' along down yonder? Your Papa holdin' out alright?" He didn't look at Myra. His wife, Mrs. Jenkins, sat in a nearby office, running through figures in a ledger.

"Right good, for the time being, Mr. Jenkins," Arden said lying as he set a glass jar of molasses on the countertop.

Arden knew they were in serious trouble with their pa now hurt and in his deteriorated condition; also considering what little money remained, and an eight month delinquency, too, on their mortgage payments. The mules were low on hay and feed. The storage closet shelves were nearly bare of the jarred vegetables they'd put up the previous fall. Yet one hope hung on a prayer. The apples were greening on the trees over in Mr. McCarver's field, and they were soon to ripen.

Jenkins mentioned, "Been nine months since they went belly up yonder in the big city. Now it's done trickled down here into the low country. Shame really. Stores is closing down, but hopin' I ain't gonna have to. Peoples is getting bad off, now. Right bad, ain't it boys?"

"Where there ain't any end in sight, it's looking like," Arden said as Cade licked his lips while eyeing the candy in the glass containers by the counter.

Mr. Jenkins took out a pad and pencil to tally their tab. He gave out no credit anymore, likewise, as the money had nearly run out.

He said, "That'll be four dollars and fifteen cents, Arden." The grocer rocked back on his heels, spat a stream of tobacco juice into a spittoon behind the counter, and watched the young man digging into his pockets.

Arden handed over the coins, mostly dimes and a few nickels while Mr. Jenkins counted slowly and let them fall into the metal can with a jingling similar to Christmas bells.

Myra studied the contents on the countertop and thought for a moment.

"Mr. Jenkins," Myra said, looking upon the chalkboard where he kept his pricing, while counting off on her fingers. "The molasses is fifty-five cents, right? The lard is thirty-five cents and the salt, ten. Both ten pound bags of flour and the coffee are sixty cents each, correct?

The oil is twenty and the candles are ten." She quickly took the pencil and pad, figuring. "That's two dollars and fifty cents even. And the jerky is a dollar eighty a dozen, but we only have seven pieces here," she said, double counting the strips of smoked beef on the countertop. She swiftly scribbled more figures and subsequently scratched a long pencil line under her remaining sum on the paper. She glanced up. "That totals three dollars and fifty-five cents."

His brows knitted into a bunch as he stroked his chin whiskers and pursed his lips. Mr. Jenkins was thin as a bamboo fishing pole with white hair, a bushy gray moustache and narrow set, beady eyes. He squinted in regret that she had caught onto his game.

Myra looked at both her brothers who were bent forward, studying her math.

"She's damned sure right, Jenkins," Arden said as he rested his hands on his hips, face reddening. He was surprised he hadn't caught it as he was generally the one in charge.

Myra held out her small hand, her nimble fingers twitching. "That'll be sixty cents back, if you don't mind."

Jenkins crossed his arms in defiance and jutted his pointy chin out toward them. "Hell, don't forget the tax, little lady." He smiled wryly.

"Since on what day of the year do you pay a gal' damned dime's worth of tax, Mr. Jenkins?" she shot back.

He flinched at the fervent language and audacity of the young girl, not much taller than a bean pole.

Reading the store owner's demeanor, Cade reached out and took the old man by his collar, pulling him up against the counter so force-fully that a suspender popped off his overalls. "That'll be sixty cent, Mr. Jenkins!"

Arden reached in the cash can himself and withdrew the coins, counting them out in his hand.

Cade pushed the old man back and the counter rattled severely. Close by, big cigars rolled off of a dime store Indian figure, the little Indian a display the size of a doll holding its arms outward to hold the thick, brown cylinders in place.

"At least Mr. Burch the schoolmaster taught us a thing or two over in that schoolhouse, seeing as how the three of us can read the front page of the Americus Gazette faster than you could read the funny section," Myra spat. *"If you can read at all, that is."*

"And we can do our figures a lot better, too, it looks like," Cade added.

Mrs. Jenkins dashed out of the office with a look of surprise on her face. "What's going on?"

No one answered.

Arden thrust the coins into his pocket. The other two took up the goods and the three walked briskly out of the store.

Arden emerged from the storage closet and held a tin of stale peanuts. He divided them out and the three ate hungrily. "Keep the smokehouse full up, you say? At least we can start with the little fawn we brought in this afternoon."

"That ain't but a few meals, it's so small," Cade replied.

Arden tossed the last of the nuts into his mouth. He said, "Cade, speaking of the smokehouse, do we have much ammo left? Like those 30/30 casings? What about our shotgun shells? Any of them?"

"I'll look and get a count, but you know as well as me, we're damned low on everything. We're out of most everything we bought up at Jenkins's, the molasses, lard, flour, coffee, and jerky. Out or short on most everything."

"Short on money, first and foremost," Myra said, "and we haven't paid the mortgage in, I can't remember, how many months now?"

"Been eight months," Arden said. "Because of the drought, we were short last year and with the added infestation, this year was worse. We have nearly nothing. We can't pay without cotton to harvest. Now we're about out of money, too, and there's no way we can make it up now."

The rain had slacked off so she let the shutters back out, pushing them to swing open and clap against the side of the cabin with a soft thud. She placed her hands on the sill and looked out to the north toward Mr. McCarver's land more than an eighth of a mile up the hill in the general direction of town. From where she stood, his robust apple trees could be seen in the far distance, covering the hillside with young green fruits revealing themselves among the twisted branches and thick leaves.

Arden stood at the window beside her and looked too. "Those are some pretty trees, ain't they?"

"*Ain't* isn't a good word, Arden." She turned to look at him.

"*Aren't*, then I guess. Miss Know-it All."

She looked back.

"And beautiful apples, too, come this autumn," Cade chimed in from behind, licking his lips and rubbing his hands together in anticipation.

"Amazing how well they held up in this hellacious drought. It ain't hardly poured in two or three years." Arden brushed tiny rain droplets off his arms that fell from the window frame above.

"Damn good thing Mr. McCarver died last year," Cade remarked.

"I'm guessing the apples are as good as eaten then," Myra added, implying the obvious.

"I hope you like apples, cause, that's all we'll have any further down the road from now."

"Apples are gonna have to do."

"I reckon Mr. McCarver wouldn't mind."

"His wife, Ms. McCarver, wouldn't either. She's dead, too."

"What about all their prime land? I guess the government or the bank's gonna git it sooner or later."

"Bout the time they come and get ours."

"Shut up, Cade!" Myra said, her mood changing as quickly as the wind shifting direction.

They pondered, the three standing at the window.

"You gonna go wake up Papa 'bout Momma, now?" Arden asked Myra. "I can hear him sawin' logs in yonder, even with the door shut tight." He let his head hang low and almost started to cry. They'd never witnessed their big brother cry before, except the morning they came to take their mother away.

Chapter 3

LEE COUNTY LAY in middle South Georgia where the western portion of the county was ceded by the Creek in 1828 to the U.S. government. The Creek Indians were pushed out onto the Trail of Tears toward Oklahoma for relocating their native heritage thousands of miles to the west. However the painful journey took many of their lives and left none with happiness, only despondent misery. The county seat was deemed Leesburg before the initiation of the Civil War. Though to the north, the greater cities of Americus in Sumter County and Albany down in Dougherty dominated the region with their larger populations and economic strength. All put together: the vast rural settings, the beautiful woodland hills, and the late-summer laid by cotton graced the landscape where the Flint River cut directly through the heart of Lee County from north to south.

In 1923, the Army Corp of Engineers began the drawn out construction of the Warwick Dam on the Flint to create Lake Blackshear. Yet the construction and consequent flooding of the surrounding land caused great loss to many landowners for the reason the government failed to alter their boundary records properly. As a result, they excluded landowners from adequate compensation for their flooded land. They also defeated lawsuits years later as the records had not been accurately accounted for and transferred. On Mac Grayson's land, some of his eastern acreage was submerged, too, and regrettably this occurred leading up to the Great Depression. Thus, the delayed-accounting of lost property was eventually neglected never to be made right by the government. Cotton was king in the south. Cotton was hard on the soil and hard on the people, in the days leading up to 1929. During the 1920s, Mac Grayson was laden with fieldwork but flush with cotton and prosperity. Although, consequences prevailed: the partial flooding from dam construction, the erosion from plowing, the nutritional depletion of his soil, the extended drought, and *then the depression,* accumulatively brought this to an abrupt halt.

In the good years, Maclin worked diligently hand-plowing his acreage along with numerous hired black men that he paid at the rate of fifty cents per day. (Of course Mac back-charged fifteen cents each if required to feed them with cornpone, fatback, or turnips). Mac had begun leading a plow-mule by the young age of fifteen, like his father Earl, although his father returned from the war less one leg, therefore Earl had hired out his work, too. With the integration of modern machinery, Mac contracted an adjacent landowner, a man named Chesley Kutner, to bring his mules and new motorized-combine harvester to strip off the cotton during harvest season. Inherently, this was part of doing business in the modern ag-industrial age. The Grayson's fields were nearly fifty acres considering the Flint had consumed ten with the filling of Lake Blackshear. Hand picking cotton had gone by the wayside with the evolution of the combine, this suitable for farms of substantial acreage well above a small cut of ten or more, depending. Mac was happy to pay for the services, simultaneously saving on time and having to manage a contingent of pickers. Using a combine was simpler, cheaper, and more efficient. Simply a smarter farming practice.

When Mac was done in the field, he came up and let Kutner on with his mules and combine to strip the cotton. He wiped his face from sweat, took the gourd and ladled cool water from the bucket. He could look out over his crops and know he had done what needed doing. He was raising his family and caring for his wife. This was satisfying to him. From that time, he could think back to their beginnings and he was happy.

At a young age, Mac met his wife Ila Mae at a county fair in Leesburg where her father was showing cattle for sale. Mac threw horseshoes with her brother that day, and fell in love with Ila that night over a strawberry tart and a cup of Cremco. As often as his time allowed, he visited Ila Mae in Leesburg, but Leesburg was a long jaunt on his jennet mule, Odessa, and she didn't much care for the long journey either. So in lieu of riding over too frequently, he proposed marriage as the most desirable option. Her father, Mathew Bradley, agreed as Maclin claimed to possess a right good lay 'o land and a roof to sleep under, after all. Mac and Ila were married the next day by the local country preacher. Mac properly took her flower that night, and they rode tandem on Odessa back to Flintside the following morning—however saddle-sore her stern became haven also ridden her massive husband for her wedding the night before. After packing fresh corn shucks into his bed mattress for added comfort, she soon became pregnant and waddled about the cabin until Arden was birthed on a stormy Monday morning. Upon her laboring, Mac ran on foot up to Wilton Meyer's place (as Odessa refused to run), and his wife, having been a midwife in her days, followed him back down to find Arden already in Ila's arms, sucking her tit. Ila had birthed Arden herself on the kitchen floor and had done a fine job of it, this made apparent by the broad smile of her round face.

Their modest cabin was of three rooms in which the Grayson family had made a home for adequate living. Low, with one window out front, it leaned in a manner that expressed the hardship that had been heaped upon it. Their great grandfather had, indeed, built the dwelling at the first of his retirement ninety-one years prior, and the place had served the generations well over the years. Given to the approach of the path up from the lakeshore, the cabin stood on a knoll among tall oaks where the lake-green water, expansive view, and cotton surrounding the property could be seen in all their beauty. The land to the south disappeared with the bend of the water. The far rolling landscape to the north bared apple trees, an abandoned barn, and woodlands of sun-berthed hills. The homestead had seen wear in its past. Time had done its job, and the life that had lived there had been good.

Paired with their land which ran parallel to the lake's shoreline, the more sizable farm of Jack Waylon graced a large enough portion of Lee County (large enough to be noted by men of greater wealth than Mac Grayson), with nearly two hundred and eighty acres of prime farmland and pasture. This property was mounted on high hills away from the lake, across the dirt road from Mr. Grayson, and it was filled with livestock from here, there and yonder. However, the gravel road separating the two properties gave way to a sudden contrast in upward topography as Waylon's land quickly raised in elevation from Mac Grayson's. This land mass also formed a land-locked separation from the bend of the lake's shoreline due to the impediment of the gravel road and Grayson's property itself.

When Arden came up the path holding a string of small lake bream, his face was like stone, his facial features still as cut granite which belied his good-natured heart as he was burdened with the task he had been called to undertake. The supposition of this, notwithstanding the grief, brought back memories from their past they had rather forget.

Arden set the fish down and entered the cabin. Through the window, he could see Myra working as he came up the steps. She was preparing a meal with the last of their cornbread in a cast iron skillet.

The cabin was plainly furnished with a ductile iron stove (which served for cooking as well as heating in the winter), a hard-worn plank table, and five straight-back chairs. A long oak counter was attached to the wall with square steel nails and supports, with a galvanized wash tub as a sink, and a water bucket nearby always on-the-ready for trips to the well. A wooden shelf for holding supplies, pewter plates, cups, some dried herbs, and other sundry things, was mounted to the wall above the tub. The fireplace had been made of fieldstones taken out of their land; well-made, assuredly, by their great grandfather and a few of his laborers many years earlier. The stone facing and oak mantle were blackened by smoke and soot from decades past. Although the place was rough-honed, it was robust and heart-warming in the days of winter. What remained that was short in accommodation had been replenished with devotion and love.

After Arden slipped off his boots and sat to rest at the kitchen table, she glanced up and caught his expression in the corner of her eye.

"What to do, Arden?" She placed her hands on her hips for a moment, but as he remained silent instead of answering her, she stepped over and stood in front of him while wiping her hands on her cotton apron. "You must go get our mother, you know this."

After some thought, he sat forward, resting his elbow on the table. "Then I best get out and tend to that wagon. It's a might broken-down as you know." He hung his head as he often would when in deep contemplation, this instant riding his thoughts on the side of sadness rather than indecision.

He thought about his girl, Natalie. He hadn't seen her in almost six months since she'd moved away with her family up north to Illinois where her uncle lived. As luck would have it, Natalie's father had lost his job at the Americus Gazette after the economy had fallen. Incidentally, Mr. Weldon was one of the only men he knew that owned a car, and this was appreciated as he had brought Natalie to visit him on several occasions. But Arden had had big hopes. He had saved and had picked out a small two room house that was for sale out toward Leesburg, but after the fall, Natalie left for Illinois and his money eventually evaporated.

Since then he and Natalie had exchanged a few letters, but he missed her terribly and knew that their opportunity of getting married, as he had hoped for, was now slim to none.

He slowly looked up.

"Cade could go with you," Myra suggested.

"Cade can't go, you know that." He rubbed his hands on his knees.

"You might need him. I'll stay. I can take care of Papa."

"You'll need Cade more than I. Cade can help get Papa around and on and off the pot, do the heavy lifting, I suppose. Do the man's work."

"I can do it. I can do *man's work*," she said spitefully.

"You can, can you? What about gathering and splitting more firewood? I have to repair the wagon. You know our woodpile is shy in the savings account. As well as our money."

"I can split a cord while you're gone. I could if I had to."

"The problem, Myra, lies out at the far tree line." He clasped his hands together and paused, letting this sink in. Sunlight was cutting through the low branches of the red oaks, into the window and into his eyes. He looked away, thinking, knowing their situation was becoming even more difficult.

He said, "The good standing deadwood is way out yonder at the tree line. That takes an ax and a mule to pull back with lengths of rope. Then the big cross-band saw and a big set of guns to cut those logs, if you know what I mean. Not to mention that set of Cole chisels. They ain't light work. Neither is the sledge."

She fell quiet and stepped back to her cornbread, considering the long and extremely difficult cross-band saw. Her forehead made faint wrinkles while her hands worked slowly. He could see the wheels in her head turning.

"You're right. I can't do it without Cade. I know. I just thought a positive attitude would help."

"Being positive and practical are two different things, Myra."

"Where is Cade, anyway?"

She was silent.

"I best go and see what needs doing." He slipped on his boots, stood and went out the door toward the barn and wagon.

The following morning as the early sun rose over the hills, they heard a loud rumbling coming down the road from the direction of Flintside. The sound was unmistakable. It wasn't the low clatter of a tractor way up on Waylon's property, not the low vibrations made by a combine or a small motorized farm implement of some kind. The whirring hum was that of a gasoline engine in an automobile. The distinctive sound only a car creates; the combination of both torque and high speed not commonly heard in farm machinery. And this sound was rarely ever heard around the Grayson property.

Cade stepped out of the privy, tying his belt, and looked up to the road that crested the ridge above the fields. Arden appeared from the barn while holding an adze. As he watched, he bent to brush the litter of wood shavings off his trousers and shirt sleeves. Myra came to hear it too, wearing her usual apron, standing in the front window of the cabin. With haste, Cade came around the house and stood out front. The three eyed one another in anticipation: Arden in front of the barn doors, Cade in front of the house, Myra in the window.

Watching the vehicle rounding the ridge, Arden set the tool on the bench outside the barn and whispered to himself, "Who could this be?"

He stepped down to the house and the three met out front. A sleek, long Nash Coup came with soft bounces and squeaks down the hill. It was painted enamel-black with a tan fabric roof and a shiny chrome ornament on its hood. They observed two well-dressed men in the car, both wearing black dress jackets and matching gray Fedoras. The car pulled alongside them, came to an abrupt halt, and the one man in the passenger's side emerged with a briefcase in hand. The other remained seated and seemed to be looking at himself in the rearview mirror, admiring his hat and neat mustache.

Cade stepped forward, but Arden held him back and whispered, "Hold on, Cade."

"Can we help ya?" Arden asked.

The man was placing his briefcase on the hood of the Nash. He didn't look at them, only studied some papers he held in his hands. The other man rested his arm out of the car window for a moment, then took a cigar from his coat pocket and lit it with a match. Blue smoke floated out of the car window. He coughed sharply, placing his hand over his mouth. Easing the big door open, he adjusted his weight in the driver's seat and watched but remained in the car.

"Gentlemen," the man said. "Nice day here on your property, I see." He actually smiled but not as an amicable gesture, only as a representation of his own self-importance. "I'm Jaren R. Rutledge, from Americus First Trust." He paused for affect. "J.R. for short," he added. He smiled again.

Instantly they understood why this man was present and had driven all the distance from Americus. They noticed the muddy tires on the Nash, and brown streaks splashed across the sides of the car. Obviously these men had been required to drive across the wide creek that intersected the road between Flintside and Desoto, the small town south of Americus which necessitated driving through while in route. Fortuitously for them, rain had been nearly nonexistent in recent months, therefore, Flintside creek was passible and lower than usual. The only other route was an extended detour requiring an extra twelve miles of travel where it could be crossed at a bridge up in Cobb.

"Who here is Maclin Grayson? Which of you gentlemen is he?" he asked.

"That would be our father, Mr. Rutledge."

Myra came and stood close to Arden, her shoulder touching his thick arm. She squinted in the morning light, looking at the man, Mr. Rutledge, and then to the man in the driver's seat. The man in the car seemed to be staring at her unblinkingly while working the cigar in his mouth hungrily. "Where then can we find your father? I...we need to speak with him concerning some banking matters. Would that be alright with you?"

Arden said, "Would be 'cept he can't speak with you right now. You see, he had a bad accident a ways back and he's in bed at the moment."

"Who the hell are you!" came a thunderous voice from behind them.

The four turned quickly, and Mac Grayson was standing in the doorway of his cabin, propped against the doorframe, wearing overalls with a toothpick in his mouth. He held himself upright with a walking cane of burled walnut. He began to step forward but paused in contemplation of the steep front steps.

"Papa!" Myra yelled. "What on earth are you doing out of bed?" She bolted to the house and up the steps in seconds. She grasped a chair from under the table and situated it behind him. Arden raced up too, and they both eased him down to sit comfortably there. He grimaced and groaned but was able to sit after a noticeable deal of maneuvering.

Myra placed her hand on his shoulder. "Don't you do that again! You know you're not allowed to leave your bed without our assistance."

"Says who?" the old man said. He let out a powerful cough, heaved forward and spat out phlegm into the yard.

"Doctor Clack did. That's what he told you!" She patted his back and he commenced to cough again.

He wiped his mouth with the back of his hand. "What does he know?" their father protested.

The man named Rutledge came to the base of the steps to make his presence known. He held out a thick file of papers for signing, apparently legal documents. Cade stepped up behind him and stood closely by.

Mac said, "What the hell do you want, Rutledge? I know who you are. Don't act naive with me."

Mac Grayson was a big man with a wide girth and massive hands like grappling hooks. His mountainous shoulders, barrel chest, and burly arms gave him the appearance of a stud bull looking for trouble. His gray hair was wavy and tossed back off his forehead. His face was wide, and his jaw hung like an iron pot under his mean face. He weighed nearly three hundred pounds, though he'd lost a few since being confined to his bed. Fortunately, his condition had improved over the period of a few months, yet his accident at the lumberyard in Flintside had assuredly disabled him permanently.

He sat in his chair in the doorway of his home, looking down at the man in the business suit and polished black wingtips.

He said, "A pinstripe suit? Really? Out here on the farm? I'm so impressed." He tapped his index finger lightly on the knob of his cane. "Tsk, tsk," he added.

Mr. Grayson was much more forthcoming than the banker had expected, so Rutledge laughed nervously and said, "Mr. Grayson. You know why we've come. You haven't paid a mortgage note in eight months. As we all recognize the country is falling into a very serious state. Most of the regional banks have called in fifty percent of their farm loans thus far."

"Horseshit."

He laughed again, this time not so discreetly. "We're simply here doing our job. This is not personal. There is no need for foul language. This is strictly a business matter so we dress accordingly." He brushed some lint off his lapel and straightened his jacket just so.

"That's all bullshit, all with the dress-up doll business your kind put on." He coughed and cleared his throat, hocked a snot wad over to the side of the cabin. "I'll pay up my debt, but in the meanwhile, I aim to have my say so."

"With all due consideration, you don't expect the bank to roll out a red carpet and invite you to dine with us on our lawn, do you? Mr. Grayson? Really?" He motioned with the file of papers in his hand, making sure Mac saw them.

Mac possessed a strong, deep voice however disabled he'd become. He glanced down and nodded. "You know as well as me that a business runs in cycles. Most businesses and farms carry a loan just for that purpose. That's good management practice, and all know this. It's common. But, I done paid down most of my mortgage to you-uns anyways up there in Americus. I been paying you loan sharks at a damned high interest rate too, pert' near twenty percent cause you had me with no other choice. You and that First National Bank in cahoots up yonder. So I'm just about paid up. Or didn't you know that? I know, cause I have my statement that says so!"

"Inopportunely, that's not how your loan contract reads. Mr. Grayson." He paused. "At any time you default, regardless if you owe just one single dollar—"

"—That don't make a damn to me."

"Do you have a copy of your contract?"

"Well, hell yes, I do." He shifted in his chair and resumed his coughing fit a while longer. The banker paused until Mr. Grayson could settle down. Mac asked Myra to bring him some water which she did. He drank and continued. "I may be a little short on cash at the moment, but I've paid you ninety-five percent of what I owe. I have a plan, and I can pay in short order."

"How short, because according to the language in this paperwork, you have exactly thirty days left, That's all. And then we'll come for it."

"You are? Where you taking it?"

"Mr. Grayson, be reasonable."

"I'll be here with my gal damned shot gun. You know that, don't you?"

"Maclin. Is that right? That is your name, isn't it? For the love of God, can't we act like grown men?"

"Hell yes, we are."

"Listen here—"

"—You listen here! With that there paperwork, you may be *legally* right at this time, *but you ain't morally right!*"

"Mr. Grayson, we have no choice. I have a number of constituents I must answer to. It's actually not *all my money*, you see."

Mac had held back his last card to play until the end of this discussion. He said, "I don't know if you are aware, Mr. Rutledge."

"What's that?"

"The Leesburg Courthouse burned down a few months ago, and along with it, many of the tax plats, deeds, and property surveys this side of the Flint River in Lee County—not all but many. My connections say the county has assessed their situation, and that my property records, in fact, are one of those that were destroyed. And that means you can't close my case until all legal components are accounted for."

This was Mac's ace in the hole.

Mac Grayson had seen his share of setbacks in his days: fire, draught, theft, the boll weevil, cut worm, loss of limb, even heart ache and death. But this bank man was like a thorn in his side.

Mac's face softened somewhat, and he resumed drumming his thick fingers on the nob of his walking cane. He paused in thought, looking up at the sky with his head cocked sharply to one side. He slowly held out his hand and motioned for the banker to hand him the papers to review.

Mr. Rutledge stepped up a few steps and reached forward with the papers.

As quickly as a rattle snake, Mac snatched his hand instead of the papers and yanked Rutledge up where he held him face to face. The papers floated to the ground in swirls.

Mac's face was as red as a radish, his eyes bulging from their sockets. "You listen to me you little varmint. You get off my land right now, or I'll pump your ass full of so much rock-salt, you won't be able to sit down for a month!" With one hand and all of his might, he flung the banker twenty feet backward where he landed with a thud in the dirt, his fedora flying in the wind. In shock, Rutledge scrambled and crawled across the ground after the papers and his lost hat.

Alarmed, Rutledge's counterpart in the Nash jumped out, yet both Arden and Cade stepped forward and made it clear he was not to advance, otherwise risk life or limb.

At that instant, Myra appeared in the doorway of the cabin with a 12 gage shotgun. Without a moment's hesitation, she fired both barrels into the morning air, and everyone ducted for cover. She fell back several feet but regained her balance and recoiled, still holding the heavy piece tightly with both hands. The loud report echoed off the hills and into the river valley. Everyone's ears were ringing. At sixteen, she stood well over five feet, about five foot six, but the Buffalo Springfield was almost as tall as she.

Rutledge was just then standing after grasping his lost hat off the ground. Myra resumed her wide stance by her father in the doorway, and yelled, "Best get movin' on Mr. Rutledge lest you want to lose you head, too!"

Chapter 4

THE TWO BOYS took Mac to his bed and laid him down. Once again, he began coughing, almost gagging. Myra vigorously patted his back and attempted settling him down. Apparently the meeting with Mr. Rutledge had disturbed him. Later she brought corn bread and fatback, but he refused to eat, rather preferring to smoke his pipe. He told her he didn't feel well. Moments later he slept.

He slept most of the time, eighteen hours per day since his accident. Inactive as he'd become, he ate but not much; he mostly smoked his tobacco pipe instead. He rarely left his room much less the house due to his weakness and the risk of taking the four steps down from the front door.

Confident and assured, he told his children the following morning he wasn't too concerned with the bank. His longtime friend and neighbor, Ches Kutner, had spoken to people in Leesburg who assured him that having a county engineer accumulate a new Library of Property Surveys might be postponed for a long time to come. Mac explained to his children that the State of Georgia was low on funding as it stood, and that having the matter corrected would take some time. With this, Mac was satisfied. It made perfect sense. He was assured he could eventually take care of the issue. As time had passed, he had always managed whatever had come their way, no matter the difficulty. But how to handle this situation, honestly, had not yet occurred to him.

Jasper John stood on a tall ladder while making repairs to the church roof when Ches Kutner approached from the road in his wagon. The long oak wagon was made for hauling, with a four-wall bed, chained tailboard, corner stanchions, and the buckboard mounted on two curled semi-circles of steel that flexed as a crude suspension for its riders.

Kutner halted his draft horses and let them eat wild thistle by the fence that fronted the churchyard. After he dismounted, the horses pulled the empty wagon closer to the fence to get at the tall weeds. Kutner was a small man with narrow shoulders, a black Irish type with tar-black hair and a fair, sunburned face. Although short on stature with thin arms, he was sharp in wit.

Jasper John came down the ladder to meet him.

"Chesley," Jasper John said.

"Pastor Tucker," Kutner replied.

"What brings you up to the church this morning?" Jasper John set down his hammer on the church steps, along with the nails and cedar shakes he was using to repair the roof.

"Passing by, on my way to Flintside to pick up a load of supplies. Saw you out on the roof here."

"You and Jessy and the little one doing alright?" the pastor asked. Kutner and his wife had recently birthed a newborn child, a little boy.

"Good as can be, considering." He removed his straw hat and wiped his forehead with a handkerchief he withdrew from his back pocket. He took a deep breath in dismay, and the pastor knew what he thought.

"Things are getting bad, I know. We all know," Jasper John said.

Kutner said, "You hear Mel Parrish up in De Soto had to move his family out?" he asked, speaking of a prominent farmer holding more than four hundred acres. "And they took Darl Smith's land back. He's gone to who knows where. All of this before the courthouse fire, of course. But Cobb Mason, over in Leslie, he's on a short list now too, I hear."

"I know, Ches, I know all about it," Jasper John said.

Kutner added, "People are saying that Americus First Trust, as a matter of fact, was down this way yesterday making calls on loans."

They moved into the nearby shade of the church steeple to get out of the sun, Kutner fanning his face with his straw hat.

Jasper John asked, "What about Mac Grayson? And his three? You know Mac is a good man from a good family. They've owned that property for near a hundred years."

"Yes sir, a long time. You know I've done work for him in past years. I've taken my combine down to strip his cotton and help them haul it to Warwick. Yes, he's a good man. But I believe years ago he took out a mortgage to run the place and now, I hope he's not in jeopardy, too," Ches said.

Ches Kutner was fairly young, middle-aged, in his early forties, with good ethics, had a farm a half-mile down the road from Grayson. He was a cotton man, too, and had suffered as all the cotton growers with the weevil and drought, now with the depression coming on.

Jasper John said, "It ain't looking good either way with the circumstances they're in. Their situation has multiplied taking into account his accident, the economy, and the condition of the cotton crop. I've been down to his place a few times to visit since his accident, and of course he's confined to his bed."

Kutner asked, "What're his children's names and ages? Refresh my memory."

The pastor said, "Arden the oldest, is 'bout twenty-four. Cade is the middle one. He's 'bout eighteen."

"And the little red head?"

"That's Myra, 'bout sixteen, almost seventeen, I'd say.

"You heard anything more since the accident as far as the circumstances? The word is hush hush with all the ones that were present."

Jasper John said, "It was a strange situation from what I'm thinking. Mac's not sure what happened. I'm not sure he's too clear on it himself."

"Somethin' doesn't sound right with what's traveling through the grapevine here in north Lee. People are talking about it, like it was *not* an accident."

"Well, I wouldn't want rumors flying around. Hearing rumors is one thing but passing them along is another. But I have to say facts could be facts. What do you think?"

"From what Carter Farnsworth said, Mac was loading his wagon with lumber at the lumberyard to repair his cotton house."

"Whatever good a cotton house is right now." The pastor smirked.

"Well anyway, Mac told me he was planning on taking in what he could by gettin' me over with my combine, even at five cents per. He wanted to see what might shake out, one way or the other. But anyhow, Mac was there a' loading wood when it happened, alright."

"Yep, that's what he told me, too, he was loading wood."

"You see, Farnsworth works for Jack Waylon, and Farnsworth was there along with Ben Dollar. Dollar also works for Waylon—they both do—and Dollar was there and saw it too. Now that time has passed on, Farnsworth has become a little vague with his story, about the occurrence, maybe cause he works for Waylon." Kutner fanned with his hat, wiped his face with his handkerchief in the hot day as they stood in the shadows of the church.

"You thinking Waylon had something to do with it?"

"This is what I gathered from speaking with Farnsworth. Grayson was loading some long truss wood from a high pile a timber. Waylon was there too in his long-body Ford flatbed, you know, the kind with the new straight-eight engine in it. Anyhow, he was there too at the lumberyard, a' loading short stud lumber nearby Grayson loading long trusses. From the way Farnsworth tells it, some other driver there accidentally backed his truck right into the side of that tall stock of trusses, on the opposite side from where Mac was loading his wagon. And the whole blame pile fell over, landing right on top of Grayson. And I mean tons of gal darned wood fell on him. Crushed the hell outta Mac and his wagon, too. He was buried."

"What about the truck driver? What happened to him?"

"Farnsworth says he took off in a hurry and fled the lumberyard not wanting to take any responsibility."

"And Grayson?"

"By the time everyone there gathered around, Farnsworth and Dollar had pulled him out and set him in his wagon bed, but said that he'd done gone limp and couldn't speak, was awake and aware, eyes moving around and such, but was damned paralyzed. Luck has it that he's now recovered somewhat, and his feeling has returned. Lord bless, he can walk a might in his house with a cane. But hell, that's about as far as he can go, Jasper."

"Well, the Lord help him I pray with all else that's going on and the crops, too. I know he's hurt pretty bad." Jasper John shook his head, thinking. "But do you believe he might improve with some time?"

"Don't know, yet."

"I suppose the Lord's only one does. What about Mr. Slade?" the pastor asked, concerning the lumberyard proprietor.

"Jasper John, you know that the Big River Lumberyard is a busy place. At least it has been until recently with the economy slowing. Commercial transport trucks are usually coming and going all day long. Contractors, freightliners, farmers, even little wagons of all shapes and sizes. Could have been any truck, Slade says. Farnsworth and Dollar are the ones that could tell you, but they ain't talking anymore about it."

Kutner wiped his head again, slipped the handkerchief in his pocket and donned his straw hat. He added, "Least Mac has the three young'uns with him, but he weighs darned near as much as a Hereford yearling. Managing him in such a small place as their cabin must be difficult."

"You are right about that," Jasper John agreed. "Now, what about the *grapevine* you were talking about?"

"Now this is just hearsay, but my wife Jessy knows Farnsworth's wife, and Farnsworth's wife says Carter was right upset about the whole episode. Actually more upset than he should have been. Jessy says Farnsworth's wife originally told a slightly different version to the story, implying Jack Waylon has some grudge with Grayson, but what the real story is we aren't clear on—saying that somehow there was a connection with Waylon and the accident. "

"Anybody contact the law, yet?"

"The thing is from what I've gathered, Sheriff Blackburn up in Americus happens to be the brother-in-law of Mr. J.R. Rutledge, the president of Americus First Trust Bank. And I hear Rutledge was down here and may be after Grayson's land too, so Blackburn probably doesn't want to interfere with Mac Grayson due to that situation."

"Damned devil, I tell you, brethren. The devil, he's always working on something."

"Listen here, Pastor. I have to get going. I know I've been out of church a while, but I'll see you at next Sunday's service. Lord we need some prayers, Pastor."

"I'm a' praying like there's no tomorrow, brother."

"Well, hell if there ain't one, pastor, then I reckon we won't have to worry anymore." He bid the pastor goodbye and rode into Flintside.

Confined and motionless, Mac lay sadly in his bed and looked out of the window up through the oaks, watching the soft clouds lumbering like migrating beast across the afternoon sky. He thought of his Ila Mae and how the many years had passed. He thought of her dark brown hair and how she would let it out at night and it would flow like a river over her shoulders and down her back.   Only in the privacy of their home would she let that beautiful hair fall. He thought back at how long it had been since he'd seen her oval face, with those pale tired eyes that smiled however long the day had been in the fields or kitchen. Despite how many buckets she had pulled from the well. Despite how much cotton they had sacked, or how much sickness had overcome their children. No matter how difficult life had become.

He smoothed his wavy gray hair back over his head. The room was sweltering although the opened window offered a steady breeze from the field up from the lake. He was naked except the thin cotton sheet that covered his waste. On a side table, an oil lamp glistened gold with a faint, flickering flame. Could he lay with her again, he was thinking? He took up his Bible and kissed it with an invocation that he would see her again. Could she know him after so long, he wondered? Would she recognize his voice? Although he doubted this, he still had hope. He fell asleep with her in his heart.

Later night fell, and he woke again.

The room was now shadow-struck with the flickering oil flame. The night sky through the wide window was a palette of purple and black, the edges of clouds trimmed with salmon-pink to the far west. Their armoire, the one she had hauled down in their wagon from a furniture shop in Americus, was the only piece of good furniture they ever had. Mid-Atlantic she had been told, probably Maryland or eastern Pennsylvania perhaps; the broadsides and fronts constructed of walnut, the interior and secondary woods a light poplar. She had loved this. It was a small size though well-made, enough for their few clothes, yet nothing to apologize for.

Her hardbacks still remained stacked in the corner on the floor, upon the shelves of the wall, and piled under the bed gathering dust as he refused to remove any memories of her from their room. Her poems and the elegy she had written on heavy paper stock was neatly folded and remained in their locked box with their other important papers and things. She had loved to read, had been taught by her mother. She had read endlessly in the winter or on Sunday afternoons at her first chance of rest.

A rounded mirror of cheval glass with chips on its edges still hung on a nail over their small table and her wash basin; the mirror he cared not to look into anymore as he didn't care for what stared back. Two pairs of his now-useless work boots edged the wall and expressed the wear of his hard days in the field. On the bedside table, the melted candles had guttered down into their holders and looked like the old man's eye sockets. His unshaven face sagged and made him look like an old dog.

He had aged but his heart was not yet gone. On early spring mornings, he sometimes thought he could smell her scent lingering on the breeze coming into their window. Was that his imagination, he thought? Or just the honeysuckle vine that grew abundantly along the fence up by the road? However, of all that remained with him, both tangible and in spirit, the memory of her loving heart was the most potent.

The dark came to him in his loneliness and what was left was silence. Shadows on the ceiling were wraiths upon his dwindling life, watching and waiting. It was as though the dark and solitude were removing him out of his virtue, let alone his hope and belief of what could have been. He reached out with his hand to touch his Bible on the bedside table, and he prayed the world could not subvert his faith that his Savior was with him that very moment. Whatever his size and strength had gained him in his youth, what now awaited was an empty shell, lost and afraid to die.

He woke when the eastern light was pink. Roosters up on Waylon's property always announced the coming of morning. He heard Myra and Cade speaking softly in the other room, a pan being put on the potbelly stove, wood going in, and the door clanging softly shut. He picked his head up from the bed.

Zirrr Zirrrr Zirrr

Zirrr Zirrr Zirrrr

Zirrr Zirrrr Zirrrr Zirrrr Zirrrr Zirrr

It fell quiet once again. Birds chirped and sang their morning song outside his window. From lying in his bed, he could see through the window and up to the split rail fence on the ridge where the road came in from Flintside. On the rise, he saw the slabs of vertical granite stones arranged as straight as a plumb line, morning shadows from the willows dancing over them, the family names cut neatly on them, and the cross of Christ chiseled in their centers. The wind blew the willows and they bent gently in the breeze. He could hear Cade's voice, now higher; now Myra speaking too, her inflection becoming stronger.

Zirrrr Zirrrr Zirrrr Zirrrr

Ping Ping Ping

The sounds stopped.

He sat and craned his neck to look out of the window. He took up his cane and sat on the edge of his bed, ran his hand back over his hair. He pushed and stood then paused to catch his breath. Supported by his cane, he stepped the few feet toward the window and looked out in the direction of the barn, but from his position, he could only see that the barn doors were opened slightly. Naked, he turned and urinated in the caught pot by his bed. His arm quivered as he held himself upright. Afterward, unable to continue standing, he returned and sat on the bed.

Zirrrr Zirrrr Zirrrr Zirrrr went the cross saw

Then the ringing of a hammer on nails.

Ping Ping Ping

Myra and Cade were talking louder now.

He turned on his bed and faced the door toward the kitchen.

"Myra! What's going on out there?" he called. His coughing spasms returned and he heaved forward gagging, coughing. When he finished, the house was silent.

He listened. No voices, no one. No sounds of the tools.

"Myra!"

Minutes later, she slowly creaked the door open just enough to peek in.

"Morning, Papa," she said sweetly.

"Could you please bring me some water?"

A moment later, she entered and sat by him on the bed with the cup. He had draped the bed cover over his waist. He drank then set the cup aside. He coughed.

"What's being done out in the barn, Myra?" he asked.

"That's Arden, Papa. He's repairing the wagon."

"The wagon?"

She pulled her long hair off her shoulders. The auburn tent glistened in the morning light coming from the window, her beautiful ambience seen in the youth of her face. Her small hand rested on his knee and she looked at her father sadly.

"Yes, the wagon. Do you remember your accident up at the lumberyard in Flintside? When the lumber gave way and you were standing under it? Do you remember what happened?"

"Course I do. That's why I'm a prisoner to this bed, in this room, and this house. And why I'll be a burden to you and the boys, maybe for the remainder of my days. I'm with a broken back. Says Dr. Clack, anyhow." He ran his hand back over his head.

"Well, the falling lumber not only crushed you but the backend of the wagon too, and busted the main crossbeam." She placed her hand on his shoulder. "Arden's out in the barn fixing the wagon."

"Needs fixing, I guess." Still sitting on the bed, he popped the knuckles of his marred hands and looked around. He noticed his dirty clothes piled in the corner that Myra would eventually have to wash.

She said, "We've decided we're not taking in the cotton this year, not after what has happened. We just can't. There's not enough to make it worth our trouble."

"Yeah, I've agreed to that. Ain't worth spittle, I suppose." He hung his head and studied the worn oak floor, the grain of the old wood, the way it swirled. "But best get that wagon taken care of 'ere we need it. Cotton or no cotton."

"Papa, Arden's going to make a trip up to Americus."

"Americus?"

She left the room momentarily but soon returned. She held a fold of paper in her hand. However brave Myra attempted to be, however young she pretended she wasn't, she could not escape her honesty. She had a tear on her cheek.

His back was bad, yet his eyes were good enough. He could still see down the barrel of a 30/30 and take a deer from one hundred paces. See the eye of a needle well enough to thread it. See and read the big print in the hymnals without his glasses. See well enough to eye an eagle in the top of a tall fir tree. And he could read the return address on the letter in Myra's hand, though she hadn't meant for him to: It read: "St. Francis Mental Hospital" in bold type across the top of the page.

Zirrrr Zirrrr Zirrrr went the saw.

Ping Ping Ping went the hammer.

"Papa, Arden is making a new crossbeam for the wagon. He'd going to fix it, and he's taking the two mules and driving back to Americus. He is going to get Momma, and we're bringing her home."

Chapter 5

JACK WAYLON KICKED the dirt, cursed and strode off down the hill. He abruptly stopped, placed his hands on his hips then half-turned, frustrated. He glanced out over his property of nearly three hundred acres from atop the embankment that fell away to the dirt road below.

"Gal damned hell!" He shook his head and spat chaw juice then kicked the thick dirt pile that had gathered on the ground around their feet. "Gal damned hell, Bobby!"

Bobby's tall drill rig was positioned on the steep incline with the truck cab facing uphill. It was running hard. The engine spat and sputtering until Bobby Womack shut it off, and it came to a slow, grinding halt. With a final backfire, it stopped dead.

"Mr. Waylon, we done dug half way to China by now. Damned near hundred and fifty feet and we still ain't hit the aquifer." He removed his cap and ran his arm across his forehead to wipe off the sweat. His boots were submerged in thick mud up to his shanks. Drill pipe lay nearby on the ground in ten foot lengths. His assistant, Jamie Ellis, just stared and held his hand flat over his forehead to block out the glaring noonday sun. It was nearly ninety degree.

"Bobby, we got to go deeper. There must be water in this ground somewhere."

"This is our third drill this week. And we got nothing."

"Gal damned drought!" He could see Lake Blackshear way down the hill across Mac Grayson's property, the water green and flowing like the River of Life.

He said to Bobby, "We've hardly had any groundwater up on this high side for two years now, since '28. My number one well went completely dry six months back. Dry as a bone, it did. And I'm gonna have to do something about this. I need a deep well pump in this ground and soon!"

"Mr. Waylon, you already have the vertical turbine pump, the head, right angle gear drive, and the gasoline engine to run it over in the number one well. We just have to pull it, move it to a better location, adjust the length of the column pipe and shafting to fit the depth, and we're good," Bobby said.

"But we haven't found any water yet."

"All the water," Bobby said assuredly, "is down in the ground in the lower topography." He pointed down the hill toward the lake. "The problem Mr. Waylon is that the groundwater has dried up along with the river. You need to be down there, over the road in that field down yonder."

Jack walked back up to the drill rig and placed his hand on the truck, leaning against the fender. The truck was a long body truck with a high, structural tripod in the rear bed where the gas engine and vertical drill rig were set up.

Waylon said, "Even worse, that field down there is Mac Grayson's property, not mine. His property runs up the side of the lake nearly a quarter mile. He's down there and I'm up here. I have two hundred and sixty head of cattle to water. And a corn crop for feed in the west field, too. Grayson ain't got nothing but a field of boll weevil cotton." He rubbed his hands together. "Like I said, I've been driving a water truck down to the landing on the end of old man McCarver's property. But it's a long way there and hauling it back is a hell of a job. The truck can't carry enough and the water doesn't last long enough."

"What does Mr. McCarver say about it?"

Jack shook his head and laughed. "Nothing, because both he and his wife are gone, both died a few years back. Their land's idle, been that way for years. No children or relatives, I hear. His property is tied up in probate court over in Leesburg, I bet you."

Jack Waylon was a handsome man, tall with a head of light brown hair, a square jawline, and a prominent cleft chin. His sharp blue eyes gleaned the property below, and he could see the Grayson cabin in the low rolling hills below his land, and Lake Blackshear, also, not far beyond. His steady gaze grew angry and he turned to look at the well driller.

Womack scratched his head while holding his cap. "If we could get down there, we could set a pump and run piping up this hill. Build a trough about here," he said, motioning his arm out over the hill, "and bring the cattle over here for watering. Maybe extend the pipe, too, just over toward the corn field and run irrigation ditches."

"In a perfect world, yes, but I know Grayson won't let me walk on his land. That would be a cold day in hell when that happened."

"Well, if Mr. McCarver is not present, let's go on that property and do the same."

"Can we run a pipe for a half mile or more from there up to here?"

"Could except it would cost an arm and a leg considering we'd have to get a half mile of pipe and a much bigger pump and engine, too."

"Well shit then. With this economy, I'd better watch my wallet, you suspect?"

"Yes, sir, I suspect so then." He slipped his hat back on his head. "Another fifty feet you think, Mr. Waylon?" Bobby asked, slipping his leather gloves on, too. He glanced over at his workhand, Jamie Ellis, who shrugged his shoulders.

Jack knew it meant another twenty-five dollars at fifty cents per foot."

"Hell, let's do it." He spat chaw and cursed. He had little to no choice in the matter.

The day's sun was fading over the horizon when Jack trudged wearily back to his house. Another day lost digging for water. From his columned front porch, he turned and watched Womack's drill rig leaving in a cloud of dust toward the road back to Flintside. He slapped his hat on his thigh and hung it on a hook outside his front door. The heavy door squeaked open and the house presented itself with stillness and silence. He stripped off his sweat-soaked clothes and boots and laid them on the floor. Naked and exhausted, he stepped in the front room and fell into a leather chair that faced the massive stone fireplace and hearth.

Aside from his frustration, the days he spent alone had taken their toll. Other than his water issues, the price of beef had plummeted in recent months and his bank was limiting monthly withdrawals, too. Word was out that if First National in Americus failed, everyone with accounts there would lose all their money, and *all would fail*. Lines were running out from the bank's doors and around the block. And no money meant no beef sales. In the worst case, he considered that bartering might suffice if he could arrange a system with the feed mill, the co-op, veterinarian, grocer, hardware supply, or even the county tax office. But if beef was valueless then what good was it now? What could the county do with heads of beef, at any rate? Fortuitously, his small steel safe which was hidden away held a fair amount of cash.

He stood and walked into the kitchen for supper. He slipped a pair of overalls off a brass hook behind the door and put them on. Thumbing the straps over his shoulders, he stepped to a tub on the counter to wash his face and hands as he stared out of the glass window to his farm.

From the window, he watched his workhands Carter Farnsworth and Benjamin Dollar coming out of the barn carrying bales of hay then pouring corn feed into the troughs and calling in the cattle.

"Woohoo!" Carter called out at the top of his lungs. "Woohoo!"

The mooing began as the cattle quickly approached in droves from the fields. Dollar turned the valve on the cylindrical water tank to fill a large galvanized bucket, and he proceeded to pour that into numerous low, elongated troughs on the ground. Finally he turned the last bucket upward and softly shook out the last drop. The pond in the east field that had served for many years as a water source for the farm, was now dry-baked clay overgrown with tall weeds. The pond hadn't contained water for many months.

Farnsworth stood motionless and watched the herd come. A dust cloud emerged and drew up in the late day air under the moving hooves of the beasts. As they came, their heads dipped and rose with their strides, ears flinching, their mooing becoming louder and louder as the rumbling arrived. A mass of brown and white hides merged as the cattle rounded the troughs and gathered to feed.

Jack ate his stew and washed it down with warm beer. Later he came out to the front porch to see his workhands off. From there, he looked out from under the cascading canopy of thick poplar that surrounded his home. Crickets whirred in the distance. The wind whispered. The sun was setting in the west.

Farnsworth and Dollar approached and stood at the base of the steps: Farnsworth stout and round-shouldered with a trimmed beard he wore even in summer months; Dollar sunburned-red, wiry and agile with a shock of black hair that hung in his eyes. Waylon handed them their pay. Wordless, they stuffed the dollars deeply into their blue jeans then turned to leave.

Waylon called them back. "Men."

They both stopped and turned.

"We didn't have much luck today, boys," he said and rested his hand up against a tall column on his white-painted porch. "And we drilled damned near two hundred feet down. The well driller finally got some water but said it wasn't enough to piss in a catch pot. Says the water table under my land has dried up."

"No wonder, boss. It ain't rained hardly in two, three years," Carter Farnsworth said nervously, knowing where this conversation might lead.

"The water tank is empty again, too," Ben Dollar said, stating the obvious, this remark only infuriating Waylon further. As if to soften the comment, he added, "I'll go first thing in the morning and take the truck and the small water tank down to McCarver's landing at the lake."

Waylon stepped off the porch and stood in front of his men. The three momentarily looked at one another in silence.

Waylon finally said, "Anyone asking anymore about the accident at the lumberyard?"

Farnsworth answered, "David Slade done said it's cleared up. States there was nothing to it," he added speaking of the lumberyard proprietor. "He says it was nothing more than an accident when that out-of-state freight carrier backed up and hit those timbers, causing them to keel over. Accident is what he said."

Unable to look at Waylon directly, Farnsworth quickly peered off into the distance and drew his mouth into a straight line because his eyes would give him away. He looked down and studied his boots, muddy and torn, then rubbed his hands on his jeans. He was unwilling to incriminate himself if any further questions arose. He preferred to agree and be done with his responsibility. He had a family and children at home. He hadn't had any part in it other than being at the wrong place at the wrong time and witnessing the unfortunate event. He didn't care to go against the grain and lose his job. He couldn't afford that.

To Farnsworth, Waylon said, "That's what I gathered too from Mr. Slade. Nobody saw otherwise, is that right, boys?"

"Nothing, no sir," Farnsworth reluctantly agreed.

"Boss, you weren't even there, were you?" Dollar said, sarcastically laughing, not afraid to smile.

Waylon nodded his agreement to their pact and told them, "You boys get on, now. I got a nice bonus coming your way for the over-time. I'll see you at first light, alright?" He turned to leave but said, "Benjamin, looks like you'll be hauling the water truck down to the lake from sun up to sun down. We must get as much on the crop as we can, or it won't be worth anything before too long. It's wilting out there in this brutal sun and action must be taken. Of course as a last resort, for the cattle we have hay stored up in the haymow of the barn, but they are ever thirsty beasts."

With a last word he warned them, "And if we can't get a pump in the ground down there in the lowland, we might be on the last train that leaves the station for Atlanta."

Waylon stepped into his house and went for some moonshine to take the edge off.

Later, he stumbled to bed, holding the wall toward his bedroom to keep from falling.

Cade rummaged through the smokehouse and the storage closet in the cabin one last time but returned emptyhanded to the table were Arden and Myra sat. Their father was snoring so that the bedroom door seemed to vibrate. The day had turned to rain which rendered a hunt unlikely. It had rained off and on for days. Having no flour, bread, molasses, cornpone, chitterlings, fatback, salted meat, or jarred greens meant no dinner, either. Their food had completely run out. The last of the chickens running in the yard had been eaten, too. Myra, the previous day, had gone into the woods to gather dandelions, wild onions, and mushrooms by the handfuls, but they were depleted also. Though Cade had fished, he'd returned with no bream or lake bass. Their remaining ammunition had dwindled dangerously low, yet some still remained. As a last result, Cade had agreed to ride a mule the following day to the Desoto Bank for the end of their father's savings which totaled five dollars and five cents, but Arden had been informed by Chesley Kutner the doors had been chain-locked and the windows boarded up, too. All the neighbors, according to Kutner, were panicked about the Desoto Bank. And no one as of yet had gotten word from the folks up in Americus as to their dire situation either.

"What the hell are we going to do?" Cade said while running his thumb down the blade of his knife.

"What about the squirrels over in the apple trees? They ought to be running the branches, gathering the unripen apples by now. I know they come out this time of late summer," Myra suggested.

"Not a bad idea, but it's raining cats and dogs right now."

Rain was hammering the tin roof of the cabin like an army of squirrels running amuck up there. Rainwater poured over the roof eve and fell in front of the open window like a waterfall.

"Bout time it rained anyway," Arden said.

"We don't need it at the time, though" Cade mentioned, admiring the gleam of the knife's metal, the serrated cutting edge, the fine wooden handle formed to his hand.

"We need hunting weather, now," Myra said.

"And more ammo, cause we're almost out."

"I guess we could cover our hunting jackets with bear grease, take out over to McCarver's and squirrel hunt in the rain. Damned the only three 20 gauge shotgun shells that are left, I'm getting mighty hungry."

"There's bird shot in the shells, right?"

"Buck shot, I'm afraid, so we might best hold off. A squirrel ain't but a meal. A good sized doe can last weeks. Besides, buck shot will blow a squirrel to Timbuctoo."

They pondered.

As a last resort, Arden went to his chest. He withdrew a square of hardtack wrapped in wax paper that he stored there, as a back-up in the event of a long overnight hunting trip that might be delayed for some unforeseen reason. Myra brewed the last of the coffee. The three ate and never knew how good hardtack and coffee could taste.

Chapter 6

AFTER THE RAIN, Cade took to the woods toward the McCarver property and walked through with his slingshot, hoping and praying he might get lucky. He wasn't too good with it, but it was worth a chance if he spotted a squirrel. Just through the tree line, he heard footsteps and turned to see Myra coming up behind with a parka over her shoulders. She stepped gracefully along the rock path and pulled her hair off her shoulders as she approached him. For the first moment in his life, he saw her as a woman. Though she was just short of her seventeenth birthday, the harsh events of the summer had seasoned her from the mere skittish child she had been in the early spring. She had matured. Not discounting her bright keenness, the innate wit she had been born with, the challenges alone in which they faced had proven that she was a worthy partner in their urgent state. She was changing. Life's trying challenges change people. Difficulty and heartache can change people, some for the good and some not so much. When one walks through life they change the world. However as they go, life changes them too.

"Arden is sleeping," she said as she came up to him.

He turned and resumed his direction along the wooded path as she followed.

"I'm worried about Momma," she said from behind.

They walked single file. Cade remained silent. He often chose silence over saying the wrong thing. He wasn't sure what to think. He was as worried as Myra and Arden.

"Arden is nearly finished with the wagon, has the big crossbeam in and is putting the bed back together. He's a good carpenter."

"That wagon has many miles on it, Myra, from here to Americus, Desoto, Leesburg, and back many trips. The bushings and axels are worn. I hope he has enough axel grease for the trip. Fortunately our mother, given the circumstances, would be a light enough load."

The three had discussed the preparing and making of the trip the previous day. With little disagreement, the plan had been cast as Arden was the oldest. Myra and Cade would be required to stay and care for their father. He certainly couldn't care for himself, much less stand for more than a few minutes and walk.

"I'm frightened what is to come, now having to manage Papa in his bed. Where are we possibly going to put her, too?"

The arrangements were made as soon as Myra had turned thirteen. Papa had his room, Myra hers, and the boys slept on stuffed pallets on the kitchen floor, which was a comfortable advantage lying next to the woodstove in the winter months especially if they had coal in the house. At one time all three had kept the same room although it had been cramped. Their father had made bunks for the boys. Myra had had her own frame with cross-roping and a hay-and-shuck mattress.

"Do you remember her?" she asked.

The time had passed on now many years without their mother. It had been strange and none of them had really understood her.

"Yes, I can remember her," he said lowly as they walked the path to a rise where they stopped and could see through an opening in the trees to the lake below.

They paused to watch the narrow lake, green with Georgia river water that had run down from the north, gathering rain and storm water as it made its way to Sumter then Lee County; to flow onward through the marshlands around Albany among the palmetto and magnolia. On to join the mighty Chattahoochee and onward through Florida, to the home the native Apalachee Indians called Apalachicola on the Gulf of Mexico. The flow of the river with a history behind it, having seen blood of civil war soldiers; the brutal history of slavery in the south; the farms and the farmers of the past and their strife to sustain and live; to carrying with it the songs of the south, African spirituals, and the poems of Sydney Lanier. The vast Flint River with all the wonders it held.

"What was wrong with her do you think?" she asked.

"They say she lost her mind. That is what Pa and Dr. Clack said. I think she was touched, though, maybe even by God, not that what I think matters."

"How do you reckon it happened?"

"She just quit functioning properly, I suppose. Nothing specific happened, Pa said. No one event marked the beginning. He said it took place over a period of time. But, as far back as I can remember, she was always like that," Cade told her. "Of course, she and Papa are nearly seventy. I'm eighteen."

Cade said, "I do remember she couldn't remember my name from one minute to the next." Through the tree tops, they saw a break in the clouds, and fine bands of sunlight touched their faces. Cade began to speak again but halted.

Myra instead said, "You know she loved you, though, didn't you?"

He shrugged his shoulders. His blue eyes resembled still blue water with light in them, so stark and vibrant, his square face and neatly trimmed blondish-brown hair whisked back and catching the sunlight through the tree branches.

She laughed. "Cade, she couldn't remember any of our names."

"Do you recall when she would stand at the stove and stare at the empty pots, not knowing how to cook? She didn't even know what a pot was for, remember?"

"She was senile, that's what Dr. Clack said. Call it what it was. She just went senile as soon as she turned fifty, they said."

"I saw her the time she went out into the yard naked and forgot her clothes."

"Papa went out and cried as he pulled her inside, shaking his head in utter disbelief. He didn't know what had gotten ahold of her, maybe the devil, he thought."

"She just repeated herself over and over, too, saying the same thing, asking the same questions repeatedly; then beginning the same line of conversation just minutes later. Saying she needed to go out to pick cotton even though it would be the dead of winter. Or that she wanted to know where her sister was, even though her sister, Mary, had died years before."

Myra said, "I know. I remember." She added, "She would stare at me silently and admire my hair. She would reach out and want to touch my hair and run her hands over it. She wouldn't speak. She just smiled and felt my hair. I guess she was completely gone and had no awareness at that point."

"During wintertime, she sat in her chair for hours and watched the fire in the fireplace, just silently watching the flames. Or Pa would set her outside in her chair when the weather was warm. But she wandered off sometimes, too, and scared the hell out of us. Remember when we lost her and couldn't locate her until midnight down by the river? She had been out there all night. Papa went about crazy looking for her. She was a handful for Papa, and he about lost his sanity too, I believe. He had to run the farm too all the while."

"I recall when the preacher Jasper John came, and they all had a prayer vigil outside of her room, but it did no good, it never improved."

"Though, she carried that Bible with her for the longest time. I believe that although she had lost her mind, somehow the spirit of God stayed with her. She couldn't make sense of anything, but at least she somehow knew what the Bible was for. She'd take that Bible anywhere but would forget her clothes."

"How long has it been since they took her away?"

"A long time. Years. Maybe ten years now."

They hadn't spoken of her for many months, maybe a year or more. It was too painful.

Cade said, "You know Momma and Papa had a son, long before any of us came."

She paused and tried not to weep. As her body was changing, her moods were also. Her emotions ran sometimes light and at other times dark. She often experienced an unexplainable welling in her chest that would arrive at any time and for no reason. But for unknown reasons at the most pointed of occurrences, she could not hold back, and sometimes this caused her to cry uncontrollably. She felt frightened with what had taken place in her childhood, concerning their mother. How they had all witnessed it and had been affected by it. Given the recent events with their father, too, she was ever more frightened. Myra was strong but sometimes weak. It seemed at times that the moon and stars even pulled her away from a settled state, and she didn't know why.

She held the emotional surge down the best she could as Cade spoke.

"They say his name was Paul. They had him long before our time. Papa said he was a fine young man."

She felt the welling coming, building in her small chest, raging, and her lips quivered with sadness. She gasped and her tears came flooding forth. She sobbed. She rested her head on her brother's shoulder, then turned and held him tightly. His arms remained limp at his side, but one hand awkwardly came to rest on her back. Cade was without feeling and had suppressed his emotions for many years, unable to cry at all. Apparently he had been affected much differently than his sister by their mother's history.

He continued, "But Paul became ill, and they don't know what took him. How he died in the cotton field. He was so young, maybe thirteen or fourteen, they said. Possibly some rare heart complication the doctor suggested."

She wiped her eyes and stood back to see Cade up close. She said, "He's buried up on the hill I know, along with Great Grandpa Samuel, Lauren, their daughter Selma and her husband Wyatt, Grandpa Earl and Grandma Nancy, all of the Grayson clan. And Chebona Bula, the Indian canoe-maker, too. I've remembered their names over the years as I've sat up there from time to time to look on them with love." She stepped away to a tall Maple tree and rested her had against the rough bark. She looked back and added, "There's room enough. You know that, too."

He looked puzzled.

"Room enough up there on the ridge for the rest of us to be buried."

"I can say I may not be joining you." He stepped back as if he were leaving.

She loved her bother, naturally. They had grown up together, had walked to the schoolhouse together to be taught by Mr. Burch the schoolmaster. They had learned to read aside one another; had read some of the same books. They had been through so much, and now, the three required each other in the most testing of times.

She stepped forward but stopped. "Not with us?" She wiped away more tears.

Though she was becoming a woman, he thought, she was still a girl in the same way.

"I can't stay here forever. I just don't feel like I fit in. I've been reading the magazines from Mr. Jenkins's store, like *National Geographic* and *Life* magazine. There is a whole other world out there, not just this broken down farm in the middle of God's nowhere."

"Where would you go? I love it here, the farm, the lake, our land. It must be worth something, fifty acres. And don't forget our father. I've never considered leaving. When I came here as a little girl, Papa took me in and loved on me. He gave me what I couldn't have. I was so sad and without care, indigent really. The only material possession I brought with me on that train ride down to Americus was my little suitcase."

"*We all took you in*, Myra. All four of us if you include our mother. You were only three years old. I was five, but I remember." He looked up through the treetops, and he watched the sun just beginning its slow decent westward.

"You say you don't fit in? You have your own blood kin here, Cade, with Arden. I'm the misfit if ever there was. I'm the one that should feel that *I don't fit in*. But I must remain here and take good care of Papa. He took care of me, and now I have to take care of him in return."

"You can't take care of him, not really. For one, he's as big as a bear. When he loses his legs, he'll need a wheelchair and will never be able to leave the cabin. Until—" He paused, turning away with the thought of it.

He said, "For now, we are having a hard enough time caring for ourselves. I know you *want to care for him*, but you know you can't. I know you're hopeful, but you are much too smart not to realize the truth."

They watched the water of Blackshear catching the day's sunlight with glimmers of gold. Birds took flight with the wind and flew into the trees across the water. A blue Herring stretched its beautiful wings and sailed by effortlessly below them along the water's shoreline.

"Let's go see the apple trees," he said after a long silence.

The sun was out from behind the moving clouds, now bright in the sky. They strode through the woods, there boots shuffling the leaves.

Ascending the hill, Cade parted the tree branches to allow Myra to pass. In a zig-zag pattern, they walked up through the trunks of large oaks and hickories. Moss grew like velvet in the shadows. Wild flowers, Golden Rule, Lady Slippers, and Wild Violet grew in between the jutting rocks.

When they crested the hill, the McCarver property came into full view: the hillside of apple trees in flower; a dilapidated barn in the far distance; and a gravel road on the far end winding its way down to a concrete landing for boat access; although the access abruptly ended in a mud flat because the water had receded far back with the drought.

"The apples are in bloom. Look, there, small green ones. It won't be long, now."

"I'm famished just thinking about them."

They walked out onto the rolling field of wire grass, to the apple trees to enjoy the shade. Just at that moment a squirrel raced into view on a branch above them. It paused to inspect them far below, its nose twitching curiously and its tail flipping in the air. Cade slowly picked a small rock and loaded his slingshot. In slow motion he raised his arm, simultaneously retracting the long rubber tubes. *Pop!* The squirrel fell at their feet, squirming. Cade swiftly drew up a long stick and brought it down on the varmint's head to finish it off. Soon another appeared; then another. An hour later, they carried their dinner, six squirrels, back to the house for cleaning and roasting on spits in the fire.

The following morning after her brothers left to fish, she helped her father to the wide doorway of the cabin and sat him nude on a cedar trunk to let the sunshine warm his face. She placed a towel over his waist and bathed him. Earlier in his room, she had set the catch pot on a low heavy stool and let him squat. She removed the waste and took it to the wood line to dump it there. From the doorway, he could look over his land and watch the water, see the trees move with the breeze. This was pleasant for the old man. From a soapy bucket of water she had warmed on the fire, she took a cloth and washed his body, his large feet, his neck and back. She washed his hair. She hung his mirror on a nail and let him shave. She made up a batch of rose water and rinsed him down in the warmth of the morning sun. She ran a comb over his head and let him brush his teeth with baking soda. Then she dried his body and helped him dress.

Afterward, the boys returned. She brought over one of their pallets. Cade helped lay him there with his back against the log wall in the big room to have conversation with them. He remained there that morning, chewing his tobacco and smoking his pipe. With the very last of their lard, she cooked a meal. Together the family ate a lunch of fried lake bass the boys had carried up along with more wild mushrooms. Though a poor family, they were happy that day.

Inside his attorney's office, J.R. Rutledge leaned his shoulder against the window frame and worked a toothpick in between his teeth while sizing up the situation. Through the second story window, the banker observed the passing traffic in the street below, cars, trucks, wagons, and pedestrians. The streets of Americus bristled with commerce: a grocer on the sidewalk stocking fruits and vegetables into bins in front of his store, merchants sweeping their stoops, trucks backing up to make deliveries, wagons of grain and feed moving through. From the window, Rutledge viewed the Americus First Trust Bank Building just down the street, this where his office, employees, and money resided. Although President Herbert Hoover on the previous day had made a radio announcement to the country at large that uncharted waters lay ahead, Americus apparently hadn't taken this into account. By the looks of the busy traffic in town, no one had paid too much attention.

Rutledge turned from the window and met eyes with his counterpart, John Paul Jones, one of the most prominent lawyers in South Georgia.

Rutledge said, "John, this is a very serious condition we're facing. I don't think it has hit the people yet, the *lay people* to be more specific, as to what's ahead." He stepped to a chair that faced Jones's desk but instead preferred to stand behind it and place his hands on the back. "Real estate in the south, especially agricultural land, has been slowly descending into a state of foreclosure for months, ahead of this stock market collapse. The drought and insect infestation along with subsequent falling prices has sent it into a tail spin. We at Americus First have been aware of this trend and aren't surprised by the sudden turn of events. However, I only suspected a sharp deflation. Not a total collapse, which may now be on the near horizon. Instead of a deflation, this is amounting to a complete annihilation of the entire country's financial backbone."

The attorney sat forward and placed his hands flatly on his desk. "J.R., as is stands I have lost over half of my wealth in a matter of months, not to mention my partners and our associates here at Jones, Howard & Marston." The attorney tossed his glasses on his desk and crossed his arms. "We must recoup all we can, J.R. What do you think?"

"The best we can do is progress into damage control at this point, the way I see it."

"I have two hundred thousand dollars tied up in your bank as is," he said, his voice ascending even higher with a tone of frustration. "Banks are already beginning to close their doors up in New York City, and I understand that a few regional banks here in Georgia have too. I fear if we don't play our cards just right, we'll close along with them."

"John, we are doing all we can to assess our position at this time," the banker assured him.

J.R. Rutledge was a well-dressed, narrow-bodied man, coal-black hair, medium height with a mustache resembling a bicycle's handlebar. He was quick to speak, and his sharp gaze was capable of conveying his mood with the least amount of guessing.

He paced back to the window, glanced out and turned to look at Mr. Jones. "In Lee County alone, we currently hold seventy-nine properties of ten acres or more and eighty percent are delinquent."

Jones said, "The problem is greatly compounded by the fact that the Lee County Courthouse went up in flames." John Paul Jones was a tall man with a pale pallor, long fingers, and a pointed nose. He smoked cigars incessantly, one after the other, and his office reeked of cigar smoke.

"Not only that but forty-six of *our properties* had their records go up in flames with it."

"As of the county's last count, thirty-something property records are all that survived. And that is because they happened to be in the annex at the time of the fire."

He asked his attorney: "So, what are we up against, John?"

"According to current case law, in order to foreclose there must be clear title and deed, but most of the official county records have been destroyed and that will hinder any immediate property transfers, foreclosures, or bankruptcy proceedings. The missing records will have to be reconstructed and re-recorded. The county must compile a new Library of Property Records, Titles, and Surveys as soon as possible."

"That could take some time."

"The first line of action would be for the county to approach the property owners themselves, each of whom should have a copy of their deed and any closing documents."

J.R. laughed. "Why would any jeopardized landowner freely produce those, knowing they are at the risk of foreclosing, and that the county obviously doesn't have a set of their own? They must realize that without the land surveys and titles, we will have a difficult challenge in foreclosing and taking our properties back."

"That's correct. And certified surveys are required to generate titles. On the other hand, some properties were granted by the government many years ago, and the land owners in those cases may or may not possess those records. Ultimately the county is responsible for holding all grants, titles, deeds, tax plats, maps, and so forth."

Rutledge said, "The property owners, however, may or may not be aware of the applied legalities, and what the law requires and what it doesn't."

"Unless they hire their own lawyers," Jones quickly put in.

"How could they afford to do so if they don't have enough to pay their own mortgages?"

"They may. Some just may be holding out on their debt obligations, not their cash. You might be surprised."

"How could the county records be reconstructed, then?"

"Accumulating them over time from bank records, attorneys, real estate agencies, and the landowners."

"Do independent survey companies keep records of surveys?"

"They could, but that is all transferred over to the county court following any property closings or title transfers. I believe some laws are pending that may change all of this, but at this time none have yet been passed or enacted." He paused then added. "I suspect a lot of laws and regulations will be changed by the time this economic crash is over with."

"How the hell are we going to proceed with reclaiming our properties if this is the case, where we can't complete a foreclosure due to a lack of county records?"

"I know it's frustrating, J.R. Another issue remaining is that governmental funding is probably limited due to the economy. This may take time that we don't have." Jones stood and paced in his office, hands thrust in his pockets. "And at the rate we're traveling, the entire country will be in the ditch before too long."

Rutledge asked, "But John, do you recall the one *specific property* that I'm interested in?" Rutledge leaned forward and straightened his pressed white shirt sleeves. "You know: the Grayson property we spoke of? The one I am interested in most immediately?"

"Yes, I've looked into it."

"As I told you a few days ago, Americus First Trust Bank has the mortgage loan documents on *that property* however it's unfortunate we don't hold a survey map. Apparently that document was entrusted to the county. And let me remind you that Mac Grayson is eight months delinquent."

"The expeditious means for that particular property would be to have the property re-surveyed, and to get the case taken in front of a judge as soon as possible. Of course the courts are backed up for months if not years."

"I'd make it worth your time. You know I'm good with my word."

"I may know a judge that owes me a favor," Jones said, smiling.

"Let's get a surveyor over there as soon as we can."

"I'll look into that right away." Jones puffed his cigar, excused Rutledge, and called in his next client.

Chapter 7

STANDING AT THE small water trough outside his kitchen door, Jack Waylon ran a bucket down and pulled up the handle. Just then through the open doorway, he heard his help, Wynonna, coming into the kitchen. She appeared in the kitchen doorway while holding her carry bag.

"Mr. Waylon, good morning," she said.

"Wynonna, why don't you get this water and take it into the house? Give me a hand, will you?"

She placed her bag on the counter and went out to carry in the water pail. She had already walked the mile up to his ranch from Flintside. There she lived alongside her husband in a converted cotton shack with little if any insulation and no windows, a makeshift stove, and an ill-flashed stove pipe that ran through the roof.

First, Jack bent down and cupped his hands to take a drink. He splashed the cool water on his face and dried with a towel he took from the rail. Setting the towel aside, he turned to see the morning sun rising in the east. Wynonna watched him as she took the pail. She knew him, had worked for him several years. His gaze was steady and his resolve often grew out of his own steadfast determination. From the constant fieldwork, his skin was tanned browned. His striking eyes were the color of blue lapis, and his short light-brown hair curled back away from his face when the wind blew.

From his perspective at the water trough, the crest of his land fell off toward the lake in the far distance. He could see Mac Grayson's house down the hill, the dim morning light glinting off its galvanized tin roof. Beyond, the lake water was dark and green. Most consequential to his rigorous planning as a cattle rancher was the misfortune of the current once-in-a-hundred-year-drought which he couldn't have forecasted. Realizing that the nearest water source was a concrete landing at the end of the McCarver land was daunting enough. Already, many daily trips more than a half mile away had been made in a truck with a water tank in tow. This task also required his workman to hand-pump from the lake into the small tank which was time consuming and inefficient. Hardly enough to sustain his many head of cattle and a quickly dwindling corn crop; the crop mostly used as feed for the beef not to mention the additional income generated at the market in Desoto.

From the ridge on which his house had been built, he looked back away from the lake toward his rolling hills to the west, to his many grazing beef and the brown wilting corn rows lined up for hundreds of yards. The wooded tree line far afield was taking on a golden hue as the early morning sun came over the horizon. Nearly three hundred acres and all of it in jeopardy considering the drought coupled with the sudden economic collapse in the south.

Wynonna took in the pail of water and put his bacon on to fry. She went to the hen house, chased out a snake with a hoe, and brought in some fresh eggs. She sliced bread and made coffee while looking out of the window to view the morning sun cutting yellow-white across the field and onto the sides of the big barn. Minutes later, Carter and Ben came up the road on foot, carrying their packs for the day. She saw them rounding the house and heading for the barnyard to begin their workday. Mr. Waylon ate and went out to meet them.

Inside the barn, with the truck's hood open, Ben was making some adjustments to the small pickup they used for carrying the water tank down to McCarver's landing.

Without turning, he said, "Got an oil leak on this head, Mr. Waylon. Gonna have to tear it down for too long."

Jack walked up behind him. "Damned old Ford. The heads always go first, don't they?"

Carter was nearby looking in the tool chest for a wrench. He came over and stood with them.

Jack said, "Lookin' like rain too."

Ben replied, "That dirt road down by the lake gets hard to deal with after it rains. If I get stuck we'll have to take down the Massey Ferguson and some big chains to pull her out again."

"Gal damned hell," Jack said. "Hell if it ain't finally raining, and I'm a day late and a dollar short." He rested his hands on his hips.

"Your daddy wouldn't have liked it, I tell you that much, Mr. Waylon. All the blamed work we've done, now the drought and prices like they are in this economy." Ben removed his hat to wipe his forehead with his shirt sleeve, already breaking a sweat.

"He would gal damned jump out 'o his grave and have a hollerin' fit. Go up to Washington. D.C. himself and yank a knot in ol' Herbert Hoover's ass, right on the White House lawn." Jack shook his head in reflection of his late father's well-known vim and vigor.

They laughed.

Carter asked, "What, he's been gone now about five years back?"

"Five come Christmas, sure enough. And seven since Mama went, too. They just up and went, left it all for me to carry on my own with no help from them."

Ben said, "Well if it matters, me and Carter here are pulling our own weight best we can."

Jack said, "Long as you keep pulling, I'll keep paying." Jack rubbed his hands together. "Ben, you better start making some trips down to the lake this morning. Least the corn up here on top of the hill has survived. Let's keep water on it for now. The rest of it—" His voice trailed off while he waved his hand away and shook his head in disgrace.

"What are you going to do about the well going dry?"

Jack's face reddened. He didn't like being questioned by his underling employee like this.

"Well, *we tried* to get rid of old man Grayson, didn't we? I backed up in my truck on the other side of that tall timber pile where he couldn't see me, and I pushed the whole damned load over on him, but that didn't work."

Carter said, "Well, actually *you tried*. We didn't have nothin' to do with it."

"We kept our mouths shut about it. That's our part in it," Ben added.

Jack pondered. "I'm going to have to go down to talk with Grayson sooner or later. Gonna have to see if I can work out a deal with him, cause he has all the water there under his land according to Bobby Womack, the well driller. But I doubt he'll go along with anything. Cause we have a history, I guess you could say."

"Looks like getting a well drilled down into his property will be the only way to survive, Mr. Waylon," Carter Farnsworth said. "Then run a water transfer pipe under the road and up the hill to here," he added. "If these beef start dying off, then..."

"Shut the hell up, Farnsworth," Ben Dollar said, looking over, watching the terse expression cross his employer's face.

"I'll figure something out," Jack said. "Meanwhile, we best get going down to the lake with the water truck."

While cleaning greens in a bowl for supper, Wynonna stood at the kitchen window and looked out toward the barn. She saw the three men standing in the sunlight in the open barn door. She saw they were making conversation; their mouths moving silently in the distance, too far away for her to hear. She noticed the grimace on the face of Mr. Waylon. Obviously the three were discussing the testy situation, she surmised.

Wynonna looked down at her work as she cut a piece of salt pork and filled a pot of water from the pail. She opened the stove and resurrected the fire with a few pieces of oak kindling. Her gray nappy hair fell about her dark Negro face and the flecks of pale pink freckles on her cheeks. Her hands were scarred from working since the age of ten when she had labored raking the gin mill floor as a child. She wasn't even sure when she had begun to work for Jack's mother many years earlier because she'd lost track over the years with her own indifference of time. Not that it mattered. They had started her in the yard feeding the chickens and in the barn milking their Holsteins. She was soon given the responsibility of doing some of the cooking, making up corn muffins, kneading bread, and cooking oatmeal in the morning. To the best of her recollection, Mrs. Waylon had been kind enough, had even given her ham on holidays to take home to her husband in Flintside; she had also been generous enough to give her days off during the holiday season although many domestic chores were required at that time of year. Mr. Waylon had been fair as well and had kept his distance, leaving the care of housework and kitchen duties to his wife. Years past and the Waylons both died within a few years of one another. After Mrs. Waylon passed, Mr. Waylon became depressed and filled his days with drinking corn whiskey which proved to be fatal. Now his son, Jack, had taken to it also with his loneliness.

Jack had been close to marriage at one time, but the young woman's family, a merchant's family from Cordele, had sent her off to college to the University of North Carolina and left Jack holding himself in his own lost time. What remained were Jack and the whisky jug paired with a full white moon in the evening sky. Once late, Wynonna had overheard him drunk and talking to the moon on a clear-skied night while sitting alone on his front porch. Many years back, Wynonna's husband had assured her that they would most likely remain underprivileged throughout their lives. But that one could make a large fortune in farming provided one starts with a large one to begin with. That one being Jack Waylon.

Through the opened window of his room, Mac heard the steady work being done in the barn. The sound of hammering and tools rang out as the wagon was being rebuilt for the trip to Americus. He heard voices and conversations; the thud of the adze and the saw cutting wood; a mallet pounding the heavy axel in; more nails being driven into oak planks. Leather plied with stress as the mules were brought from their stalls and strapped to the new harness bar, just for their fitting. Bridles jingled with handling, one mule braying, the other shaking her mane to shoo the flies off her neck. More low voices, those of Cade and Arden discussing the coming days ahead.

This saddened his heart. The thoughts of Ila Mae lingered in his head, a montage of images both old and new, sorrow binding with an unsure hope of what may come. He smoked his pipe and thought. Would she arrive in a state of shock with a complete loss of her functions? Or could she possibly know him, even though she had not when she had left?

From what Mac remembered, Dr. Clack along with his assistant came to drive her in his car to the state home in Americus for much needed care—as much for her sanity as for Mac's. Dr. Clack pled with the staff on duty, as only one more bed was left available in the institution that quarter. To state his case, Clack had insisted that both Mr. Grayson's father and grandfather had served the nation as war veterans. How could the State of Georgia neglect the families of war veterans, he had argued? For all intents and purposes, the family was unable to care for her any further as senility had taken her mind—to the point of her memory failing without the hope of healing, and her husband unable to cope any further after years of attempting to help her. The children were young and couldn't understand the final outcome as it was, Dr. Clack had insisted to the doctors on staff.

With or without Ila Mae, Mac had issues of his own. He was powerless to rid his respiratory ailment of coughing which usually occurred during the sleeping hours. This resulted in a lack thereof, and his days passed with dazed dozing, tobacco smoke, and sweat-soaked bedcoverings in the hot, humid house. Just as the days came and went, his children did as well. Hindered by the circumstances as much as he, they did what they could to care and cheer him up. But his back was permanently broken, and the feeling in his legs came and went. A reoccurring numbness throbbed in his pelvis, and he often couldn't feel his toes. Dr. Clack had come to visit and gave him tinctures and dissolved powders for his cough but without much affect. The doctor administered a morphine shot to ease the pain in his back and gave him morphine tablets for later use. He also noted his growing bedsores, so he suggested that Myra clean him as often as she could. What the long term outlook revealed was discouraging. They simple did what they had to.

As a result of the workplace accident, David Slade, the owner of the lumberyard had arrived with his wife bearing an apple pie as an apology. He assured Mac that numerous freight trucks had come and gone the day of the timbers falling in. Slade went as far to say that one witness watched an unmarked black flatbed quickly leaving the yard after the accident, but that most everyone present was concentrating on freeing him from under the tons of wood, not what trucks were coming and going at that moment. In closing, the business owner offered his position of liability: that it was known to be unsafe to move and load cut timber in the lumberyard without the assistance of a lumberyard employee. To that Mac assured him that the stack of lumber had been quite stable, until someone from the opposite side caused the pile to keel over by backing in with a large truck—one coincidentally that he was unable to see as the timbers were piled so high. However, fair or unfair, this had transpired months earlier, yet Mac was unable to come to grips with what he was to do moving forward. Was he going to die in this bed with Ila Mae beside him, unable to care for her, his children, or his land?

Evening arrived. Mac asked them to come and sit with him. The boys came followed by Myra. Cade and Arden sat in chairs they brought from the big room. Myra eased down beside him on the bed after pulling up the fresh bedsheets to his chest, the ones she had put on that morning. With her compassionate green eyes, she told him as much as her words: that they loved him and meant the best. Myra was so different from her brash insensitive brothers, most likely her own mother's nature and affection coming out; a mother she could barely remember but one she sensed in her heart from time to time. Myra at three years of age had been the sweetest thing Mac had ever seen as she stepped off the train that late day just before Christmas after riding so many hours from Atlanta. The look of sheer anticipation on her little face; how innocent she had been.

"Arden," he said. "You and Cade move this here armoire." He shifted up onto his elbows, motioning his hand toward Ila Mae's heavy walnut cabinet. "There's some things under it I need to show you three."

The boys slid it aside which revealed a loose floorboard. Arden stooped and removed the board to find their Papa's box where he'd left it. The box was unusual with its carvings of elephants and coconut trees, from India their father had told them—a gift from a fellow officer in the U.S. Navy, a gift to their great-grandfather, Samuel Grayson. A pad lock held it securely, and Mac told them where to find the key, atop the window frame mounted in the exterior wall.

"Give it over," he said, his hands out.

Arden closely resembled his father with his wide, square face, heavy-set frame, and thick muscles. Arden handed him the heavy box, and he opened it on the bed.

"Here," he told Arden. "This is for mother."

It was her gold wedding band he took from the box, a band with a beautiful diamond. He had presented the belated ring to Ila Mae several years following their wedding, as he did not have one on the day he proposed their marriage to Mr. Bradley, her father. Upon Mr. Bradley's approval, he immediately married her then rode her on Odessa from Leesburg all the way home to Flintside.

Mac said, "This is her ring. This originally come from Americus. You take it and sell it to a jewelry shop up there, for no less than twenty dollars. If you can't get that much, you bring it back with her." He paused. "With her a-wearing it, alright?" Arden took the ring and slipped it into his pocket. "You'll be careful with it, now, you hear." Arden nodded his understanding.

"Cade, you come here, son." Cade slowly stood and came to his side, his deep blue eyes like quarry water, his locks of blondish hair combed back off his forehead, his face sunburned red. His stature was tall, almost a head above Arden which was so unlike Maclin. "You know your Mama's mind went not long before you were born. Her memory couldn't hold a thing from one minute to the next. Wasn't no fault of her own she went like she did. Plum crazy and not knowing one person from the other. She had no idea what she was doing. I'm almost sixty-nine, and she is too. We had Paul. Then years later you three came along, Arden being our second after Paul died. Cade you were next. Then we got Myra from that church in Atlanta, thanks to Jasper John, his brother up there, and thanks to God with Jesus and his twelve disciples, I suppose."

He smiled at Myra.

"Cade," he said, "here is some good cash I've been saving for hard times. And, well, if this ain't hard times here, then I don't know what is." He took an envelope from the box and gave it to him. "You take this and you take care of yourself and Myra both. Arden is going to Americus and should return in a few weeks, depending. But we need to be prepared." Cade stepped back and sat.

"Myra, darling." He sniffed back his nose and a tear fell. "I have for you three this property deed that I inherited from my father—this land, our heritage and our homestead. This is for you and the boys." He held the fold of paper in his hand as he spoke. "Now, you never turn this over to J.R. Rutledge at Americus First Trust, you hear me? This is yours, here. I done paid them by far most of this mortgage, and we'll figure on paying up the rest as soon as we can. It may be a year or two, but we will. This little box is as safe a place as any for its keeping." He patted the antique wooden box.

He ran his hand in the box and pulled out a tattered booklet. "This here is my mother's journal of the Grayson family history. Keep this and read it to your-uns. Add in your parts too, and never let this go. Also in here is an old war medal of Grandpa's, one he earned in the War of 1812. I suppose it ain't worth much except for the blood that was shed for it. Keep it too and never lose it. "

Lastly, he removed thin pieces of paper he found in an envelope, and he told them, "This was your momma's set of poems. And her elegy she called it. She named this *Lee County Elegy*." He held up the yellowed paper made of old pulp stock with her handwriting on it. "This is Paul's. This was your mother's and this belongs to him."

He addressed the three. "Momma's coming home. In what condition, I'm not sure other than the doctor up yonder seemed to ascribe her good physical health to their care, and that she is able to travel. Arden, you take good care of her and watch out for foul weather. If the weather turns, you stay put until the time is right to bring her on. Cade will give you money enough for the trip."

Night had fallen darker, and the three left him to sleep with his morphine. Mack had a haunting in the night while watching the shadows of tobacco smoke in the flickering of his oil lamp. Seeing her face and her sad, oval eyes of brown; watching images of yesteryear in the shadows moving on the rafters of the old cabin; hoping she might come back to him likened to her old self before she had left him in her mind. Dream-cast the night moved into the wee hours of morning, and he ran through the fields after Ila Mae to come home with him.

Chapter 8

YOUNG ARDEN TOOK up his burden such as a farmer does his mules to carry the load he must. Leading them on a journey from home and taking with him what he could of his life and remembrances of his mother, packing his sorrow on their sway backs for the woman that he had loved but never understood. And for his father, a good man yet a shadow of his former self. Arden, a determined trooper like his pa, took what burdens came his way, made the best with what he had, and plied from their roots a better means by which to overcome. Maybe revealing his own blindness to believe they could survive and that she could possibly remember them because his father, though well-deserving, was still praying for her. That somehow God would giveth and never taketh away. Arden wasn't much more than a farmer's hand but he determinedly faced the world alone. He held his own Bible in his own heart. Yet suffering under his own infirmity of having fictional illusions of hope, somehow, led him to greener pastures however difficult his journey would become.

Weeks earlier, Doctor Clack had pulled him aside and explained that Mac was poor in health prior to his paralytic accident, with his chronic respiratory ailment, digestive issues, and weight. They all admitted he was gravely ill and needed rest. But why, for days leading up to his departure had Arden been leaving the barn for his father's smoke-filled room whenever he could? Maybe more often than he should have, delaying his duties of repairing the wagon, assuring that somebody was with him as his siblings were out scavenging for food or fishing at the lake? Not wanting to chance him facing the forever-after without a familiar face to give him assurance, possibly that he might be nearing his last day. This was an instinctual intuition and he felt an obligation. However, Arden certainly didn't want any credit. Myra and Cade were doing all they could. But he would expect the same for himself one day if he ever bore children of his own. He was still young. But his father had been blessed for most of his life, trials though there had been at times.

Cade stood by the door, one hand on the doorframe and the other on his father's shoulder. He had brought him and set him on the sturdy cedar trunk in the doorway, to see out on the land and green water of Blackshear. To see his son off in the refurbished wagon, colors of old wood and new in a sturdy patchwork crossing the yard behind the two mules. Arden wore a brown coat and his dark suede hat although it was late morning in the warm yellow sun. His gear was packed and rolled in a heavy canvas tarp under his buckboard. The mules, Bess, a bay jenny, and Big Joe, a sorrel john mule, were both sturdy and well cared for. Arden in the last hour had ridden into Flintside to the tack shop and very luckily traded a jar of sorghum with the fat Mr. Wells for a set of new bridles—obviously Mr. Wells was stocked-up on many bridles but short on sorghum syrup for his griddle cakes.

Myra was awash in tears though she attempted to hide them behind her hands. She went out to the wagon and handed him a canteen of water he had asked her to fill from the well. Through the branches of the massive red oaks that grew aside the small cabin, morning light glinted into shadows on Arden's strong face.

"Weather's good, brother," she said to him. "Cade gave you enough money, don't you think?"

He nodded his consent.

Inside the cabin Cade stood watching, steadfastly loyal not to leave his father's side at such a moment. He thought it better to remain with him. Rather for the support and his undying love for Mac, or just as well for his tentative awkwardness and unsure bearing. He wasn't but a young teen. At times he had difficulty expressing himself and often made comments that did not come out exactly as intended. He knew how he felt. He just couldn't say the words in the right manner. For this, he often took a low profile as he desired the appearance of being thoughtfully wise, instead of opening his mouth and removing all doubt.

"Son," Mac said, turning to Cade and patting his hand. The old man smiled, and his unshaven face drew into long furrowed wrinkles like the farmlands of Lee County.

"Arden's a-going now." Cade stood beside him.

"Arden, look here, boy!" Mac belted, leaning forward through the doorway, rubbing his knees. "Listen, son. You take good care. I know you're the man around this farm, and I'm counting on you, boy, you hear?" Though Mac was infirm, the timbre of his voice was strong.

"Yes sir, Papa. I got it under control. Shouldn't be any trouble at all. Cade and Myra need to stay put and take care of you here." He wore a black pair of his only Stetsons, the ones he'd had since his nineteenth birthday when his massive feet had finally quit growing. However aged and road-weary, regardless of the work done in them, they had a sturdy character much like Arden. Well-made and reliable.

Myra still stood by the wagon, her thin wrists poking out of her sleeved cotton shirt she had outgrown. Her hand-loomed wool skirt was thin and worn. Her lap was sprinkled from the bit of flour Arden had bargained for, the flour she'd used to bake a few morning biscuits. However indigent, she was graceful.

"Arden, we're waiting on ya'll to get back home," she said, clasping her hands together.

"I'll be as quick as I can, Myra."

"I'm preparing a place for her in with Papa. We're going to make their room while you are gone."

"We can take care of them both, don't you think?" But he could read the reservation in her eyes. Though young, she was smart and practical; a good judge of place and situation, he had learned.

Mac said, "You get up there." He rubbed his hands on his knees, chewed his lip. "I know we ain't been up there in a coon's age, but it never seemed too much good with her just staring at the wall and not at us. Not knowing our names or who we were."

"I know, Pa. We've been over that as many times as there are stars in the sky. It ain't your fault or any o' ours, either." He squinted in the daylight and pulled his hat forward. His long curled hair fell out and lay on his broad shoulders. His face was dark and bronzed from the recent days he'd spent in the sun.

He said, "I'm going down the road, Papa." He nodded and turned the mules out, and they pulled forward with the squeaking of the wheels and creaking of the old wagon frame. He waved over his shoulder as they made their way up to the road on the ridge.

He felt he might be leaving his father, maybe for the last time. He grieved for his father and his misfortunes, for the family and the suffering they had endured. For the hope that had been taken like a thief in the night with his injury and the lack of any future left for him. Splayed out on his bed; now an invalid in constant need of this and that; please go here and go there; fetch me this but take that there; know I would if I could but I just can't. Thank you, thank you. His pride all but left to the buzzards without the Ila Mae of their youth that he so needed now.

Arden soon made the outer road after passing the marsh. He pulled into Flintside and traffic was light, a few wagons coming and going, an older Ford parked in front of the boot shop. The lumberyard was quiet for a change, its chain link fence running for hundreds of feet into the distance. He knew Desoto was just across the line in Sumter County, the first place the mules would have hay and rest, a good six or seven miles further. He needed food too, and although he thought to stop at Jenkins's store, he decided against that knowing he might not get a fair deal. As he passed through town, he peered down to study the contents of his leather pouch to make sure all was in place: his billfold, money, writing paper and a pencil, the letter from Dr. Roberts at the infirmary, and his mother's wedding ring securely placed in its small velvet box.

Leaving town he crossed Flintside creek, a wide ford with gushing water and lilies dancing in the breeze. The creek bed looked to have been cut through the terrain a hundred thousand years in the past with its rocky moss-covered embankments and huge oaks bent over the water's edge. He drove onward up a hill and the terrain leveled out, the road as straight as cut timber into the dark fold of trees up ahead. Along the way the mules' harnesses pulled and creaked with the tension of the leather. Their heads dipped in unison with their strides, hooves clopping the ground as they went sending back dirt and sand. A copperhead slithered across the road into the scrub, but the mules drew back and waited then continued on.

He was unsure of his task, not knowing what his reaction might be at the first sight of his mother. It had been a long while since they had made the trip to visit her. In his very early years before she was gone in her mind, he recalled she'd held him tightly in a sling while picking her way through the cotton fields alongside his father and their hired help. He remembered her carrying him in the sling, the cotton sack over her shoulder, and the black women singing beautiful spirituals as they went through the hot sun. As he grew, he carried the water canteen around the field, brought out corn fritters for everyone, or ran errands here and there. Before too long by the age of eight, he was promoted to wagon driver, and he went into town for supplies with a list in hand.

He could remember her bathing him in the Flint long before the building of the dam. She cooked the finest brined venison roast over an open flame. She made apple tarts and apple pies; flatbread in the wood oven; flour biscuits with sausage and gravy. By firelight, she read to him at night the passages he loved from *Homer's Iliad* of Achilles and the Trojans, verses of Virgil and Foster, too. Stories of Twain's *Huckleberry Finn*, and *Twenty Thousand Leagues Under the Sea* by Verne.

As of this trip, Arden hadn't seen her for well over a year, maybe two. The doctors had not discouraged them from making the long three day wagon trip into Americus, yet they hadn't encouraged them either. The family had dutifully visited the hospital on several tentative occasions, possibly three or four visits over the years. However, the trips had seemed futile as she was not well. The doctors were officious and pragmatic, even stern in their demeanor, but they seemed to lack a bedside manner one would expect from a professional healthcare provider. Whenever the family had gone to visit, the air of the place was awkward as the hospital was unlike a medical treatment facility but more of a ward for human animals. Most of the patients were not cognizant of their surroundings and made little sense when they spoke. One, for example, stood in the corner and talked implicitly to the wall. One sat in a chair and made continual, repeated motions with their arms, over and over while blathering nonsense. One man walked about day after day and repeated to anyone nearby, "I do believe you're right. I do believe you're right," although no one was paying him attention, just nudging him aside whenever he got in their way. One unusual woman refused to remove her coat even to sleep, apparently under the impression she would be leaving at any moment. Their mother stayed in her room and kept to herself, making abstract drawings with a pencil and paper, mostly just scribbling. She made hundreds of them and the staff even taped a few of the better ones to the wall. She appeared to read books too, however she stared at the pages and inanely turned them without purpose or reason. She couldn't remember anything that happened the minute prior. No conversation could be had. His mother had always been good natured, though, and was far from resistant or belligerent. She had become completely incompetent, yet somehow she had kept her good-natured side and was easily handled. It had been extremely difficult, to say the least, for young children to understand what was much later termed in the medical field as being the early onset of Alzheimer's disease. But they did what Dr. Clack had suggested and luckily the hospital had taken her in.

A squeaking Ford jalopy passed him on the narrow road to Desoto, and he pulled aside in the weeds to allow them passage. Other cars also came and went but the passengers paid him little attention. Along the ride, the trees of the forest hung over the road and threw shadows at the mules' hooves as they walked. After leaving the realm of woods, level open fields came into view and stretched out as far as the eye could see. Field hands were little brown images painted against a pallet of clouded blue sky on the horizon as they worked their way through a vegetable grove. Far in the distance, a cabin lay on the crest of the land and he could see smoke from it low and flat, seemingly unmoving in the windless day. The sun had reached its meridian and had begun its descent westward when he came upon a man carrying a shotgun and walking with two hound dogs on the roadside.

"Mister," Arden said from the wagon as he approached.

The old man stopped, slid his hat back off his forehead and wiped the sweat from his brow. "Going coon hunting out yonder," he said, pointing into a thick band of woods off the road. "Got some big 'uns in there, I know."

"Coons? What good are they, Mister?" Arden had had the pleasure of tasting coon once before, and knew it to be about as good as tasting the foul end of a horse's ass.

"Coon is good for the fur, son. Makes a good coon hat or home-made shoes in the winter."

The old man looked to immediately need a pair of his own, as his were leather remnants of old boots with cording wrapped and tied in all directions to help hold them on his feet. He stood square in his shoulders and his britches were cinched at the waist with a wide belt resembling a razor strap. He removed his hat and his thick gray hair stood like bristles on a hemp brush. He glared up at Arden, and his face looked such as old leather, faded brown and worn.

"Nice looking dogs," Arden said, speaking the truth, looking at their fine coats.

"These two, now they can tree a coon faster 'n a bullet comes out of a rifle barrel." He chuckled at his own comment. "And you?" he asked.

"I'm just passing through to Desoto, Mister. Good luck with your coonin', now."

Arden flipped the reigns but the man holding the shotgun seemed suddenly interested in the contents of Arden's wagon bed. He peered into the bed as the wagon passed, noticing the canvas roll. He bent over the sideboard and sniffed deeply. He said, "Smells like you got some biscuits on board there, sonny."

Arden was taken aback. How had the old man discerned the smell of the biscuits Myra had given him for his trip that morning? All rolled up with his belongings in the canvas tarp? Maybe he hadn't; maybe he had just assumed so.

Arden turned to look as he passed the man holding the big gun. The man smiled but he didn't have a tooth in his head, just a round oval for a mouth and small slits for eyes.

"You take care, now," the old man said and continued on his way, the hound dogs close to his heels.

Much later in the day, the town of Desoto came into view and he was pleased he'd made it this far. This was farther than he'd been in quite a long time as Desoto was the best place for shopping, farm equipment, hardware, good tools, or gasoline. Having had little money on the farm, any trips into Desoto had been postponed as there were no funds except for absolute necessities such as food and lamp oil—most of which could be found in Flintside.

Chapter 9

MYRA CAME AND brought his supper, a cup of simmering squirrel meat and onion broth, but he wouldn't eat, so she left and went about her business. As usual, he coughed and wheezed. Took his handkerchief and wiped his mouth then loaded his corncob pipe and smoked. Watched the light change as the day merged into gray twilight. The walnut cabinet had been moved back against the wall with the elephant box replaced under the floorboards.

The leaning of the long narrow cabin was made obvious by the uneven slope of the wooden floors as the foundation had settled over time. This condition caused the walls to stand unevenly too, and the doors had had to be planed-down over the years to prevent them from hanging-up. The leaning of the narrow house seemed to cause the hot breeze to inherently creep into the front door at one end of the house in a manner that carried the dust up to the ceiling in the big room and down the wall into Mac's room at the other end. Voices also seemed to carry that same way, along the emotional currents from one end of the house to the other.

He heard their low voices by the stove. Though he couldn't hear their words, their tone and sharp inflections told him all he needed. The rise and fall of their cadence told him of their concerns.

He called them in and asked them to bring the chairs again.

"Myra, I want you to go into Flintside for me."

She leaned back in her chair attentively, hands in her small lap.

"Up there in Flintside, down Old Leesburg Road 'bout a half mile on the right side there is a big house that is painted white."

This right away caught her notice because not many houses were ever painted, as paint was very rare and expensive. The thought of a painted house made her pause, why she would be going there. She had seen this house of course as she had made the trip into Leesburg on numerous occasions. Yet, for whom or what purpose would be cause enough to go there confounded her at the moment.

Mac said, "That is the house of an old friend. We go back a long way, even before your time. His name is William Tullman, and he is a lawyer that retired years ago. He is from Albany but made his retirement in Flintside as he got a good bargain on a right big piece of land over there."

Mac paused, wiped his mouth then went on. "In about 1915, he had a heart failure in Flintside and I rushed him and his wife up to Americus, driving my mules day and night to the medical hospital there, and I might have saved his life in the process. Now in return he has been generous to me as I've needed some advice a time or two. He's a nice enough fellow, and I believe he can help me again. I want you two to go up there and talk with him about the Americus Bank and what our options are here with J.R. Rutledge breathing down my neck. You explain the situation with the Leesburg Courthouse burning down and all of that. You tell him we have a legal deed but owe the bank yet a small amount of money."

Cade glanced at Myra and they exchanged a concerned look. Cade said, "Papa, this Tullman fellow still lives up there with his wife? I believe I know who he is. Is he the tall man that drives that beautiful tan car?"

Mac shifted his weight in his bed and sat up on his elbows. "Yep, that's him. He comes into town driving that '28 Chevrolet National. He usually wears a long pinstripe waist coat and silver-rimmed specs."

Myra asked Cade: "Was he the old fellow that helped us get the rock out of Little Bess's shoe that afternoon? When she was hobbling up a fit?"

"Yep, that's the one," Cade agreed.

Their pa said, "You go up there in the morning and knock on his door. You tell him you're Mac Grayson's two. He'll let you in, I'm sure." He coughed. "But not too sure about the wife. I ain't seen her in a long while. Maybe she's gone in the way up wonder to be with her kin." He looked out of his window into the early evening sky now brushed with wind and gray clouds.

Cade asked, "Should we say a bit about the lumberyard accident, do you think? Him being a lawyer and all?"

"I don't know what to make of that, son, like I said. I was just at the wrong place at the wrong time, I suppose. Much was going on in the lumberyard, people workin' and trucks being loaded. Lots of voices and noise. It's a big place. I don't believe I have it in me to address the problem that a way with a lawyer. I'm too old and too short on cash. Probably don't have much of a case to take on Mr. Slade. As he said, I was loading my own lumber at my own risk. That about says it." He reached for his pipe and tobacco pouch. "Cade, you-uns get on up to Mr. Tullman's first thing tomorrow about this bank problem, you here?"

"Will do, Pa," Cade assured him.

"You take good care of your sister too, son. Now that Arden's gone, you're the one in charge around here," he said, although he looked quickly at Myra and held her gaze for a long moment.

Mariah Moses was a poor little pickaninny, raised in Leesburg in the low marsh that skirted the city's southern limits. His father had been poor too, and his grandfather a slave in Lee County before the war. He and his mother had moved out of town and were occupying an abandoned sharecropper's house that edged a fallow field set way back from the highway. A few years earlier, his father had died in a farming accident. His father had mangled his arm in the gears of a moving combine, and when the bleeding couldn't be stopped they dragged him aside and covered him with a blanket until the end of the workday to retrieve for a burial later. Fortunately, Mariah's mother soon landed a coveted housekeeper's job at the Mangum farm a ways up the road, as Mr. Mangum was partial to pretty sugar-browns with petite figures and sumptuous bosoms. He often paid handsome bonuses too if the work was done just so, so she soon learned. Mariah had been through the second grade in the local one-room schoolhouse for Negros, but he instead preferred to work from time to time on the Mangum farm too, when there was work enough to keep him busy.

His mother was proud of Mariah, too, because he'd been so smart and had schemed himself five whole dollars for doing what that big white man had paid him to do. Five dollars, Mariah thought. He hadn't made five dollars that whole summer, he knew, since dropping out of school. He would do almost anything for that amount of money. That's like striking gold, hitting pay dirt, or robbing a bank. Five dollars, boy o' boy. The big man approached him, and he didn't even know he was standing there until he touched his little shoulder. The man had wandered in through the basement door of the Lee County Courthouse that morning, offering Mariah to play a practical joke and run through the streets screaming that the courthouse was on fire.

Earlier that morning, the county judge had come down and told Mariah to simply watch the boiler chest with the coal pile, to keep the coal flames just so high, as he held out his hand at Mariah's kneecaps, showing the little boy just how high. But the judge was only paying twenty-five cents for the day.

Patiently, Mariah watched the white man set the pile of clothes then the timbers afire which quickly spread overhead to the floor joists. The flames began to roar in no time, the wood cracking and popping with immense heat. Soon there was a wave of black smoke so thick Mariah couldn't see, and he overheard loud voices and the floor above them rumbling with boot traffic. The big man then told Mariah, "Run, boy, run! Run and tell everyone that the courthouse caught on fire! Then you meet me out behind the stables on Tuft Street and I'll pay you the five dollars to keep you quiet!"

Five dollars, he thought. He didn't believe he'd ever seen five dollars all in one place all at one time. What could he do with five dollars? Well, his momma knew. She went out and bought herself a new dress and pretty flowers in a vase, some candy, and a jar of whiskey too, that's what. Not to forget an apple pie for Mariah. Besides, she had heard from the housekeeper of another farm that the fire had been set by the mayor's brother because the money stolen from the City of Leesburg had involved him too, as he had worked in the city's purchasing department. Apparently the mayor and his brother were embezzling money from the city through the purchasing of goods and services. So, to keep her mouth shut, she deserved a slice of the pie, too.

Arden was weary from his road trip, buckboard-sore and thirsty. It was late afternoon, so he dismounted the wagon then walked by the Wayside Inn in central Desoto on his way to the grocer. The streets were covered with gravel as the roads here were built for horses and wagons, although he knew Americus was paving roads up there with the onset of the automobile crossing the state. Things were changing quickly. Things had to change as the automobile was propelling the country as quickly as the automobile could shift gears, albeit the recent sudden halt in the economy had caused the country to plow on its brakes. Desoto was larger than Flintside in all respects: a small granite courthouse centered the square; the streets were lined with cars and wagons; storefronts of many types rounded the square; a newer gas pumping station had been built on the corner.

As he entered the grocery, he took his pouch and strapped his waist belt through it for safe carrying. Circling the shelves he took some food items and next paid at the cash register. After a minute of gleaning a few magazines at the bookrack by the door, he left to take care of his mules. He led them by Big Joe's bridle as they pulled the wagon to a small stable around the corner. He gave the attendant two dimes and filled two feedbags with grain then slipped them over the mules' heads. The attendant made small talk as the mules fed. Minutes later, the attendant tossed a pile of hay at the mules' front legs and they fed on that. Arden wandered back to the inn and went in for a drink. Prohibition was the law of the land, but he knew it could be had with the right connections and for the right price. Moonshine was rampant in South Georgia and though he had partaken just a few times, he was far from home and needed a tonic to calm his nerves.

When he entered the Wayside Inn, the waiter working the small restaurant took in Arden's age of being about twentyish, and he smirked. Three others were sitting at small tables, sipping from clear glasses colored with Coca-Cola. They glanced up simultaneously then looked back at each other, shrugging their shoulders.

"What can I do for you young man?" the waiter asked.

Arden said, "What are you serving up today, Mister?"

The three looked at him again, glanced to the waiter but remained quiet. The waiter slowly strolled up to the front plate glass window while drying his hands on his service apron. He looked up the street one way then down the other. "Anybody seen Jarvis?" he asked the three, speaking of the local sheriff.

One man said, "I believe he's gone over to Leslie to the jail there, to pick up that horse thief he wanted to get. To bring him back here to Desoto. I passed him on the way in and had a word with him."

To Arden, the waiter said, "Just serving up Coca-Cola today, my friend."

Arden reached his hand over to the next table and asked the man sitting there, "You mind?"

The man hesitated and gave the others a look for a consultation. They said nothing, just stared and frowned. The man slowly handed Arden the glass and Arden sniffed it.

"Coca-Cola? Is that right?" he said. He handed the glass back. He glared the waiter down.

"What are you offering then?" the waiter asked.

"What's the deal?" Arden asked. He removed his hat and set it on the table.

"Corn whiskey." The waiter wiped his hands on his apron. "Gettin' a quarter a shot."

Arden swallowed hard, reached into his pouch and withdrew a Standing Liberty Quarter. He knew Myra would shoot him between the eyes if she was aware of his squandering this money.

Once again, the waiter looked over his shoulder through the window, hesitated and went to the kitchen. They heard a cabinet door open, bottles moving, pans and plates sliding around. He emerged with a jug, carefully poured a shot in a small glass and mixed it with Coca-Cola.

He brought it over and took the quarter.

Arden didn't hesitate. He tilted his head straight back and shot the entire load in one single gulp. Then lowering his head, he released a sharp belch and let the drink work into his bones. The warmth began in his gut and slowly spread outward through his body, into his arms and legs, finally reaching his fingers and toes with a tingling sensation. The tension immediately released him from the work and worry that had gripped him for days. His body slumped. He rolled his head in a slow circle around his shoulders and opened his eyes.

One said, "Damn good shit, ain't it?" He smiled.

The other two laughed. "Damn sure is," another agreed.

They all burst into laughter but Arden didn't. He just watched.

The waiter lifted the jug with a question marking his face.

Arden motioned him over, pulled out another quarter.

He took another hit, set the glass on the table and looked around.

The youngest of the three said, "Name's Billy James." He smiled again.

"Arden Grayson," he replied.

"What's your business here in Desoto?"

"Heading up to Americus to see some family."

"Whereabouts you coming from?"

"Down south of here on Blackshear. Just a day or so back."

The young man looked over his shoulder and spoke quietly. "My uncle's got some good shine out at the house. For a good price, I mean."

"No thanks buddy. I'm heading down the road."

He left and went for his wagon and mules. Thirty minutes later, he cleared the Desoto city limits and found a glade off the roadside to set camp. Before long, he had a fire going and strips of pork belly hanging from a long spit he'd whittled out of a thin tree branch. Just then he looked up and saw a crescent moon rising in the sky.

Later by the warmth of the fire, he observed the silver stars in a sky as black as ink. He lay on his back, looking upward. Millions of crystalline stars across the heavens filled his eyes along with the tears of his misgivings. That he had not known his mother while in his prime; or rather that she hadn't known him. That he wished they could have; and added to this, his doubt he had been empathetic enough, even as young as he was. The months and years had wasted away with her in her deteriorated condition. Their father was at a loss as to what her final outcome might be while considering the family's future having to deal with her. Arden, Cade, and Myra, all had been too young. Their mother and father were much older than their school friend's parents. Arden had been six when Cade was born, but by that time, Ila Mae was fifty years of age and her mind was already going. Years later after struggling with her, Mac had gone and urged Dr. Clack to take action. At his young age, Arden was unable to fully understand, though he knew he loved his mother regardless of her infirmity because she had loved him first. Days spanned into weeks and months. Then many years went by.

"You always take your Bible wherever you go, son," she once told him when he was a boy of five. "I mean, not in your hand but in your heart, do you hear me?" She sometimes read her tattered King James to him at night by oil lamp, stories such as Daniel in the lion's den, and the ram-horned trumpets bringing down the walls of Jericho; stories such as Moses standing on Mt. Pisgah to see across the Jordan to The Promised Land, and of King Solomon constructing his great temple from the tall cedars of Lebanon. Schoolmaster Burch was teaching Arden well, she knew, as she could hear by the way he read *The Tale of Peter Rabbit*. Sometimes she had Arden read back to her, and they would exchange readings at night, turning the pages of young children's books. At other times she read *Doctor Dolittle* to him. They read about the doctor's adventures and his preferences of treating animals over humans; how he could talk in their languages to better understand the world as it was. "Dr. Dolittle was smart, too, Arden," Ila Mae once told him. "I wish we could all see things in the way that the animals do. No war, no hate, no greed. Things would most likely improve if we could."

Ila Mae had been a sweet woman; beautiful in her youth with walnut eyes and a long dark mane; flowing hair which was let out only in the privacy of her own home; nor would she allow her hemline to rise an inch above her ankles; nor allow another man to lay one finger on her under any circumstance, even as a friendly gesture upon her shoulder. She had been raised to be a good healthy farm girl but suffered the same fate as her own grandmother with senility. She had become lost, not knowing her own self or anyone else.

In earlier days with her Christian faith, she had known Bible verse by heart and recited it from time to time by firelight or at the supper table. As for art, she wrote poetry and pressed wild flowers. She meticulously glued the flowers into decorative arrangements on paper and framed them with hand-made frames of oak and bark she constructed in their work shop. She had had sepia tone photographs made of her and Maclin with infant Arden in her arms, on the front steps of their cabin when a photographer came out door to door, selling pictures. She had never had her picture done, and she was amazed at the box camera, its accordion shaped lens, and the automatic flash-powder tray used to create light when the pictures were taken.

She and Maclin had passed many cool evenings sitting on the river's shoreline with a picnic basket of sweet rolls, butter, and tea. Sometimes she heated cheese toast on the stove or would serve Arden fresh milk with cookies at night when they read their books. Then after time, their routine began to wane, and she slowly became distant and strange, keeping mostly to herself, talking to herself and hardly paying attention to Maclin or Arden anymore. After all, she was well up into her years, much older than the other children's mothers at Mr. Burch's schoolhouse. Their mother, Ila Mae, had appeared much like the other children's *grandmothers* with her aged face and gray hair, the way she carried herself and spoke with the other younger mothers. Arden had been told the story of Paul, the older brother he had never known, the one that died long before his upbringing on their farm in Lee County.

Through the trees out on the road, an automobile passed. The late night traveler came and went, the car tires crunching on the gravel, then all was quiet. Arden stirred the coals in the fire and added a few more oak branches to liven it up. He took a piece of beef jerky from his bag and chewed on it slowly, reminiscing.

He sat back and remembered Natalie and her long yellow hair, her fair complexion, and the pale freckles that dotted her pretty cheeks. They had met at a church camp meeting in Desoto and were struck by one another at first sight, Natalie with her light-green eyes and Arden's dark head of hair pulled back from his handsome face. They sat far back from the tent and festivities and sipped tea with mint leaves while they talked and began to know one another. Over time, they kept in touch through letters. They also met in Desoto as Mr. and Mrs. Weldon drove from Americus sometimes on Sunday afternoons to shop while they allowed Arden and Natalie to lunch at the Wayside Inn.

He had told her of his father's land and that he expected to inherit it one day, and that he had plans and dreams to succeed. But she could have cared less; she just loved to look into his deep dark eyes. One afternoon he received an unexpected letter from her, that she was being moved to Peoria, Illinois as her father had taken an editor's job at a newspaper there. Naturally Arden was devastated, and though she had written on several occasions, she had gradually faded away into the distance though he thought of her often.

He fell off to sleep by the fire that late August night. He pulled his parka and wool blanket up over his shoulders and dreamed of Natalie and their days at the Wayside Inn.

Chapter 10

CADE AND MYRA walked the road leaving their farm by Mr. Waylon's property. They could view his tall house on the hill, the red wine barn as long as a big train car, and rail fences running for what seemed like miles. Obviously he was a wealthy man as seen by the breadth of his land, from here, there and back. From their perspective down on the road, the cattle looked to be well over two hundred head, their soft white and russet hides gleaming in the morning; the cows chewing their cud, flipping their tails with contentment, grazing the pasture of thick grass. A small aluminum wind mill the size of a large sombrero spun in the wind, telling anyone that cared which way the wind blew.

"Mr. Tullman is supposedly nice enough, 'cording to Pa," Cade said anxiously.

They walked along the road, and he ran his hand over the tall grass tops at the roadside. He pick one and slipped it in his mouth, chewing.

"I suppose he won't mind us," Myra said, but remained quite as she had been all morning.

After a while, as they made their way into town, she finally added, "I'm worried sick about all this. I mean, how are we going to take care of Mamma and Papa at the same time? How can we manage her, too? Are we going to have to bar her door and keep her confined? You know she just wonders around aimlessly. She may be a handful. Our hands are already full. We are heaving Pa around as it is." She began to cry at the thought of it. "Forget about school, right? Cade, there is no way we can do this—"

"—but you have to, Myra for now. You and Arden."

"Just me and Arden? What about you?"

He pursed his lips.

She said, "We have Pa, now Ma, and the bank is on us. We have little money to speak of, little food except what we can take from the land—"

"—but, for now, we have each other and that counts for something."

She was surprised by this unusual display of confidence from Cade suddenly appearing from some hidden place she wasn't aware existed. She noticed the change in his attitude whenever Arden wasn't on the farm. Finally she added, "You're right. But we're in a bad place, and I'm not sure how much longer Papa can make it, anyway."

"When Ma comes home, he may be revived."

"That's going to wear off, however, after the day-to-day chores set in."

"Well, he can talk to her don't you think?"

"Even if she doesn't understand a thing he's saying to her?"

They walked through Flintside. Mrs. Jenkins was sweeping her storefront, but she wouldn't acknowledge them until she gave them a shy look then turned and went inside. Mr. Slade was out cleaning his office windows at the lumberyard but his back was turned. The tack shop had a few customers. The boot shop was quiet. As they walked the half mile down to the lawyer's house, a few buggies passed but their passengers paid them little attention other than a quick wave as they went by. The flatland woods were filled with tall spruce, maple, and poplar. Yellow pines were gathered in groups, the tall and their saplings in great big swaths. The ground was sandy and palmetto thickets covered the landscape in every direction. Southern oaks tunneled the dirt road and Spanish moss hung from the trees like torn flannel.

Soon they approached a grand two story house that revealed itself behind a long run of Blackjacks on the side of the road. The white-painted home possessed a front porch running its entire length, and two brick chimneys standing handsomely atop the steeply pitched roof. A pea-gravel driveway punctuated by a circular turnaround in front of the porch invited the eye up from the road to the front door.

"This is lovely," she said as they climbed the front steps.

They wore their usual frayed clothing and worn boots, all they could afford after the money went low with the drought and cotton prices as they were. *Like their Pa had told them years back: they were land-rich but money-poor.* Now, with the depression, this was not even the case. Their land wasn't worth much either. At best, she had primped and pulled her beautiful red hair up into a classic, neat bun. She had put on the only decent cotton blouse that she owned though it was stained.

Cade knocked and they waited. Bird song came from the trees. The breeze whispered. An old truck could be heard clattering down the road as it passed the house. Moments later, Mr. Tullman came and opened the door. He was a tall-framed man, almost as tall at the doorway. But they were surprised because he smiled before he spoke.

"You are Mac Grayson's, am I right? Let's see, Myra and Cade if I remember correctly."

"Yes sir, Mr. Tullman," Cade replied.

Mr. Tullman stood in a pair of overalls, wearing boots, not his usual attire.

"Excuse me. I was heading out back to my garage to work on my Chevrolet. But since you've come to visit, I suppose that can wait." He smiled again and stood aside. He said, "Come in you two and make yourselves at home. What can I do for you this morning?"

They stepped in and were amazed at the scale of Mr. Tullman's home, the furnishings, high ceilings, and polished wooden floors. He led them to a sitting room and offered them a glass of tea which they nervously declined.

He sat slowly across from them. His face was kind but his posture wooden as if he were deviled by a skeletal ailment of some kind. He placed his arthritic hands on the arms of the chair but he did not rest against the chair's back. His neatly combed hair was iron ore gray, almost blue in tint. The white beard he preferred was course but closely trimmed to fit his elongated face. Regardless of his age, his expression was aware and his perceptive gray eyes alert.

"Mr. Tullman, our Pa has sent us to speak with you," Myra started, but her voice faltered from indecision as she wasn't confident how to present herself or their situation—for once at a loss of words, Cade noticed.

To break the ice, Mr. Tullman initiated their conversation by saying, "I realize your father has had an accident. And I'm sure the advent of such hasn't been easy for you. I've spoken to David Slade at the lumberyard, and he made it clear that an out-of-state freight hauler caused the accident but apparently left the scene, and they haven't been able to identify him yet."

He chewed his lip and looked at the two, Cade with his long posture and Myra all knees and elbows. He said, "I'm also sure your father has expressed my loyalty to him as he most likely took part in saving my life some years back, for which, I am forever grateful. I'll do whatever I can from my position to help."

For the reason Mr. Tullman had been so frank and forthcoming, Myra relaxed and said, "Thank you, Mr. Tullman for your help. Lord knows we sure could use some about now."

"So, what is it I can do, Myra?"

Cade spoke instead. "It's not the lumberyard, but the bank, Mr. Tullman. You see, we've paid down almost all of our debt, but because we are currently a little late in paying, J.R. Rutledge at the Americus First Trust Bank wants everything back, lock, stock, and barrel."

"I thought this might be the other reason for your call." He stood and went to the window to look out at his property. He slipped his hand in his pocket and turned back. "I realize Mac couldn't make the trip on his own and apparently he trusts you to take a message back."

"Yes, sir, that's right," Myra said. "But are you aware of the court-house burning down in Leesburg?"

"Most certainly, and in your case it should be a good deterrent for due process, but for *how long* is to be determined. It could be to your advantage depending on what you can do in the meanwhile to make a remedy regarding your finances. The banks have legal rights just as the land holders do."

He looked at them. "I'll tell you this. I'm a retired lawyer. The only office I have anymore is in an upper room of this house. I haven't seen a courtroom in many years. I'm nearly seventy-five as you could guess. I'll tell you what I'll do, though. I'm driving up to Americus in a week or so for other unrelated business. But I'll call on Mr. Rutledge to get a feel for the situation, maybe put a good word in for your father. Nothing in writing, mind you. But I'll let you know what he has to say. How is that?"

"Sounds fine, Mr. Tullman, fine with us," Cade replied, happy with their conclusion. He looked at Myra.

Myra said, "I don' reckon Mr. Rutledge will be very cooperative."

"Why is that?"

"My Pa, with one arm and his broken back, threw him about twenty feet through the air out of our front door and into the yard, that's why." She even smiled.

Mr. Tullman smiled, too. "Well, he probably deserved it then."

On the return trip, Myra and Cade stopped in Flintside to collect a few necessities. With what remaining savings their father had given them from inside the elephant box, they realized frugality was at hand. The more urgent concern was Mr. Rutledge's promise that only thirty days remained until the bank would exercise their right to evict. And in thirty days, what then? Where would they go? How would they eat? How could they transport and care for their father and mother in their conditions? Would they be forced out to the roadside to see their father die there? The future was unknown, and any number of events could cause a series of derailments beyond imagination.

"I need to pick up some lamp oil and tobacco for Papa," Myra said as they neared Mr. Jenkins's store. "You better wait out here, alright?" She remembered their last encounter with Mr. Jenkins, and his attempt to swindle them out of valuable pocket change that had caused such an outrage from Cade.

Cade wandered off and Myra entered the store. A small bell rang as she pushed the heavy wooden door open.

The general store had been an establishment and landmark in Flintside for many years. It was owned and operated by Mr. Jenkins and his wife who lived in the upstairs apartment. The building was constructed of oak clapboard and was painted dark green with two steel-barred plate glass windows flanking a wide front door. Among food supplies, the stock also included general hardware, feed, light farm supplies, and apparel. Other than selling merchandise, the store also served as the local post office where the U.S. mail was delivered. On this day, several vehicles were parked on the road, a car, a stake-body farm truck, and a buckboard wagon drawn by horses.

As Myra entered, several townsfolk were shopping and conversing while standing at the checkout counter. Mr. Jenkins was busy assisting an elderly man with heavy sacks of meal that he was carrying to the man's car. He didn't notice Myra come in as he passed her while talking with the man and discussing the usual subjects such as the price of cotton and feed and the weather outlook. She went to the shelf to take a can of lamp oil, but as she turned, she bumped into a man standing behind her. She looked up and Jack Waylon was carrying a sack of chicken feed on his shoulder. He stopped, turned and smiled.

"Myra?" he said. "Well, I haven't seen you in town for a while. How are you doing?" Jack noticed that the young lady had grown considerably. She was nearly seventeen, and the last time he could remember seeing her, she had been a little-girl-version of who stood before him now.

"Mr. Waylon?" She held the can of oil, pulled a lock of hair from her face.

"Myra, it has been a while. Tell me, how is your pa doing? I know he had his accident a while back. I've been meaning to come visit, but you know. Running a large cattle ranch is time consuming." He set the bag of feed down and rested a hand on her shoulder. "I hope he's seen some improvement by now."

"Well, Mr. Waylon, thank you for asking, but he hasn't improved much more than walking a few steps with his cane." She looked at the size of this man, tall and wide-shouldered, the way he towered over most other men. "But, that certainly hasn't hindered his opinion of things, you can imagine."

"Oh, I know he can say a piece, that's for sure," He smiled. "Now, tell me. Is your momma still in the home up in Americus? I know it's been a while, years actually. The tragedy of her health took everyone by surprise. It certainly did me. She used to come into town a good bit, and we spoke on a regular basis."

Myra elected to keep their conversation to a minimum, desiring to avoid any discussion regarding her mother and Arden's trip to bring her back home to Lake Blackshear.

"She remains in the hospital there. Fortunately the state has taken good care of her, and we visit her from time to time."

Jack could see there was no resemblance between Myra and Ila Mae, as Myra was tall and slender with a fair complexion and hair the color of amber. Of course, he knew Ila Mae wasn't her biological mother.

Everyone knew Myra had come from a broken family, and that Jasper John had arranged the informal adoption with Mac and Ila Mae through his brother and a church in Atlanta many years earlier.

"Listen," Jack offered, "if there is anything I could do for you, don't hesitate asking, alright? Right now I'm dealing with a critical problem of my own with no water on my land, among other things—well everyone is dealing with something or another, I suppose. And you with your father, it ain't easy, I'm sure."

"I appreciate that, Mr. Waylon. I really do, but no thank you."

Before departing with his feed, he added, "As for your farmland, though, you have access to water down there in the lowlands by the lake. I wish I was down there too as we badly need water up on my high ground." He tipped his hat toward her. "Considering all, that's one problem you don't have to contend with."

"If the boll weevil hadn't gotten us the way it did, I suppose we could have used it."

"Heck, right now, we're driving a water truck down to the landing to fill a tank up."

"Well, Mr. Waylon, if I could, I would let the water run up hill to you."

He caught her sarcasm and frowned. "Maybe we could work out a deal of some kind. I could put a well in and run a water pipe up to my cattle. Then compensate you in some other manner."

"Oh, you mean bring a rig in and equipment? Drill on our land?"

"I know you must be short on everything as you ain't got any cotton. But if you had, it wouldn't matter much cause come harvest you won't get but five cents a pound, they're estimating."

"You'd have to bring that up with my pa, then," she said weary.

"Well, seeing as how he and I stand, I don't think I should. You know we don't see eye to eye, don't you?"

"I suspect I do."

"Well, that was before your time, I reckon." He lifted his feed bag onto his shoulder. "Who's making the decisions around your farm these days? Arden, I guess."

"No, that'd be Papa. He may be immobile but he ain't stupid yet."

"Well, I'll see you around, little miss," he said and went out the door to his stake-body work truck.

Days later, J.R. Rutledge returned to John Paul Jones's office for a meeting. He sat in front of the lawyer at his desk as they continued their previous conversation.

Mr. Jones said, "J.R., I have some promising news that may play into your favor. Our firm has handled many, not all, *but many* of the property sales over the past years in north Lee County, and, of course, we have retained all of those files, documents, and surveys for our records. Earlier this week, I had an associate in our firm look into this, and he has produced the records of one particular property that may help you," he said wryly.

"This pertains to the Grayson property, right?"

"Correct. I have an engineer with the county on his way over to discuss the matter. He should be here any time."

At that moment, Mr. Jones's secretary knocked and entered. "Mr. Browning is here for his appointment."

"Send him in, Martha. Thank you."

Beau Browning, the county engineer, entered wearing kakis, a blue oxford, and a pair of muddy field boots.

The lawyer said, "Mr. Browning, this is J.R. Rutledge, the president of Americus First Trust. Thank you for coming."

The two shook hands and straightaway sat across from Jones in two leather chairs.

The engineer began by saying, "Mr. Jones, thank you for calling me in. The timing couldn't have been better. I was just wrapping up some work at the municipal department with the county. And, by the way, I certainly do appreciate those new Goodyear tires you had put on my truck yesterday. My wife was pleased about them, too. And when the wife is pleased, well," he said, laughing sheepishly. "That goes without saying."

"Good deal, Mr. Browning, good deal."

Jones looked to Rutledge. "I've spoken to Mr. Browning ahead of time, specifically about this."

Jones took a thick cigar, lit it with his kerosene lighter, puffed and continued. "J.R., I have in my possession the closing records of a specific property that we handled a few years back—in 1925 as a matter of fact. What is promising is that this land I'm speaking of lies directly adjacent to the Grayson property, and it was owned by the former Cline McCarver." He sat back proudly and said, "Mr. Browning, can you assist us with explaining, please?"

Browning leaned forward and said to the lawyer, "Mr. Jones, because you hold the records, the dimensional property description, and the survey map for the McCarver land, this will prove very beneficial as I can show you."

While motioning with his hand, Browning said, "Gentleman, if we could move to this trestle table over here against the wall?"

The attorney promptly turned to his credenza behind his desk, retrieved a thick file and a roll of paper. On the nearby table, Browning took the liberty of sliding aside some law books and notepads. Jones came and set the contents on the long table in front of the other two.

The attorney said, "I have discovered that Jones, Howard & Marston closed on the McCarver property seventeen years ago, the property that is directly adjacent to Grayson." He opened the file. He presented the documents, the property description, the closing statement, and title information which had been neatly done on an Underwood typewriter.

Jones continued, "As you can see, Kline and Grace McCarver purchased their property from a William and Betsy Stanford in November of 1925." He also rolled out the beautifully hand-drawn survey map, the name Theodore Giles & Company, Surveyors, Americus, Georgia, in the lower title block.

Browning held the drawing and stood between them to present the information. "Here gentleman is the land in question."

"Very good," Rutledge said. "Please explain."

Browning said, "Mr. Jones has informed me you are explicitly interested in the Grayson property, which is beside the McCarver property, is that correct?"

Rutledge nodded.

Browning continued, "As you can observe on this map which Mr. Jones has kindly provided, we obviously do not have a detailed survey of the Grayson property." He pointed, and the other two followed his index finger as he ran it over the paper map. He added, "However, on this map, you can see the adjacent property next to it, wholly represented as the *Certified Survey Map* of the McCarver property."

Rutledge slowly nodded while nibbling his thumbnail.

Browning went on. "Now then, so far there apparently hasn't been a survey record found for the Grayson property due to the incident of the courthouse fire. Yet I can produce it easily enough because I have the McCarver survey. Let me explain. Can you see how Lake Blackshear creates the *eastern boundaries* of both properties? Well if you notice, the county road creates the *western boundaries* of both because the road very precisely intersects the lake on the northern end of McCarver's land and the southern end of Grayson's. Understand that when the dam was built and this land flooded, it nearly overtook the road but not quite. So there you have it, the lake and the county road encompass both properties, creating the semblance of an elongated oval split in half width-wise. In other words both properties are alone, side by side, inside an oval circle created by the lake's shoreline and the county road. If I can resurvey the McCarver land then the lake and road do the rest. The final step would be to survey the Grayson land by process of elimination. I will have to enter their land and mark it out. Then I would have a Certified Survey Map of their land as well."

Jones said, "The McCarver land is likely in probate at this time because the McCarvers had no Last Will and Testament, nor any children or family, so it is probably tied up in a long line of other cases awaiting the court's attention."

"How does that affect us?" Rutledge asked the attorney.

"Fortunately, none whatsoever. We aren't foreclosing the McCarver property are we?"

"No, not the McCarver's. It's the Grayson property I'm most interested in at the moment."

"Besides J.R., for the money you're paying," Jones said, "I know a judge that can move your case directly to the front of the line." He chuckled and puffed his cigar.

Mr. Browning said, "May I ask, why the urgency, Mr. Rutledge?"

J.R. turned and quickly replied, "The *first reason* is that Grayson humiliated me in front of my vice-president by physically removing me from his property. Threw me on the ground and ruined my suit, too. Then his daughter threatened me with a 12 gage shotgun by blasting it into the air above my head. That is my *first reason*."

"How is Grayson's payment record?" Jones asked.

"Eight months delinquent, but ninety-five percent of the principle is paid down. Apparently from what I've gathered, his great-grandfather earned the land by means of a land grant by the U.S. Treasury for his military service in the Navy."

"Ninety-five percent, how unfortunate."

"I don't give a damn. I'm going to take every last grain of dirt he owns."

Browning asked, "The question presented next is: What can the bank do with the numerous properties in Lee County once you've foreclosed them? No one will be able to buy them, not in the state of this economy. The properties will lay dormant unable to produce cotton, corn, or livestock. And in turn, they will then be worth even less."

"That could be true for the time being. But don't worry, Mr. Browning. I have plans for the Grayson property. That particular piece of ground, as I've stated, is almost paid-off so I can get it for nearly nothing. You see, many of the loans that my bank has called in aren't but ten or twenty percent paid-down. Those properties are more of a liability than an asset. But the Grayson property? It is one beautiful piece of land as you will soon discover."

Rutledge returned to his office, down the street to the Americus First Trust Bank Building. He nodded graciously as her entered, first to his employees then his secretary. When he stepped into his private office, his young daughter Bethany, his *second reason*, awaited him there.

"Diddy, how did it go? Are we on our way down there now, Diddy?"

"Not just yet, darling. Not just yet."

Part Two

Chapter 11

THE FOLLOWING MORNING, Arden packed his long-suffering grief and trepidation into the wagon and rode out at first light behind Bess and Big Joe. The day was clear up ahead and looked promising for the ride, but his spirit was not free as his burden was heavy. What could he possibly do with his ailing mother? He hadn't seen her in well over a year. How difficult could the challenge become dealing with a mental convalescent? What would people think? Could he manage and contain her in their wagon for the three day trip? How could they care for their ailing parents when they had trouble enough caring for themselves?

Americus was yet another eighteen miles barring the time to stop for rest, to eat and tend the mules. For an extra twenty cents, the stable hand in Desoto had left hay and a feed sack in the wagon bed. In the case they did not come across a meandering stream, he could provide the mules water from his canteen by pouring it into a pail he had carried along. The road was long. They would be fine, the beasts of burden as tough as they were.

The lay of the land was mostly even with a few houses and barns along the way. After a while, the topography out of Desoto climbed steadily in elevation until the wagon crested the flatland and Arden could see for a half mile or more. In the distance, the landscape was vast and open. The road was direct as an arrow, and its trajectory held the earth's curvature straight into oblivion, disappearing into the sky on the far horizon. The land was the color of pale straw and olive-green. Singing birds traced the edges of the fields and darted from one stand of trees to the next. Gathered against a roadside fence, a herd of black cattle grazed and chewed their cud without a care while watching the wagon slowly pass. Spring wildflowers were fading in the late August sun. The country air was humid; the morning sky indigo, cloudless and serene.

Once underway and traveling at a good pace, he noticed a long line of dust rising up from the earth into the sky. Coming in his direction, it appeared to be another wagon on the road ahead. After some time, it came closer into clearer view as the driver approached while spitting chaw out to the side of the road. As they neared, Arden pulled aside to allow room, but instead the man halted his team with a pull of his reigns.

"Young man, where are you going?" the old man asked. He wore a pair of faded coveralls with a pocked suede cowboy hat, a red scarf around his neck, and a tobacco pipe poking out of his top pocket. He turned, spat again, wiping his hand across his mouth.

Arden was confounded that the man even cared. The previous day he had passed other cars and wagons but no one else had taken a breath to speak with him.

"Headin' north to Americus to see my kin. And you?"

"Headin' south away from Americus." He spat again. "Ain't nothing good up there anymore. The lines at the banks are strung out like long ropes along the streets. People are panhandling looking for scraps. They say the cotton will be no good. Won't bring three cents a pound they say. No one has the money." He spat again.

"I reckon I'll have to go anyhow. I have a duty to undertake." He looked out to the road ahead. "We lost all ours to the weevil, too. Damned beetle." Arden hadn't been aware of the air in the city yet, but this man was apparently telling him.

"None of it is good, young man. I suppose your kin'll tell you that when you arrive."

"I suspect so then," Arden said with a tip of his cap.

"Good luck, son," the old man said and rode on.

Away from the flatland, the terrain began rolling into hills. Soon trees began draping the road with long shadows. A creek came into view and he pulled the team into the weeds so they could drink under a line of hanging willows. He dismounted and stretched. A minute later, a deer fawn wandered out of the brush. He moved slowly and went for his Colt pistol in the canvas roll, but it was too late as the fawn dashed away at the sound of his rustling. According to the old man in the wagon, everywhere you went was under strain. In response to this, he thought to have the Colt revolver handy anyhow, so he hid it under the buckboard in his folded jacket.

Later, afternoon came. After more mileage, he halted to feed his mules and eat apples and jerky. Then he resumed his journey and rode the buckboard as the red dirt road passed slowly away beneath him. It was a good time to read, and he took his pocket Bible from his jacket to read passages and pass the time. Clouds were beginning to build in the western sky, and he hoped the weather would hold out for the remainder of his trip. The land was rural with little population. Fields of corn were chapped and dry. Sparsely grown cotton ran for miles in all directions, their imminent demise seen from the lack of rain and infestation. The thought of all which was lost weighed heavily on his mind; also knowing long nights of winter eventually loomed ahead which would allow more time for dark reflection. He was uneasy with what lay ahead and what he must face. Not just the coming days ahead but for the months and years as well.

The following afternoon into his third day, Arden neared Americus. As soon as the road widened, cars sped by in red rolling clouds of dust while honking their horns at his mules for taking up their fair share of road. The rural outstretches quickly began yielding to dense farmland and housing. Tightly-fenced properties, storage barns, and small commercial warehouses came into view. A cotton exchange building with a row of loading docks lined the road. Vertical gasoline tanks and a pumping station for automobiles were on a corner across from a grocery and clothing outlet. His wagon came to a set of railroad tracks, and he grimaced as the old wagon bounced harshly over them. He realized that too much of that could break a wheel and perilously strand them in the middle of nowhere.

After entering the city, the dirt road abruptly changed into pavement. Soon, a long run of brick buildings came into view and paralleled the road on each side: many merchandise stores, an icehouse, and an inn with shady oaks out front. Municipal buildings were built of concrete block. Further on, a two-story granite courthouse looked to be newly constructed. On one street, he passed the Windsor Hotel and on another, the Rylander Theater. Further on, beautiful antebellum homes were set between thick leafy trees. Electrical lighting fixtures fronted the buildings and homes, as electrical power was being brought into the rural regions of South Georgia from the big cities up north.

However, crowds were gathered on the street corners, people of all shapes and sizes in every kind of dress. They seemed to be discussing the downturn of events, now that nearly a year had passed since the stock market had collapsed. Men puffed cigars in lingering clouds of smoke. The homeless stood on the sidewalks while guarding their suitcases. In the heat, some women wearing winter coats held large paper sacks in one hand and a child's hand in the other. Further on, lines had formed at the bank door and people were shouting. A fight broke out and the crowd fanned away. Shocked to see the state of affairs in Americus, he noticed a few teens in dirty clothing loitering along the sidewalk, apparently lost and without parents. Droves of vagrant men in ragged clothes from the countryside walked the streets with their hands thrust into their pockets. They meandered through the city while gazing hopelessly into nothingness. Some people were digging into trash cans. Arden could see the sad loss marking their empty faces and hollow eyes; the look of desperation and fear, the look of abandonment and devastation.

He drove on, and a train station came into view where more bystanders were crowded even deeper while awaiting a train. Two attendants were pushing them back from the tracks. In the glaring late day sun, he noticed a long line ahead of him leading toward a church with a boldly painted sign that read: *Bread — Half Loaf Per Man.*

He knew where to find St. Francis, just another block and to the left, by a row of administration buildings and across from a gothic Presbyterian Church with an ancient graveyard. The St. Francis Sanitarium was state-operated, one of only three in the entire state they'd been informed: including Central State Mental Health in Milledgeville and Crawford Long Hospital in Atlanta. Although his last visit to St. Francis had been earlier the previous year, he could not have put it out of his mind even if he had tried. With that horrid memory etched into his brain, he needed no city map to get him there.

After arriving, he realized it was late afternoon. He tied up to the hitching rack in front of the hospital and fed his mules. Other horse-drawn wagons were driving by. Cars were parked in assigned spaces alongside the building. Across the street from the hospital, he could see the breadline entering the rear of the Presbyterian Church from the direction of the rail station.

The two story hospital was utilitarian in its design, a wide redbrick facade with office windows on the lower level and a few vertical slit-windows on the upper level. Two black steel doors centered the building where weather-stained urns had been placed for decoration but the vessels were empty of any greenery. As he removed Doctor Robert's letter from his roll, he looked up. From the small vertical windows on the upper level, he noticed the faint images of ghostly faces staring down at him, pale faces with gaunt expressions and dark eyes. A chill ran along his back and he held his breath as he watched. One image waved forebodingly, and he thought it might be his mother.

Arden was tentative as he approached the front doors. Having planned in advance the night before, he had made a bed pallet in the wagon with what he had: his bedroll, some burlap produce sacks he'd brought along for padding, and his coat for her pillow. He could stretch out on his rain parka on the return trip which would be fine for him. If the weather turned, he had a bull hide cover prepped with grease as a rain repellent. Under those conditions, she should be dry although uncomfortable for the long ride home. At night they could sleep under the wagon, too, if worse came to worse and the rain became too heavy. Other than that, according to Dr. Roberts, the hospital's food supply and medications were nearly depleted. What medications, Arden knew little of, nor what good they were. Without the proper medications, how was he to care for his mother if the hospital could not either?

He entered the dimly lit building and came to the front desk to wait. Right away he noticed the electrical lights as power was non-existent south of Americus down in Lee County. The lobby was austere in appearance with chairs and a threadbare couch he didn't desire to sit upon, rather preferring the floor if need be by the looks of the furniture stains. The lobby was small and confined with two separately locked doors exiting in opposite directions. The walls were drab gray and windowless. From the lobby he heard strange voices, bumping sounds and moans, sharp intonations of discussion then silence and demented cries of rejection, even screams of grave disruption.

Soon a nurse arrived while straightening her dress as if from a tussle. She sat at her desk and attempted to right her hair bun pinned to the back of her head. "Yes, can we help you?" she asked though distracted. She seemed to be looking for a file of paperwork in a stack of others. After a moment she relinquished her search and looked up again.

Arden rubbed his hands on his dirty trousers and paused nervously. After an awkward lull, he said. "My Name is Arden Grayson. We received a letter from Dr. Walter Roberts a few weeks back." He handed the letter to the nurse and waited as she read it. "I was ordered by my father to come here as soon as I could to get her, so I could take her back home to Lake Blackshear." He licked his lips, hoping he had done well in representing his dear mother.

The nurse glanced up quickly and held the letter. Her expression changed from darkness to compassion and hospitality. "You are Ila's son."

"Yes, I am." Arden's face was youthful and sunburned from his long ride. Though tired, his eyes were bright and hopeful. He had come so far and the time had arrived for him to be a man.

The nurse said, "I loved your mother." She glanced back at the letter and said, "I'll return in a few minutes."

A long while later a doctor and an orderly came with the nurse. They entered in single file, but the look on the doctor's face alarmed him. The three stood shoulder to shoulder. The nurse looked at the doctor then to Arden.

The doctor began by asking, "Mr. Grayson, how is it you have traveled to Americus from Lake Blackshear?"

"In a small draw wagon with two mules." He looked over the three. "You must be Dr. Roberts," he said.

"No, I'm Dr. Carlson."

"Where is Dr. Roberts, then?"

"Mr. Grayson. We are sorry but Dr. Roberts has been transferred to Richmond, Virginia to take up a position there."

"And my mother?"

"We also regret to inform you that your mother died some weeks ago. Her health turned too quickly, and there was nothing we could do. I'm sorry."

"She has died? How can that be?" He was devastated.

He said, "She died unexpectedly. We couldn't prevent it. However, she must be buried as soon as possible as she has deteriorated into a foul state. Her body has been kept in the morgue in the basement without the availability of embalming fluids, and I would not recommend you taking her in a wagon back to your home as she couldn't make it all in one piece."

Arden froze, stunned. He felt as though he had been punched in his gut with the blunt end of a shovel handle. He gasped and put his hands to his face.

He looked up and said, "She died and is now decomposed? We came as soon as we could. I had to repair my wagon for the trip and prepare for the ride. Prepare my mules and my roll. It is a three day trip. And well, here I am for her!"

"I'm sorry, Mister Grayson. For what it is worth, she was nothing but in a vegetative state as it was. And then she had a sudden turn of physical health. I'm very sorry. I know you have done your best. But we did ours as well. I'm sorry."

"What now?"

"Well, there is the cost of the twenty dollars mentioned in the letter."

"The letter says twenty dollars to release her but she is dead."

"You must pay to release her."

Arden turned and cried, put his hands on his hips and shook his head as confused as he was saddened. He had not planned for this. Not for her body's condition or for her death. What could he do?

He turned back. "Why do you need to release her? She has died. Where could she go?"

"To burial, Mr. Grayson," the doctor replied, now the one confused.

The doctor was odd, a tall man with a sad expression as his mouth seemed to form a permanent frown that drew long lines down his face. The orderly was thick with large arms and narrow-set eyes. Standing with them, the nurse was older but seemed to have a surprisingly pleasant disposition given her occupation in a state mental hospital.

"Where to then if I can't take her with me?" he asked.

The doctor seemed curt. "I recommend to the church cemetery across the street. As a matter of fact, they only have a few plots remaining. But the fee is twenty dollars, also accounting for her back-expenses."

"What if I can't afford it, then?" Arden knew that he held the money. Cade had given it to him before he left.

"Our burial plots at St. Francis have been full for years now. We would have no choice but to take her to the stockyard for a dumpster there. The state has left us with no other choice. We are broke."

Arden was now more than stunned. He was shocked. "Alright then, but it's late. I'll return tomorrow with the money."

"Well, we would prefer you pay now and meet us first thing in the morning. The digging must be done." He held out his hand for the cash.

"I'll be in the church graveyard across the street at daylight. But I won't pay until the job is taken care of and she rests in peace."

The doctor smirked. "No sir, it will be twenty dollars now or we won't be able to dig her grave and furnish a small tombstone with her name on it. That's cheap, considering." The doctor's hand remained outward.

Arden agreed and paid the twenty dollars though he was reluctant. Twenty dollars was hard to come by and the family had little money remaining. Yet he withdrew it from his pouch and handed it to the doctor.

"In the morning, Mr. Grayson," the doctor said with a stern nod then left with the orderly.

The nurse said, "I'm very sorry."

Chapter 12

JACK WAYLON STOOD on his land, on the hill overlooking the Grayson property down below and Lake Blackshear further in distance. The Grayson land was so elegant, he thought, the manner in which it rolled up and along the narrow lake. Many hundreds of yards across the water, the land ascended softly off the lakeshore into the surrounding hills of north Lee County. The air was hinting of fall and the late morning was cool and refreshing. After some thought as to his plan, he returned to the house. Wynonna was in the kitchen preparing the meal he had arranged. She had arrived early to fry the chicken golden brown, to mash the potatoes with extra butter, to stew the green beans and make up the skillet cornbread just right. She had packaged the meal in a straw basket with plenty of decorative napkins, and she even tied a yellow bow on the handle as a women's touch.

"Mr. Waylon, if this can't win their hearts in this time of shortage and depression, I don't know what could." Her hands were wrinkled and coarse, the sweat on his forehead beaded from the hard work and heat. She slid the back of her hand across her face to push her gray hair aside. "And I done made up a fresh batch of tea with fresh lemons from the store."

Jack usually did his own grocery shopping and knew the lemons had cost plenty. She had returned with little coin change from Jenkins's, but it didn't matter as she could hardly count anyway. He said, "Looks mighty good, Wynonna. Mighty good. I'll take it down and see what I can work out." He leaned forward and took a whiff of the chicken.

"I left out some pieces for you too, don't worry."

"I suppose this is as good a time as any. Might as well git 'fore this cools off." He took the basket and went out the back door. "I'll return, hopefully with a deal."

"Sho nuff, cause them cattle sho needs some water up here. Looks like the pond out in the field has puddled-up a little with the recent rain, but that is far from enough, Mr. Waylon." She followed him to the back door to see him out.

"You git on back to work now, Wynonna. Time's a wasting. No lollygagging, now."

He went to his flatbed Ford, drove out down the hill and around on the road to Mac Grayson's house. He knew he was running out of options. He'd thought the wood pile in the lumberyard would have done him in, but as fate would have it, the man was still alive.

In the orange sun, Cade came up the path from the lake holding only his bamboo pole. From the front steps, Myra could see him with no fish on his line. Her stomach growled constantly. She was so hungry. The pantry was completely empty. After a final attempt at bird hunting, there were no shells left for the shotgun. Papa's elephant box was now empty of money. What little remained, the few dollars he had saved was being reserved for the bitter end as they were attempting to live off the land, what little it could give them. Over the last few days, all three of them had been severely sick with running diarrhea. From the forest mushrooms possibly, maybe the squirrel from McCarver's apple trees, maybe too many green immature apples. Myra thought if she saw another apple she would die of stomach cramping. Her monthly period had returned on schedule, and she had no choice but to use rags from the toolshed, ones she'd washed the best she could.

Cade was dejected as he came through the door. "Fish just ain't biting this morning. I don't know what the problem is other than the lake water is brown from so much rain, and they don't bite worth a damn when it's like that."

"Damned rain is right," she said. "We can't win either way. Not enough for two or three years and the crops suffer. Now too much and the lake is muddy."

"Water level is risin' a little every day, now. It's up higher than it's been in a year or two."

At that moment they heard the sound of a truck coming down the ridge. They looked at each other with caution.

Cade said, "That's Jack Waylon's truck. I can recognize it from a mile off. He drives up and down the county road like he owns it. You can tell it's him."

"What in the devil is he doing down here, though?" Myra said.

Inside the cabin, Cade stood in the door light, taller than ever. His shoulders had broadened over the summer and his face had matured. With age, his stubble was becoming prominent now that he was nearly nineteen. When he turned from the doorway to look at Myra, she suddenly saw him in a different way. His blue eyes were brilliant, and his voice had deepened considerably. Since Arden had left, he appeared more confident and outspoken. Maybe the tough conditions had hardened him. But this day he was now a man, she finally noticed.

"Waylon ain't nothing but trouble, if you ask me."

"I guess we better go see what he wants," Myra said.

"Wait, Myra, you stay here. Let me go out, alright?"

She crossed her thin arms and nodded her agreement but said nothing.

Cade went out and stood in their yard, waiting. Waylon pulled around and his brakes squealed loudly as he came to a stop. He stood from the truck and held a basket in his hand. He was tall and broad with sharp blue eyes.

"Cade, how you doing, son?"

"Mr. Waylon, what can we do for you today?"

Waylon approached slowly, knowing he wasn't welcomed on this property due to Mac's disagreements with him. Over the years, Cade and Myra were unclear as to every decision and knew their father wasn't at all times forthcoming with his reasons. With due respect, their father had been reserved but with an undeniable authority that had been passed down from his father and his father's father.

As far as disagreements, their father on several occasions had protested Waylon's farming practice of pulling down scrub and dead timber from his land to theirs. (It's always easier to accumulate timber when pulling down hill). Waylon would burn the wood close to their fence line which, in turn, created the nuisance of dense smoke over their cabin and barn. In another instance, his cattle escaped the fence and trampled much cotton over which Mac became irate. Mac even threatened to shoot them before Waylon took care of the problem but failed to compensate Mac for his loss and aggravation. In addition, there had once been a property line dispute. But Waylon finally gave in after Mac threatened to get William Tullman the attorney involved. Waylon had taken it upon himself to redirect his driveway further into the Grayson land for ease of access up the hill from the road. Naturally, Mac disagreed, and he placed large river rocks there to prevent further encroachment.

But were these reasons enough to hate the man? To not allow him onto your property? Naturally, many occasions cause any number of neighbors to disagree at one time or another. Farmers in close proximity to one another were notorious for land or farming disputes. This was a part of land management and home ownership.

For this and for what other cause, their pa despised Jack Waylon.

Jack opened by saying, "I know it's been difficult caring for your pa, Cade. I know we've disagreed in the past but we ain't never really caused either any real harm, do you think?" Waylon stood in front of Cade almost eye to eye. Waylon could see he'd grown considerably. "Now, I brought this down here as recompense, as a compromise, if that's okay. Let bygones be bygones, ain't that right?" He handed the food basket out for Cade to take.

Cade licked his watering mouth at the sight of the friend chicken. He reached out and took the basket by the handle. He said, "Looks real nice, thank you."

Waylon looked up and saw Myra standing on the front steps as pretty as she was. Myra was growing up too, beginning to shape up nicely. He had noticed this the previous occasion when he saw her at the store in town. Her hips were now more becoming, and her face had matured from that young-girl-of-last-year into a women with her breasts now poking up high and her gate more mature when she walked.

"Myra," he called out. "I brought something good for you three to eat. How's your pa doing?" He took a cautious step forward to test the air, and she smiled slightly.

"Well," she replied, "doing 'bout the same I reckon. He's able to get out of bed a little but can't go too far yet."

Jack was disappointed. He had hoped for better news.

With her amicable reaction of at least speaking to him, he slowly walked up to the base of the steps and awaited an invitation to enter. When she saw the food basket Cade held, she smiled. "Mr. Waylon, how nice of you! Come on in, will you?"

Cade went up first. "Tea in mason jars, too," he said to Myra.

When the three entered, Mac was standing in his bedroom doorway, propped against it while holding his cane.

"What the hell do you think you're doing, Waylon? And who the hell said you could put one foot on my land?"

"Papa, now calm down! Look! Look what he has brought us!" She ran to his side with a chair from the table to help him sit.

Waylon could see the demise on his neighbor's face, the look of defeat, that he had lost much weight and was gaunter than he'd ever seen him. His pale complexion showed his lack of being in the sunlight. His eyes were deeply set and weak with dark circles and a glaze over them. He looked like a dying man. He could barely stand much less be a threat.

"Well, Mac, listen here. I'm just being neighborly, that's all. I know times are tight. I'm tight myself, but I wanted to bring you something good to eat."

Just then Cade couldn't wait and he took a piece of chicken.

"Put that back boy!" Mac hollered.

"Pa? What? We're starving, Papa." He looked desperate. "I mean what harm could this do?"

"Plenty what's been done in the past you may not be aware of."

Waylon quickly said, "Listen, Mac. I'm sorry for your accident. I really am, but we all have to move on. You know my uncle lost both his eyes in a farming accident years back. And he was blinded. But gal damned, Mac, he didn't hate the world and everyone in it because of it."

"Hogwash, I hated your ass long before that." He coughed severely and reached for his pipe from his pocket, but Myra came and said, "No Papa, this tobacco pipe is what might be killing you!" She yanked it away.

"Myra!"

"No, Papa. Not right now. You settle down."

"Mac," Waylon said softly, stepping forward. "I know you are strapped with no cotton to sell. I know it ain't but three or four cent right now, depending on who you talk with. But, listen here, I need water and you've got it down here in the lowland ground. You know my family has had water in our big pond up there for as long as we've owned our land, but the creek leading into it has never dried up like this. This drought is bad, Maclin, real bad. Now, I'm bringing you this dinner in hopes you might come to your senses, cause we're both in bad shape and it ain't getting any better."

"That's all you want. You didn't bring this dinner as a will of a good heart. This is bribery, Waylon."

Cade said, "Pa we ain't ate much of nothing for days now, maybe three or four. And we got Momma coming back home with five mouths to feed."

"Papa, I'm sorry but we must eat," Myra said, and they sat at the table in front of the basket. She began to cry and this broke his heart like a violin on the strings of his soul.

Waylon said, *"This is from my good heart,* Mac, but we have to work together now. I have the food but you have the water. Just let me bring my driller down tomorrow to drill and set a pump. We'll run a two inch transfer pipe under the road and up the hill to my cattle and we'll work out a deal. Water for food. What do you say?"

"Papa?" Myra said, wiping away her tears.

Jack Waylon turned to look at her. She looked into his blue eyes for a long moment, and something in the back of her mind nudged her, but what she wasn't sure, something in his eyes.

Cade said, "We have to eat, Papa. We have no food." He stood and went to their father.

Mac said regretfully, "You do what you must, then." He looked away at the wall and shook his head in sadness.

Myra came and brought him meat, but he refused to eat.

He said to Waylon, "After this, Waylon, you stay off my land or you'll get a bullet in your backside for trespassing."

"Papa, why can't you cooperate?" Myra asked while eating.

Mac advised, "Cade, you get back down to the lake in the morning and you'll catch some bass. You catch a slew and we'll salt 'em good in the smokehouse. We got a little money left to buy some more buckshot, and we'll get us a good doe to salt, too. Ain't too late to put some turnips in the ground, either. We ain't done yet, Waylon. As long as I got a breath in me, Waylon, I ain't done just yet."

The following day, Myra trudged into town and purchased shells and turnip seed. At noon, Cade left through the woods and hunted deer for hours from the low branches of an ancient apple tree. It was said the apple orchard had been planted by the Creek Indians long before the coming of the white man in South Georgia, and that the trees had proliferated and some were estimated to be a hundred years old. Cade expected deer to come for the apples on the ground as they usually did in the fall rut, as they had for many years since the beginning of the ages. Though indeed they came, the deer were unfortunately too far off in the distance to be brought down with scattered buckshot.

Also, the previous night, he and Myra had discussed their dire situation and were convinced the squirrel meat was responsible for their stomach ailments, thus they avoided any more of them. Later, Cade attempted fishing but was hardly successful, returning from the muddy water with a few small lake bream. With the days cooling and sky overcast, Myra went to the barn for mule dung and to dig a small plot with a shovel out in the sun. She scattered in the manure, planted the seed, and brought water up from the well. With this, she expected for the turnips to be up and on the table before the end of November, if they could wait that long.

Myra stood from her work, brushed the dirt from her hands, and studied the turned ground she had watered. Turnips were a good fall plant, a two month crop in the south. Turnip greens were easy to grow especially in loose fertile soil with good sunlight. She heard someone from behind, and she turned to see Jack Waylon throwing his leg over their fence, coming off the road on the ridge. He stepped by the small Grayson family gravesite on the hill and came through the trees and thick ivy. He wore a nice cowboy hat, denim trousers, boots, and a stylish tooled leather belt. He had a long piece of wire grass in the corner of his mouth that he was casually chewing on.

"Mr. Waylon? I thought we agreed you were to stay clear of our property." She stood straight and put her hand on her hip.

"Myra, I don't mean you or your family any harm, now." He smiled. "I know your father and I got sideways over my driveway and his property line, but it really was a small issue and we corrected the problem without too many harsh words. It wasn't but a few feet of road that were being contested. Heck, a few feet of road out of fifty acres? And I attempted compensating him for the trampled cotton, but he was too proud to accept it. Is it really all about that? I believe he's just jealous over my success, that's all."

She followed him into the shade of a cottonwood at the bottom of the hill. The shade was cool and the shadows of the tree brushed along their faces as they spoke.

"My Papa is a hard-headed man, I know, but—"

"—Myra, Myra, listen. Your father's old and his health is not the best. Before too long, the dealing is going to be between the two of us. And your brothers, of course. I believe we can be a benefit to one another if we could just get your father's pride out of the way and go about making some smart business decisions."

"I'm sorry Mr. Waylon, but I must abide by his rules for now. You just can't come down here and rewrite our relationship by dismissing him because of his age or health. He may be in bad shape at this time, but his condition has improved slowly. He is getting around the house better. His mind is good mostly. He may surprise all of us."

"Either way, if he's up or down, someone is going to have to think logically over the situation. Myra, I got two hundred and sixty head up wonder and that means meat and income. You don't have a bucket of dirt to sell. I'm just here to make sense of our circumstances, girl."

"I appreciate that but you best go on, now."

She tossed her hair off her shoulders and nodded in the direction up the hill for him to leave. He looked her over and slowly turned.

"Time will tell little lady, time will tell."

Chapter 13

Jasper John rode from his home in the backwoods of Flintside and came down to the Grayson farm on his mule. The old mule had a bad hip. The pastor's weight made her list from time to time, so as a precaution, the pastor slid off and led the rest of the way on foot. After coming down the hill, he lashed her reign to a sapling by Mac's cabin and looked about. The air was quiet, just the sound of the wind up from the lake. He walked up the front steps, paused and banged on the oak door with his fist.

"Maclin!" he called, but no one answered.

A moment later: "Yeah, come on around the side, Jasper! I'm back here."

Jasper John rounded the exterior of the cabin to the backside where the oaks and cottonwood grew. He came around to the window and looked inside. He could see Mac lying on his daybed, a burnt-out cigar stub between his fingers.

"Maclin, you doing alright?"

Jasper John was an elderly man with a leaning posture, age-spotted arms, and sad brown eyes like two swirling knots in a piece of old barn board. He however carried himself in an air of ease with a good-natured spirit and kind smile. After forty-five years, he had retired as an employee at the Martha White Flour Mill in Leslie to become a pastor at Mount Olive Church.

Mac said, "Not worth a shit, Jasper John, to tell you the truth. I've seen better days. My back hurts from the time the sun rises, and I can hardly walk."

"Well, you won't need them legs when you get up yonder, my man. No sir. You'll fly away, Lord, you'll fly away." He smiled.

"Who the hell says I'm going to heaven?" He laughed. "I didn't know God had decided that, yet. The jury's still out ain't it?"

"Lord, Maclin. If ever a man went up to heaven, It'd be you. You done taken in these children and did what needed doin'. That's what I say."

Mac chewed on his cigar stub. "They ain't been too bad, Jasper. Good thing I got 'em now, I'll tell you. Now Myra, she's as sweet as a bee's honeycomb. She's got some good blood and a good heart in her, too. It's a good thing Lester took her and put her on that train down to here when he did," Mac said, speaking of Jasper John's brother with the Methodist Children's Home in Decatur outside of Atlanta.

"Yep, she was a little thing. Needed a good home and you said you'd take her. You're a good man, Maclin. You done good."

"Wasn't easy but we did alright. Arden was a good boy from Ila, and he took to Myra pretty well when she became part of our family."

"Arden looks like he's cut from the same slab of rock as you, Maclin. You two favor one another. Same face and eyes, same build."

"Yep, he's mine alright," Mac agreed.

Jasper John rested his arms on the window sill at eye level with Maclin in the bed in his room. Standing on the outside of the cabin in the shade, Jasper was nice and cool.

"Where are Myra and Cade, anyway?"

"They're out rooting around. Cade's hunting or fishing, I'm sure."

"Now, how is Cade doing? He's getting along alright?"

"He's a good boy. A good hunter and worker, too."

Mac sat up on the side of the bed. Myra had sewn an extra-large pillow cushion he used. Mac propped it up and turned toward the pastor.

"Speaking of Cade, Waylon was down here yesterday. He wants to bring in a drill rig, equipment, and a pump for groundwater."

"Sounds like a lot of tearing up to me."

"I didn't like the idea."

"What's in it for you?"

"He's offering food and money."

"Best take him up if it gets too tight."

"Hell, he should have offered that years ago, Jasper."

"You believe Cade will ever catch on? He looks just like his daddy."

"I'm afraid he will."

"It was a shame. But you couldn't have proven anything."

"I was up in Macon for a while, at the big yearly farm equipment auction with Mel and Chesley. Well, Ila Mae had been awfully sick with her stomach ailments. She turned up pregnant the next month, and I knew right off it wasn't mine. Wasn't hard to figure out. But she had already lost her mind. She didn't know what she had done. Chesley's wife was supposed to have been down here watching after her while we were gone. Then as the years passed, Cade grew up to look just like his daddy, Jack Waylon."

"I suppose Waylon, that bastard, took advantage of the situation."

"Yep, must have, Jasper. We're so remotely located down here by the lake. There aren't that many people around here. And, well, it took a few years to figure out. I guess I started with the process of elimination."

"Couldn't have been too many options, it appears."

"We'll never know the details. But Ila Mae had no idea. She didn't even know me when I walked through the front door with her mind gone like it was. But I couldn't prove anything. By the time Cade turned ten, I was sure. I'll say this: no one in this family has blue eyes and stands well over six feet like Cade does. But I'm keeping my mouth shut. It is water under the bridge, and saying something now wouldn't prove anything. I'd just cause grief and a whole lot of hurt." Mac chewed his cigar stub, frowning.

"You're a good man to do what you've done for these children, Mac. You're a damn good man."

"As long as our little secret about Cade stays between you and me, Jasper, I'm fine with it."

Early that Tuesday morning, Beau Browning the county engineer drove from Leesburg in his Ford truck. He came through Flintside and steered down the road by the marshes. With a map, he located Cline McCarver's land just as the morning sun was rising over the tree line. He had his instructions and the files from Rutledge and Jones. They were paying him to map and survey the McCarver property so that the Grayson property boundaries could be deduced as a result. Fortunately, the law firm still possessed the records from the McCarver's original purchase which included the survey map. In their meeting, Browning had informed them that if he were allowed to re-mark the McCarver property, he in turn could recreate a survey of Grayson's simply by using the lake and the county road to do the rest. The plan was to produce a certified map and bring it to a judge's attention in order to allow foreclosure on Mac Grayson, therefore reverting ownership back into the hands of Americus First Trust Bank, essentially J.R. Rutledge and then his daughter.

Edging the weeded fence line in his truck, Browning stopped at the chain link gate which had been padlocked. He nudged his truck bumper up and slowly pressed the accelerator. The truck surged forward and snapped the rusted chain, opening the gate to the property. From there he could see the old McCarver homestead, a small clapboard house with a low single-ridge roof and a narrow front porch supported by three oak posts. He drove along the gravel drive that wound its way up to the house. He parked and stood from his truck to see the land. Further down the rolling hill, the land met the lakeshore. North, the fields were fallow and overgrown. To the south, apple trees with red and golden fruit graced the hill in the distance. A beautiful piece of land he thought as he rounded the truck and placed his hand on the fender.

Before long, he had gathered his survey equipment. In the truck bed he threw back a gray canvas tarp to reveal his tools: a transit, boundary pins, mallet, a compass inside a flat wooden box, a large circular measuring tape, and his prized theodolite. He pulled them out along with his backpack and set everything on the tailgate. From the cab he withdrew the property files and the original survey map provided by the attorney. Next, he folded out the map on the hood and studied its contents while slowly turning to look over the land to get his bearings. On this day, he had preferred that his journeyman assist him, but he was unavailable due to other assigned obligations with the county. This would require more work from Browning, but he didn't mind. He preferred being in the field rather than an office, so he soon set out to begin the job.

The McCarver property wasn't but thirty acres, once used as a farm years earlier. The old barn sat on the hill and stood against the morning sky, warp-boarded, abandoned and alone. A barbed wire fence surrounded it, the gate leaning with indifference in an outward direction. Old wooden troughs and rusty hitches lined the yard. An empty corn crib rested on the crest of the hill in the sun. The land was quiet, the sky cloud-strew, white and gray.

Browning was a healthy man with a swoop of dark hair and a handsome, angular face. He wore his field gear, sleeved-shirt, canvas pants, and high-laced Herman Survivors. As he strode through the thick overgrowth down to the waterline, the weeds folded back to make way for him through the field. On his shoulders he carried his transit and theodolite with the pack hanging on his back. The large circular measuring tape and boundary pins hung from his belt clips and clanked softly on the way down. In his hand he took the map and planned to be done with his work by the day's end.

Cade woke early to stoke the embers in the stove. He was the first to wake so he was slow and quiet. The cherry wood snapped in the morning embers after he put it through the iron door, the aroma sweet and pleasant as it drifted through the cabin. Always his first thought when waking, he was hungry and his stomach growled. However, finding food had become a constant struggle. He thought to visit the orchard once again to hunt for deer. The previous day, he had eyed a few whitetails with their fawns, but they had been too far away for the shotgun to reach. Shotguns were well suited for dense underbrush but could also be used for open fields although for short range only. Fall was the rut season, and he hoped the deer would soon begin moving. He had one 30/30 rifle casing left, one he had saved for the right occasion. If the deer was out of range for the shotgun, his rifle could do the job.

He set out with his Winchester strapped over his shoulder. Minutes later he was at the tree line and up the hill through the woods. He came through the low scrub and over the hilltop where the apple orchard came into view. The trees' thick trunks were knurled and bent, their bark shiny and peeling back in layers. Apples were cast over the ground, and he expected this to bring the deer in for feeding by noontime.

At the edge of the field, he climbed on a low branch of a large apple tree with a clear view of the land. Up on the rise, the roofline of McCarver's abandoned house came into sight. He saw the broadside of the barn and the fence running around the end. Once settled, he waited patiently. He knew a deer hunter must be enduring with little movement, as deer can easily detect a human's presence. Knowing the deer crept down from Waylon's land and into the orchard, he would be vigilantly watching in that direction.

Cade's mind wondered back as he looked through the tree limbs into the field below. He pondered his thoughts. He pensively considered his life on the farm with his family and the hardships they had been through. He considered his two siblings, how different the three of them were but also how managing given the difficulties they had undertaken. Arden so like Pa in his demeanor and stance, the way his hands hung at his side and the expression on his face when he turned to look at you; his slow movements that seemed to create the most efficient amount of work; his powerful arms and back usually as strong as two men put together; his reserved silence until he had a piece to say to which most men would usually listen; also the manner in which he held his ground regardless of the circumstances, unyielding and firm-postured.

Myra was different in a graceful way; long flowing movements; smart; and even elegant in an innocent kind of way although she wore plain clothes and the same shift on most days. She lit candles in the window, collected wild flowers for a vase, hand-made beautiful Christmas cards. She loved animals and wildlife in nature's settings, especially beautiful horses. She was fascinated by all natural elements in the world. Her emotions flowed like the Flint River, swirling and cascading, pooling in silent places, raging in storms. She had auburn-red hair and a freckled complexion, striking eyes like green sapphires in the night.

Cade felt close to his family but apart at the same time. He usually stood off in the background, questioning, listening, and weighing his thoughts before speaking. Myra on the other hand was so outspoken and precocious; and Arden so self-assured and resolute. Cade felt insecure at times, even different and alone, such that some other sense greater than himself called him to be someplace else, though he did not know where or why. Something beyond the cotton fields and lake seemed to pull him away, but for when or where, he was at a loss. He had been a part of the family and was certainly included in all its aspects, but at a distance, he thought; near but far too in the same way. The day to day living in such a remote place seemed to lull him into a dream of a better future far away. He'd seen the *Life* and *National Geographic* magazines in Mr. Jenkins's store and could only imagine what more was out in the world.

He adjusted his position on the low tree branches to wait out the day for deer to come down the ridge. Morning cardinals, thrashers, and mocking birds darted about the trees, angling to get a peck of fresh apple from the tree. A cool breeze came off the lake and rustled the leaves. Fish were jumping on the surface of the water and he wished he had a pole. However, after a while of waiting, he noticed a curious man coming up the lake's shoreline while carrying survey equipment over his shoulders. This piqued his attention and he squinted to better see him coming up through the tall grass.

Chapter 14

ARDEN LEFT THE hospital, dejected and saddened. After such a long ride in a crippled wagon led by two old mules, he had given it all he could. How was it that Dr. Robert's letter had arrived only weeks prior although his mother's body lay decomposed in the hospital's morgue without having been embalmed? Putting the timeline together, this meant she must have died within days or even hours of the letter having been written by the doctor. Why not the courtesy of a follow-up letter stating her untimely death? Maybe she had died before he had written the letter. Arden was at a loss for reasons.

He rode his wagon out of the city and found a narrow swath of woods between two dairy pastures. He weaved in and was sure to be secluded behind the trees, thick vines, and ground scruff. Soon he was unloaded. He tended to the mules first, detached them from their harness bar, lashed them to trees, fed and watered them. He took his canvas roll and dragged it into the woods to be safely hidden under broken limbs and leaves. He removed his small Colt pistol just in case and slipped it under his waist belt. Given to the desperation of circumstances, he wanted to be prepared.

He decided to return to town to look for a restaurant. The streets were filled with wondering souls and hungry people. Arden wasn't well-dressed, only wearing his rural farm attire he used in the fields. No one paid him much attention. He looked much like everyone else.

He found a place to eat, a hole in the wall named the Overland. He nudged into the back corner and sat at a small table. The place was crowded with mostly well-dressed businessmen and their wives. A waiter was working through the patrons, carrying trays of succulent steaming food. Arden's mouth watered. He took a menu and ordered fried catfish and potatoes, the least expensive item on the menu, yet his best meal in days. Later, he returned to his wagon and mules. He bedded down and slept for the night.

The early light woke him at dawn. He packed up, went into town to the Presbyterian Church and graveyard. He parked the wagon on the road and hitched the mules to a rack there. He found his mother's gold and diamond wedding ring in his pouch and slipped it onto his small left finger for safe carrying—the wedding ring Papa had given him before his departure from the farm, to sell or return to the ring finger of his mother as a good omen. He had preferred the latter.

From the road, he noticed two black men in the graveyard that were digging a grave. A mound of red dirt began to pile to one side of the hole in the ground. An hour passed, and the more they dug the further their bodies went into the ground until just their chest and heads were visible as the dirt flung out with their shovels and the motion of their arms. Arden walked across the street but no one was available in the hospital lobby. The doors were locked this day.

Finally a wagon came from behind the hospital carrying her casket, being driven by an orderly dressed in stark white clothing. This was a different orderly than from the previous afternoon, an orderly Arden hadn't yet seen. Unhurried, he looked in both directions as he crossed the street onto the church grounds. Arden left his mules and went from the road to meet him. Arden slowly walked out through the tombstones toward the burial site near the rear of the property. As he passed through, he noticed many of the weather-eroded grave markers were dated as early as the 1600s.

Driving down the gravel road that encircled the graveyard, the orderly steered around to a stop where Arden and the two black men stood. They had finished digging the grave and were wiping the sweat from their dark faces. As if on que, an elderly pastor emerged from a side door in the church's chapel. Wearing all black, he had gray hair and a thin beard. He came with a Bible in hand and a cross hanging from his neck. His expression evoked his austere nature of discernably contemplating God's wrath on mankind and the end days to come.

As he approached he said, "You must be Mrs. Grayson's kin." He smiled and this surprised Arden as his gesture belied his appearance of stern reflection.

"Yes sir, that's me. I've come to see my mother off."

The pastor looked down at the deep hole in the ground and tightened his lip. A tear formed in Arden's eye. He knew this was his last time with her. She had been a good mother despite her infirmity.

"God is with her, my son," he said, assuring Arden of his strong conviction.

The four laymen: the two black men, the orderly, and Arden took the pine casket and placed it next to the gravesite.

The pastor read passages from Palms and the Book of John then took dried rose pedals from his pocket and tossed them onto the wooden casket. The black men respectfully bowed their heads when the pastor prayed for Ila Mae's soul to be taken into God's arms and His kingdom forevermore. Apparently they had been raised to be God-fearing. However, the orderly glanced off into the distance, scratched and yawned.

After the pastor had recited a short eulogy for Arden, the orderly pointed nonchalantly at the casket with a question. "Care to have a last look?" Obviously, the orderly had done this a time or two in the past.

Arden thought to open the casket yet decided against that. Not wanting to see her in such a decomposed state, he considered how awful that might be with her lying gray and stiff, no telling how badly off she might be. He thought about the diamond ring he had placed on his finger, but he hadn't the nerve to open the pine box and place it on her finger. This ring had been toiled for in the cotton fields, his pa had told him. It had been purchased as a representation of his love for her—a belated wedding gift years after their formal commitments to one another in a local church in Leesburg. Despite the ring, Arden wished to say a speech, but no one of significance was there. He did not know what to say other than, "I loved her. We all did."

The pastor smiled as if happy with the circumstance. He said, "Don't grieve, my son. God is with us. And if you are with Him, you will be with her again."

Then with ropes, they slowly lowered her into the cold earth and began to fill in the dirt one shovel full at a time. The black men nodded respectfully to Arden and continued their work.

Had he done his duty, he thought? What else could he have done? Would this suffice his requirement to care for his mother? Would his father be proud enough given the conditions? The doctor at the hospital had said she was unfit to travel because of her decomposed state. In his right mind, could he have returned to Lake Blackshear with her body crumbling into pieces with stench and rot? For the love of God, how?

She was buried, and the pastor threw on several remaining handfuls of earth then turned to wipe the dirt from his hands as he strode away. Arden watched him leave. He said nothing else. The black men, solemn and wordless, nodded once again and left with their hats in their hands. The orderly sat on his buckboard and took up the leather reigns wrapped around the wooden stanchion by the seat. He looked up as if to study Arden's face. He squinted in the daylight.

Arden said, "Twenty dollars then I suppose, for the cost of her burial—twenty dollars for you, the black men, the pastor, and the plot of ground. I suppose that's the going rate. But that surely appears awful expensive if you had asked me."

The orderly appeared confounded. "Twenty dollars? You paid for this?"

"Well, yes, I did. We received a letter a few weeks back from Dr. Roberts claiming the cost of twenty dollars to release her due to impending expenses, and now her burial. I got here as fast as I could, but she had passed."

"Oh no, Mister, she died a long time ago. Months ago, as a matter of fact." He looked concerned. "You didn't know that?"

"Hell no, I didn't." Arden was furious.

"Yep, she died a long ways back."

"So the burial plot here cost twenty dollars, right?" he asked.

"Oh, no. That's donated by the church to the State of Georgia for the ones out of the hospital over there. Ain't no cost to bury anyone here. The church will even supply the small tombstone with her name engraved on it. That's all donated. Maybe it costs fifty cents per nigger to do the diggin'. That's about all."

"What about Dr. Roberts. What would he say?"

"Don't know. He's gone. But it looks like you got hoodwinked." He looked down at the freshly turned earth on the ground.

Arden said, "Are you sure my mother was in that casket?"

"I wouldn't know that. I'm just the wagon driver."

Arden looked downward, realizing the casket was buried five feet deep, now too late.

He ran across the street into the hospital entrance and confronted the nurse. She claimed to leave for the doctor but never returned. The doors from the lobby were tightly locked. Although he pounded on them with all his might, no one came to answer. His pounding seemed right in place with all of the other horrific sounds coming from within the sanitarium's interior walls.

Arden was disgusted. Twenty dollars could have gone a long way in the current state of the economy—could have paid for Dr. Clack's visit, a week's worth of groceries, more shotgun shells, so much more. He left the hospital and took his team. He edged into town, hungry and looking. He needed a last meal before riding out south back to Blackshear. He returned to the Overland for lunch, thought it would be best.

He found a seat at the table in the back. Apparently corn whiskey was rampant although it had been outlawed years earlier in the Prohibition. One man beside him was eating buttered biscuits and drinking a small bottle, however early in the morning, not even noon.

While nodding toward Arden, he asked, "Care for some?" He smiled. "It's just a quarter a nip."

Arden wasn't much of a drinker, but he was slowly becoming one, he surmised. He had been through much in the past weeks, had been confronted that very morning with his mother's unexpected burial and her eulogy. It wasn't in his moral compass to do such, the way his pa had taught him—although, this was his only chance, now alone and grieving.

He nodded. "Alright, hit me up."

The man took a small shot glass and poured. Arden gave him the coin and took the drink in one shot. He winced and turned to the fellow. "That'll work, I appreciate it."

Arden ordered a cheese sandwich. Moments later it arrived and he ate.

The man with the corn whiskey said, "Any for me?"

"Get your own. It cost thirty cents, that's all."

"I had my biscuits. I think I'd rather drink." He smiled again and drank more.

"Where you from?" he finally asked.

"Down south in Lee County." Arden took a toothpick and worked it between his teeth.

"What you doing up this way?"

"Business to attend to, that's all." He looked at the small bottle of whiskey and thought about it. Instead he said, "Guess I'll get going."

"What's the hurry?" the man asked, slurring his words. Obviously he'd already had too much to drink.

"No, hurry, I suppose."

"Say you're from down in Lee County, is that right? Lee's a big county."

Arden nodded.

"What's your line of work down there?"

"Cotton farmer."

"The weevil has killed 'bout everything in the field, you know. I'm a mechanic and work for a local shop here in Americus performing equipment repairs. Everyone's runnin' low on money and it's been awfully slow." The mechanic's hands and fingernails were stained with black grease. "Say the drought is bad too ain't it?"

"Real bad, like everywhere, I guess."

"My uncle works for a big farm down that a' way. Down near Lake Blackshear, as a matter of fact. Works for a man named Waylon who owns a cattle farm. Ever heard the name?"

Arden quickly looked over and studied his face. His eyes were red and glassy, his pallor pale from too much drink. Arden smartly replied, "No, can't say I have. What's your uncle's name?"

"Dollar. Ben Dollar," he said.

"What about it then?"

The drunk said, "They say they been drilling for water but the aquifer up on their land done ran dry—says it's too deep down in the ground and they can't get to it."

"Is that right?" Arden sat forward, listening carefully.

The drunk lifted the bottle again and took another deep slug, finishing it off. "Damn good stuff," he commented quietly, as if to himself. He looked at the empty bottle and frowned.

Arden said, "We got water but the weevil took its share. That's mostly what did us in."

The man looked at Arden, his eyes askew with drunkenness.

"Anyway, between you and me, my Uncle Ben says they badly need water from way down on this neighbor's property but there's some dispute between his boss and this old fart down there. Says this Waylon pushed a pile o' lumber over on him in a lumberyard down yonder, trying to get rid of him." He laughed. "Old fart wouldn't keel over though, they said." He smiled and hiccupped. "People just need to get along is all I say."

Arden considered this carefully. Had he heard this correctly? Was this a coincidence? A gift from the unknown? An answer to the question of his father's accident? As to how it actually occurred? His face reddened and he considered his options.

"What did you say your name was? I don't think I caught it."

"Name's Cotter Rye." He stared at Arden inquisitively.

"Cotter Rye. I'll have to remember that." He paused and said, "You say these men tried to kill their neighbor?" Arden wanted to be sure to remember this man's name.

Suddenly the man looked away, his expression turning grim, as if realizing he had said too much.

Arden thought that he may have to inquire with the authorities about this. "You say you work at a local garage here in town? Did you say the name?"

He turned back to Arden, closed-lipped. He said nothing.

Arden waited.

Finally he spoke. "I didn't say."

"Well, that's claiming a lot, claiming to know of an attempted murder," Arden said.

The man quickly stood to leave, but Arden grabbed his shirt sleeve. The drunk yanked it away and hurried out the door. When Arden went after him, the man had disappeared into the crowd and down the street.

The waiter called out as Arden stood in the doorway of the restaurant. "That'll be thirty cents, buddy! Where do you think you're going?"

Arden fumbled with his belt pouch. He threw thirty cents jingling across the countertop and he ran out the door. By this time, the man had disappeared into a side alley. But Arden quickly sprinted after him down the street and into the alley.

"Hey you son of a bitch!" Arden called out but the man was gone.

The alley was crowded with homeless men standing in circles, smoking cigarettes while discussing their situations. Some were huddled around a fire pit, roasting some type of meat resembling small rats on long spits. Others were gathered in the back sharing liquor. The walls of the dark alley were lined with brown mold and moss. The stench of unbathed bodies filled the air. The acrid smell of burnt wood blew in his face and stung his eyes. He covered his nose and worked his way through, looking. In the rear, he found a narrow division between two buildings, and he emerged onto a small backstreet lined with trash cans. He spotted the drunk rounding the corner of a warehouse. When he rounded the corner to follow, he was hit with a wooden board across his head and he fell, stunned. He looked up to watch the drunk running away.

"Hey, you bastard, come back here!" he yelled.

Without further thought, he pulled his Colt pistol from his belt and fired. The man went down on one knee, stumbling, but he stood and limped away. At that moment, several men were leaving a blacksmith shop across the street where broken down farm machinery and wagons were parked out front.

"Hey, boy, what's going on!" one hollered as they ran across the street.

Arden stood, dazed. The drunk hobbled off down the street and quickly disappeared behind a fence, apparently suffering only a flesh wound. Arden's forehead was bleeding.

The men approached him cautiously. One said, "Put down your weapon, son!"

Arden let the pistol fall to the pavement. Two of the men held him by his arms. One went into the blacksmith shop to call the police. Minutes later, Arden found himself in the back of a police cruiser heading for the police station. Because of the desperate atmosphere of the city, the men had suspected him of armed robbery, and they called the Americus Police Department to take care of the matter. Arden attempted to explain his situation to the blacksmiths and the policemen, but no one would listen. The police officers confiscated the Colt pistol and quickly placed Arden in handcuffs then drove him to jail.

Chapter 15

MYRA STEPPED DOWN to the lakeshore to fish with Cade's bamboo pole. She had dug up worms in the side yard and put them in an old coffee can. She waited patiently standing on the shore, looking into the deep green current. The water had risen moderately with the recent rains but the lake wasn't near full pool.

After a while she pulled in a few small bass though hardly enough for a meal of three. She realized their condition was becoming critical with no food or money remaining. They had been ill to their stomachs and their faces were drawing gaunt. Nonetheless, she had gone up to Jenkins's store to attempt trading a few yards of unused cotton cloth for food, but Mr. Jenkins had simpered at this saying he needed no cloth, that the clothes on his back were holding up just fine. She suggested he could sell the cloth in his store but he told her he sold no cloth. She offered to sell him two fine candle stick holders made of brass, but he declined. She proposed to do any needed work for him, possibly sweeping or cleaning the premises. Maybe assisting in unloading goods from the supply truck when it came in, or helping stock his shelves to relieve him of that chore. He only laughed and told her that that was his wife's department. As a last resort, she removed a prized turquoise-beaded necklace from around her neck, the only jewelry she owned, and he gave in paying fifty cents for it. Then he shooed her off his premises before she could impose any further. Although she tried to find work elsewhere in town, none was available.

Their land was despairing and what little cotton remained had wilted on the plant. Now, after second thought, she wished they had bagged the last fifteen or twenty pounds and had ridden into Warwick on Bess to the weigh station. The ride would have taken from dawn until dusk for only one dollar, but every single dollar was now needed. Had they not bought the cotton seed in the spring from the farmer's coop in Desoto, had they not toiled to plant their acreage from one end to the other, had the drought and weevil not consumed their crops, then their family could have survived the brutally harsh winter of 1930-1931. Without cotton to sell, their cash had run out. With nothing to sell or barter, they stood little chance of survival on their land. With just days remaining until the bank was to come with law enforcement to exercise their right to evict, Myra was in tears as she sat on their front steps awaiting death to arrive.

From the steps, she heard her father in the house coughing and wheezing. The pipe smoke had bellowed out of his room for weeks until the tobacco had finally run out and he began complaining. Yet, she told him none was left, that *nothing was left*. And that she didn't know what to do or which way to turn. He suggested they take their farm equipment up to Flintside and attempt selling it. She informed him they had no way to get it there as the mules were with Arden. She told him the farming season was over, and no one had money, anyway.

"No one needs farm implements, Papa," she said emphatically. "It is the fall season and no farm work is being done at this time, at any rate."

"Someone could get a good deal."

"But no one has enough money, much less enough food to eat. I hear Mrs. Barton has locked and boarded up her home and has left Flintside without any discussion, and no one knows what has become of her. They say that the Darl Smith family was forced out to the highway with only a few suitcases to carry. You know Mel Parrish and his wife and children went to Americus to catch a train up to Atlanta, but no one knows for sure how they got there or if they made it. I suppose we'll never know."

He coughed and reached for his pipe, but paused. "Tobacco is plum out, ain't it?"

"Gone, Papa. Everything is gone." She whimpered and turned away.

"Any money left in my elephant box?"

She knew her father was becoming delirious. They had previously discussed this on numerous occasions. She went to the stove and took the last stale piece of corn muffin and brought it to him. He took it and ate, drank from a water cup on his bedside table.

"I'm going back down to the lake to fish, but we have no fish hooks left. The last one broke. I'll have to go out to the work shed and scrounge up some wire or something to improvise a hook." She stood to leave.

"I bet the fish'll be a biting." He smiled positively.

"Oh, Papa," she said, holding back more tears.

From the hidden branches of the apple tree, Cade watched the surveyor for a while as he worked in the field and drew a long metal tape along the ground. At the shoreline, the man took an iron mallet and drove an orange-painted stake deep into the earth. He drew the mallet high in the air, and Cade could hear the clanking of iron on the large steel stake. Cade dropped from the tree and approached him as he came up the hill. When the surveyor looked up, he saw Cade coming.

They met half way up from the lakeshore and stood in front of each other.

Cade said, "What's your business out this way, Mister?"

Cade held his 30/30 by the forestock with the barrel facing downward toward the ground. The surveyor was laden with equipment and carried a long, folded transit and a theodolite over his shoulder.

"I've been sent out to measure this property. I understand the former landowners have passed away and this property is uninhabited. They wanted me out to re-mark the boundary lines. Something about probate court."

"The people that lived here died? I didn't know that," he said wryly, of course knowing they had.

"That's what I've been told." The surveyor studied Cade. "What about you?"

"Just doing some hunting, trying to work on supper."

"You didn't know the McCarvers, then?" he asked tentatively.

"Heard of 'em, I guess." Cade shifted his weight and looked warily down the hill at the orange stake driven into the earth that he knew marked the division between the McCarver property and his father's.

"You live around nearby?"

Cade thought carefully. "Up yonder in Flintside. Come down here to the orchard to hunt squirrel and deer. They like the apples." He threw the man an innocuous smile, not wanting to reveal too much.

The surveyor seemed to relax. His face glistened with sweat in the sunlight. He asked, "Then do you know the Graysons? Maclin Grayson?"

"Heard of him, I believe," Cade said vaguely.

"He lives down that way, doesn't he?" the man asked, looking southward beyond the tree line into the dead cotton field.

"I suppose so," Cade replied, trying to sort things through in his mind, knowing this was no friend but a dangerous foe. He asked, "What's the purpose of all the equipment?"

"I have to use these instruments to mark the boundaries."

"And the paper file and the paper roll?"

"This is the property file and the survey map I am recreating."

"What does that have to do with the Grayson's then? I'm just curious."

167

"Well, it will define their property from the McCarver land."

"So, who sent you out here, then?"

"Americus First Trust Bank." He smiled, not realizing Cade's name was Grayson.

Cade tensed. He swallowed hard and looked away.

"You said you know the Graysons, right? That is their property, isn't it?" the man asked.

"Know of them, that's all," he said. "They're not any kinfolk of mine. I reckon they own the land as far as I know. It doesn't make any difference to me, I guess." He turned to leave.

To be more explicit, the surveyor added, "This work is actually over some dispute with Grayson's financial obligation to the bank is how I understood it. Not that it matters." He smiled. "As long as I'm not trespassing on your property, that's all."

"It's not my land. I just hunt here. No matter then," Cade said, nonchalantly turning back as if disinterested.

"I'm just doing my job here." He nodded courteously and adjusted the weight of the equipment over his shoulder.

Cade said nothing else. He tracked up the hill and climbed into the tree again. He settled down and watched the man for a while laying out his measurements. After more work, the surveyor drove another orange stake at the top of the property and used all his might to do so, the mallet gleaming in the sunlight as he repeatedly brought it above his head and down onto the stake. Cade winced at each ring of the mallet as it struck the steel driving it deeper into the earth.

After this, the man lifted his gear and looked about eyeing the land and the tree line toward Cade's property. He turned, slowly walking further along the hill in the direction of the cabin which perked Cade up. He sat up watching. The surveyor was now on *their land*, not the McCarver land. For some reason, the man abruptly stopped and seemed to be scanning the horizon. He consulted his map for a moment, slowly running his finger over it.

Cade cringed at the thought of this man on their property. He recalled the banker J.R. Rutledge, dressed in his fancy suit, coming down and demanding that their father sign reams of paperwork on the spot without the presence of representative or a legal counselor. How imposing and unfair it was, the manner in which the bank man attempted wielding his authority in such a way. Although the terms of the bank loan had not yet matured or come to pass. After all, his father told his children that ninety-five percent of the debt had been paid down. And that he had never been late on a single payment, until the great depression had come upon them and the entire nation at large. Cade found it unimaginable how it was right to ban a near-paralyzed man from his family home of three generations, out into the road without a loaf of bread to eat. Apparently the land (all land) was currently nearly worthless due to the big collapse. What was the bank's hurry, anyway? Cade grew furious as he thought through these occurrences, how it had come to the point of utter desperation and greed. His face reddened, and beads of sweat dotted his forehead in the shade of the apple tree.

Cade lifted up his rifle and set the long barrel over a branch at eye level. He looked down the sites and found the surveyor's back come into view. He considered having been on this land since childhood. Also that his great grandfather had been awarded the parcel by the U.S. government for a life of dedication to the service of his country—but how it was seen as being righteous to take the land from a good man, not known for dereliction but of hard work and pride. Cade looked down the sites of the gun and steadied his hand. He drew a long breath and held it while slowly counting to five. Without further hesitation he pulled the trigger, firing, and the survey man fell over forward like a sack of cement, dead.

The police took Arden to the police station that was located in the center of the city next to the courthouse and other municipal buildings. They hurried him out of the police car and into the back where the prisoner intake was located. The two police officers took him by his shoulders, threw him into a holding cell and slammed the steel door with a loud clang.

"Buddy, we already have enough of you farm boys coming into town and making trouble," one said gruffly.

"Got our hands full with all you troublemakers," the other said.

Arden rebuked, "Gal damned! I tried to explain that my father was the victim of an attempted murder down in Lee County, and that man knows the perpetrators."

"Likely story, son. We've heard 'em all now, ain't that right, Jester," the other said, laughing while sitting at his desk to fill out a report.

The policeman, Jester, leaned his hand against the brick wall and leered. "Sounds about right. Heard it all, now."

The jail was a dark and dingy keep in the rear of the Americus police station. Dim lighting hung from the ceiling, casting shadows on the gray walls and jail cells that lined the corridor. Several other prisoners were in their cells either sleeping or quietly mulling about with their hands in their pockets. One man beside Arden snored so loudly that Arden kicked his cell bars with his boot to wake him.

"Shut the hell up!" Arden said.

"Better settle down there, boy. You think kicking and cussing is gonna git you out of here, you'd be wrong," Jester said.

"What's the charge, then, that I'm being jailed for?" Arden asked.

"Assault with a deadly weapon," Jester said, lighting a cigarette.

The other officer writing the report looked up from his paperwork and added," Gonna be a while until we can get him in front of a judge. The whole city's out o' hand, and we have a long list of cases ahead of this one."

"I told you my wagon and mules are out by the Overland restaurant."

"We'll get 'em. Don't worry. We could use a team of mules." He laughed.

Arden held the cell bars and took a deep breath. He noticed his mother's diamond ring on his left small finger, the ring he had meant to put on her finger for the return trip back to Blackshear. He hung his head and looked at the dirty concrete floor then back to the hard bunk where he would be sleeping. "Gal damned hell," he whispered to himself.

Myra came up from the lakeshore carrying their washed clothes in a basket. She strung them on the clothesline in the side yard. She pulled a water bucket up from the well and took it into the kitchen. She washed the kitchen and potbelly stovetop then threw the wash water out of the window. She heard her pa snoring in his room. Thankfully the strong scent of tobacco smoke was not present as the tobacco had finally run out.

A while later she sat on the front steps of the cabin to rest. She sat and sulked. Her fingers were marred and her dress was worn. She also couldn't help but notice that her work boots had seen better days. One of the soles had become nearly detached and required mending. She realized that if she delayed repairing the boot, the condition would only worsen and become more expensive to fix. She had no choice but to return to Flintside to the boot shop to have the cobbler take a look.

After her chores, she walked the mile into town as her boot sole flopped on the dirt road with every step. She missed having little Bess to ride but Arden had taken the mules with him to Americus. His temporary trip had caused her and Cade much torturous walking to town and back, so she looked forward to their soon return.

She walked into the boot shop to meet with the cobbler then she stepped out to sit on the wooden bench to await the repair. She would have to pay extra as an expedite fee because the boots were the only pair she owned, so she couldn't leave them to return later in the week. Luckily on her prior trip into town, she had sold her turquoise necklace for fifty cents to Mr. Jenkins, the one her father had given her the previous Christmas. With this, she could pay for the boot repair.

As she sat on the wooden bench outside the boot shop, she noticed a few cars coming and going and several wagons being pulled through by horses and mules. The lumberyard wasn't too busy, just one freight truck with the lumberyard employees working to load his lumber. The local schoolhouse could be seen on the edge of town; it was shut down as school wouldn't resume for several more months until harvest ended.

Moments later a long flatbed Ford came and parked in front of Jenkins's store. Jack Waylon stepped out, went in, and emerged with a handful of mail. Because the general store also served as the post office, she imagined Mr. Waylon came to retrieve his mail on a regular basis as he ran a business and cattle farm. She watched him thumbing through the mail bundle before sitting in his truck to return home. He instead glanced up and noticed her in front of the boot shop. She tensed as he tossed his mail onto the truck's front seat and came in her direction.

As he approached, he was working a toothpick in between his teeth. He turned from side to side to look about town, then down at his boots and back up to her. He smiled amicably. She adjusted her weight on the hard bench. Her shift was worn and stained. She sat barefooted with her feet in the dust by the side of the road. When he stepped up, she threw her hair back over her shoulder and crossed her arms.

Jack said, "Myra? What are you doing in town?"

"Mr. Waylon, probably the same as you, I suppose. Getting what needs getting." She didn't smile but rather frowned and looked away.

"Myra, I mean you no ill will. Why do you have to take up such an attitude with me?"

"I don't have to, I just do."

He glanced off in the distance and looked back. "If there is anything, and I do mean anything that I can help you with, please let me know. I realized your pa is in bad shape. Like I said, I'm sorry for his accident, but I have no bad feelings for him or you."

She finally looked at him.

He said, "What are you here for, anyway? Looks like you've lost your shoes."

"They're being repaired as we speak."

"Lord, Myra, are those the only pair you have? You can't come back later?"

"No sir, it doesn't look that way, does it?"

"Myra, I know you have worked hard down on your farm. I suspect you deserve more than what you have."

He stepped into the shop. She waited and wondered what he could be doing. Minutes later he returned with a new pair of boots, low ankle lace-ups, good leather, pliable soles. While catching her anxious gaze, Jack set them on the ground at her feet.

"Try these on for size." He smiled again.

"Mr. Waylon," she said surprised. "What on earth?"

"Try them on. They look about your size."

She was flattered. She hadn't had a new pair of boots in years. The ones she owned were falling apart. "Mr. Waylon?"

"Go ahead, Myra."

She couldn't help herself. She slipped them on and they were a perfect fit. She stood and walked two circles around him.

"Well, I can't believe this. I mean...."

"Myra, these are yours. Maybe one day you can see me for who I am. I'm a friend, not a foe."

She noticed the rich, brown leather and how they shined; the pointed curvature of the toe and how feminine they were, not with the round bluntness that a man's boot possessed. They were practical but attractive, beautiful really especially to a poor farm girl. Much more so than the old clodhoppers she owned. So much more that she might have said 'elegant'.

She looked up at him. "I suppose you're just being nice because you want to bring a drill rig down on our land."

"Could be, but your pa won't allow it, so I suppose I can plant a seed of friendship with you for the time being, can't I?"

She could hardly turn him down. She was a poor pauper, and if she let her pride get in the way, she would never forgive herself or forget this beautiful pair of boots. "Thank you, Mr. Waylon," she said, accepting them.

"Please just call me Jack. That's fine." He smiled again.

He entered the shop and paid five dollars for the boots then explained to the cobbler the others weren't worth repairing. The cobbler tossed them in the trash, thanking him.

He came out and said, "You need anything else here in town?"

"No sir, I don't."

He laughed, "And none of this 'sir' talk, alright then? Just 'Jack' would be fine. Come on, let's jump in my truck and I'll take you back home."

They bounced along the dirt road, out of town, and down the declining terrain toward the lake. She couldn't take her eyes off her new boots, at how shiny and brown, at how well they fit on her tired feet. She wiggled her toes inside them and couldn't help but smile.

"Now, there you are, Myra. I like that smile. You see, I ain't that bad am I?"

She looked out of the truck window into the passing woods and said, "I guess not, no. Maybe I've been a little too cold." She turned toward him. "My papa's a proud man. He has his ways."

"I know. I've known him for many years."

"How old are you Mr. Waylon, if you don't mind me asking?"

"I'm forty-two."

"Do you remember my mother then? I know your own father and mother died not too long ago."

He nervously glanced away and held his composure while looking into the distance through the truck's windshield. He clearly recalled the afternoon he had found Ila Mae aimlessly wandering the ridge road, innocently picking wild flowers and how he had taken advantage of her severe mental weakness. He had carefully led her unaware down into the shadows of the tree cover and forced himself on her. (Actually it had been just a stern nudge, and he had helped her fall gently backward into the thick pine needles). She had looked up at him while on her back, disoriented and disconnected, not knowing any better as he pulled her shift up. The act had only taken a few minutes as she stared inanely up into the sky with that blank expression of misunderstanding in her eyes as he rode her gently in a smooth rhythm. Not all that bad, he later considered; harmless really.

Afterward, she wandered back toward her farm, dazed and confused as if she were lost although she was already unaware of what had just occurred. Their ages were far apart, but Jack was a lonely bachelor and had his needs. She was well up into her years and had lost their first son, Paul of thirteen, not long before this. She was pretty though, he thought, for her age. Well, at least pretty enough. The community knew of her condition, that she had grown senile and had completely lost her cogitative thought. Nine months later, she had had Cade. But Jack kept his distance, not knowing what he had created until years later when Cade grew to be an absolute, striking image of Jack.

Individuals that never encountered senility, face to face, would scoff at this event, but those that have experienced the disease firsthand could understand the utter devastation the disease could render. A person with Alzheimer's disease is completely hopeless, lost in self, reality, and time. They become impossible to communicate important information with, impossible to reason with, or to simply talk with. The diseased doesn't realize what occurred a day ago, an hour ago, or even minutes beforehand.

Jack looked at Myra and told her, "Yes, I remember Ila Mae. That was a shame. Now with your Pa in his condition, I can't imagine." He frowned while holding back his secret, holding in forever the crime he had committed.

However, she held back her tears too, not knowing what the future might hold for her, her father, and her family. And she was completely unaware of what Jack had done to Ila Mae. "We just don't know what to do. You knew that Ila Mae's coming back home soon, didn't you? Arden should return any day now."

"Whatever happens, Myra, I'm here to help, like I said." He knew Ila Mae was incapable of remembering him just as she was unaware the day he had raped her.

Jack returned Myra home and let her off by the split rail fence on the ridge. She thanked him profusely and he drove away back up to his farm.

Cade went numb. He had expected to lose his self-control and begin panicking, yet conversely, he sat in the apple tree and stared out for a long moment. Numb. The afternoon sky was growing gray with cloud. Black crows flew over the fields, small black specs pricked in the distance against the far tree line. To the north, the outline of McCarver's barn stood in the southern sky, broad and sun-washed yellow. The lake moved lazily southward, birds flying over its smooth surface with wings of freedom.

Cade slid out of the tree and walked up to the body of the engineer. When Cade approached with his rifle, he saw the man's limbs akimbo at odd angles as he had obviously fallen over in a mishap-position, probably dead before hitting the ground. Crimson blood ran from the back of his neck where the bullet had entered in the exact center of his nape. Good shot, Cade thought. Now what?

He let his rifle fall to the ground. He quickly looked about, down to the lake, up to the tree ridge, out toward the barn and abandoned house—no one was there, nothing, no moment to be seen anywhere. He placed his hands on his hips and licked his lips, now reconsidering his actions. Without further delay, he threw the man's body over his shoulder, took his 30/30, and trotted as swiftly as possible toward the abandoned house. After the several hundred yard trek, he found the man's truck parked in the gravel driveway with the keys still in the ignition. He dropped the limp body on the ground and searched the man's rear pockets. His billfold contained seventeen dollars in cash; his front pockets, coin change and a small note pad. Before leaving, he leaned his rifle against the truck to retrieve later.

He returned to the site and dragged the surveying instruments deep into the woods, except for the large iron mallet. Down in a ravine, he covered the transit and theodolite, the tape measure and pins with dead tree limbs, leaves and dirt. As quickly as possible, he returned to the field and sprinted down the hill to the shoreline with the mallet in hand.

After a good deal of work, he dislodged the orange stake and swiftly ran it uphill toward the barn. After crossing hundreds of yards of ground, he turned to look back down the hill from where he had come. He had traveled a long way up from the original survey pin location where the surveyor had marked. He was much closer now to the abandoned house and barn. He edged along the lake, located a good spot set off from the waterline, and drove the pin deeply into the earth. He made his way back to the site where the surveyor's body had lay. On the topside of the property he repeated his actions, running up elevation toward the house and old barn. He stepped along the roadside and drove the stake there into the hard clay. He had essentially gained many, many acres of ground by relocating the property boundaries up the hill.

Nonetheless, he made one last trip and returned to the truck with the paper files and survey map left on site by the engineer. For safe keeping, he slid them in the truck cab behind the long bench seat. Without much delay, he found a rag in the truck and tightly wrapped it around the man's head to prevent blood from smearing. He tossed the man's body into the truck bed and covered him with the gray canvas tarp.

He jogged back over the field, through the woods, and to the cabin. Myra was just coming down from the ridge wearing her new boots. She saw him running from the wood line and noticed the desperate expression drawn on his pale face.

"Myra!" He came to her and took her shoulders as they stood in front of the cabin.

He led her away, down toward the lake where their father wouldn't overhear. Drying blood streaked his shoulder and back; sweat ran down his face, and his eyes were wide with fright. He briefly explained that the bank had sent a man to survey their land in preparation for the foreclosure. He told her what he had done, that he had killed the man and had moved the stakes farther up the hill.

He ran into the house and grabbed a leather carry bag from the storage closet, took his knife and a few other belongings. Minutes later, he walked out of the cabin and down the steps to the well where he washed off. He turned to leave and explained that he must go. As he went, he quickly yanked numerous wet clothes off the clothesline to take with him. He told Myra that he was going away, *that he had to go*, but that he was not sure when he could return.

She called out to him as he ran toward the woods and the orchard, but he wouldn't stop or look back.

She ran behind him, reaching for his shoulder but he wouldn't slow.

"Cade! Cade! Come back," she called.

"Myra, no! I have to go! Leave me alone!"

As they came to the tree line, she stopped, winded.

"Cade!" she called out one last time but he had disappeared into the fold of trees. She was now unsure when, or if, she would ever see her brother again.

Chapter 16

ARDEN HADN'T SPOKEN to anyone. He dozed in the holding cell but was given only water and a few pieces of bread to eat. The day stretched on, and he heard many voices and much commotion in the station though he couldn't see anything from his cell. Later that afternoon near sundown, he was relocated down a set of stairs to the jail basement which did not make him happy. The police had not formally charged him, nor had they spoken to him regarding his status.

Down in the basement, two short rows of cells lined a narrow corridor. The walls were made of mortared granite rock, and the cell bars of cold roll steel. The basement was subterranean and the darkness quickly overcame him as the only light with which to see streamed from small rectangular windows at the top of the wall. Grayness and dank air hung in the place; defeat, sadness, and forlorn hope, as well. He could feel the underground depth of the basement when he breathed. The air was thin and hard to pull into his lungs. Seeping water from the foundation dripped down to the concrete floor and puddled at the end against a wall. As they escorted him to the end cell where the floor was wet with rain seepage, he passed several dark faces in the dimness, only seeing the whites of their eyes as he stepped by.

"You're in here, Grayson. Cell eight," the officer said. The other officer left.

"Don't I get a phone call? Or at least a public defender to speak with?"

"No public lawyers are available. County ain't got the funds and can't afford them right now." He closed the cell door and locked it. "Phone, you said? Your folks have a phone at home? Country folk ain't got any phones, so I doubt that." He laughed, thinking he was clever.

The officer left and the basement grew deathly quiet. One man off in the distance coughed. Another sneezed and Arden heard the echo. Lingering smoke drifted through the air and he smelled the faint scent of tobacco. He heard low voices and water dripping. There was little light even for reading. The floor of his cell was a puddle of cold water, so his leather boots would soon become soaked. He slipped them off, set them on a shelf, and crossed his legs on the sturdy wooden cot. There was no blanket or pillow, just the hard wooden surface of pine board. And a galvanized two gallon pail for excrement. No running water in the basement existed.

The cells were divided by concrete walls and fronted with steel bars. The cell opposing Arden's lay vacant. Yet in the one down, a man's dim silhouette crossed in the background but Arden couldn't see him; it was too dark. At the top of his cell wall, he looked up to see a small barred-glass window that was no larger than a man's head. On the ceiling, shadows danced through it from what appeared to be wind in the trees at the back of the lot. He looked around. His cell was dank with mold. A few doors down, a man coughed and wheezed, sniffing back his nose. Another moaned. Through the metal door at the top of the stairs, a timbre of voices resounded in the upper rooms of the station, and they seemed to carry the intonation of anger.

From the adjacent cell, the sound of a sick old man came. When he spoke, his dry raspy voice sounded such as slowly rubbed sandpaper over drift wood. "Boy," was all he said, but Arden didn't respond. Arden could hear his labored breathing but he couldn't see him, so he stepped to the end of his bunk to look out, only seeing the man's hands grasping the bars which looked like old tree roots holding creek rock.

Almost inaudibly, he said, "Boy, tell me your name."

Arden paused, not wanting to converse at the moment. He thought he might need to do some praying first.

The old man said, "Tell me what brought you in today."

Arden took a deep breath.

"Son, can you tell me your folks' names, then?"

He refused to speak.

Minutes later, Arden heard the quick scratch of a match and smelled the acrid scent of sulphur in the air. Tobacco scent lingered in sudden clouds of gray; smoke rings drifted out of the cell, more clouds of smoke. He said, "Listen, you might as well. You'll be here for a while."

Arden stood on his bunk in his socks, and placed his hands against the tall block wall between their cells. "What do you want?"

"Name, maybe?" More smoke.

"Arden Grayson from Lake Blackshear."

"And—"

"Aggravated assault with a deadly weapon. It's all horseshit though."

To the old man, he said, "And you?"

"Name's Arnold Wiseman."

"What's your deal, Arnold? What are you in for?"

"I was the Mayor of Leesburg."

Arden thought back. "Seems I've heard the name Wiseman before."

"Yep, I was in court the day the courthouse burned down months ago."

"In court for what?"

"Misappropriation of city funds." He coughed, blew more cigarette smoke, and grasped the bars tighter with his wilted hands.

"Misappropriation?"

He spoke but weakly. "They were going to hold my trial three months back in Leesburg Christ Church which is the court's temporary location. I was out on bail but they caught me at the train station here in Sumter County in Americus, attempting to flee for Atlanta. I was not allowed to leave Lee County as a part of my bail, you see. Did you know they have policemen all over the train station because the crowds are hard to control? I've been waiting here for two months to return to the Lee County jail, but so far they haven't come for me, and this food here isn't worth a damn, nor is it nearly enough."

"Got a wife and family?"

"Did, but she's divorced me. I'm too old anyway. She doesn't give a shit, is probably happy about it. I wouldn't know. I haven't seen her since the courthouse fire. She's getting the house, land and bank accounts." He puffed, blew more gray clouds.

He said, "I had to hit the tracks. Everyone wants out, up to Atlanta where there are lots of soup kitchens and government breadlines. Even maybe work to be had. I hear the highways up toward there are lined with old farm trucks and people camping on the sides of the roads, in church parking lots or anywhere they can get. Transient encampments are what they call them. Anyway, lots of homeless everywhere, they say."

"Got a lawyer?" Arden asked.

"Had one. But my luck ran out and my money did too."

Cade walked swiftly through the orchard and up the hill to the truck where the dead man lay in the bed. He placed his wet clothes and bloody shirt in the back then the leather carry bag up front in the cab after retracting a fresh shirt to wear. After climbing in, he turned the ignition key and the truck jumped to life with a loud clatter and a plume of petrol emissions. Without wasting time, he steered in a semicircle and drove to the road and back toward Flintside. He found a cap on the dashboard and slipped it down over his eyes to disguise himself when he drove through town.

Having made several trips north up to Americus, he knew the route and required no map to find his way. Thinking back, he had driven several trucks in the past and knew how to work the pedals, shifter, and clutch. During previous harvests, Chesley Kutner had brought down his combine to strip the cotton. He also drove a stake-body transport and trailer for hauling the cotton into Warwick which was the closest gin and weigh station that side of Albany. Mr. Kutner had shown Arden and Cade how to operate the vehicle, and as a result, Cade had driven the truck to Warwick numerous trips for hauling the cotton to market.

After reaching Desoto, he decided to rid the surveyor's body in case he was pulled over by law enforcement. First, however, he required food and something cool to drink. Easing outside of town, he found a remote location and parked the truck in the rear of a warehouse, then walked into town for a meal. He left an hour later and soon located a backroad that ran alongside the rail tracks. Where the road ended, he dumped the surveyor's body in a ditch then covered it with heavy logs, limbs and debris. By mid-afternoon, he left the Desoto city limits far behind in his rearview mirror.

Along the route, he expected to run across Arden with his mother returning in the wagon but was somewhat alarmed when this did not occur; however also relieved that he wouldn't have to explain his new truck. He suspected some unforeseen issue had arisen, or that some trouble had transpired in the last minute of their journey. Of what trouble, he wasn't sure. But, he stopped to ask several road-walkers if they had seen a wagon with a young man and a crazy old woman, but no one had.

By late afternoon, he reached Americus and was astounded with the many wayward vagrants that had come from the surrounding farmlands to find work or free handouts. The streets where filled with unemployed sharecroppers and land tenants. He drove past the train station, and the city had set up barricades and policemen to prevent rushes to the trains when they pulled in from down south in Albany.

At the mental hospital, he had visited Ila Mae with his pa a few times in the past. Although his mother had not known him from birth, and now would not know him if she saw his face, Cade certainly felt obligated to check that Arden had come to take her with him. She had been Arden's mother more than his. Then again Cade was her son and she had birthed him. And having been told by his father, however, that he had been fed with her breast was reason enough to want to love her even though she hadn't know of his birthing just months after the fact. This proved she had been old enough to develop senility, yet by a miracle of God, strong enough to bear a child without compromising her health. He had noticed her mentally-stricken behavior while living on the farm, though he was just a tot old enough to ride an ass donkey. Yet, it was unadmitted later in his youth that he had found her pitiful and was ashamed of her.

He located the state run facility after asking directions on the street. He arrived and went to inquire, but after much pounding on the doors, no one came. He attempted walking around the building's exterior, but a locked fence prevented him from doing so. He waited for a long while, and after more knocking, a nurse finally came to let him in.

She explained that the doors were kept bolted for safety purposes; rather for the security of the patients or the doctors, he wasn't clear. She further explained that Mrs. Grayson had been buried across the street in the church's cemetery and that her son had left without her. She offered little more information and suggested he cross the street to the church, but Cade found the church also locked with no one there. He was perturbed. After a lengthy search, he found her name cut into a rough piece of marble atop her freshly dug grave at the back of the cemetery, and he grieved silently, alone. Not as much for her but his father, saddened how it had transpired in the end.

At her graveside, Cade hung his head and said a prayer. Having been unable to see her one last time, he was now ashamed for not having cared more. The nurse in fact explained that if he had arrived earlier, he could have seen his brother. As the circumstances prevailed, he apparently almost had. So, Ila Mae had very recently died, the nurse confirmed. And when Cade left the hospital that day, another family was just arriving to pay their twenty dollars as well. Obviously, twenty dollars was the going rate.

However, now the question remained: where was Arden?

Cade found a backstreet where to park, yet he hardly slept on the truck's bench seat while curled in a fetal position and using the leather carry bag as his pillow. He tossed and turned throughout the night, nervously wondering where his life might lead. Wishing he had possibly taken a different course instead of acting on emotion when a prudent course of action would have been wiser. Yet there remained little doubt the bank was going to foreclose and evict them. The bank man had said that much; that only weeks and days remained of their stay at the farm. Would they come with a sheriff and deputy holding a pistol? Could they physically heave them off their own property if they refused to leave? How far would they have to travel? How could they remain together if there weren't four walls to hold them together? On the other hand, Cade felt as though he was destined for a life out on the road, anyway, given the outcome that was in store. He had also anticipated Arden's return to Blackshear to assist his sister with the cumbersome duties ahead. Yet, where Arden had gone was unknown, and his return was now uncertain.

Cade thought: would he ever see his father again? His brother? Myra? His cabin home on the shores of Blackshear with the blue herring and sky hawks? Would he see the rolling meadows of the orchard and the woodlands thick with deer and wild berries? What of the field of white cotton reaching in all directions? Where could he possibly go? Where would he find his meals when the surveyor's money ran out?

How could he survive? Time would only tell, he knew; time would likely write its own ballad.

From what he'd gathered, Atlanta was the place to go. There was no farm work in the south anymore, and the city was their only hope. So he planned to travel in that direction as soon as the sun rose the following morning. He wrote Myra a letter as to their mother's passing but that Arden's whereabouts were unknown. In addition, he wrote in his letter that he feared for his freedom if ever an investigation was pursued and the engineer's final ending was discovered as a result. He wrote that he planned to travel north to Atlanta as he'd heard there may be work available there. Later that morning, he dropped the letter in the U.S. mail and left Americus in hopes the letter would find her well.

Myra was beside herself with anguish. Having been in such a rush, Cade hadn't taken the time to bid his father farewell. Maclin fell asleep and when he woke in late afternoon, he asked where his son had gone, but Myra held it from him until nightfall. She hoped by some miracle he had reversed course and had come to his senses. Myra ran the possibilities through her head. Before filling a bowl with wild dandelion and polk for their evening meal, she ran up to the orchard and stopped to look, but she noticed nothing unusual. After she returned and told her father, he was distraught and he cursed.

He sat on his bed with his feet on the wood plank floor. He hung his head and drew his eyes up to Myra.

She said, "Cade has gone, Papa. He said he killed the man from the bank because he was laying out survey markers for J.R. Rutledge. And the surveyor, not knowing Cade was one of us, stated he was there because Americus First Trust had sent him. Cade explained that he disrupted the man's work by relocating the boundary markers further up the hill."

Mac said, "He has killed the man? What the almighty hell?"

"That's what he said." She was as distraught as he.

Mac thought for a moment. "Holy hell, Myra. Gal Damned. And he moved the property lines, too?" He pinched his lips tightly and looked away. "Well, I don't suppose McCarver would have liked that."

"What does it matter, Papa? Cline's gone and so is Grace."

"Well, they never did bare no children. Why, we didn't know. But she never had a child with him."

She helped him stand with his cane and walk to the table by the potbelly stove. When he sat, he grunted with discomfort. He turned, placing his hands flatly on the plank table.

He said, "When Arden comes with Mamma, I'll send him out to find Cade. He must have went up to Americus. Where else could he have gone?"

"Papa, if Arden leaves again to go back to Americus, I'll have to care for you and Momma by myself, then. But, we have no food and our wood supply for the stove has dwindled. While in the process of hunting for food, Cade has neglected the woodpile. I'll have to go out and gather wood soon, but standing dead wood is what's needed to burn hot. Rotted wood from the ground is not much good. I'll need to go out and up the hill. There is a thin dead oak there I might be able to cut down that would make good firewood. It's becoming cool in the evenings and we'll need good heating wood for the stove." She reached down and felt the side of the large iron stove, noticing it was cool and needed tending.

"Arden will be home soon, darling. Don't worry. He can get the woodpile up."

"What about Cade, then? He's not going after Cade? What are we going to do?"

He said nothing, not know what to say or how to say it anymore.

She was hesitant, but she added, "Why not let Mr. Waylon bring down his drill rig, Papa? What hurt could it cause us?"

Her father looked at her with stern agitation. "Myra, I've made up my mind, now. I've told you he ain't allowed on this here land. He's caused us great trouble in the past, and he's taken advantage of me for many years."

"Taken advantage? How has he done that? So, he encroached a little on our land once. He burned his scrub brush down here on top of the ridge. His cattle once trampled our cotton. His roosters wake us at the crack of dawn on Sunday mornings. But he's taken advantage of us, intentionally?"

"I don't want to talk about it anymore." He turned and looked away.

"Papa?"

He refused to speak anymore. Instead, he let out a burst of coughing and she came to pat his back. She went out to the woodpile and brought in a few pieces of dry wood to put in the stove.

Later, they ate their polk salad in silence, not knowing what tomorrow might bring. She helped him back to bed and she went out to sit on the front steps to watch the stars in the sky. Since the air was cooling she took a wool shawl to drape over her shoulders. She looked up into the heavens to wonder. The stars seemed to be cast before a black window in the sky, and the clouds moving across the full yellow moon were such as shadows before the emotions of her life. Drifting, clouding the view of the future, moving like wandering gypsies from yesterday toward tomorrow. She looked up and the eve of the roof was angled and dark against the night. Stars were like a distant ocean as the trailing Milky Way was strung from horizon to horizon.

She thought of her adoptive mother, her last memory of Dr. Clack coming to take her to the hospital in Americus. Myra had been so young. It was years ago. She was standing by Maclin's leg, holding him in fear and misapprehension. His arms were outstretched, holding both Arden and Cade, and the family just watched in silence as she was driven away.

9

They next day came and they were hungry but there was no food left to eat. No shells or casings remained in the storage room. No fish hooks or a mule to ride into town. She had expected Arden and Momma to have returned by then, but she hadn't heard any news of their whereabouts.

The night before in her small room, the room the three siblings had shared before her adolescent years, Myra was up late. She sat on her cross-roped frame and corn-shuck mattress, watching her candle quietly flicker. Above all, her heart sank the most for Mac, her adoptive father. She had loved him since the first day when she stepped off the Atlantic Southern passenger car in Americus with her small suitcase and wearing her only pair of shoes. The train came into the station and the conductor assisted her off; he had been such a nice and attentive man on the lengthy ride down.

Maclin was there with Jasper John and his wife, too, with Maclin grasping a baby doll for her to hold. One they had bought at a five-and-dime around the corner from the terminal. Having come from a loving mother herself, Myra, even at the young age of three, immediately felt their love and knew when she saw goodness because she had an instinct from an early age. She had smiled and hugged the doll as if it were her own child, and they took her home to Flintside in Jasper John's wagon.

As soon as they arrived, the babysitter opened the door and she met Arden and Cade for the first time. The three stood bright-and-wide-eyed for a moment, staring at one another until Arden, then at the age of eight, reached out and hugged her. However there was a strange woman there who lingered in the background but hardly spoke. Sometimes the old woman wandered around in the cabin aimlessly, staring into space, her expression as blank as wallboard. Though she was harmless and never touched Myra, the old woman frightened her at first until she got use to her. Over time, Myra grew to understand that Ila was part of the family, actually a part of the man named Maclin, yet it took her years to comprehend the truth and to see the circumstances under which the woman existed.

From the beginning Mac took care of Myra and made sure she was happy. Myra remembered a toy horse he gave her, one that rocked to and fro on a set of rails like a rocking chair, and how she had loved it. He had taken her out into the fields, out to the barn to see the mules, and by the river shore. He carried her on his shoulders up the ridge and along the road. Although later, she could recall his complaints concerning the government and how the river swelled up and became a lake over a year's period, how it grew and covered the land, too. The first time she witnessed him lose his composure was upon receiving a formal letter from the Army Corp of Engineers. She had naively asked if the Army of Engineers were men with guns and holsters, with bombs and grenades. He couldn't help but laugh at this, and he had picked her up tossing her in the air, both of them laughing.

However after all of the years on the farm, Myra still contained distant and faint memories of her early childhood at the age of three, of her biological mother and father from the big city of Atlanta where she had originated. Faint memories too scary to recall as she grew deeply saddened at the thought of them. But sometimes, she couldn't help but venture back.

She could vaguely remember. She could faintly recall that her mother was tall and had long flowing red hair. And how her father went out to work early in the mornings and came in so dirty in the evenings, too dirty to sit in the house and that he would wash outside with the water spigot. That she rarely saw him because he worked almost every day from sun up to sun down; she could remember that. That he was a slender man with black hair and a closely trimmed beard, and often too tired or busy to take much time. Of her faint memories, however, the most prominent was her mother's sickness. How she fell ill when Myra was little, but that the doctors could find no reasons for it. Her mother remained in their kitchen and was usually cold and squatted by the heat of the stove even on summer nights. She had become sick to her stomach and retched vilely into pails by her bedside, night after night. She slowly became a shadow of herself and gradually faded away such as wildflower petals on a late fall day. Her mother slept in her bed and was unable to get out, her arm outreaching for Myra to come to her, but Myra was too scared for her mother's face had become skeletal in appearance.

That's when the time came. They talked about what to do and they soon came to take her away, the women in the church. They had met her mother in her time of need, and her father had apparently been unable to cope and work-like-a-field-mule at the same time. They had to eat didn't they? And the church pastor came from the Methodist Children's Home of Decatur to take her and transport her to the train station.

One last faded recollection came to her, even though she was now close to the age of seventeen; the memory had been too long ago in the past to recall clearly. She had been so young, only three. Putting the past back together in her mind had become ever more difficult, like gluing back the pieces of a shattered glass bottle. She wasn't absolutely sure, but she thought she recalled having sisters, two older sisters. Something with the sisters and playing with a cat that sometimes sat high on the fence and licked its paws; Myra remembered this. Or were the two girls perhaps the neighbor's children? She wasn't so sure, now. However, she most assuredly remembered other girls, much older than her, maybe eight or nine years of age. And how they laughed, played with colorful ribbons, and tied them in her hair.

At one time, Myra had asked Jasper John what he recalled about her past. But his recollection wasn't too clear, only knowing his brother in Atlanta at the time was busy managing the adoption of many children, not only hers, as the Methodist Children's Home in Decatur was an institution specifically dedicated to such causes. Jasper John apologized but informed her that his older brother had since passed away, and with him, the details of her history in Atlanta.

Myra fell off to sleep. The night was windy and a full orange moon rose in the clear, dark sky. The red oaks over the cabin rustled in the cool air, and low branches scratched against the rusted tin roof like fingers in the night. Owls hooted in the distance, and the lake glistened as the moon rose and paled to candle-white in the sky over the farm.

Chapter 17

CADE WAS A contemporary man of action. He'd taken exploit into his own hands and was now engaging his future and life. He was driving up the highway toward an unknown tomorrow in another man's automobile with a map in hand. Having driven through Americus, he had seen the train station and the masses, the police presence, and the crowd control underway. The station was lined with homeless families, numerous fathers and mothers with a multitude of children while holding onto what belongings they could carry. Attempting to board a train Cade knew would be difficult, time-consuming, and risky. Cade wasn't aware of his status, if he was a wanted man, or if the engineer he had dumped in the woods was yet considered missing.

After much thought to the matter, he settled on a plan, located a gasoline station and filled the car's tank with the assistance of the station attendant. He purchased a state map in the station's office while paying for the gas. Cade hadn't ventured any further than Lee or Sumter County in his entire eighteen years, and he drew up his courage to do so. He gripped the automobile's steering wheel as he drove north onto the highway in the general direction of Atlanta.

After traveling five miles through the countryside, he merged onto a second highway, in the northerly direction of Oglethorpe and Montezuma. This highway became more congested. There were many vehicles on this road, cars, farm trucks, and horse drawn wagons moving down the side of the weeded shoulder. The mechanized convoy moved at a slow pace, and he bided his time. He noticed many groups of farm trucks gathered in campsites along the way; campsites of small tent cities in church yards, abandoned warehouse parking lots, and in glades on the side of the highway. These groups were set up with tarps, tents, and fire pits where people stood in circles while roasting meat on long wooden spits. The tent cities were lined in long rows with children running amuck and men standing in circles in deep discussion; women tending their cooking and a few police cars from the cities of Oglethorpe and Montezuma riding through to monitor the crowds. Apparently the economic crash had affected not only Lee County, Cade could surmise, but many others, too, reaching far and wide. The boll weevil, severe drought, the depression, and the rampant rate of farm foreclosures had caused many of the farms and businesses to shut down. This put many farmers, land tenants, and sharecroppers, with their families, out to fend for themselves on the highways. Many cars were broken down, old jalopies unable to cope with the mileage. Several had been abandoned in roadside ditches or parked on side streets and left to rust.

Only a few dollars remained in his pocket, and he realized the gasoline in his tank would eventually run low. He glanced through the engineer's billfold and found a driver's license and a business card: Beau Browning, County Engineer, City of Leesburg, Georgia. However, no more money was found. He pulled to the side of the road and parked at a bridge. After looking over his shoulder, he tossed the billfold and the engineer's paperwork, along with his 30/30 rifle, into the river below. Now the last of the incriminating evidence was history other than the license plate mounted to the rear of the truck.

Did he languish for the engineer shot dead then left in a ravine by the railroad tracks? Not hardly considering their debt was nearly paid although the bank had insisted on retaining the entire acreage regardless—this being without the slightest negotiation or flexibility considering the unprecedented economic conditions. How was this fair? J.R. Rutledge had simply arrived at their doorstep, un-appointed, expecting a signature of agreement to whatever altered terms they desired. How unjust.

After a long day, he found a side road and a tree that he could park under to stretch out on the truck's bench seat. Yet beforehand as the sun was setting, he walked through a field to a nearby transient encampment where many other wayward strangers were parked and gathered while cooking over fire pits. He befriended a boy about his age and they discussed the evolving conditions. The boy told Cade his family had come from Bainbridge, south of Albany, and they were driving to Atlanta to look for work and charity. He clarified that his family had left a feed store behind, and as a last resort, his farther had chained the doors shut in hopes no one would burglarize the property. Cade explained that his father's farm was soon to be foreclosed, and that he had had no other choice but to go out to look for work and a new future.

Fortunately, Cade purchased a meal of fire-roasted chicken from the boy's father and ate quickly as he was famished. Cade spent the evening with the boy. They sat on the tailgate of his father's truck. They watched the crowd moving by and noticed the young girls and people talking in the night. Fires were ablaze in the distance. Gray smoke drifted over the trees. Cooking could be smelled, the scent of sizzling beef and fowl, roasting corn and onions. As the night darkened, laughter grew. Whiskey bottles were being passed around. Banjos players and fiddlers were heard over the crowd of voices. Some were singing gospel songs, others folk music and slow ballads. Around a bonfire, one group began dancing like gypsies at the rhythm of a fast-strumming guitar. Some were hollering, 'Yahoo! Yahoo!', and the dancers went faster and faster. Two pretty girls sidled up to the two boys and sat with them to enjoy the partying. Cade almost stole a kiss with one but missed his chance when her father found her and called her back to their encampment. Much later, after the evening came to an end, Cade returned to the truck and slept in the cab for the night.

Often death calls at a time that is most inconvenient, taking with it one's soul before the living knew what had come and gone. Its long cold fingers reaching down to one's bed, holding them in its grip as the living looks on helplessly yet is useless to ward off the danger.

Myra woke late after sunup and noticed her father wasn't coughing as he usually did in the mornings. She went into his room with sleep in her eyes and checked to see that he was alright. The cabin was cool and quiet. The light was just coming through the crack under the door. But when she entered, he was lying in bed, propped against the wall. He was slumped to one side and holding his Bible, his dead eyes fixed on the ceiling, looking into distant eternity beyond the world of the living. The candle beside his bed had pooled down into a flat circle of white but was still aflame with small tongues of orange and yellow. His still eyes were slightly open but glassed-over, his mouth ajar with drool running onto his chest as if death had come most unexpectedly before he could rush it away.

She ran to his side and heard someone crying then realized it was herself crying. With both hands, she grasped his thick arm and pulled at him hopelessly, shaking him but he wouldn't wake. The feel of his lifeless body was ridged and his skin, stone cold. But, the stillness in his face and his muted expression told her all she needed. The Bible fell from his hand onto the floor with a soft thud. The room was as still as death until the candle flames stirred softly as if awakened. What could she do? She cried, sobbing, shaking her head in disbelief. Papa, she called out but he wouldn't answer. She threw herself onto his chest and held him. Oh Papa, she cried.

Only wearing her night shirt, she went to the front door and flung it open, looking out. The day was fresh, sky clear. She saw water fowl inflight over the lake, the sun rising behind the trees, the fields silent and empty. No one was about. She ran to her room, quickly dressed and slipped on her new boots. She returned to him and looked at his large nude body partially covered with a white sheet. He was pale as a bowl of bread dough. His limp arms and legs were splayed outward, the look of his last breath upon his face, lifeless, as still as a gravestone. All she could do was cry. She had loved him. She covered his entire body and face with the bedsheet. After little hesitation, she left.

She went up the hill toward the ridge. She threw her leg over the wooden three-rail fence and ran up onto Jack Waylon's property, up through the tall wire grass onto the steep embankment. Jasper John's was way too far, well over a mile away, she thought. So, she trudged in long strides over the damp ground, tears streaming down her face as she wiped them away. No one remained on the farm, and she had no idea as to when her brother might return, although they should have long ago. Cade had departed too, for who knows where, possibly for good after murdering an innocent man in a throw of prideful emotion. She'd been left on the farm to fend for herself, starving and alone. Now her father had passed away that very morning without a final word of goodbye. How could the rapid turn of events been anticipated?

The hill was steep, and when coming over its crest she could better see the Waylon home more clearly than ever before: it's beautiful architecture with white-painted clapboard and tall chimneys of red brick, the many rooflines and gables, the long front porch and gingerbread railings. She slashed her way through the thick grass and came up to the barnyard. To the west, his many head of cattle were spread out far afield as they grazed in the early morning light. Chickens and roosters ran in the yard by their coops when she strode through walking quickly by the large barn, smokehouse and his flatbed truck parked on the side. She came to the back door by a small water trough and peered through the glass window. A large black woman was there with her back turned, preparing food for the morning. Her nappy hair was gray and her apron off-white. Her hands were working busily kneading bread atop the flour-sprinkled countertop.

Myra softly knocked and the woman turned, startled. She glanced over her shoulder and her thick brows drew up in surprise. She came to the door, unlocked the latch and turned the door knob.

"Chile, what on earth?" she said, placing one hand on the doorframe.

"I'm Myra from the Grayson farm down yonder. Is Mr. Waylon here this morning?"

Myra had seen this woman a few times walking up the road from town. But she had never set foot too far onto Mr. Waylon's land before; much less had she ever considered walking into his house. However, she could feel the warmth of the woodstove in the corner, smell the fresh bread, see the morning light streaming in the kitchen window. Then she heard the movements of someone in a nearby room.

Mr. Waylon came around the corner and his mouth fell open. "Myra? Is everything alright? What are you doing up here this morning?"

She only shook her head silently and wiped the tears from her face. Unable to find her words, she stood in the doorway, thin but five and a half feet tall.

He came to her and put his hand on her shoulder.

"Myra, what's happened? What's the matter?"

He asked her in and shut the door behind her. His face was clean shaven; he smelled of shaving lather and mint toothpaste. His hair was neatly combed and he stood well over six feet, looking down at her.

Finally she said, "It is Pa...."

"What is it? Has he fallen?"

"No." She shook her head and took a long gasp, holding back her grief.

He saw the look in her eyes and knew.

"Tell me, Myra. What has happened now?"

"My Papa is dead. He died in his sleep during the night. I woke and he was lying in his bed this morning, cold. I didn't know what to do."

"Where is Cade, Myra?"

"He's left. He left days ago but I don't know to where."

"What about Arden and your mother? What about them?"

She frowned. "They should have returned days if not a week ago. I haven't heard. No one has sent a letter."

She leaned forward inconspicuously, and he took her in his arms and held her in an awkward moment of connection. She sobbed and cried. However hard she tried, she couldn't cease. He patted her back. Wynonna went for a glass of cold water and brought it. Jack and Wynonna caught each other's eyes over the top of Myra's head and they both frowned. Reaching out, Myra took the glass and drank.

"Myra, are you sure?" he asked.

She nodded. Her eyes were bloodshot and deeply set in her small face. She held the water glass with both hands.

They heard voices. Jack went to the kitchen window to look out. Just then his workhands, Carter Farnsworth and Ben Dollar came into view, walking around the house toward the barn. Jack asked Myra to wait in the kitchen, and he left through the door.

Wynonna said, "Chile, what happened honey? Do you know?" She untied her apron and set it on the counter.

"My pa has been sick with a coughing he couldn't rid. And he had an accident in the lumberyard several months ago which broke his back. It's been up hill ever since. I didn't believe he could go on like that in his state, and, well, he couldn't. He's gone now. And my oldest brother should have returned days ago with my momma from Americus. The weather has been good, and I don't understand what could've delayed their trip back home."

"Listen, hon, we can figure out what to do." She went to the window to observe Jack and the two workhands talking. Myra could smell the bread in the wood oven, and her mouth watered.

Wynonna turned from the window. "Lord you must be hungry, aren't you?"

Moments later she had fried bacon in a skillet, scrambled eggs, and slathered butter on slices of warm bread. She had milked the cows earlier that morning so she poured a glass of milk, too. She set a place at the breakfast table in the next room and Myra sat to eat.

"Thank you," Myra told the Negro woman.

"My name is Wynonna. Call me Wynonna, chile." She smiled warmly.

Myra devoured the breakfast and Wynonna could see the girl was famished. So she returned with the fresh bread loaf and Myra ate half of it.

Later Jack returned. He said, "I'm riding into Flintside for Jasper John. Myra, you stay put with Wynonna and I'll be back."

He quickly left in his flatbed down the drive.

Wynonna cleared the table and led Myra to the front porch to sit on a bench by some flower planters. They heard Mr. Waylon's men working in the barn, the sound of hammers on nails and wood.

Wynonna said, "Why don't we sit for a spell, chile? It is best we wait on Mr. Waylon and Jasper John to return. They'll know what to do."

Myra sat at the end of the bench. She was pale and still, holding the bench's arm tightly with one hand.

"Tell me what happened."

Myra explained how she had discovered him in his bed, and she repeated that he'd been ill for quite some time. How difficult it had become taking care of him but that he had quit consuming food but preferred smoking his pipe rather than eating, until the tobacco ran out.

"Tell me about your daddy," she said.

"He was a hard worker. He provided for us and a means to live on the farm. We grew cotton and he made a good life. His father was a war veteran and his grandfather was too. He took us to church and saw that we had good schooling. He was a little rough around the edges but he had a big heart. Now, I'll have to figure out what's next." She whimpered and wiped more tears away.

"What are you thinking?" she asked.

"Well, first things first, I suppose. We have a burial ground on our property. Our family is buried down there along with an old Indian named Chebona Bula. When Arden gets home, I'll have him make a pine grave marker for Papa until we can afford one cut in stone like the rest."

"Yes, I've seen the graveyard for up here on the hill. In the wintertime, I can see it down through the bare trees over the ridge."

"But the bank now wants our property because we're late paying."

"A lot of folks is, they say."

"But, I'm gonna miss Papa. He was everything."

"How do you mean?"

"Other than Mr. Burch, the school teacher, Pa taught me everything I know. He's taken good care of me. And I so hated to see him with a broken back. I suppose that hurt him the most and he obviously couldn't take the pain and morphine anymore. I came from a poor family up in Atlanta when I was a baby about three years old. My real momma was very sick. I can't even remember the last time I saw her."

She turned away and sobbed, coming to the realization that the course of her life had suddenly changed with a magnitude in which she could have never imagined just months before. With both hands, she gripped the edge of the bench's seat between her legs and she bent forward to stare at the floor as her tears fell.

Wynonna scooted over and held her. "Now, now," she said in a soothing voice.

"My Papa has legal papers and such in a hidden wooden box that I wouldn't know what to do with. The bank is threatening us. I don't know where my brothers have gone." She sniffed back her runny nose, held her hands over her face. "Now my pa's gone for good and I don't know what to do."

"Listen, I know how it can be. I lost my papa years ago in a terrible way," she told Myra while looking closely into her eyes. "And I miss him to this day."

"What happened?" she asked.

"This was years ago, *many years ago*, mind you" she clarified. "He was in Leesburg when a protest broke out, the blacks against the white Ku Klux Klan. They took him and his friends and lynched them in trees in the town square. I wasn't there. I was with my Momma and sisters at our shanty, a sharecropper's shanty west o' town over near Sasser. But them men got away with murder, I'll tell you. The whole town seen it, the sheriff too. An he done nothing about it, they say. They say it was justified because the niggers was makin' trouble. But wasn't no one making trouble but the Klan. They used to come out and burn crosses in our church yard and scare the devil outta everybody there. Then they came one night and burned the whole church down. They's just a bunch a hateful men, that's all. They killed my Papa and his friends, one of 'em the church preacher."

"That's awful," Myra said.

"I'll tell you, there must be a special hell for anyone that'll murder a preacher man. A man of God. A disciple of the Word of God." She placed her hands in her lap and looked down solemnly. "My Papa was a good man, too. He was good to my Momma and us little 'uns." She smiled.

"Where do you live now?"

"My husband and me, well, we made our home the other side of town. We rent an empty cotton house from a man over that way. Pays him five dollars a month. It ain't too bad, I guess. We've made a stove and ran a smoke pipe out the roof good enough. It leaks some but it's better than nothin' I say."

"You been working for Mr. Waylon a while, then?"

"Oh yes, worked for his folks from way back, too. I'm a deal older than Mr. Waylon, I guess you can see. I can take care of him and myself if I have to. I walk up every morning from town, 'cept on Sundays."

Myra noticed the old woman had strong arms and hands, a tough disposition and a determined spirit. Her face was drawn, her cheeks sagging from age, but her eyes were the color of gold and she seemed wise and caring.

"What about your husband?"

"Oh, that's Hezekiah. He's a good a man as I could find. He done worked over at the grain mill at the railroad line where they unload grain feed. He's reliable. He's been working there for nearly twenty-one years."

"Any children?"

"No, none a them. We don't know why. I 'spect that's the way God wanted it. No chillens." She frowned.

"Mr. Waylon seems nice enough, but for some reason my Pa and Mr. Waylon didn't get along. My Pa, well, he was hard headed they said." She frowned away more tears.

"I don't know why, but some people just don't take to other people and you can't figure why, even when there seems no reason at all." She wiped her hands on her shift and gazed into the distance of the fields.

"Mr. Waylon ever been married?"

"No, never. He's had his acquaintances, two or three, but he never seems to get around to closing the deal. He's right testy at times, and busy too. I reckon marrying ain't fo' everybody."

"He has a big farm and a lot to deal with. Seems he would have, at least needing the help with himself and the land."

"He's too single minded, has to have everything his way. I doubt I ever knew a woman that could marry him and then put up with him anyway."

Myra fell silent. Wynonna stood and went in the house. She returned with some nut bread and shared it with her. She was so hungry she ate most of it, too. Later they saw Jack coming up the drive with Jasper John and his wife, Ella, riding alongside him on the long bench seat of the truck. They parked, and Myra ran to the pastor and he took her up in his big arms as Myra wailed.

Chapter 18

THEY WENT INTO Mr. Waylon's farmhouse and sat in the big front room. Myra sat by Jasper John on a long couch that faced the fireplace and she cried. Tentatively, Jasper John rested his arm around her shoulder and patted her softly.

"Now, now, little Myra, you hush. I'll get a message to Dr. Clack to come as soon as possible. Then we'll get your pa taken care of. We'll go down and see about him and taking him out of the house. "

He looked up at the group. They knew what difficulties lay ahead for Mac's three children. Jasper John, his wife Ella, Jack, and Wynonna all exchanged glances, knowing the size of the man only guessing what his weight might be.

Jasper John Tucker was a temperate man with strong hands but a gentle touch. He was known in the community for his good heart and downright good preaching, able to stir many a hardened souls from the pulpit of Mt. Olive Church. He'd done his share of community work and was loved from near and far.

He said, "Myra, you are a part of our church family. You are with us now."

His wife Ella said, "Myra, where are Cade and Arden?"

She told them of her brothers and their journeys away. Of how she was inadvertently left alone to care for her father without their help,

Cade obviously expecting Arden's soon return from Americus to handle the situation.

Ella looked at her husband and frowned. "We need to go down and take a look, I suppose."

Jack asked, "Pastor Tucker, how long to get the doctor here? Do we need to wait to bury him?"

Jasper John said, "We should have a legal Certificate of Death and that comes from a doctor, generally speaking." He patted Myra affectionately on the back. "I believe we should. And there is also the issue of Arden's return and how long to wait. We wouldn't want the body to fester, though. I don't suppose there will be the money for a proper embalming. Everyone at church is short on money, too."

The five of them took Jack's flatbed down the hill to the Grayson cabin, Myra riding up front on the long bench seat with Ella while Jasper John and Wynonna rode in the truck bed. The day had grayed and a light mist had begun to fall. When they pulled up and went to the front cabin steps, Whip-pour-wills could be heard in the trees, calling for rain. King Fishers were clacking as they flew over the lake water while looking for a meal of fish. Crows in the distance cawed in the treetops.

They went in to observe him in his deathbed. Face covered with the sheet Myra had pulled over his body, he was as still as the night, his soul having left for the doors of heaven.

Jasper said, "We should pray. Looks like he's gone on to be with the Lord. He deserved it."

Jack remarked, "I'll be durn if I could blame him with the shape he was in."

"In the first place, his lungs were weak and he had trouble breathing," Myra said.

"Let's pray then" Ella said.

"Let the soul of this man be taken into your arms, dear Lord Jesus," Jasper John began.

He prayed a fervent prayer for his friend and Myra's adoptive father. Myra wasn't purely religious. Yet she had given it some thought while in church. Especially during the camp meeting the previous summer in Desoto and wrestling with her own spirit in the summons of good prayers as she had been called to the altar. How she had felt singled-out while under her own convictions, although many were present, stove-up with apprehension in her mortal heart, pondering what Jesus might be thinking of her because she had been adopted.

She remembered the preacher saying, "God gave you your family to comfort your human lot, as a token of his own suffering and love. For in love they were conceived and bore for you and your togetherness. But we are all sinners, alone or together." Was he speaking to her directly, she had thought? How could he have known her mind, this man standing and preaching right in front of her? The preacher had continued on saying, "He gave us the gift to raise our voices in His undying praise, because there is more rejoicing in heaven over a few saved sinners than over a hundred that have never sinned." Had she sinned, she had thought while kneeling at the low wooden altar? Once she had cheated off Lena Hardwick's math paper in Mr. Burch's classroom. Once on a cold winter day, she had lied and told Mac she had been to class when she had, in fact, skipped school over to Lena's as her folks were out of town. There they partook of tobacco and wine for the first time, and Myra became sick to her stomach and returned home as pale as the harvest moon.

Myra cast her eyes around the room to look at their faces, friends and possibly foes she hardly knew. She watched the Pastor praying softly, and she wondered what was to become of her, would God take care of her or would she have to care for herself?

As Jasper John's prayer droned in the background, she thought, how could her father have done this? Couldn't he have awaited Arden and

Ila Mae's return? And to know what had become of his son Cade? Her father had stood among her and her brothers, but now it would feel differently. How could she mourn for him without them? How could she be strong enough to endure his death and their departures at the same time? She wasn't strong enough to grieve for all three of them, she didn't believe.

They agreed to wait for the doctor. Myra dug in the cabinets and found a box of talc. She patted it on his body then covered him with a blanket to rest. Afterward, she told them she couldn't sleep there with her deceased father like that, and Ella suggested she come with them to their home for the evening.

So she gathered a night bag as they stood talking. Jack agreed to return if needed with his workhands, but Jasper John assured him members of the congregation would be plentiful, that Mac and Ila had been loved by many. He said they would take him to the church for a nice visitation service then up the hill to his family plot for a burial there. Jasper John never recalled seeing the likes of Jack Waylon's shadow standing in the door of his church. So, he offered for him to come to Mt. Olive for a visit, and Jack promised he would consider the invitation in good time.

They closed the cabin windows, placed a padlock on the door, and nailed a note to it warning Arden in the event he returned with his mother. Myra went with Pastor Tucker and his wife to their modest home, past Flintside in the direction of Desoto. After riding through Flintside, they soon crossed Flintside creek in the pastor's old wagon and found the narrow path leading into a soft valley where their log home stood.

Ella Tucker was a small woman with a kind face and soft, pale eyes. Her hair was gray but shinny and thick, which she wore in a bun. After they dismounted the wagon and put the mules into their shack, she said to Myra, "You can stay here with us." Her hand reached out to Myra's shoulder. Her heart expressed her compassion. "We'll take care of your pa's arrangements and work out a deal with the carpenter for your father's coffin. He's a man that has been working with us for a long time, and he will understand that you are indigent and have no money."

The gravel road ahead of Mr. Tullman was washed with rain, and the rubberized windshield wiper worked diligently in the afternoon deluge. As the wind rose up, the fabric roof cover of the car flapped, and the headlights were illuminated only to warn any oncoming traffic out of Americus of his fast approach. Fortunately, the roads north were good and the lay of the land flat out from Flintside and Desoto.

Mr. Tullman was taking the long drive into Americus for conducting much needed business. He was concerned for his valuable collection of antique stamps and gold coins that he stored in a dry, safety deposit box inside the First National Bank. Also there were important papers, savings bonds, his will, and deeds to various properties he owned. Considering the state of the banking industry (and from what he had read in the *Atlanta Constitution*) William thought it was best to remove his collection and papers before it was too late as the bank's doors could close unexpectedly. A few in New York already had. As it stood, withdrawals were being limited across the board, but luckily he kept much of his cash buried in steel containers in the woods behind his home. Also there was his continuous need for blood-thinning medicine and nitroglycerin tablets to ease his angina. These he purchased every few months. Aspirin was all he could take for his arthritis though it didn't help much. William had a daughter who lived in Birmingham with her family, but his wife had died unexpectedly of illness a few years earlier.

He was going to pay a visit to his stockbroker for advice as well as to commiserate and lick his wounds from what was left of his once bullish portfolio. Other than his banking and retirement planning, he also came into Americus from time to time to get a taste of the city life however congested it was. He would stay a week or so and eat at the good restaurants, shop and see old friends. Yet, one advantage of living in a rural setting such as Flintside was the tranquility and beauty. But this wasn't without its drawbacks as services were limited such as having a phone line, plumbing, and electrical power—although the previous year he had paid handsomely to have a waterline run from town together with having his house piped for modern plumbing conveniences. After much local discussion and articles written in the Desoto newspaper, the phone and powerlines were due to be installed but as of that time, this had not occurred. He put up with this partly because he'd been raised on a farm in rural Albany without them, and partly for the reason he had paid close to nothing for his vast acreage.

In 1925, he had endured a lengthy jury trial and saved a local politician in Albany from a corruption conviction which left the man broke other than the land he owned in Flintside. So as payment, Tullman took the land and retired but hoped the public services would soon be completed. However in the 1920s, progress was antiquated and slower than expected in the rural south.

While in Americus, one additional exercise that required his attention was to visit the Americus First Trust Building. He planned to meet with J.R. Rutledge to discuss the matter of Mac Grayson's land as he had promised Myra and Cade several weeks earlier. Could a compromise be negotiated? Could common ground be reached? According to the children, the principal was nearly paid off. He would see what he could do.

After departing the First National Bank with his collections and papers, he made his way through town to Americus First Trust and hoped by chance he could meet with J.R. Rutledge. Fortuitously he was in his office, but Mr. Tullman had to wait an hour to see him.

When William entered his office and shook his hand, J.R. recognized the retired lawyer immediately.

"Will, what brings you into Americus First Trust this afternoon?"

Rutledge offered him coffee but he declined.

Tullman sat stiffly in the black leather chair across from his desk.

Years earlier, the two men had participated in mutual closings of several properties in the Sumter and Lee County vicinities—a few farms, land parcels, and private homes in the area.

"We haven't spoken in a while. I thought I would stop by."

"You're not here just to check on my health now are you?" He laughed, lit a cigar and puffed, watching the lawyer. He asked, "How have you been doing, Will? I know you lost Mary Ellen a few years ago. I hope you are doing well, though."

"Yes, she got sick. I brought her up to the hospital here in town, but she never was able to leave. She went downhill rather quickly, and the doctors did their best to just make her comfortable. Thanks for asking. And you?"

"Sarah is doing fine, keeping up with her gardening and bridge club. Bryant and Mark are both in school at Emory University in Atlanta. Bethany has married a young fellow connected to a large family business here in Americus. Ever heard of Lockhart Textiles?"

"Yes, the cotton textile plant south of town."

She married Glen Lockhart's oldest son, Glen Jr. They're looking for a home where they can lay down some roots."

William said, "As you know, my daughter Milly lives in Birmingham and married a doctor up there. They have two children who are both in college, too, at Auburn University."

"Birmingham? Is that right?"

"Yep, and it's a long drive there, I'll grant you that." He laughed.

Rutledge knew something was under contention. The old lawyer certainly wasn't making a social call. The banker said, "What can I do for you today, Will?"

"Years back I had a mild heart attack. I don't know if you were aware of this. Anyhow, a neighbor fellow of mine happened to be in town when it occurred, and he drove me in his wagon all the way here to the hospital. Unfortunately, my car was in disrepair, otherwise I would have had him drive me. No one else with a motor vehicle was available that we could locate although we stopped by a few farms on the way out but were unsuccessful in finding anyone. I was in much pain and he ran his mules to near death to get me here." He paused, coughing out the cigar smoke that J.R. expelled from across the large mahogany desk. Then he added, "And I am greatly indebted to him and his family for what he did for me."

"Whom, may I ask are we speaking of, Will?"

"The name's Maclin Grayson from Lake Blackshear."

J.R. turned a shade of red and swiveled in his chair to look out of his second story office window. Without turning back, he asked, "So, I suppose this is concerning his land and the foreclosure about to happen. Am I right?"

"That's correct, J.R. As a matter of fact, I understand he owes little to nothing on his mortgage as it is."

The banker turned to look at the lawyer but said nothing.

"You're not going to push Grayson out onto the highway are you, considering his failing health and the condition of the cotton crop this year? If I know Mac, his account has been well-maintained throughout the duration of his debt obligation, is that correct? Now you are going to take advantage of his family? Without the slightest variation in his loan? Without the first negotiation?"

"Yes, you are right about his payment history. The debt has been paid on time until recently, but currently he's nine months behind, Will. It's not all my money, you know. It's not just my decision but the board's too. I have only so much leeway."

He placed his arms on his desk and clasped his hands. "The payments are *eighty-seven God damned dollars a month*, Will. He's backed up nearly eight hundred dollars by now. That's a hell of a lot of money, especially in today's money considering the state of this economy.

We're up to our necks in delinquencies. How can we differentiate one account from another? How can we discriminate in one case but allow leniency in another?" He puffed more blue-gray smoke into the stale air.

William suggested, "Let's adjust the terms and make a new loan. His family has owned the land for almost a hundred years. What do you say if I kick in a hundred bucks? Would that help take care of the new loan documents?"

"Hell no, not now, it's too late."

"What about the Lee County Courthouse burning down? How does that affect this?"

"It doesn't because we have all the information we need to proceed without it. As a matter of fact, we have a surveyor out there drawing up the property so we can finish it. My firm has a local judge that will take the case and prioritize it, so we should have the matter taken care of in short order."

"Why the urgency, J.R.? You must have a hundred or more cases that are currently delinquent."

"I have to admit, I have a special interest in this property, that's why. This is my bank and what I say goes, as long as my board agrees." He puffed on his cigar and let the smoke linger.

"You have only *so much leeway*, right?"

"And I'm leaning that way, it appears."

"Can I take a look at Mr. Grayson's contract and loan documents?"

Rutledge grinned slyly. "Will, I understood you were retired, isn't that so?"

"Does that mean I can't look at his loan?"

"Really, Will, that's out of the question." He puffed smoke, rocked back in his leather chair and looked at his cigar admirably. "Besides, Will, there are only days remaining until we take the property back."

Just then the banker's office door opened and a young girl's face peeked in. "Diddy? Are we ready to go?"

"Hold on, honey. Could you please wait in the lobby? Just give me a few more minutes while I wrap things up, alright?"

She nodded and closed the door then left.

"My daughter, Bethany." He smiled sheepishly. He stood, took William by his arm and led him to the door. "Good day, Will. It was nice to see you. You take care, alright?"

Mr. Tullman left unsatisfied with their conversation and went out to his car to return to Flintside.

Just as Tullman descended the staircase to the lobby, he passed a well-dressed man on his way up. Rutledge was preparing to leave for the day as he had a trip planned to Flintside with his daughter and son-in-law. However, the associate from the bank's management department arrived in Rutledge's office before he could leave.

"Mr. Rutledge, do you have a minute, sir?" the associate asked.

"No, I'm sorry I don't, Mr. Armstead. I was just leaving."

"It's important, Mr. Rutledge." Armstead was a dapper young man, slicked blonde hair, a nicely fitted suit and polished black wing-tips.

Rutledge held his briefcase and draped his dress jacket over his arm, ready to shut and lock his office door. "What is it? I'm going out of town with my daughter."

"Well sir, it's about that fellow Beau Browning, the county engineer we had surveying the McCarver property down in Flintside."

"Alright, what seems to be the problem, Armstead?"

"Well, I didn't know if you were aware of this, but it appears he has gone missing."

"Missing? What do you mean missing?"

"Just that, sir. According to the county he's been missing for nearly a week. He hasn't reported to work in days. They have gone to his home, and neither he nor his truck is there."

"What about the survey? Does the county have that?"

"Well, no sir. That's our problem. He also has the McCarver property file with him. Rebecca gave it to him."

"The file and all the contents?" Rutledge was becoming concerned. This was not good to hear just before taking their trip to Flintside.

"Yes sir, apparently he has the file with him. According to Rebecca, he told her he needed the paperwork and the dimensional property description so she gave him the entire file."

"Then you get over to the county and get this taken care of, Armstead. This is extremely important."

"I'll try again sir, but I was just there this morning."

"Browning will show up. I've been told he's a reliable man. My lawyer has worked with him before on other cases. Right now I have to go. I'll check back with you tomorrow."

"Alright, sir."

"Get this taken care of," he told the associate, pointing a finger at his chest and holding his gaze for a long moment. He locked his office door and met his daughter and son-in-law in the first floor lobby.

Cade drove up the highway passing old abandon farms and people walking along the roadside. One group of men claimed to be out of work from the paper mill in Albany, and they hitched a ride in the back of the pick-up, yet this only caused more gas consumption. He was already running at half tank due to poor gas mileage. Later in the day, Cade approached a town by the name of Fort Valley where they eventually pushed the truck to the roadside after it ran out of gas. Cade parked the truck behind other abandoned vehicles that had suffered the same fate.

Predictably, Fort Valley was much like Desoto or any other small town in size and amenities, with many of the wandering homeless vying for food or shelter. After a lengthy walk he located the railyard, but a temporary fence had been constructed at the station to prevent illegal, un-ticketed individuals from boarding without paying. With the few dollars left in his pocket he managed to purchase a train ticket for Atlanta, and the following morning he took up the rails to the big city to the north.

Arden had been held in the Americus City Jail for several weeks without an opportunity to contact anyone much less to speak with a legal aid. The officer that delivered their meals (if one could actually consider them meals) offered little conversation. He used the excuse that the city simply lacked the funds to afford food, much less public defenders, and that the few lawyers they did employ could only do so much. Arden slept during the day as it was quieter although he had no mattress, only a filthy blanket to cover with. At night the jail became loud and lively as the drunks and trouble makers were brought in during those hours. The mess pot he'd been furnished was only removed once every few days, and the basement of the jail stunk of the prisoners' shat and diarrhea.

On the seventh day, an officer by the name of Crandall came to check on him but overlooked his cell's condition with the puddling rain seepage from the building's foundation. Instead, he asked about his health, but Arden mentioned nothing other than the fact he was beginning to starve at which the officer laughed. Arden also insisted he deserved the right to at least contact his family as to his whereabouts. To his surprise, Officer Crandall later returned with a paper, pencil, and an envelope. He suggested Arden write and address a letter home which he did in short order. Yet, the officer didn't return until the following day. After a sad deal of pleading, the officer agreed with Arden to take the letter and put it into the outgoing mail.

The officer took the letter to his desk and lazily placed it on top of an opened Americus Gazette he'd been reading. However he was immediately called away to another pressing task inside the department. Later that afternoon another officer brushed by Crandall's desk, and the newspaper along with the letter fell to the floor. That night, the janitor threw the pile of newspapers and the letter into the trash, and Crandall entirely forgot about Arden. Days later, the officer went on medical leave, and Arden's letter never made it to Myra and Cade in Flintside but went to the city dump instead.

Chapter 19

THE DOCTOR TOOK five days to come by car from Leesburg as other emergencies and obligations prevented an earlier arrival; doctors in rural areas were hard to come by especially in hard times. Dr. Clack was a man of short stature with a rotund waistline. He had a head resembling the shape of a lightbulb and a receding hairline with a widow's peak and a bristled gray goatee on his chin. He waddled when he walked and carried a large, black satchel with a zippered top where he stored his equipment and medications. After he finally arrived, his thick glasses glinted in the sunlight when he spoke to Myra in their yard in front of the cabin. Although he was awkward in appearance, he was well-respected and had been visiting Flintside to see patients for a number of years.

Myra was living at the Tucker's, making herself useful with cooking and chores alongside Ella, the pastor's wife. Mr. Burch's school was soon to start, and she was debating if she would be able to return. School usually resumed after the fall harvest, yet seeing as how there was little to harvest, school could be beginning sooner than usual. Jasper John was retired from fulltime work and his only responsibility was attending his flock at Mt. Olive. To pass the time, in his workshop he whittled toy ducks from poplar wood and painted them various bright colors then sold them at Jenkins's store as novelty pieces. One morning, Myra went out to observe him working, as he carefully carved a wooden form while the wood shavings fell gently onto the sawdust floor of his shop.

He had said, "Myra, we're going to get you out of this mess one way or the other. I suppose you could stay with us, but we don't have enough room for your momma, Arden and Cade, too—supposing they return soon enough. Someone, I'm a-sure with a charitable heart would be able to help you-uns, but I know like everyone else, all are durn short on work, food, and fixins, too. And your momma could be difficult as she wouldn't be able to lend a hand for chores and such."

He let more thin shavings fall onto his shoes as he moved his way around the duck, the sharp chisel slowly working in his rough hands. His shelves were lined with small paint cans and brushes, tools and other things. The work shed was small with a rusted tin roof and a double door opened to the morning sun. He had expressed his concerns more than once. After all, his late brother had located Myra in Atlanta years earlier. He had sent her to him as she was up for adoption due to her impending situation of becoming homeless. Although she was now grown and Mac Grayson's daughter, he felt responsible for her, but he couldn't take care of her brothers too, he realized.

When Doctor Clack arrived, Myra was already there coming up from the lake. He had parked his Chevrolet by the fence and had walked the several hundred feet to the cabin. However, his crankcase oil was leaking profusely. He carried extra oil cans in his trunk and checked his dipstick regularly. However, he preferred not to allow the mess to drip onto his patients' properties in front of their homes.

"Myra," he said, reaching out to pat her shoulder as she was now almost as tall as he. "I'm real sorry to hear about your papa. I know he had a severe accident and it couldn't have come at a worst time."

"It was awful, Dr. Clack," she said and wiped her damp eyes.

They unlocked the front door and stepped into the house but were immediately overwhelmed by the stench she hadn't expected. She placed her hands over her face to prevent smelling the noxious odor. The doctor took out a handkerchief to cover his nose. She quickly explained to the doctor they hadn't had the funds to afford the embalming process and so forth. He assured her not to feel singled-out, that it had become common with the depression now in full swing and people short on money among other necessities. Furthermore, he added that his practice had, in fact, evolved into a charitable organization as people hadn't the money for food or much else. He mentioned Mac and Ila Mae had been paying patients for many years. Not to forget Myra and her brothers' past medical needs, as well.

He inspected the body in short order and wrote the certificate. In the meantime, Jasper John brought an oak casket down in the bed of Chesley Kutner's truck along with Chesley, Wilton Meyer, Daniel Bray, and Thomas Burch the schoolmaster, all members of the local church. This required all six men to heave the heavy body of Mac Grayson into the casket and the casket out of the cabin. Myra covered him with a blanket. Jasper John suggested that the church visitation be waived considering the decomposed state of the body, and that the service instead be held on the Grayson farm with plenty of room with which to breathe. They all agreed, so in lieu of taking him to Mt. Olive, they carried the casket on a tilt-bed trailer into the barn for safe keeping until the following day for the service.

Myra cried again at the site of her father. He was as pale as ashes from a hearth, with a slick purplish tinge to his face such as the sheen of dirty oil skimmed across water. She knew she would take one last look before they dug his grave and set him in the earth forevermore, before the Lord came and took him to a better place.

The following morning she arrived early to prepare. A young fellow, a well-drilling man by the name of Bobby Womack came along with his assistant, Jamie Ellis. Both of them were longstanding members of Mt. Olive and Jasper John had sent them over to help out. They arrived in Bobby's loud rigging truck, but they parked up at the ridge on the side of the road and walked down to the farm. They met her out front and introduced themselves. Bobby mentioned to her that he had recently worked drilling up on the Waylon property, but that they had been unsuccessful in finding water due to the severe drought conditions. She told him she certainly understood this, courteous not to reveal the previous conversations had with Waylon himself, wanting to spare the two of this neighborly contention that had nothing to do with them.

Bobby was a young man about twenty-five years of age, medium height and broad-shouldered with locks of dark hair tossed over the side of his tanned face. Jamie was much younger with a slight build, closer to her age, but shy and soft-spoken.

They went to the barn and opened the door but quickly turned away from the awful smell, Bobby and Jamie almost gagging. She suggested they bring out the trailer and coffin to allow the stench to clear in the air. Both men heaved forward and rolled the trailer out of the barn into the morning shadows of the barn roof.

She opened the house to air it as well, the door, shutters, and the windows, too. She and Ella had made up small cakes the previous evening, and the pastor's wife would be bringing down jugs of tea also for the funeral's attendees. Myra expected quite a few of the congregation to arrive, and she had to do with what she had. Bobby and Jamie went about the yard with rakes to sweep out the wood chips. Then they pulled weeds out by the fence to make the place more presentable. Myra located the heavy sack of lime in the storage room of the barn and poured the dry powder down the privy hole in the outhouse. The three of them went up to the road to search for wildflowers and Queen Anne's lace for a nice vase arrangement. Next, Myra suggested they make a trip over to the orchard to gather fresh apples. After she came with a few baskets from the storage room, the three went through the woods up to McCarver's land.

Before long the baskets were brimming with colors of red, orange, and green. Bobby had climbed high into one tree and tossed the apples to the ground. Jamie attempted catching them in a basket but missed several as they bounced downward and askew through the branches. Myra happened to look upward into the late-morning sky and noticed a trailing circle of buzzards overhead for some unfortunate creature off in the field, this certainly not unusual out in the countryside. She could see the green lake below and she noticed a family of gray fox making their way along the shoreline while hunting. In one tall apple tree they spotted a black and gray hornet's nest and they made sure to avoid that, rather walking in the other direction.

As the funeral service was scheduled for later at one o'clock that afternoon, they had plenty of time to spare. On the return trip back down the hill to her farm, Myra told them of her life on the farm with her father and brothers and the recent circumstances of them leaving but mysteriously not returning. Bobby and Jamie knew Arden and Cade from Mt. Olive, and Bobby told her he feared for her and her future situation there.

When they reached the trees at the wood line, Myra noticed the buzzards now flying low over the treetops, landing in the branches and disappearing over to her property. They walked quickly and emerged through the forest to see buzzards landing and marching around her father's coffin on the trailer. They sprinted over to the barn, waving their arms and yelling.

Now near noon, the day had grown hot with the sun high which had brought the coffin out from the barn shadows and under the heated sunlight. That is when the circle of buzzards had appeared. Because of the stench of the coffin, the birds had come to scavenge. Luckily the breeze was setting away from the barn, down toward the lake, but it was well into the day with the sun hot and high in the sky. They must have smelled it from miles away, she gathered, as wild animals have uncanny, extra-keen senses. There must have been a dozen of them setting along the ridge-pole of the barn and three perched directly on top of the coffin. More were on the ground circling the box hungrily, bickering and screeching.

Myra began chasing one around the barnyard like it was a turkey, waving her arms but it just lifting off the ground enough to dodge her and go flapping back up to the roof of the smokehouse, merely agitated. Several took flight from the ridge pole and landed on the coffin right in front of her. She burst out yelling and swiped her arm forward as quickly as she could, but the buzzards lifted off screeching and flew back up to the ridge pole.

"This is horrible! Get away!" she hollered.

"Jamie!" Bobby called out. "Go get your firearm out of my truck!"

Jamie ran up the hill and quickly returned with a .38 pistol.

"Shoot the bastards," Bobby shouted.

Myra ran to the barn and returned with a rake, screaming and waving it in the air toward the ridge pole.

Jamie hesitated. So Bobby took the gun, quickly checked it for ammunition and fired-off six loud rounds into the air. The buzzards took flight, more than twenty of them, into the sky.

"You dirty bastards," Myra called out, shaking her rake at the departing birds.

She let the rake fall to the ground and began to cry. She placed her hands over her face and bent forward, heaving. Bobby came and held her. They vaguely knew one another from church and around town. He was older, but his arms around her felt good and comforting.

"Take it easy, Myra," he said. "It'll be alright. They're just a bunch of no good vermin. We got 'em gone, didn't we now?"

The boys pushed the trailer and coffin back into the barn and shut the doors for the time being. Guests were expected soon. Myra went into the cabin and busied herself. She got the stove going with kindling, straightened the place up, fluffed the pillows in the sitting chairs by the fireplace hearth. She went into her room and gathered herself together, dressed, combed out her hair, and splashed cool water on her face from the well. The boys brought up the flowers and apples and set them on the kitchen table. Ella soon arrived on her mule pulling a travois sled made of long tree branches. She brought in the cakes, tea in jugs, some cookies purchased from Jenkins's, also nice glasses and plates she had packed in a box from home. She arranged the flowers in several pottery vases and spread out a cotton table cloth from the storage cabinet. She found a large flat bowl for the apples and washed them off in the galvanized kitchen tub after several trips out for well water. Myra was glad to be getting the function underway. Before long, Jasper John came dressed in his Sunday best, well-shaven and bathed, his shoes shined. He held his Bible in his hand, but when Myra saw him coming through the door, she ran to him and held him and began to cry once more.

He took her and they sat alone in front of the fireplace.

Quietly she said, "How can I bury my Papa today, Jasper John, without my brothers? Where are Arden and Cade? This isn't right, it just isn't."

"Myra, the Lord works by his own time schedule, that's all I can say. We don't know when or why. He just does."

"What am I going to tell them when they return? That I couldn't take care of him on my own? That he was too much trouble and place the responsibility on their shoulders? Or that I just let him die and didn't know what else to do?"

"That's nonsense. He just went, but you had nothing to do with it. He was tired and ready. He just went on and went, that's all." He held out his large, burly hand to her and she took it. He drew back his own tears, restraining himself, thinking of his old friend.

"Are you going to preach a service, Jasper John?"

"You know I will, Myra. That's my job here."

"Then say a piece for my brothers that they have gone far and are missing."

He agreed and they heard someone coming.

They turned to see the first arrivals, the elderly Wilton and Ruth Meyer coming in the door. They were a gray-haired couple with many children and grandchildren to their name. The Meyers lived up the road toward town and had been family friends of the Grayson's for decades. Wilton grew produce and had a grape vineyard for making homemade wine. His wife, Ruth, was a heavyset woman with a kind face.

Wilton nodded and greeted Myra.

Ruth said, "Myra, we are so sad to hear about Maclin. We sure did love him and we know you did too."

"Thank you, Mrs. Meyer. I appreciate that."

"You know I was here for Arden's birth many years ago. But, actually by the time Maclin had come for me, and I came running, Ila Mae had already birthed him right here on this kitchen floor." She smiled genuinely and added, "Although, I was Ila's midwife too when Cade was born. And he was a handful. When Cade arrived, it was in the middle of a cold February day with snow on the ground. It was so cold we had Ila laid out on blankets in front of a blazing fire. Your daddy and Wilton were out splitting wood, and I was in here birthing Cade."

"I know, Ruth. Thankfully you came. I don't think my father could have done all that on his own."

They laughed.

Then they heard heavy footsteps and turned toward the door to see Jack Waylon coming in, their second arrival. Behind him were his paid workhands, Carter Farnsworth and Benjamin Dollar. The Meyers stepped aside and made way.

"Myra," Jack said. "I am awful sorry, darling. I just wanted to come and express my condolences." *Sorry?* Yet she didn't know how sorry he really was.

"I know, Mr. Waylon. Thank you." She stood from her chair and straightened her dress. Her long auburn hair was pulled up in a bun with a yellow ribbon. Her dress was pressed linen, one that Ella had lent her as they were almost the same size. Ella had taken the time to hem and press it the previous night.

Jack turned toward his men. "Carter, Ben, you two head on up the hill to the burial site with Jasper John. He'll show you were to dig the grave." He turned toward little Myra and added, "It's the least I could do, now."

He looked toward Jasper John. "We brought our own shovels."

"We appreciate that, Jack, we really do," Jasper John said, not knowing to whom he would have assigned the task from his congregation.

Carter and Benjamin left with the pastor to do their work.

"Myra, I have something for you," Jack said. He went to the door, stooped on the steps, and returned with a dozen splendid white roses from the florist up in Desoto.

"Oh, they are beautiful, Mr. Waylon. And so creamy-white. Thank you for your thoughtfulness." She could see the meaning in his eyes.

"Myra, just call me Jack. That's fine, remember?"

She blushed and Ella put the flowers in a tall pottery jar then set them at the center of the table.

Chapter 20

MANY FRIENDS IN the community arrived. They filled the hillside in the shade of willows where Mac's grave was placed beside his mother and father. The carpenter that had built the casket also carved a thick oak grave plaque with a floral bunting and decorative inscriptions. He had painted the work with coats of off-white enamel which paired with the white roses placed atop the casket, the roses Jack Waylon had brought.

The weather was fair. The choir sang classical gospel songs such as "Victory in Jesus", "Shall we Gather at the River", and "The Old Rugged Cross". Myra had been greeted by everyone, so Pastor Tucker spoke a fine eulogy and softly closed his Bible at the closing of the service as they lowered the casket into the earth with rope. The choir then sang two closing stanzas of "What a Friend We Have in Jesus" while Myra wept.

Afterward, they departed either on foot, by horse or mule, or car. Myra was disappointed that Mr. Tullman hadn't made the funeral, but she understood he had gone to Americus, as ill-timed as it had been, just as he promised he would weeks earlier. Jasper John and Ella were the last to leave, and they invited her to come with them. But she refused and explained she needed to be on her land simply because it belonged to her now. Though times were hard, some friends had brought gifts such as coffee, cakes and pies, smoked turkey, pork sausage, a few loaves of bread, fresh eggs, and a pack of sweet butter she would store down in the cellar by the well. Maybe enough food to get her by for a week or more.

Later she sat on her front steps and watched the night. The sky had grown gray with light clouds. The empty fields were quiet. A cool breeze came with the hope of autumn in the air, and she knew the fall leaves would soon color red and gold. Crickets whirred in the distance. The darkening sky soon grew heavier, and the wind lifted a notch. She stood and went into her room and heard the first rain drops falling on the roof.

She sat on her bed and lit a candle. She knelt down and took out a small suitcase from under the wooden bed frame, the one she'd brought down from Atlanta on her fateful train ride some thirteen years earlier. She'd kept the suitcase as a storage box for her memories; a few photos that Ila Mae had the professional photographer take; a blue ribbon her real mother had given her before she had died of the strange illness; a beautifully decorated church bulletin from the local church in Atlanta. And finally, a thick 8" x 10" manila envelope, an envelope she hadn't opened in years.

Inside the suitcase's contents were drawings she had created as a child; a story she wrote at the age of seven of her and a talking dog; a set or pressed wildflowers she'd made; a school report sent home to Maclin written by Mr. Burch accrediting Myra's excellent progress in school to her dedication and devotion.

Finally in the back she withdrew a handwritten missive from her biological father, one he'd written to her before she'd left Atlanta at the age of three. She had not read the letter in years because of the pain and misunderstanding it brought. For she hadn't grasped its meaning until years afterward when she eventually realized that coming to Flintside had been for her own good; the realization that they hadn't sent her away because they didn't love her, but because they did; for the irrevocable reason that they couldn't have possibly provided for her due to the conditions under which they had suffered and couldn't control.

Dearest Myra,

It has been extremely difficult to write you now that it is too late. It is because we loved you so much that we had to send you away. The most that I could hope for is that one day when you grow up you will understand this, as times have been hard and life too short. I love you so much that I do not believe mere words alone can express my remorse. I considered leaving you this letter to express our sincere misgivings that both of our hearts are broken over the circumstances. And that I must send you away with Pastor Tucker to his brother in Americus as they are good people, and they will provide a good home for you there. As it is now, I can hardly breathe, and your mother recently passed away because she was unable to survive. You are three years old now, and I hope one day you will find this letter and empathize its meaning and know I speak the truth. That we loved you with all of our heart.

I met your mother years ago at our place of work, in Atlanta, in a textile factory by the name of Worthington Textiles. After considerable time there, she departed and found work elsewhere, but I remained on as a maintenance supervisor for many more years. As the case has transpired, it has now been discovered there is suspicion of severe environmental dangers involving toxic chemicals at this industrial plant, which apparently has sickened many of its employees. We are not sure yet, but the circumstantial evidence is strong and mounting, however no one can yet prove our case. This case they say is unprecedented from a legal standpoint, and new measures and laws are underway in the legislature to protect the American workforce operating under such dangerous conditions. Understand that many of the employees became too sick to hold their jobs, and quite a few have passed away since, including your mother. How and why I survived longer than she, although I worked there for many more years, is not understood. However, the doctors and attorneys involved are highly concerned that many of the retired employees from Worthington are either sick or have passed away. So for me as well as many others, it is now too late as the poison and sickness is irreversible.

Your mother was a good woman and loved you very much. We were both torn but made the decision before her death to send you away for safe keeping, as I can't work anymore, let alone stand up. I am extremely sick to my stomach and have lost copious amounts of weight, just as your mother did before her last days. I have little money remaining to support myself or even to pay a doctor. The kind pastor Tucker and the women from the church have been so helpful. I've been staying at Mrs. Ross's home down the street as I was evicted from our rental due to my lack of income. Thank God Mrs. Ross is a Christian woman with the church.

In parting, I love you and I will miss you more than you could ever understand. I hope my health one day recovers enough so that I can make the trip to Americus to visit.

With my most heartfelt love, your father, Willis Burns

She folded the letter and returned it to the envelope, then slid the suitcase back under her bed. Outside, the rain increased to a steady rhythm. She latched her window closed and watched the flame of her candle flickering against the rafters. She thought of her mother and hoped when she died that she would be waiting for her at the doors of heaven.

She could not remember her face, but she could feel her love in her heart, and she believed that they would meet again on some distant realm faraway between the stars.

She considered her frightful position in life, the way it had suddenly transpired into catastrophe. She thought of her seventeenth birthday just weeks away, but how she felt alone, isolated, even abandoned. She had been left on this barren land, stranded in the middle of nowhere, with winter coming on and the days growing shorter, too. Having lost the only father she had ever known, yet also missing the one she hadn't. Not knowing where her brothers might be, or if they would ever return.

The fields were barren and windblown, the barn empty of mules or a wagon. She had hardly a stitch of clothes, and only the gifted food remaining to eat. She didn't know what would be left if the bank came to take everything away; no idea what lay on the horizon; how she could support herself; or what may become of her. There simply appeared to be no recourse or redeemable solution. She certainly wouldn't want to rely on Pastor Tucker. She had already been passed down from one family to next, from one mother to another. Yet once again she was in a disastrous situation with no promise, hope, or a foreseeable conclusion in sight.

Utterly frightened were the words that came to mind though she attempted pushing them out. However, desperation and panic were on the verge as well. This situation had arisen unexpectedly, however her resulting sentiments certainly hadn't. For the reason that everyone was gone, she had no feasible means by which to subsist alone, with no other opportunities in store and no one to help; no one there to hold her hand and guide her through the night. She was only a teen, now alone, with little direction, no one to steady her and assure her that everything would be alright.

Ella had been sweet enough. But Myra had only known her from a distance through infrequent church gatherings and a few kind

232

conversations. If all else failed, which apparently it already had, she would be pushed to knock on the Tucker's door to beg a meal and also a bed on which to lay her head. Reduced to a wayward pauper, desperate and alone in the wilderness of the great depression.

She rolled over in her bed and sobbed, scared and lost. She grasped the bedcover and wiped her damp face in the candlelight. The rain came heavier with a pounding on the roof, raining more forcefully than it had in a long while. She cried herself to sleep that night and dreamed of a land with no tears or fear, one where all present stood in the light of their dear Savior's throne.

So much time had passed since Myra had eaten a delicious lunch. She almost cried with joy when she sat in front of the plate of eggs and sausage, slices of buttered bread, sweet cakes and coffee; the food that the family friends had brought. However, not long after she wiped her plate clean with the last slice of bread, she heard the reverberation of a car's engine approaching on the hill. She noticed it wasn't the muscular baritone of Mr. Waylon's truck, she was certain of this. But more of a moan such as a modern car's engine, one she was sure she recognized. After quickly clearing the kitchen table, she went to the door and flung it open just as J.R. Rutledge's Nash came into view around the end of the fence. She gasped, not knowing what to do. Had he come with a sheriff to evict her off her land? Well, no, apparently not, as there was no sheriff or police car in tow behind him. Then what could he want?

She ran into her father's room and took the 12 gage from the gun rack then returned to stand in the doorway—incidentally, where she had stood during his previous visit while she held the same gun, yet this time without ammunition as it had been used up. By happenstance, Mr. Rutledge on this occasion would not be aware of this variation and would assume the gun to be fully loaded.

On the front stoop, she took her stance and held the firearm with both hands, but her knuckles whitened as she squeezed her grip. In the breeze, her red-auburn hair lifted back off her shoulders just as Rutledge opened the door and their eyes met. However, what startled Myra was the striking voluptuous brunette that stepped out followed by a handsome man from the backseat which was quite her equal in appearance. J.R., rather proud and assured of himself, had already forgotten his previous engagement with Myra. Rather he stepped toward the cabin but stopped at the sight of the feisty redhead holding the dangerous weapon.

Myra took a step down from the landing and shouted, "What do you want, Mister?"

She held the piece and turned her thin frame at an angle just enough to allow the long barrels to point slightly over their heads. J.R held his arms outward to brace back Bethany and her husband. The look on Bethany's face was priceless, a look of perturbed discomposure, as if she would demand what low living creature should be on her soon-to-be property.

"Mrs. Grayson!" J.R. called over. "Now, you better *remove that gun.*"

She stepped down another step and they backed up two. "You better *remove yourself off this property*, Mr. Rutledge." Myra had never found such gumption so deep in her gut. She wanted to be brave for her father and family, although she was shivering at the thought of her predicament standing alone to protect their land.

In the meanwhile, the three had determined that standing behind the car might be best. So, from behind the Nash and over the roof, Rutledge said loudly, "With all due respect, Mrs. Grayson, you will soon have no legal rights to remain on this land. As I told you before, your deceased father's signature and contract with our bank is essentially the adversary here, not I. You see, your father made a legal agreement with my bank and has not met his obligations. This is not my doing, but the laws of the State of Georgia that predicate the terms and remedies of the banking industry. Don't take offense with us, take it with the law. IT IS THE LAW."

She remained silent, listening.

"Your property is soon to be for sale and to be sold."

"Who is going to buy it then Mr. Rutledge? There will be no one. No one has the money. That's what Pastor Tucker has told me."

Bethany stood a little taller and primped her dress, exchanging looks with her husband.

"Well, this is my daughter and she is here to see it."

Myra said nothing.

"I assure you, that gun will do you no good other than to get an innocent person hurt, and you possibly taken to jail—maybe for the rest of your life. You're going to fight a losing battle, I'm afraid."

Myra let the gun lower. She looked at the young woman not but three or four years older, so well dressed with bright, striking eyes and a stunning outfit of royal blue and cream.

Rutledge continued, "Rather you go on your own, or be thrown off this land by the sheriff is up to you. I'm sorry, but it's the end of the line. I have the law one hundred percent on my side. Shoot me if you want but that won't change anything other than a murder conviction and a life of imprisonment for you."

Myra sucked in the cool mid-day air and let her blood ease. She realized he was probably right, the rationale being that he had the law in his corner. She was smart enough in this instance to let her good sense override her pride. She realized then, too, that words can be stronger than guns. Finally, she relented and let the gun barrels point down to the step where she stood.

She said, now calmer and more clearer-thinking, "Alright then. You come with your daughter and take my land and give it to her. Obviously she's more deserving. I can leave but I have nowhere to go. Not where I can have my own life, except out on the highway where I would starve for all she cares."

"That's not our intent for you to starve."

"Where will I go, then?"

"I'm sure you could find someone with charity to take you in. Besides everyone here is dying. Or has died." He smirked but she couldn't see him well from her point of view.

"And I can go live in someone's closet, I suppose, and live an indentured life and leave this place to her and let her have what my family has built for nearly a hundred years?"

He said nothing more. Slowly they emerged from behind the Nash and took several tentative steps forward. Myra bent and set the gun at her feet flat on the step. They approached slowly until they were at the house.

Bethany said, "Well, hi there."

Myra attempted to restrain herself but one tear rivulet fell off her cheek. "Alright. You come take it."

Bethany paused. She had never witnessed such a dramatic event and certainly hadn't seen such a poor, ill-dressed girl in her life. Her private school and family's country club was worlds apart from this place. However, she turned to see the wonderful view of the lake and the soft roll of the land, the forest on the hillside and apple trees in the distance.

"Come this way," J.R. quietly told his daughter as he motioned his hand so they would follow away from the cabin. Soon they had reached the crest of the rise that overlooked the land, and they began a quiet conversation regarding the beautiful lake and property, a conversation which she couldn't hear from the front steps. Their backs were turned, and Myra watched them with J.R.'s arm around her shoulder and her head nodding vigorously. He slowly reached his other arm outward and crossed it before the couple in a semicircular motion as if a gesture of encompassing the entire property before them. Their heads nodded in unison, and their conversation livened. However, Myra had been left behind to wilt in the sun and slowly fade away.

She considered her options and her mind slowly changed. In a flash, she took the gun into the cabin and set in on the fireplace hearth. She darted out the door and up the hill by the gravesites. One leg then the next, she crossed over Jack Waylon's fence and ran up the hill toward his farmhouse.

Chapter 21

SHERRIFF JARVIS IN the city of Desoto had his plate full with the upswing in crime since the falter of the economy. The unemployed and farm-less had become creative with their means of making a living which kept the police department working overtime. Jarvis didn't need another report of another missing man, this one named Beau Browning, an engineer with Lee County who had mysteriously vanished. Sheriff Tanner from Leesburg had sent him the message stating the engineer's home had been searched and there was no sign of the man anywhere. The message stated the engineer had last been assigned a surveying job near Lake Blackshear, not far from Desoto, and Jarvis reluctantly went out to investigate. After he and his deputy searched the McCarver property, no sign of the man or his equipment could be found. What concern was it of Sheriff Jarvis if the man Browning had some kind of financial or familial issues and had taken to the road as so many in the current times? People were disappearing left and right, so what should he do about it? Jarvis left the McCarver land with no further intention of searching elsewhere as he had other pressing issues at the moment.

Myra came in the kitchen door so quickly that Wynonna dropped the salad bowl when she turned.

"Chile, it's you again! What in the world are you doing up here? Every time you show up in here, you look scared to death." She looked at Myra, well over five feet tall, standing in the kitchen.

"Wynonna, is Mr. Waylon here? I need to speak with him if he is."

She stooped to retrieve the bowl, stepped to the kitchen window and peered out toward the barnyard. "I believe he may be out in the barn looking after his tractor. He said somethin' 'bout needing a new ignition switch. I know he went up to Desoto yesterday to get some parts." Wynonna rested her big hands on the counter while looking out beyond the barn to the fields.

Myra went out the door without another word. Wynonna watched her heading with a determined purpose across the barnyard, her long red hair trailing behind her. The old woman shook her head in thought, wondering what the girl might be after.

When Myra walked through the open barn doors, Jack was fiddling with wires on the console of his Massey Ferguson tractor. He glanced up and immediately noticed the look on her face.

He stood and set a screw driver on the seat of the tractor. "What is it, Myra? What's wrong, now?"

"Jack, it is Mr. Rutledge from the bank. He's come to say I have to leave in the next few days. That I'm being kicked off our property. He's down there right now with his daughter telling her the place is going to be hers, and that he doesn't give a damn about me or my brothers." She swiped back a lock of hair from her face and stood with her hands on her hips. "Do you think you could help me? I don't know what to do now."

He took a rag off the tractor's fender to wipe his hands. He stepped over to see the strain on her face. She was so young but determined because she was growing up that very minute before his eyes and turning from girl into woman now that the world had been heaped on her shoulders.

She bit her lip and said, "Can you come with me?"

"Alright, let me get my keys." He went into the house and came out motioning for Myra to get in his truck. They went down the hill to the ridge, around the end of the fence and parked behind the Nash. They strode to the cabin to see Rutledge coming up the path from the lake followed by his daughter and son-in-law. Jack and Myra went out to meet them coming into the barnyard.

"Mr. Rutledge, I'm Jack Waylon, the Grayson's neighbor from up the hill."

J.R. held his fedora in his hand and stopped to look at this tall man he'd never met. Bethany stood by his side, an impatient look on her face. Her husband loosened his necktie and held his hand over his forehead to shield the noonday sun.

J.R. said, "We were just on our way out."

"Well, hold your horses, Mr. Rutledge. We need to talk a minute before you go."

"I don't suppose we have anything to talk about. Our business is done here today. It's a quick hour and a half back to Americus where I have a meeting at the bank."

"Well, I don't think your business is done just yet. Myra tells me that you plan to take this land back."

Mr. Rutledge pursed his lips and rocked back on his heels. "Well sir, we have little choice because the Grayson's can't make their loan payments. Now, if you don't mind—"

"—well, I do mind."

Rutledge attempted to pass by Waylon, but the man stepped in front of them.

"Myra has nowhere to go, Mr. Rutledge."

Myra looked at Jack and back to Rutledge.

"Well, Mr. Waylon. That really doesn't concern me, to tell you the truth. Half the farmers in this county can't meet their debt obligations, nor could Mr. Grayson. I have my own problems."

"How much do they owe you Mister Rutledge? Tell me that."

He was now face to face with Waylon, and he looked up at the size of the man, well over his head. "What concern is it of yours? What does it matter how much it is? There's little time left, anyway. Listen, I must get going if you don't mind."

Jack placed his hand on his shoulder. "How much?"

Rutledge gave in. "Close to eight hundred dollars, seven hundred and eighty-three to be exact, just for the delinquent payments plus nominal penalty charges."

Jack took a deep breath and glanced away then down at his boots, thinking. He looked up. "Seven hundred and eighty-three dollars?"

"Due the beginning of next week, or else."

"Well, I tell you what, Mr. Rutledge, how about I cover the seven hundred and eighty-three, how does that sound?" He looked at Myra and her mouth fell open. She stepped closer and placed her hand on his arm, looking up at him.

"Myra?" he asked, but she remained silently spellbound, staring unblinkingly at him. He glanced back at the banker.

Rutledge said, "Well that's not possible, because—"

"—Damned if it ain't. It doesn't matter where the money comes from. Hell, if it fell out of the sky she could still pay it and be caught up, am I right?'

"Diddy..." Bethany said looking at her father, but instead paused while gauging the situation.

Jack said, "As a matter of fact, I can have it to you by tomorrow afternoon. How does that work?"

Rutledge exchanged looks with his daughter. "We're busy at the bank and we weren't actually expecting that, *you see*—"

"—*No, I don't see.*" Waylon stepped forward, almost chest to face with the short banker. "I believe Myra has the legal right to pay up, doesn't she?"

"Then what about future payments? There are roughly twenty remaining. She'll be behind again in no time." Rutledge was beginning to raise his voice.

"Well sir, I won't allow it. I'll make sure the payments are made."

"Would you mind telling me who you are and what business you have here? Why it makes a damn to you?"

"Yes, I would mind." He locked eyes with the banker and held his gaze. "I will tell you this much. I have nearly three hundred acres up there," he said, tilting his head back over his shoulder in the direction of his land but keeping his eyes on Rutledge. "And I'm damn sure not in foreclosure. And I have plenty of money to pay what I want and spend any damn way I please. Am I making myself clear, Mr. Rutledge?"

Rutledge backed off and swallowed hard.

"Expect me up in Americus tomorrow mid-afternoon to pay you what is owed to date."

The banker looked at the disappointment crossing his daughter's face. He reluctantly removed a business card from his wallet and gave it to Waylon. The banker had no choice but to concede. He hadn't expected this last minute intervention, but rather expected to own the property in a short time at a fraction of the cost considering the loan was nearly paid off.

"Have the figures together when I arrive, Mr. Rutledge. You will be in your office won't you?"

He nodded reluctantly. "Mr. Waylon? That is your name isn't it? Mr. Waylon, listen—"

"—*No, you listen!* I don't want to get my lawyer involved, either. I expect your full cooperation. I'll be there with Myra tomorrow afternoon. If there is a problem, I'll promptly have my lawyer get in touch with you. His name is Trent Sanders out of Desoto. And when I need him, he usually comes quickly as we've had a dealing or two in the past. And trust me. He knows his way around a courtroom."

Rutledge agreed and left with his daughter bickering in the background. Myra turned to Jack and thanked him profusely. As they watched the dust of the Nash trail away, Myra breathed a sigh of great relief, having been again rescued by Mr. Waylon.

The following day they drove to Americus and paid the amount in full which the bank requested. Along the way, she watched out for Arden coming with their mother but saw no sign of them. After leaving the bank, Jack drove to the mental hospital and the staff nurse informed Myra of Ila's recent death; but that she'd been buried in the church cemetery, and Arden had left town without her. She made no mention of Cade, however, as she hadn't been on duty the day he arrived.

Naturally, Myra cried over the news. She took Jack and walked to find the grave marker with Ila's name cut in stone. She prayed silently as Jack stood by and allowed her the time to take in a reflective moment. With her regret, she frowned as they stepped away and climbed into his truck to drive back home.

Just before closing, Mrs. Jenkins finished stocking the shelves and sweeping the floor. Mr. Jenkins met the U.S. mail truck in front of his store and took the cardboard box from the driver with his customary nod. The truck drove away, and Mr. Jenkins returned into his store to sort the mail as he usually did every Monday through Friday, except on weekends and holidays. The U.S. Post Office paid him a monthly fee for using his general store as the Flintside Post Office, for handling and sorting the mail to insure a timely delivery to all the local residences. Behind the counter a wooden grid of small boxes was arranged for distribution. Often Mr. Jenkins would do the work after hours for the next day's mail.

On this evening, he was going through the mail and he noticed a letter to Myra from Cade, the post mark being from Americus, Georgia. He'd heard from Mr. Waylon that Cade had left the Grayson farm unexpectedly and no one knew what had become of him.

"Look here, Darlene," Mr. Jenkins said to his wife.

She stepped up to the counter, holding a broom in her hand. "What is it?"

"A letter from Cade Grayson here to little miss Myra. Tsk, tsk," he added.

"Was that the kid that came in here with the other two and grabbed your shirt, all about that misunderstanding with you miscounting their change? When the Indian cigar display spilled all over the place?"

"That's the one alright."

She smirked.

"To hell with the Graysons, those little smart-assed kids," he said. He took the letter and slipped it under the checkout counter to hold it there.

"Maybe that will teach them a lesson." He smiled, and his wife returned to her work of cleaning their store.

Days passed, and Myra made do with the gifted food from the funeral. Late at night, rain had begun to come more frequently. She sat in bed, biting her nails, listing to the rain while wondering what had run through Cade's mind when he'd pulled the trigger. What could have provoked him to the point of murdering a man? She knew Cade was concerned about the bank. Yet was that enough alone to cause such an act? Myra didn't know he had had that kind of violence in him, or where it came from. Was it bravery, or cowardice? She certainly knew he possessed a strong fortitude, and the bank's dealings had been underhanded, there was no question about that.

She was also concerned regarding Jack Waylon's commitment to actually pay her mortgage notes, although there was only twenty or so remaining. She certainly had no way to pay—this was obvious. But she had an inclination as to why he would keep his promise.

The morning after having these thoughts, she heard his truck coming down the ridge to her property. She heard the crunching of gravel under his tires and the squealing of his brakes as he rolled to a stop, then the hollow sound of the truck's door closing and his boots soon coming up her steps. He knocked softly, and she opened the door to see him with his hat in his hand.

"Myra, good morning. Can I come in?"

She stepped aside, and he eased the door further open as he entered.

"Listen, we need to talk." He patiently drummed his fingers on his hat brim.

"I suppose I know what about."

"I did my best to clear up your bank situation, but like I told you on the ride back from Americus, I durn sure need water and I can't get it out of my ground up there."

She didn't have to make him ask. She knew. "Alright, I thought this might be coming. Go ahead and bring down your men and their drill rig. But I hope you can drill out by the road, not too close over here by the cabin. I suppose it will be loud."

"I appreciate that, Myra. I'll see what Mr. Womack can do. I don't think that will be a problem. You're so close to the water down here, drilling about anywhere should be fine" He licked his lips reluctant to delay any longer.

"Go ahead, I understand. You've been right nice with your financial aid. It's the least I can do."

The following morning, Jack came with Bobby Womack and Jamie driving the mobile drill rig. The previous night, more rain had fallen and the road was wet, so the heavy truck rutted a little as it entered her property. Before long they had the drill tower up, the bracings out, togs in place, and an auger bit in the chuck. They neatly set out drill pipe on the ground and donned their gloves. After several unsuccessful attempts, the gasoline engine finally rumbled to life and roared when they put the power to it. After an hour of drilling and Jack hovering around the rig, they finally hit water and it came gushing out. Later in the day, the pump had been installed. They dug a trench across the road, and ran the transfer pipe up to where Jack had pulled over the holding tank with a chain off the hitch of his truck. By sundown the tank was full, and Jack had a big smile on his face. Soon the cattle came to drink in the troughs he had scotched-up along the ground. The following day, they would install a 3-way valve and run the piping farther up the hill. This to fill the pond and to water what remained of the late August corn before it entirely wilted away. Having to take a truck down to the lake, as inefficient as it was, had grown tiresome. Jack was glad to be done with that.

As the men closed down the rig and loaded up tools into the truck, Myra stood by watching.

"You look worn out," Myra told Bobby with a laugh as he slipped off his gloves for the last time and threw them in the back. He was covered in mud and sweat. His shirt was soaked through, and the muscles in his arms glistened in the late daylight.

"A good day's pay is what I say."

"I bet you do pretty well."

"Yep, I bought this rig from a man down in Oakfield. I've been running it for several years now. But the way things have slowed down, it's been tough. Luckily, Mr. Waylon has kept me busy. Making enough to feed myself and pay my house rent."

"Where is that at?"

"This side of Desoto, not too far just over the creek passed Flintside. I got a little place out a dirt road a piece. At least the roof doesn't leak anymore since my landlord put a new one on last spring."

"I've never held a job except for what needed doing around here."

"It's not too hard once you get used to it," he said modestly, just making conversation. "But I don't think there are too many jobs available these days the way it looks."

She wouldn't know where to look if she had to, she thought. Without having any transportation, Flintside would be her only option, and not much could be offered in a small town like that.

She stepped closer. "You from around here?"

"Out near Leslie. I use to work for Jimmy Tines until I got this rig going. I also do home repairs on the side if I can. Like carpentry, cabinetry, masonry, and such. If'n you ever need any." He smiled. "I have tools and I have references, too."

He was not only handsome but capable too, she thought. She noticed his tanned face and dark green eyes. "I appreciate you coming over and helping out before the funeral."

"You're welcome, Myra. Pastor Tucker sent me over."

Just then Jack came down the hill in strides. "Don't pack up just yet, Bobby. We have a pipe leaking up here on the hill."

Bobby shook his head and went back for his gloves. He turned to Myra and said, "Looks like we ain't done just yet."

She smiled. "Alright you better get on and finish. I'll talk to you later, then."

He turned and took some wrenches back up the hill.

Chapter 22

THE FOLLOWING MORNING, a steady rain fell. Jack spoke with Carter inside the barn while he worked on Jack's short bed truck, repairing the engine head. Parts were scattered on a nearby workbench, and Carter was bent over inside the engine compartment.

"It don't look too good, Mr. Waylon, seeing as how you plopped down all that money to bail that girl out." He was turning a wrench.

"Getting to that water down there was priceless, Carter. I just can't put a price tag on that." After second thought, he recanted and added, "I suppose I've paid for it, though, about nine hundred dollars so far after the late penalties were added to it."

"Was it worth that much?"

"My cattle are fifty to a hundred dollars a head. So go figure. If they started dying off, well that could add up pretty quick like. And don't forget all the wear and tear on this little short bed."

"I know. I can't. I'm here repairing it right now. I have to say, it done a good job hauling all that water up from the landing. And like you said, she paid the price, too, needing a new head in her."

"But now it's started to rain again, and I wonder if the drought is finally lettin' up?" Jack frowned. "If it has, it's got a long way to go."

"Hmmm, maybe so," Carter said.

"It rained yesterday and it's been raining since this morning."

Carter just kept working as Jack stood by. He said, "What's that lady going to do now, you going down there and paying her mortgage every month, too?"

"It's just for a year and a half, but I need to give that some thought. I suppose I could put her to work up here."

Carter lifted his head out from the engine compartment, grease and dirt smeared across his face. His eyes were brown and his dark beard was neatly trimmed. "Doing what?" he asked.

"Helping Wynonna mostly, I guess." He shrugged his shoulders.

"I bet you she could make up a nice bed." He smiled and his eyebrows danced.

"Carter, don't go there." Jack frowned again.

"Yeah, I guess you could put her to work, then" he agreed though disappointed Jack didn't see it his way.

"She needs work to do. Her pa is gone, so she won't be taking care of him anymore. She has no farm work to do, and her brothers have taken off to who knows where."

"So you paid nine hundred dollars. How many payments are left?"

"Twenty at eighty-seven dollars per month."

Carter went to the bench and found his notepad and pencil. He was good with numbers and smarter than Jack gave him credit for though he had had little schooling. "Let's see. That's damn near eighteen hundred dollars plus the nine hundred which totals twenty-seven hundred dollars, Jack." He laughed.

Jack replied, "You're right."

He scribbled more figures. "That's like paying one hundred and thirty-five per month for a year and a half to rent her land for water until the loan is paid off. That is if the drought goes on another year, but it's going to end before too long. It has too."

Jack thought about that. "You're right, Carter. I need to put her to work up here on the farm."

Carter set the pencil down on the workbench and went back to the truck. He turned and said, "She can come out and help me anytime she likes." He smiled devilishly, eyeing Jack.

"Don't count on it. Besides, you're married."

"Since when did that matter?" He laughed again.

"Since you getting kicked out of your home that it does."

"I'm just bullshittin' you, Jack. She's too young." He bent forward and went back to work.

"Damn right." Jack abruptly turned and left toward the house through the rain.

The following Sunday was peaceful. Myra swam at the lakeshore and lay in the sun to catch her breath. She wore nothing but a long, cotton gown and her small pink nipples shown through in the sunlight. She heard Jack's work truck coming down the hill so she went up to see what he needed. They had been running the well pump intermittently during the days as required. The equipment really hadn't been too much mess or imposition, only a little noisy at times, not as bad as she had thought it would be.

She walked up the path from the lake with her arms crossed over her small chest, covering herself. Jack stepped out of the truck.

He met her on the yard. "I thought I would come down and check on you."

"I'm alright. I caught a few bass yesterday and gathered firewood. I salted and hung the fish in the little smokehouse. Hauled water up from the well, watered my turnip greens and flowers, washed out the cabin, too." She stood in front of him, her hair damp and glistening in the sunlight. "I reckon I'm getting along alright."

"You have any fresh vegetables? Any fruit for breakfast?"

"Well, not much of that." She realized how hungry she'd become with swimming. She had eaten the fish, and there was little food left from the funeral.

"Why don't you come up and eat with me, Myra?" He shifted his weight and pushed his cowboy hat off his forehead. His cowboy boots were marred and his jeans worn. His sleeved shirt had front pocket flaps that were pointed down in the corners.

"Well if it wouldn't be any trouble, I guess I could."

"Alright, you get dressed and I'll wait."

"Wynonna isn't there today, is she?"

"No, she don't work on Sundays."

"Well, I didn't know you were the type that cooked."

He smiled at her for the first time. "You'd be surprised. I have to sometimes."

They drove up to his house and walked in the back kitchen door.

"Don't we come in the front door?' she asked teasingly.

"No, we're just family and workhands. The uppy-ups come in the front door."

"Well, I'm not either. And I ain't any uppy-up."

"Let's just call you our close neighbor, how's that?"

"Sounds good to me."

They spoke cordially as he fried-up pork chops in a cast iron skillet on top of the woodstove. To the side he simmered greens and rutabagas, heated bread inside the stove. He ran to the cellar and brought back soft butter then poured glasses of lukewarm tea.

Myra stood at the window. She observed Carter and Ben coming in from the field, pulling a trailer with mules, hauling some fencing and gear.

"Doesn't look like the hands will be joining us for dinner. There aren't enough chops I don't believe."

"No, they'll have to take care of themselves back at home. They're just working a little weekend overtime. Looks like they're done for the afternoon, though."

She watched them unloading the wagon and hauling the tools into the barn's storage room. They wiped the sweat off their faces with a cotton towel.

"Either one married?" she asked as he filled their plates.

"Carter is. He has a wife and kids."

"And Ben?"

"He's a bachelor. I believe he has a girl over in Sasser."

They went out and sat on the back porch where a long plank table was situated. He said, "I thought it was nice out this afternoon. We might as well sit out here."

Carter wiped his face with a cotton towel they hung on a hook aside the tack, harnesses, and bridles. They unloaded the wagon, stacked the last of the fencing in the yard then led the mules in the barn. Ben stalled them at the far end, gave them apples, one for each. From inside the barn, they could see Myra and Jack eating at the plank table outside the house.

"Looky there at Jack and Myra," Ben said after splashing his face with cool water from a bucket. He stood inside the partly closed barn doors. He took the towel from Carter and wiped his face too.

"No shit, brother. He's done got the girl up here eating off o' his fancy plates."

"Sure enough. He done set a place with a nice dinner and look at those tall glasses of tea, would you?"

"He ain't never done that for me," Carter commented while brushing off his jeans with the palms of his hands.

"She's a pretty little thang, ain't she?"

"Can't be but a day older than seventeen it looks to me."

"But a grown up seventeen, I bet you." Ben went to hang the towel on its hook.

"You think she's a grown-up yet?"

"She might be if she's been fooling around with those schoolboys, like the schoolboys I used to know did with young girls."

"Might be but it's hard to tell."

"Might have to watch her walk from behind, and see if she swings her sassy ass just right. You can tell by the way they swing it is what I say."

"Well, I'll make sure to take notice next time I get a chance to walk behind her."

They laughed.

"Beats all to hell, don't it?" Carter said, now in a more serious tone as he watched them talking on the back porch. A thin band of sunlight glinted through the gap in between the old barn doors and cut yellow across his eyes as he watched the house.

Dust lifted in the gleam of the sunlight coming in, and their shadows silhouetted against the storage room wall as Ben came around Carter's back to watch, too.

Carter said, "He tried to kill her father by pushing a load of lumber over on him, but now he's gotten his well water, and they're dining in style like they're in New York City without a care in the world. Look at 'em." He scratched his close-cut beard.

"But she didn't know about that," Ben said. "She's clueless." He shook his head. The bangs of his black hair hung off his forehead and fell just to his eyes.

"Well, I ain't saying nothin' about it. We just keep to ourselves and pay them no nevermind." Carter looked at Ben. "They say her no good brothers ran off to California and left her here."

"California? That's way up north, ain't it?"

"Out west, I believe."

"Hell, I saw a globe once at Mr. Burch's schoolhouse, but I can't remember."

"Cause you's only nine when you dropped out."

"I had my Pa's farm to work. What's the use in geography when you're hungry and got to put food on the table?"

"You got a point," Carter said. He paused and added, "Look a there, Ben. He's pouring her more tea from a pitcher." He nudged his coworker in the ribs. "Ain't that sweet?"

"I believe he's buttering her up good."

"I'd like to butter her up myself."

"You're a dirty old man, Carter Farnsworth. You ought not be talking like that. What if Laura heard you?"

"Maybe she'd join in."

"Shut your nasty mouth!" He snickered.

They looked out across the barnyard. Carter said, "Oh no, they're a laughin' about something now with what they're talkin' about. Look at him smiling. Who's the dirty old man, now?"

"I guess all three of us. Mmmm, she is sweet, yes sir."

"Anybody ever tell you that you got a dirty mind, too?"

"What I learned, I learned it from you." He looked at Carter seriously, but Carter pushed his shoulder away.

Jack said, "I'm concerned about your situation, Myra, with Cade and Arden gone off. Maybe they'll show up but maybe they won't." Jack sipped his tea. He took the tea pitcher, leaned forward and poured more into her glass.

"I don't know what has happened. I fear they've gotten into some trouble but I can't imagine what." Myra sat across from Jack at the table alongside a row of laurel growing by the back porch.

"I suggest you come and work for me up here. I believe you could help out Wynonna. You know she's getting up in age and has trouble

254

stoopin' and fetchin' and getting around. She's best in the kitchen cause she can cook-up a mess of supper."

"I suppose that would be alright. It's just a quick walk up from my house to here, and I know you'll be helping out with my payments and so forth. For the well water, like you said." She took a bite of pork and savored the flavor by shutting her eyes, but she didn't want to appear too desperate. She added, "I believe Arden with come sooner or later, and together we could pay you back for your generosity." She glanced down toward her land in hopes that he might, by chance, be coming up the hill that very moment to say he was home.

"Well, in the meanwhile, you'll have to make plans otherwise. I believe it's best to plan ahead don't you? Unless you'd rather run up here every time something comes up. Better than you rooting around in the field for polk or fishing in the lake. Unless you like polk and a limited diet of bass." He laughed.

She laughed with him, but she was inwardly torn with her conflicted situation.

"Can you handle splitting up enough firewood for the winter? How's your wood supply, Myra? I bet you can split a cord a week." He smiled again.

She genuinely laughed at this. "Not hardly. I'd be lying if I told you I could." She ate more greens and a piece of savory ham hock.

"Why don't you plan on coming up in the morning and I'll get you started with Wynonna? I'm afraid she might have to retire soon anyway."

"Oh, I doubt that. I've seen her work. She's healthy enough for the time being, isn't she?"

"Let me put it this way. I think you would be a great help to her and me both. How is that?"

"If you say so, Mr. Waylon. I'm good with it."

"Just Jack. No more Mr. Waylon, alright?"

"Alright, if you say so."

Later she returned down the hill. When she entered her cabin she was struck by the realization that she might have the opportunity of a lifetime, that Mr. Waylon's proposition might be her saving grace. Having come from Jack's sumptuous house, she was suddenly aware of how spartan and plain her cabin appeared, how worn and dilapidated it was. The leaning of the structure, the condition of the old stove, the stove pipe being so crooked and out of plumb. How the interior was drab and outdated, the furniture so threadbare and the floor so splintered. How could she live and support herself on this barren land? How could she grow cotton? Let alone have enough to eat in the meanwhile? She went to her room, sat on the bed, and was frightened by the thought of her bleak future and which way her life might turn. Exhausted from the tension, she fell asleep and slept through the afternoon, waking later to find the cabin still and eerily quiet.

Part Three

Chapter 23

ON A SEPTEMBER morning, Cade reached the outskirts of Atlanta on the railroad up from Fort Valley. When boarding the train the previous afternoon, the conductor had filed all the men, women, and children up the ladder into the dented-up boxcar. However, the boxcar was built for livestock rather than humans, and it stunk of dirty animals, urine and dung. The space however was comfortably populated. Yet as the train stopped in Macon and Forsyth gathering more passengers, it became cramped with standing room only except for the elderly, woman, and younger children that were allowed to sit. Having to relieve oneself presented another problem. Those in urgent need hung their rear ends out of the railcar, and everyone turned away as the business was done.

By early morning, the boxcar's door was dangerously rolled halfway back to allow for ventilation and cooling. Also, during the night there had been a jam ahead on the tracks, and the train had had to idle during the dark morning hours until the line could be cleared of another train. This was difficult as standing allowed for no sleep, and everyone was exhausted when the train finally rolled again at five a.m. Later, as the train approached and the sun rose, the countryside gradually transitioned from a rural landscape into being vastly populated. Sparse farmland soon evolved into a city of industrial factories, commercial buildings, and houses with roads coming and going in all directions.

Cade stared in amazement as the train slowly entered the center of the city. He stood at the boxcar door and gazed out at the size of it, the buildings seemingly touching the sky at twenty to twenty five stories. They were massive structures, all together as large as a mountain standing tall in the presence of the city. Many modern cars and transport trucks drove the roads coming in and out. Hundreds of busy pedestrians walked the paved thoroughfares in every direction, some pushing produce and vendor carts, some wheelbarrows or loaded dollies. Bicycles, buggies, and horse-drawn wagons were moving along the streets, too. The homeless vagrants milled about in the streets, dark alleys, and city parks. Fires were lit in tall barrels where men in rags stood in circles. Soup kitchen lines were strung out for blocks. Cade noticed the front steps of a local church being used as a gathering place for the homeless to sit and commiserate. The streets were lined with many businesses in buildings with concrete and brick facades, with wide steps and metal hand railings, with their names painted across the top in bold white letters. Advertisements were everywhere. Signs and billboards abounded. They read: Tobacconist Shop; Mill Belting & Supply; Southern Exchange Building; Dalton Auto Sales; Gate City Tack and Gear; Atlanta Ice House; Mallard's Provisions; Herndon's on Peachtree; and Smith's Barber Shop.

Others in the boxcar were watching too, their mouths agape. Many had never seen the big city, and they stood spellbound watching it come into view. Apart of the train, other cars up ahead included plush passenger cars, and the passengers' heads could be seen poking out of their windows. Cade's pulse raced and he had no idea what he would do once off the train. He knew he was hungry, yet he had only one dollar remaining in his pocket, the last bill from the surveyor's wallet.

The train arrived and slowly entered the Atlantic Station Center which was a massive terminal pavilion, open-ended with a domed top that spanned hundreds of feet in length and several hundred wide; wide enough to allow for six parallel train tracks to run through it. The incoming tracks had come from hundreds of miles away, traveling from all over the United States. The tracks entered the city and came through both ends of the station which was centered in the commercial district of town. Roads and highways ran aside the tracks and buildings for cars, trucks, and freightliners. Cadillacs, Fords and Chevys were seen driving the streets. Traffic conductors were directing traffic in all directions. Many passengers were seen disembarking on the loading platforms. Overhead, a torn American flag flew in the afternoon sky above the terminal.

Cade took a deep breath when the thrust of the steam engine echoed with a powerful timbre as they entered the station under the pavilion roof. Followed by bursts of hot steam, the train pulled to a grinding halt and the wheels squealed as it came to a full stop. Other gleaming locomotives were parked alongside one another in the terminal. Behind the locomotives, adjoined railcars stretched out in lines for hundreds of feet from the station.

Everyone in the boxcar immediately began climbing down with women handing their children to the men on the pavement below. In the sudden chaos of departing travelers, porters with wheeled carts were soliciting the wealthier passengers to carry their baggage for tips. Appearing through the mass of people, a newspaper boy came selling newspapers. The station was abuzz with bustle and hectic congestion. A man outside the terminal had a cart from which he sold hot sausage rolls. Another was selling soft pretzels and bottles of Coca-Cola packed in ice.

Cade stepped into the streets and turned a complete circle in awe of what he saw. The city was thriving and pulsing with commerce and life. Hundreds of people were coming and going in all directions. Some were greeting one another and talking. They were waving and smiling, too. He noticed that other pedestrians, however, passed by with unsmiling faces, apparently troubled by their demanding schedules. They made quick eye contact and gave stern expressions but moved quickly on. Carrying briefcases, books, or newspapers under their arms, they seemed too busy to chat while making their way onto other important destinations somewhere else in the city. Although many people were in threadbare clothing, a few wore stylish attire fit for the times, quality suits and shiny leather shoes with polish and style.

Cade walked aimlessly through numerous streets, watching and looking. Restaurants were side by side, and his stomach growled with the scent of cooking meat and sizzling onions. Shops and clothing boutiques were everywhere. Streetcars and buses moved along the street. Gas streetlights ran from one corner to the next.

He soon came upon a commercial warehouse and noticed long transport trucks backing up to loading docks. There was a uniformed guard at the main gate where the trucks entered the lot, and when the guard turned to address one truck driver with his paperwork, Cade slipped by. After some looking, he made his way to the end of the dock where one truck with the name Southeastern Freight was just backing in. Next he noticed a worker pulling on some gloves to unload the truck. Cade jumped up on the dock to talk with the worker.

"Hey, Mister, it looks like you got a lot of boxes to unload. You need any help?"

The man was an Italian type, dark with hairy arms and closely set eyes. "Well, I ain't supposed to but we happen to be short-handed today." He glanced over his shoulder. "Hey, Harry!"

His supervisor walked down the loading dock. "What is it, Tony? What do you need?"

"This kid here says he wants to help out." He simpered and nonchalantly nodded toward Cade.

The supervisor said, "Alright, it's your lucky day, kid. And I mean *real lucky* cause we don't let just anybody in here. And work is hard to find these days, let me tell you."

"I'll do whatever needs doing," Cade told him.

"Alright, listen. You unload this truck in an hour and stack these boxes up against that wall inside there, and we'll pay you a dollar."

"What if I can't?"

"Fifty cents tops. It's up to you. If you can get it done in an hour, the dollar is yours."

Harry and Tony departed to attend other work and left Cade to do his job.

Myra began work on the Waylon farm one week after she had buried her father. Although distraught by the recent events, she was now relieved there was hope for a future. As it stood, little remained on her barren land that she could make use of because she lacked the money or resources to do so. Let alone men or a few mules to lead a plow.

Before long, she began to favor the old Negro woman as she showed her around the house and farm, little by little. They began in the house with basic cleaning chores and kitchen work preparing meals. Myra soon learned Wynonna was strong and healthy despite what Jack had said to the contrary. The previous spring, Wynonna had planted a sizable vegetable garden close to the house. Soon she and Myra were out in the sun working and weeding, picking and cleaning the produce in a tub placed on the back porch. Often Wynonna cooked lunch for the workhands, too, but they ate away from the house, either out front at a table under the poplars or in the barn when it rained. Jack owned two Holstein cows and milking became Myra's first job every morning when she came up at sunrise. This allowed Wynonna flexible time in the morning to arrive later than usual, and she found this delightful.

Of course, Wynonna made a weekly pay, but Myra's parity was structured differently—considering Jack was paying her mortgage for the remaining duration. He adjusted her pay to compensate in the form of living expenses, clothing, and meals. He assured her that if she needed something extra, he would consider paying what was needed. For example, Myra went into town to Jenkins's store once per week to get her father's mail. In September, a property tax bill arrived from Lee County, and Jack agreed to pay, as it wasn't too much, only thirty-two dollars.

As time went, he continued pumping water from Myra's well to fill his tanks and pond. After further study, he installed a long, two inch diameter hose from the pipeline and dug furrows with the tractor to irrigate the corn rows. The corn was mostly for cattle feed, and the stalks at the top of the hill (those that had survived the brutally dry summer) were dressed with delicate golden tassels standing the corn about five feet tall—not too disgraceful considering the drought that had been in progress. In the end, the well saved what remained of the corn and the cattle too.

One evening, Jack and Myra sat on his front porch after the day had ended just before she left for home. She had finished her last chore of replacing all the spent candle sticks throughout the house and filling the oil lamps. He offered her a glass of tea and invited her to sit for a moment before she left. A dark storm front was rolling in from the west and thunder could be heard bellowing in the distance. On top of the hill where the house had been built, from the front porch which faced westward, gray slanting lines of rain such as linen threading could be seen miles off on the horizon.

They spoke briefly of such routine subjects as the corn crop, the cattle, Wynonna, and Myra's adjustment of working for him. The conversation soon faded and it became quiet. Crickets whirred, the sun was setting, and the breeze began to lift.

She was about to say goodbye when instead he spoke.

"Looks like heavy rain is coming tonight, don't it?" Jack chewed a chaw of Red Man and drank whiskey at the same time, never minding to spit in the spittoon much, Myra noticed.

"Sure does. We need it, though" she said.

"It'll cool things off," he added.

Jack Waylon slowly chewed his tobacco. He was a rough-cut countryman who liked simpler effects but had grown shrewd when it came to running his farm and business. Many farmers grew thick beards, refusing to shave especially during the busier summer months and through harvest. But Jack kept his face clean shaven which Myra thought was much more attractive, regardless, even if he was more than twice her age. He was stout with big arms and rough hands, a strong man apparently with a body like steel. And what could a little tobacco juice harm if he didn't spit, but rather swallowed instead sometimes?

"Look at that sky would you?" she said. She sat on the wooden bench and Jack in a side chair made of wicker with a cushion sewn by Wynonna. "Look at all those colors. Pink and purple, orange and red. Even gold and yellow. Almost all the colors of the rainbow out there."

"Pretty sight, ain't it?" He sipped his drink.

"Makes you wonder about God, don't you think? All of that beautiful out there he made for us. I suppose he loved us with all the attention he's paid to us down here. Considering the diversity in the world."

Jack sipped again. "We have a slice of it right here in Lee County, I have to agree. I'm appreciative."

"Me, too." She watched mocking birds in the tree tops, chasing one another, dancing through the leaves. "You ever think of God much? Ever give it much thought?"

He remained silent, thinking.

"Ever been to Mt. Olive? I've been going off and on since I was a child. Pa always took us when he could."

"No, never been to Mt. Olive, Myra."

"Why not?"

"I guess I have my own Bible in my own home."

"Do you ever pray?" Myra was introspective having recently lost her father.

"In a manner I do, I guess. I think and contemplate and wish good for people." This was the best he could say although it wasn't necessarily true. Sometimes he had trouble talking with people, and he didn't know why.

He chewed his tobacco and looked at her. He noticed her youthful face colored by the early evening light; her long silky hair that fell like a beautiful horse's mane over her shoulders; her striking eyes that were like jewels in a jeweler's display he once saw in Americus.

"I pray but not much ever comes of it," she said. "I don't know if God protects me or not. What do you think?"

He thought for a moment. "God protects those that protect themselves, I suppose. I reckon a man has to make amends when he checks out of here, though. I'd say that." Jack licked his lips and looked away into the late afternoon, seriously considering what he had done to Mac Grayson and how dark he knew he could get inside. Was there a possibility that could change, he thought? Under the right circumstances?

Jack had been an only child. When he was young, his father had allowed him little say so and would thrash him severely over the least infraction. Once during the winter of his twelfth year, his father told him he needed culture, that he was too awkward and unfinished. Jack had left school at an early age as many farm boys did to work on their family farms. But according to his father, it wasn't Jack's farm work that needed much help, just his refinement.

With this, his stubborn father had a music teacher come once per week. (As his father had been raised in a musical family and had learned the clarinet during the winter months of his younger years). His father told Jack about this, of him learning the clarinet when he was a young boy. Jack explained however that he didn't care much for music and such things. Yet, his father sat him in front of the fireplace in a wooden chair with a fiddle he'd bought and insisted that he learn to play the instrument or else. After this, following each workday, Jack wasn't allowed to leave the chair for any reason until bedtime except for supper, tending the fire, or to make water. For that entire winter, he took music lessons from the local teacher and attempted playing the fiddle but was unable to master it. By the end of that February on a Friday night, his father beat the hell out of him for failing and threw the fiddle in a closet—where it remained to that day alongside his father's clarinet gathering dust. At least his father eventually passed away and Jack inherited his farm.

"I think about God sometimes, but when I die, I hope I will meet my real mother in the way up yonder," Myra said.

Jack, of course, knew Myra had been informally adopted by the Graysons when she was three years of age. The entire community was aware of this. He said, "I hope so too, darling. That would be nice now wouldn't it?" In the shadows, he shook his head at this childish thought and frowned.

"You lived out here all your life?"

"Born and raised on this land. Born on my momma's bed upstairs. Began working this land since a young age. Been out working since I was knee high to a draft horse. The first job I had was milking our Holstein, Maggie. Of course she's gone now."

"I had a dog once. His name was Browny. He was an old hound of Maclin's."

"The one with the droopy eyes? I remember him. He got old, though, didn't he?"

She thought back, happy.

Just then the rain began falling, slowly at first then harder with heavier drops. It blew in on the front porch and they quickly stood as it came now in a sudden torrent.

"I better get going, Mr. Waylon!" The wind whipped up in the tree tops, sending leaves asunder. "Looks like bad weather is on the way! I have to go!"

"Alright, you take care!" he called out and watched her leave.

She ran quickly around the house and down the hill.

Just then, a boom of thunder burst in the distance, followed by streaks of lightning across the sky. The rain quickly built and came in a fierce rush, the sky turning from dark to black in moments. She bounded down the hill and almost fell as she could barely see. Over the fence and then the ridge, it only took a minute.

By the time she reached her cabin she was soaked, dripping wet and cold. Inside on the counter, she found a dry cloth and wiped it across her face. She had no fire in the stove, but she gathered what little dry kindling she had. With paper, she lit the kindling with a kerosene lighter though it was too little too late. Having spent so much time working at Jack's, she had neglected her own chores and her remaining wood was depleted.

Angry thunder clapped in the west and she cringed. Lightning lit the sky with fury, and the wind began to whistle then moan. After a minute the house began to creak with the powerful, shearing force of the wind against its sides. More thunder came and the ground shook, frightening her. Running into her room, she looked about then climbed under her bedframe and pulled the bedcover off, curling into it on the wooden floor. She felt her small, hard suitcase against her back, the one she had brought with her from Atlanta, the one with her mementos and things inside. She turned and held it to her chest, assured not to let it go.

More thunder rumbled, this time closer, and the house shuttered violently. She could hear the plates in the cabinet rattling. The cabinet doors swung open with the concussion of the thunderous roar, and ceramic plates fell out onto the cabin floor, smashing into pieces. She shrieked! Suddenly she heard the tremendously loud explosion of lightning striking nearby, and one of the red oaks outside the cabin came smashing down on the roof, collapsing it and crushing the ridge beam. Myra screamed! A massive limb crashed into her room with a tremendous force, the leaves and branches filling the space instantly, so quickly she could smell the distinct scent of rain mixed with tree bark and foliage. Tree branches bent in and struck her face, but she unsuccessfully attempted pushing them away.

The night was black, and the wind-driven rain began pouring into the cabin in waves, over the floor and her, too, under her bedframe. In a moment she was soaked, her head a mass of hair and leaves. Slowly she stumbled out with her suitcase from under the bed and clawed her way forward. She climbed through the tree, little by little, working her way over the rough branches and finally the trunk itself. She managed to make it to what remained of the front door and out into the horrid night.

She was ripped over with bloody scratches and debris, but she was grateful she'd made it out alive. The wind continued to shrill and scream through the trees. Momentarily, she glanced up and saw the clouds moving quickly overhead in the sky. More rain fell and stung her eyes. For a brief second looking upward, she caught a glimpse of the moon peeking through a slipstream of rushing clouds, but then it was gone again covered in black. Lightning lit the night white, and for an instant she could clearly see the crushed cabin and the monstrous oak on top of it. She let out a scream, turned, and ran back up the hill to Jack's while holding her suitcase.

Chapter 24

THE FOLLOWING DAY was clear and blue. Birds were singing in the trees and the morning heat was rising, but the ground remained sodden from the tornado the night before. A few trees were blown down along the ridge but fortunately none were lying across the road hindering access from Flintside. Trees branches and leaves were scattered everywhere across the ground at Jack's house, over his driveway and the hill toward the lake.

He followed Myra down to her property, and they stood for a moment in complete utter silence to observe the cabin's destruction. Myra turned, put her hands over her face and began to cry.

"Lord have mercy, Myra. I'm afraid it's gone," was all he could say.

The huge tree had fallen squarely through the cabin, crushing it in two. The tree's branches stretched out wide enough to extend past both ends of the house, making the house appear diminutive, like a doll's toy under the mass of trunk and limbs.

He added, "Myra, you were wondering about God last night, remember? Saying you didn't know if he was protecting you or not." He turned to look at her torn face. "Well, girl, there's your answer, cause you damn sure could of been killed." He shook his head in astonished dismay.

"But, Jack..." She faltered. "Can't we—"

"No, Myra, we couldn't. I'm sorry, darling, it's too gone. There ain't enough left. Hardly any walls left to begin with."

The stone chimney had fallen entirely backwards, so far back they couldn't see it from where they stood in front of the cabin.

He added, "Chimney's plum gone, too."

She cried softly.

He thought to himself that Myra and her family hadn't the money to replace the structure. Not now. The cost would be too exorbitant. But he didn't say this.

"I guess you'll be staying with me, darling. That's all there is to it." His arms were crossed on his chest. He knew the cabin wasn't good for much of anything now other than firewood. He wouldn't have said that, but he thought it.

"Wait," she said.

She slowly walked up the two remaining steps and climbed on her hands and knees into the front door then disappeared into the mass of leaves and limbs. Moments later Jack heard her say, "Jack! In here!"

He made his way in, following her voice. He crawled and stooped when he came into where Macklin's room had been at the end of the house. He saw Myra's small face in the shadows.

"Could you please help get this walnut cabinet away from the wall?" She pointed. He walked on his knees through the tree to Ila Mae's broken armoire.

She said, "We have to move this out of the way, Jack. There're important papers under it."

"Papers?"

"Yes, in a box. I'll show you." She attempted moving the heavy cabinet but it wouldn't budge.

"Here," he said. He turned and put his back against it. He shoved with his legs and the cabinet slid a foot until it halted at a downward tree branch. He turned and leaned his shoulder against it, turning out the cabinet further.

"There! Right there. Hold on." She slid the loose floorboard away and retracted Maclin's elephant box.

"These are my parent's papers in here."

He looked at the padlocked antique box and nodded his head. "Alright, good deal. It appears it's in good shape. No damage."

The partial roof over their heads was all that was left, the original roof now mostly nonexistent. The daylight was streaming into the room, shadows dancing over their faces under branches and the structure's broken frame. The interior wall of Maclin's room was still intact but the exterior one had fallen outward.

She knew how important and valuable the box was. It had contained Ila Mae's wedding ring (which was with Arden, wherever he had gone), the property deed granted to Samuel Adams (Maclin's grandfather), Nancy's Journal (Maclin's mother's writings of the Grayson family history), Ila's poems, and the Lee County Elegy originally penned by Ila Mae many years earlier, written for her deceased son, Paul, her first son before Arden.

Myra scrambled over to the fallen exterior wall, knowing the lock's key had been hidden atop the window frame. She quickly crawled out of the house. After a lengthy search of digging through the leaves, she located the shiny brass key.

She slipped it into her pocket. Jack came out behind her from what remained of the demolished house. He handed her the box, and they went around the front to have a last look.

He said, "Myra, this is the damnedest mess I've ever seen. I'm just glad you weren't hurt."

She stood with the elephant box in her hands, her face bruised and scratched, her arms shredded over from tree limbs, her cheek swollen, her hair a mess. But she was in one piece and alive. "I made it, Jack." She smiled weakly. Although she was excessively tired having slept little the previous night in one of Jack's spare rooms.

"I reckon we go back in there and get what we can cause you'll be staying with me and Wynonna, at least for the time being until you can figure something out. What do you say?"

"I suppose I don't have a choice. I'm sure I would be welcome at Jasper John's, but their house is about as big as shoe box."

Jack put in, "And you're working for me now, aren't you? That'd be a long walk from Jasper John's, anyway. I suppose you and Wynonna could maybe walk up together from town in the mornings if that were the case."

"Maybe she should stay with you, too."

"Wynonna's got Hezekiah. I don't think he'd approve o' that, do you?"

"I suppose he wouldn't."

"Well, then. . ."

They found what they could, a few wet clothes, a pair of old boots and such, about all she had. They walked up the road to the driveway, avoiding the direct route up the steep hillside.

When they arrived Wynonna was there.

She saw them coming up the drive and into the front yard where she stood hanging laundry on the clothesline. She said, "Oh my Lord, look who we got here. Mmmmm, look at you, girl." She tried to smile. "I guess life has a way of changing course with the least regard for what we might have to say about it."

She placed a bedlinen she was folding back in the basket and let Myra come into her arms while she cried and sobbed.

A few days later, Myra went into Flintside and down to Mr. Tullman's house. She found him in his backyard reading, sitting in a chair in the shade of a chestnut tree. She told him of her experience in the devastating tornado and that she was now living and working at Jack Waylon's. He explained he had been in Americus during the time of her father's funeral and regretted missing the service and seeing everyone. In addition, he assured her he had come down to her farm after his trip, but that she hadn't been there at the time, and he didn't know where to find her.

"I want you to know, Myra, I did the best I could to deal with J.R. Rutledge concerning your mortgage and the foreclosure notice."

"Well, it doesn't matter anymore, Mr. Tullman. Mr. Waylon made an agreement with the bank because he needed access to my property to set a well pump. With the drought, he hasn't been able to get groundwater up on his land, and I've allowed him onto mine to do so. When you came down to the farm, I was assuredly up at Jack's. I've been up there a good bit lately, working."

"He's drilled on your property? And he's run pipe up to his?"

"Yes sir, it was a fair deal the way I saw it. I could have lost my land, otherwise." She stood in a faded floral shift and the new ankle-high boots Jack had given her. Her hands were clasped as she spoke with the elderly man.

He set the book in his lap and removed his glasses. "Do you have anything in writing, Myra? With his equipment on your property and so forth? Has any timeframe been agreed to? In other words, do you know how long he plans to be there?"

"No, no paperwork has been done. I really didn't give that much consideration. I don't think it'll be a problem, though. Besides, it has been raining more and more, and I believe the drought may be coming to an end soon."

He paused and thought more. "You say he has paid the delinquent mortgage you owe to the bank?"

"Yes, sir."

"And what of the remaining payments?"

"He's going to pay them, too. There are only twenty more, but he's pleased with our agreement. He says he wants to assure he has access to plenty of water for his cattle and crops. He believes the drought could as well continue, and he doesn't want to risk it otherwise."

"As long as he lives up to his end of your verbal agreement."

"I believe he will."

"Well, I'm glad it has worked out in your favor. I believe your pa would be mighty proud of you. Sounds like you have a good business mind. You know I was very fond of your mother and father. I would help you in any capacity I could, if ever you needed me." He looked out reflectively into the large swath of woods behind his house, the continuation of the nine hundred acres that he owned. He said, "I'm glad no one was hurt in the tornado."

"It was one heck of a storm. Some trees are down along the road up from my property into Flintside, sure enough, but none that wouldn't allow access."

In addition, she explained that Arden and Cade had both gone missing. She told Mr. Tullman that in Arden's case, it was so unlike her brother because he was known to be a young man of staunch reliability and good judgement. Yet, understandably, she omitted the fact she was acutely aware of Cade killing the engineer, and that Cade had also relocated the survey markers further up the hill in the process—although she knew no further details about the man or what Cade had done with his body.

Obviously, she had been distraught over the occurrence: how quickly Cade had run in to grab a travel bag and wet clothes off the clothesline before leaving that fateful day. How he had been very brief as to what had taken place. And that he departed in a flash likely never to be seen again.

Now she held the constant fear the sheriff might arrive with a litany of questions she couldn't or wouldn't answer. She had sat on her bed many past nights, going over this again and again in her weary mind, biting her nails and praying for the best. Thus far, the lawman had not come, but he still could, she realized. She could only speculate if she would be connected as an accessory, or even an accomplice, eventually charged for withholding information, or hindering the police who would be in search of her brother.

Myra left and told the old lawyer she appreciated all the efforts he had made on their behalf.

"Alright, well, you take good care Myra," he told her. "And let me know if you need me. I should be here." He smiled and watched her go.

She departed his company and returned to Flintside.

While walking through town, she passed Bobby Womack in his drill truck leaving the lumberyard. His truck was loaded down with wood and tin roofing, and he noticed her coming up the road as he pulled out.

"Hey there, Myra. How you doing?" Sitting in his truck, he tipped his hat to her. His arm was hanging out of his truck window, and the light breeze blew back the dark curls of his hair as he slowed to a stop.

"Bobby, you look busy as usual. What are you working on today?" She cocked her hip out and rested her hand there, smiling.

"I'm working on Thomas Burch's house. You know he bought old man Barker's place, right? Down by the schoolhouse? Anyway, his roof's about to go. I'm hauling down some timber and roofing tin. I'm re-roofing the place. It must be a hundred years old."

He parked on the roadside, jumped out of the truck cab, and tightened the tie-downs to double-check that his load was secure. His suntanned arms worked the tie-downs, and she could see the muscles in his arms ripple. His big hands were scarred from much work, and sweat was damp on his cotton shirt. When he turned to look at her, he ran his hand through his hair, and she saw his intense deep eyes up close. He was a good bit taller, well over six feet.

He said, "Drilling is seasonal work, mostly in the warmer months during farming. I do construction off-season, masonry, carpentry, interior home finishing, cabinets and such, like I told you. It pays pretty good and I like it."

"You know your way around a toolbox, I bet."

"Well, I try to. I have a shop back at home with some tools, and hopefully the knowhow to use 'em."

She laughed. "I believe Jack Waylon might need your assistance. He has a few things that need tending to."

"He knows where to find me. I'm busy for the next few weeks. But he has Farnsworth and Dollar, right?"

"I suppose they're just farmhands. I don't know about fine carpentry and the like. Jack needs some cabinet work I think. His kitchen could use some help."

"That's a real fine home he has."

"It's real nice. A far reach from where I came from."

"Me too, Myra. That makes two of us." He smiled and revealed a straight line of good teeth. "Listen, I have to get going."

"Good seeing you. I'll see you around, Bobby."

"Nice seeing you, too, Myra. Take care of yourself."

He climbed in his truck and she watched him drive away.

Arden waited for weeks but hadn't heard back from Myra and Cade concerning the letter he had written, the letter he had entrusted Officer Crandall to deliver into the care of the U.S. postal service. Officer Crandall, however, had neglected his duty and had misplaced the letter. He rather gave little more thought to it, and instead, left the police department on medical leave for an extended period of time. Arden's apprehension was not only for himself but his family too. Knowing the bank was intending to foreclose weighed heavily on his mind almost as much as his own distress as to why they had not come to see about him.

Days passed in the dungeon of the police station with no word from the outside. Arnold Wiseman, the corrupt Leesburg mayor, had been retrieved back to Lee County from Sumter after having spent months in Americus awaiting transport. Arden had a new cell neighbor by the name of Richard Walker, in for burglary, but other than knowing of one another's offenses, they had spoken little. The more it rained, the more water came into his cell and filled the floor. Other cells were being affected too, but complaining to the staff went in one ear and out the other. Also, because of this, Arden's catch pot wasn't emptied as often as it should have been, and the basement stunk even more. Yet, the gold and diamond wedding band of Ila Mae's (the ring Mac had given him upon his departure from Lake Blackshear) remained on Arden's finger. It had remained there ever since visiting the gravesite of Ila Mae in the church cemetery. Otherwise, the police had confiscated his pistol, his money pouch, as well as his wagon and mules, Bess and Big Joe.

Arden complained whenever they brought the daily meal, but they assured him if he didn't quit, they would refuse him food. So his complaints had subsided into appreciation for what little food they allowed the prisoners to have. Time went on bitterly, and Arden had to bide until the situation could improve.

October came in with the hint of fall as the evenings cooled and days grew shorter. Rain was becoming more prevalent, and Myra watched the rain drops falling from her new bedroom window in the upstairs of Jack's house. She and Wynonna had re-arranged one of the guestrooms, threw fresh bedcovers on the bed, wiped down the window glass, and aired out the upstairs by opening the windows. Later, Jack and Myra rode to Desoto. Myra took her earnings and bought much needed clothing and a pair of shoes. Having suffered the failing cotton crop, Myra hadn't had the money to do so for quite some time.

Although she had lost her family and home, she was eager to move on with the prospect of a better future, for at least herself. She would dearly miss her father and brothers although she hoped Arden and Cade would one day return to gather again. Notwithstanding, she had also become resigned to the fact that her pa had actually been sick for years prior to his accident in the lumberyard. His upper respiratory issues with coughing and wheezing had probably come to fruition sooner than later with the complications of his broken back. Thus, his final ending had been greatly predicated on a lifestyle of excessive tobacco use and would have taken its toll either way. Rather chewing, chawing, dipping, snuffing, smoking cigars, pipes, or the occasional cigarette, Maclin had done himself in. Even in his last days while often preferring to smoke over eating a meal.

Her father had raised her with the word of the Bible, often reading from its pages after supper in front of a warm winter's fire. Once in earlier years he had made claim the fields were christened by the hands of their Savior, sun-ripened and sweetened by the first breath of autumn in the fertile land on the shores of Lake Blackshear. However, in the good years, before most was lost to misfortune and the cabin's roof caved in, the days were as prosperous as they were long. Well enough, although the land was difficult and the labor sometimes endless. Yet, the agricultural demise in the south due to infestation and drought had brought all of that to a grinding halt coupled with the onslaught of the Great Depression. Myra dearly missed her pa, having now lost much of her life, even her family. As a result of circumstances out of her control, she was now starting life anew on the wide-reaching land of Jack Waylon.

Jack was a busy man, tending to his farm and herd. Up at the crack of dawn and in the field with the rising sun, he was ever moving as raising livestock was a seven-day-per-week responsibility. This workload often ran late after supper, too, and in some cases to midnight. His life was hemmed in with an endless accountability for his herd, breeding, land, crops, business dealings, equipment, water needs, and employees. Not to mention the loneliness.

As a matter of practice, he traditionally hauled his trailer filled with cattle to sell at the stockyards down in Albany on a bi-yearly basis. However, the price of beef (as with all livestock) had fallen to historical lows. So he had preferred to hold his stock instead, hoping the market might soon improve. His vet was required to make calls more often than he wished as his cows were with endless needs and difficulties. He grew not only acres of corn, but Wynonna had reared a sizeable vegetable garden in the side yard and kept a chicken coop, too. Contractors often came and went; delivery and cargo trucks sometimes. Carter and Ben often made errands into Desoto for various requirements. Life was demanding and as a result, Jack often washed his long days down with corn whiskey while sitting on the front porch in the evening. Myra began joining him to talk as they were the only two left after Wynonna, Carter, and Ben had gone for the day.

Jack, initially, didn't know what to do with Myra. She was fairly well-educated and well-spoken in comparison to most her age in South Georgia. Mr. Burch was a good man and teacher. He had done his best as a county employee to run a schoolhouse properly. Most of the locals dropped out of school before the age of ten as farm duties took precedence over an extended education outside of basic reading and arithmetic. Myra, on the other hand had liked schooling, learning, and even reading. Her father had allowed the extension of her schooling beyond the age of ten until she was sixteen as he realized Myra was exceedingly bright and could one day benefit from it. However when she moved to Mr. Waylon's to work, she determined she had gone as far with school as she desired. She informed Mr. Burch of this and though he was disappointed, he wished her well with her working ambitions. He told her she would be missed around the schoolhouse as she had been one of his brightest students.

From the beginning, she took on more than Jack anticipated she might, as he soon learned she was not only capable but smart as well. Outside of her chores alongside Wynonna in the house and garden, she soon began taking on more of a management role, more out of inadvertent necessity as Jack was so busy attempting to stay above water with running his farm. On one occasion, Jack had a mechanical problem with his truck while in Albany and was delayed in returning for an appointment with Bobby Womack, the well driller/ pump repair man. Myra managed the repair issue and the payment to Bobby, as she knew where Jack kept his on-hand cash: in a metal tin, bottom drawer of his desk in his office.

One afternoon while Jack was in Desoto with Carter and Ben, Myra watched a fox burrow under the wall into the chicken coop. She went for one of Jack's shotguns, loaded it, and stepped out to shoot the varmint in the act. Wynonna was frightened by both the animal and gun, having never shot a gun before, so Myra took care of the situation. When Jack returned later that afternoon, the dead fox was hanging by a nail on the back porch.

On another occasion when Jack was off the farm, a washing machine salesman arrived at the front door and made a demonstration for her while Wynonna shied away and remained in the house. Myra, having tired of washing much laundry herself, negotiated with the salesman on the spot and talked him down from his original asking price of $45.00 to $36.50. She immediately ran to Jack's office and cleaned out his money tin. They set up the manual machine on the back porch by the table and were soon doing loads of laundry. Later, following his return from Desoto, Jack became furious as Myra had taken the liberty with the decision and the money to buy the machine. However Wynonna praised her, and they showed Jack how well it worked. This household addition soon proved to be very efficient and time-saving, not to mention easier, and Jack became enamored with Myra's abilities, wits, and good decision-making.

After hours, Jack sipped his whiskey, and Myra took up needlepoint as Ella Tucker sometimes came to visit and she showed her how. On the front porch, Jack and Myra began conversing as the nights grew cooler and the sight of autumn soon arrived in full color. Carter and Ben kept the woodpile high, and fires were soon blazing in one or more of the fireplaces located throughout the farmhouse. Wynonna often tended to them just before leaving for the day to walk back home on the other end of Flintside. The addition of having Myra on the farm had allowed Wynonna to slow her pace which she relished. She soon began arriving later in the mornings and leaving earlier in the evenings. Times had changed on the Waylon farm, and Jack was glad of that.

Upon one particular visit by Ella when she came to needlepoint with Myra, Jack was off the farm. (Earlier, Jack had set up a table and large oil lamps where they could work). This afternoon Myra made ginger tea and scones to have for their fellowship, and they sat contently talking about various subjects. Ella mentioned she was originally from Leesburg and had met Jasper John at a town hall meeting of locals. Furthermore, she expressed they had never conceived a child but were unaware of the reasons why.

Then Ella revealed a secret truth to Myra, one she had withheld from the community for many years. She told her that initially she and Jasper John were to have taken in Myra as the adoptees, but that they were unable as she had been plagued by medical issues and expenses the previous year. As a part of this decision, Maclin, in the last days, offered and agreed to the placement instead, even hours before Myra's arrival by train. Otherwise, under different circumstances, Ella told that Myra would have belonged to her and Jasper John, not Maclin and Ila Mae. Myra cried at this revelation and expressed her thankfulness either way.

They needlepointed and ate their scones, sipped their tea then set their work aside for a break. After Myra returned with more scones, Ella told her more about her family; that she had family as far away as

Lexington, Kentucky and in Chattanooga, Tennessee, too, but that she had lost touch with them over the years as they were so far away. As a last mention, she told Myra of the strangest event that had recently happened to her immediate family in Leesburg. Myra asked what it could be, and Ella told her the story.

Ella mentioned this occurrence almost as an afterthought.

She had a second cousin on her mother's side that lived in Leesburg but had strangely disappeared—and no one knew where he had gone or what had happened to him. Ella said the family had contacted the police department and they issued a wall bulletin for the missing man. But as of that time, he hadn't been located and had rather disappeared into thin air. Both Ella and Myra agreed that due to the disastrous economy, the stories of people gone missing had become commonplace. Yet, Ella insisted she had heard that her cousin was stable and gainfully employed.

Myra asked, and Ella said his name was Beau Browning, an employee with the county, although she did not articulate in what capacity because she didn't know. Myra said she had never heard that name before, and that it was a shame this had happened. Myra asked and Ella had replied that her maiden name was, indeed, *Browning.* Myra paid this no more attention and shrugged it off. She went to the kitchen for more tea and never heard another word about it. She was unaware, and the reality never occurred to her, who was Beau Browning?

Chapter 25

CADE FOUND A squatter's camp, a homeless community of sorts where he could live under the viaduct and railroad bridges on the north end of town. The week before, he had attempted unloading the freight truck in an hour for a dollar as the foreman had offered. But the job had taken well over three instead, and, in the end he had been paid only fifty cents for his work. This left him exhausted as the previous night he'd stayed up all night standing on the train that had been stopped on the tracks awaiting entry into Atlanta.

Soon after arriving in Atlanta, he located where and when the bread and soup lines began, so he spent much of his time waiting in them. Later in the week, he had fortuitously landed a job shoveling coal into the flatwork furnaces at Atlantic Steel, but working eighty arduous hours a week for such meager pay was growing tiresome. He would arrive back at the homeless community late at night to wash in the nearby creek and hang his washed clothes over a makeshift clothesline. In his only change of clothes, he stood with others around metal drums of fire, spit-roasting any meat he could get which was often fatback or ham hock he bought at the backdoor of the butcher's shop. The community had a leader by the name of Sam the Man, and he owned a large pot he cooked rice in, and many paid for a bowl in the evening to accompany whatever else they had to eat.

Cade constructed a makeshift hovel out of plank wood and a sheet of corrugated tin. He located these materials in the city dump which was just under the railroad bridge leading into the marshy end of town where the coloreds lived. He was able to afford a handful of nails at a hardware store to begin the project. He built the two-wall structure in the inside corner at the rear of two adjoined buildings that faced the street above the viaduct. One of the building's basements served as the steam laundry for the local hospital across the street. A steel vent pipe from the boiler's feed tank ran out of the building and up the exterior wall to the roof where it vented its steam. As a measure of survival, Cade had constructed his shack so that the hot steam pipe ran through it by notching out the metal roof. This served as a heat source and later proved to be helpful in the colder evenings as fall set in.

One evening he returned from the steel mill and found his only pair of spare clothes stolen. He was forced to wash his filthy, soot-caked overalls in the creek then stand near-naked, wrapped in his threadbare blanket at the fire until he could afford a new set of clothes. Until then, his washed-pair were still damp in the mornings when he left for the mill. Fights often broke out and he stayed well away, however, in one case he had to fend for himself one night when an old man attempted stealing his supper as he had stepped away from his spit on the fire to relieve himself in the shadows.

Life was hard living hungry and lonely in the bowels of the city, yet he feared what his status could be. If the law might be searching for him, or if they had located the survey man's body buried in the ditch at the railroad siding. All in all, he hoped what he had done could help his family. He had relocated the property markers in their favor as the McCravers had passed away. Imminently, the county would have taken the land, otherwise, to sell at auction after the probated case was closed. Thus, what matter did it make? He had done what he had. Now he was on his own which had been his dream to begin with. At the moment he struggled, but he soon hoped to get back on his feet. However, for the time being he was shoveling coal at the steel mill.

Sunday evening came. Myra had read away most of the rainy afternoon while lying in bed in her upstairs bedroom. The house was so large and she essentially had the entire upstairs to herself. She had never lived so comfortably. After reading, she made supper and Jack came to eat. She hadn't seen him much that day, had only heard him in the house and out in the barn while tinkering. When he came in the kitchen, he brought a handful of wildflowers he had picked in the field and presented them to her.

"Jack, thank you. That's sweet," she said more in actual appreciation than as a formal curtesy. He had been so good helping her, to get her on her feet.

"I thought a table setting would be nice," he remarked as she put them in a vase with water.

"I want to thank you for all you have done," she said when she turned and placed them in the center of the table.

He held her arm and smiled. She could smell the scent of whiskey on his breath, but she didn't hold it against him. He was a hard-working man and had caused her no harm. He had been generous with his time and resources, his home and land, his financial support most of all even though he had taken water from her land and benefited from it.

"My pleasure, Myra," he said.

She thought she noticed a gleam in his eye, yet he went and sat at the table to eat. Later they retired to the porch and she picked up her nightly needlepointing. Jack usually provided good conversation and was generally talkative although she felt awkward in the sense that he was so much older than she.

Later in the week she ran into her friend, Lena Hardwick, a girl she knew from school. They met by the road in the center of town in front of Jenkins's store, Myra having ridden a mule in to pick up groceries, Lena having done the same to visit the boot shop. They lashed their mules to a hitching rack and stopped to speak. Myra thanked her for attending her father's funeral, and Lena assured Myra she would come out and visit from time to time when she had the chance. Myra updated Lena, however, on the cabin having been demolished in the tornado, her new work arrangements, and now living at Jack Waylon's.

Myra although expressed her apprehensions with Lena of the disparity between their ages, but how comfortable, nevertheless, Jack had made her. What was she to have done, she innocently proposed to Lena? She would have been otherwise homeless, and Jack had been generous considering the situation—more put on the spot, Myra actually felt, as one day she had had a home and the next it lay destroyed in pieces on her property. Where could she have gone, she asked her friend? What else could Jack have said? But Lena could offer no solution. Therefore, Lena agreed Myra couldn't have done any more considering the circumstances. Lena had been up to Desoto and Americus with her father, she told Myra, and had seen the devastation, the dispossessed, and the businesses boarded-up. Times were hard.

"By any means possible," Lena told Myra. "Lots are in bad situations, and it is difficult to survive they say. Times are hard. You must do what you can."

"I suppose I have. Actually, it's been real nice. I must admit that his house is so comfortable and warm. There's a small bathtub to pour hot water into, water that Wynonna heats on a fire pit outside the house. The bed is so comfortable too, not just corn shucks or anything like that, but a real mattress. He has plenty of chickens, milking cows, and a big garden. Turnip greens and collards are coming in, and down in the cellar we keep smoked pork fat handy for seasoning. He has plenty of tender beef steak too that he salts in the smokehouse. He's a good cook himself, I have to admit. Probably better than I am." She giggled.

"Well that sounds good, Myra. I'm glad things are working out for you. You know my grandfather sold his land right before the big crash and got top dollar they say. Now the whole family lives with my uncle, my father's brother. He has a large house up in Cobb and I'm doing well, thank you. My Uncle Harris favors me, I know, cause he's always holding on to me and such, making sure I'm being taken care of."

She turned to glance over her shoulder then whispered, "I help him out and rub him and his back too when it's sore as he has back ailments and such, and he usually gives me a dime for it." She laughed and clasped her hands together. "So far so good is what I say. My father still works at the Lockhart textile mill up in Americus, although they cut his hours, but he's still gone working a lot. You know my mama passed away a few years back and now my aunt's sick, too." She smiled. "But listen, a girl does what a girl must, isn't that right?"

To that Myra replied, "I'm working hard and tryin' to make my keep, that's for sure. Jack has been so nice and things are looking good. So far so good, like you say."

"Does he have any wife or children?"

"Why no, he's never been married. At least that's what his help told me."

"His help?"

"Wynonna. She comes five or six days a week and does cooking and cleaning."

"Listen girl, you work it, alright? Sounds like you're in good so stay where you are. I'm under a dry, warm roof myself. Where we use to live, the walls were thin with no insulation and it was so cold on winter nights. Now at my uncle's house, it's snug as a bug in a rug, I'll tell you. I ain't goin' anywhere, and I'll do what needs doing in the meanwhile. We have firewood, hot water in a tub, mules to ride, three meals a day and sometimes wine, too."

Lena was an attractive brunette with crystal blue eyes and soft por-
celain skin such as a store-bought doll in a merchant's window up in
Americus. She possessed beautiful teeth as white as Staffordshire ceramic that lit up when she smiled, and a contagious laugh, too, that
everyone noticed. Myra, with long flowing hair and jade-green eyes, was
as much a picturesque pose as Lena, with her striking looks and graceful
lines. The two young girls stood in the center of Flintside, and men both
young and old were turning to see them.

Just then Carter Farnsworth came into town driving Mr. Waylon's
short bed, and he stopped in front of the lumberyard to run inside.
Moments later he emerged with a paper sack of goods. As he was opening
the door, he glanced up and noticed Myra and Lena standing in the street.

Lena was just whispering, "Who's that? He's right handsome don't
you think?"

Myra said, "Oh, that's just Carter. He works for Mr. Waylon, you
know."

Myra watched and he drove over, rolling down the truck window.

"Hey there, ladies," he said, tipping his cowboy hat.

"Carter, what are you doing in town?" Myra asked. Lena smiled too.

"Just getting some hardware. A little project I'm working on. Staying
busy." He put his arm on the window frame and flashed a smile.

"Doing what?" she asked.

"Working on the stovepipe in Jack's kitchen. The flashing needs
repairing up on the roof."

"Speaking of the stove, did you smell Wynonna's crackling cornbread this morning?"

"Mmmm, I sure did."

"I'd like a piece of that with some butter, it smelled so good."

His face brightened. After a long pause, he replied, "I'd like a *nice
little piece of that, too.*" He smiled slyly as he looked her up and down.

Their eyes met and he held her gaze, but she quickly looked down and made no reply.

"How does that sound?" he asked.

She glanced away and laughed but remained silent, at a loss for words. Lena looked at them both and smiled during the awkward lull.

"I'll see you around," he said, smiling and tipping his hat.

He drove away, waving at the two young ladies.

"Well, he sounds like the flirty type," Lena said.

"I really don't know him, but he's been working for Jack Waylon a long time. I know that." She watched him drive away out of town.

"I bet it's a good job he has. Mr. Waylon has a big farm and lots of cattle. I wish my brother up in Nashville could get a job like that. He worked at a horse farm, but lost it not long ago. Nobody's buying fine quarter horses anymore. Not in this economy, anyway."

"Lots are out of work, I know."

They went into the shade of the boot shop's awning to get out of the sun. Lena wiped her forehead with the back of her hand. Myra unbuttoned her blouse a few buttons and opened her collar.

Lena said, "Did you know Myrtle Strickland and her folks were evicted and lost their home because they fired Mr. Strickland at the flour mill? I hear the bank foreclosed and now they're up in Mr. Parson's barn, living in the hayloft. With hardly a stich of a blanket or a bed, without an outhouse nearby. Nowhere to make a fire, either. Ain't got any food they say, so Mr. Strickland has done his best to hunt up game, but now he's taken sick, too. Mr. Parsons is a widower and retired from the school system up in Desoto. It's a pretty bad situation too up there, I hear."

Myra swallowed hard and attempted hiding her astonishment for the blatant reason she'd been so close to the same fate as Myrtle, whom she well knew from Mr. Burch's schoolhouse. Myrtle so close yet so far away, now.

Both girls agreed school was now a pastime, and that other fulfill-
ments required their attention at the moment. Although, in addition,
they spoke of the fun and friends they had met there. Myra reminded
Lena of the yearly square dances in Desoto they had attended, and the
boys they had encountered there, too. Both specifically agreed on their
earlier spring trip that year, that the night had been fun. In turn, Lena
mentioned the Jackson boy she met, and Myra chimed in mentioning
the Tanner boy likewise. Myra told her the dance had been enjoyable,
but she explained she only gave the Tanner boy kissing and cheap feels
in the last minutes of the night before boarding Mr. Burch's truck with
the others to return home. On the return trip, Myra had whispered to
Lena what she had heard secondhand about the means of schoolboys
and their sexual compunctions, but that she hadn't succumbed to one
yet. Yet, Lena rolled her eyes and added that it depended on the young
man in question. And she told Myra what she had done to the Jackson
boy earlier that night behind the town hall which left Myra looking
away, speechless. Over time, however, Myra had begun to understand
that things such as this took place. Now she was less shocked when she
heard such tales from her friend Lena.

Both waved goodbye and promised to catch up later.

Myra left Flintside to return to the farm. She rode her mule on the
dirt road in the early evening light, alone among the trees bent over the
road. The eastern sky was bruised purple-black and the west was colored
yellow-gold as the sun set. Myra felt empty and filled in the same breath,
having lost so much yet having gained such promise, too. Relieved that
she was under a strong roof, assured she wouldn't have to perform weird
acts such as Lena with her uncle or scrounge like Myrtle while living
in a livestock barn. Myra also carried with her a sense of want for she
remained detached, a single entity in a lone orbit such as a distant moon
in the evening sky. Cast astray into wayward obscurity without her roots
or a means by which to reach back.

What of her brothers and their lives now? What had taken place? Why hadn't someone written to her? Without someone, Myra knew she would become impoverished, not by lack of necessities to live but the necessity to be loved. Thrown into loneliness rather than solitude, which is a much graver fate. At least she had a home now, even work, even Wynonna and Jack, but solitude would encompass her until the sun could shine no more if she couldn't find someone. As the days went, she visited the grave of her father and cried for him and his fatal ending, how he had gone on that early morning without a word to her. She had discovered him lying dead in his bed, not a breath left in him as he stared into eternity far away from this world.

When she reached the farm, she rode into the barn, stalled her mule, and walked into the house. The place was quiet. She went and found Jack playing solitaire in his den, drinking his evening whiskey. She came in and smiled. But he could measure the sadness in her eyes.

They looked at one another for a moment in silence.

"Myra, why don't we play some cards?" he said.

She thought, why not, so she sat and he dealt out a hand of hearts. They played round after round, and he spoke of his family, his mother and father. He told her of his time growing up on the farm. He explained that his father had forced him as a child to play the fiddle, although he had despised the instrument and swore he couldn't get a good sound out of the thing even after months of practice. He told her of his days in his youth and how he had learned to ride and break horses. He had even been on a rodeo circuit through Georgia and Alabama years back, he told her; in his younger years, in his prime. He explained this was how he received a permanent limp due to a severe bull riding injury. With this, she told him she noticed that he sometimes limped, and she'd wondered why.

As the evening progressed, he displayed his ability to perform magical card tricks, and she was astonished at how many ways he could fool her and pick her card every time from anywhere in the deck. In one display, he showed her his slight-of-hand trick, with three cards he tossed in front of her on the table. But no matter how hard she tried, Myra couldn't guess the right card. One peculiar trick he performed, he slid a card into a small box, but when he opened the box it was gone, yet the next time it was astonishingly in the box again. He asked her to take the card, and when she reached her fingers in, he quickly snapped the box shut before she could, startling her, causing her to hoot with laugher. When he opened the box once more, the card had again disappeared until he slowly withdrew it out from under Myra's chair cushion and she gasped. How in the name of her Savior had he done this? She was at a complete loss. But she demanded he tell her his secret. He laughed and firmly assured her that he was done for the evening although she wanted more.

The light from the oil lamp was dim and the golden hue cast shadows on his handsome face. Although older, he was a good looking man she had to admit, with a defined jawline, square cleft chin, and wideset intelligent blue eyes. His shoulders were strong and rounded yet trim. His hands looked familiar to her though she didn't know why as she watched him holding the playing cards. The way he looked at her caught her off-guard. For a fleeting moment she thought she was looking at Cade of all people. She had never noticed this, and it was strange observing him in the dim light of the oil lamp. She blinked and looked once more. He cocked his head questioningly, but rather sipped his drink and remained silent. Was her mind playing tricks on her just as his card games had? She blinked rapidly and refocused his face. Had it been so long since she had seen Cade that she was hallucinating, wishing him there? Maybe she was tired; had had a long day of work on the farm.

"What is it Myra?" he finally asked.

"Nothing," she said although she kept her eyes on him.

Jack went to the kitchen and poured another whiskey. She looked suspiciously at the deck of cards but found nothing out of the ordinary.

Later, she left for her room and read by lamp light on her bedside table before falling asleep.

Out from the afternoon sun, Carter took the mules and fed them in the barn after a day of working the fence line, handling repairs. The tornado had downed some trees on a section of fencing in the west field. The previous day, he and Ben had been out with the saw cutting the trees away. Yet on this day Ben had taken a sick day, and Carter was picking up the slack with the work that needed doing. He put the mules in their stalls and fed them. After drinking from his water canteen, he stood in the open barn doors to see Myra coming out of the farmhouse. She strode across the barnyard while holding a small box of tools she had used to repair a latch on the kitchen's pantry door.

"Oh, hey there," she said, startled when she came into the barn. "I thought you were out working on the fence today."

"I'm done with that job," he said, hanging two bridles on their hooks by the tack and gear.

"Get all the fence rails back on?"

"Yep, fence repairs today. Probably mechanic work tomorrow on that damned short bed. I fixed the head, now it's idling rough so I'll have to take care of that next. The well pump transfer pipe is leaking again, too. I'll have to get down on the hill and take some big wrenches with me—probably needs a new pipe union, I think." He wiped his face with a towel.

"How about you?" he asked.

"In the house, dusting and waxing furniture." She followed Carter into the big storage room and returned the tools to the large tool chest under the shelves.

He retrieved his hat and backpack which he usually carried with him from home every day. He turned and said, "Must be nice in that cool house doing light work. I been out in the sun working my ass off."

"I guess that's why you make the big pay seeing as you're the top hand around here." She smiled.

"I heard about that new washing machine. Wynonna said you bought it yourself with Mr. Waylon's money. Even without his approval."

"He's glad I did now because it works so much better than washing by hand. It saves a good amount of work and time, too, and I think he's pleased with it."

Carter stepped over, facing her. He said, "It's been nice having you around, Myra. Jack seems a little more at ease these days. I think you've taken some of the worry off his shoulders with him being so busy."

"Wynonna does her part, too."

He could see her modesty.

Implying credit toward Wynonna, she added, "She's showing me around. She's been working on this farm for many years. I'm just her apprentice."

"Well, in all those years, she's never had any say-so like you." He was adjusting his backpack straps, ready to slip them on.

"That's not true." She watched him. "She's just a little shy."

"I noticed you sure ain't, though" he said, smiling devilishly. He took a slow step forward.

Myra noticed his good looks in a hard kind of way, the way he had scars on his hands and even his face from a tough life. His small eyes were dark as coal, flat under his square forehead and thin brow line; his temples smooth like stone; jaw perfectly angled, his beard black and closely shaven.

"Maybe you could go out with me next time in the back field to mend the fence. We could get out and away from the house for a little while. Out from under Jack's thumb. What do you think?"

He looked her up and down. Saw a timid inflection in her face, one he'd never noticed before.

"Well, I not sure what for."

He stepped closer, his broad chest almost touching her face. He let the pack slip out of his hand to the ground. He bent his face down to hers, but she quickly turned away and looked at the barn wall, still as a rabbit in the briar.

"Come on now. Don't you know a handsome man when you see one?" he said quietly, reaching out and gently taking her shoulders in his big hands. "Come on, now. How about a little kiss?"

She pulled back, suddenly surprised, but he restrained her in his grasp. "Myra, now be sweet with me," he said softly.

"Carter! Stop this." She pulled back but he wouldn't release her.

He rather took her in his arms and attempted kissing her again, but she whipped her head aside and inadvertently butted him in the nose, drawing a few drops of blood.

"Stop it, Carter! What are you doing?"

At that very moment, Jack appeared in the storage room doorway.

"Carter! What in the hell do you think you're up to?"

Carter's arms fell to his side, and he shrugged disappointedly. "Jack? What's wrong?"

Myra quickly stepped away and stood by Jack.

"What's wrong? What do you think?"

"Myra and me was just talking that's all." He licked his lips nervously, wiped blood away from under his nose with the back of his hand. "Just getting along that's all."

Jack looked at Myra momentarily. He turned back toward Carter and said, "You better watch yourself, son."

"I didn't do anything wrong, Jack. She's just a little country girl. Been making eyes at me all along."

"Myra said, "Not hardly. Maybe in your imagination I have." She backed up a few more steps through the wide door and stood outside the storage room.

Jack turned to her. "You go on back inside, Myra. I'll take care of this. It won't happen again. You go on, now." He nodded out toward the barnyard. She left, flipping her long hair off her shoulders as she went.

Jack slowly approached Carter. "You best watch yourself, Farnsworth. If ever I hear of you pulling something like this again, I will send you packing. You understand me?"

"Jack, we was just—"

"—Don't give me that line of bullshit, Carter. I saw what was happening." His face reddened at his employee's audacity to attempt relegating the circumstances.

He turned, strode out of the storage room into the barn. Carter reluctantly followed. Jack placed his hand against the barn wall by where the tack hung. He leaned forward and looked down, frowning. "Carter, what in the hell would Laura think? What the hell would she do if she ever caught you? Well, let me tell you. Your ass would get kicked out of your rental, that's what." He finally looked up.

"Jack—"

"—Shut the hell up and listen to me." He crossed his arms. "If I ever hear of this again, your ass is fired. Then what? Huh? You won't have a job that's what. And jobs are damned hard to come by these days, ain't they? Before long, you, Laura, and your two little ones are gonna be out walkin' the road without food or shelter. Am I right? And you won't come begging back up here with me. No sir. I won't allow it. You're gonna be out on the road or riding the damned rails, you and your family. Do you want that?" He stared unwaveringly at his employee.

"No sir, I don't," Carter said, capitulating, tightening his lips and swallowing hard. "No, sir."

Jack pointed his finger in Carter's face, shaking it. "You better watch out, son."

"Well, Jack. Do you remember how we covered for you at the lumberyard? I didn't say anything about that, did I? I saw you back your truck up and ram that pile of timbers that keeled over onto Mac Grayson."

Jack violently grabbed Carter by his shirt and pulled him forward where they stood eye to eye. "You better keep your damned mouth shut, Farnsworth, seeing as how I write your paycheck. Any word about that and you'll never step foot back on this property. Do you hear me? You think about your job here and what it means for your wife and children."

"I've worked for you now almost ten years, Jack."

"Well, let's keep it that way. You working for me and not out walking the highway. From the way it looks, you make damn good pay considering this economy. They say it's never been this bad, and I ain't sold a head of beef in ten months."

"But come on, now. Ten years I've been here, so how does this little scat already have seniority over me?"

"She don't. But, just watch yourself. Let this be a warning." Jack turned and left Carter breaking a sweat in the shade of the barn.

Chapter 26

A COOL MORNING came when two officers brought Arden out of his cell and up to the courthouse. He squinted when the sunlight hit his eyes. In cuffs and leg irons, he was led across a backstreet into another building to the courtroom.

He was placed at a table in front of the presiding Judge Henry Lucas, a district court judge of Sumter County. Arden was taken aback when, from a side door, in walked Cotter Rye and two older men, Cotter Rye being the young man he had met in the restaurant and had also attempted shooting. Cotter refused to look at him. Rather he was nicely dressed, clean shaven and sober, much different from when Arden had last seen him.

The judge said, "Mr. Grayson, we have gathered here today to bring your case to court."

Arden began to speak, but the judge shut him up.

The judge said, "Mr. Grayson, you shall only speak when asked to. Understood?"

Arden had no choice but to stare contemptuously.

The judge continued. "We haven't the money currently to afford a public defender. The ones we have remaining haven't been paid in a month, so you can guess what has happened to the rest. Knowing these circumstances, today we are considering this an informal *arbitration, not a formal court hearing.*" He coughed and took a long sip of water. "Mr.

Grayson, we have here today Mr. Cotter Rye and his father who is a long-standing local merchant in town."

He nodded and winked toward the two of them sitting at the opposing table. "We also have here with us Mr. Chester McCall, the owner of the blacksmith shop where the crime occurred. Now, according to Cotter, you attempted robbing him at gunpoint and shot him in the leg in the process. Fortunately, the bullet just grazed him and he was generally unharmed, however, this certainly doesn't alleviate any responsibility from your part. What have you to say? Please stand and state your case, but first tell us why you were in Americus."

Arden stood and Cotter finally met his eye but quickly glanced away. Arden first explained his business of coming to retrieve his mother but that she had died by the time he arrived. After this he went on to say, "I met Mr. Rye at a restaurant named The Overland. We sat next to each other in the back and struck up a conversation. I told him I was from down around Lake Blackshear and he told me he was a vehicle mechanic here in town. I noticed him drinking a bottle of corn whiskey and that he was drunk, and he told me—"

"—My son's never been drunk, Judge Lucas. I don't believe he's ever taken a drop of whiskey in his life." Cotter's father was now standing behind their table with his hat in his hand. "This young man is going to stand here and make up a whole line of bull it looks like to me, now isn't he?"

Judge Lucas said, "Dallas, he has a right to state his case. We must listen to what he has to testify. Now have a seat and hold on." He nodded again at Dallas Rye and turned toward Arden. "Go ahead, son."

"Like I said, I met him at The Overland, and we just got to talking. You see, my father had a suspicious accident at the Big River Lumberyard down in Flintside some months back where a stack of heavy lumber was caused to fall on top of him. This almost killed him, but instead, it severely paralyzed him. Which I don't know could be worse—to be dead or paralyzed."

Arden nodded toward Cotter and added, "In our conversation, Cotter happened to mention he had heard of a man down near Flintside that had had a very similar accident. But Cotter said he heard this account from his very uncle who, as it turns out, happens to work in Flintside for my neighbor, Jack Waylon. And Jack Waylon I have known for many years. Not realizing I knew Jack Waylon, Cotter explained to me that he was told by his uncle that it was *not an accident* after all but that it was *done intentionally*. Once I let on to Cotter that I was highly interested in his story of this attempted murder, he suddenly became aware that I might be connected to the victim involved and that he had said too much. So he chose to leave the restaurant rather quickly in order to avoid me and any further questioning. However, *seeing as how this was my father that Cotter was talking about*, I wanted to know more. But he ran away, such as an accomplish would who was withholding information in a criminal investigation—"

"—Hold on a damned minute, Henry," Dallas said to Judge Lucas. "This is all talk. Is this the contrived imagination of a deranged idiot here, or what? Can you believe all this horse manure? Who could?"

Judge Lucas rose from his bench and pointed at Mr. Rye. "Dallas, hold on a minute. You can't have these outbursts in my courtroom, now. Sit down or I'll have you removed."

"Henry, come on, now," he implied more softly as he took his seat. "You and I go way back."

"I know Dallas, but I've warned you. This is a court of law, here."

The judge looked toward Arden then back to Mr. McCall who sat beside Dallas and his son, Cotter.

"Mr. McCall. What do you say?"

"Yes sir, I was walking out of my shop over on Simpson Street and I saw the whole thing. This man over there pulled his gun and shot at

Cotter here while he was running away. He tried to shoot Cotter in the back like a coward would, I think. For what reason, I'm not too sure. I'm not aware of any robbery attempt. But sure enough, *he attempted shooting him*. I saw that much."

The judge said to Arden, "Son, this is about it. This is all we have. It's your word against the victim's. It looks like this witness, Mr. McCall, saw the shooting. Regardless of the reasons involved, outside of self-defense, I see this as an attempted murder in the second degree. For this, I'm charging you, and your sentencing trial will be held sometime later. Then the county will make arrangements to have you transported to the state penitentiary in Atlanta. But at the rate we are going, it may be a long time before we can get you back in court and then up to Atlanta. So, Mr. Grayson, it appears as though you're going to remain our guest for a while longer."

Arden stood and slammed his fist on the table where he sat. "This man has information about the attempted murder of my father! What are you going to do about that?"

"Bailiff!" the judge called.

The bailiff and another officer removed Arden from the courtroom and returned him to his cell in the jail basement. Having already served much time in the county jail, Arden was devastated by his circumstances. How had he not been allowed some form of legal counsel? How could a judge charge him for a felony crime that had not been tried with a proper jury in a court of law? What were his options, if any? And lastly, why hadn't his father or anyone else responded to the letter he had sent through Officer Crandall weeks prior? Arden had no choice but to return to his filthy cell to await word and help.

As Dallas and Cotter left the courtroom, his father whispered quietly, "Never again mention to anyone anything about Uncle Ben down in Flintside working for Jack Waylon. Your mother would have another

fit if her brother's name ever came up in any conversations again. You
better keep your mouth shut from now on."

Saturday morning, Myra informed Jack it was her seventeenth birthday.
When she told him, they were at the breakfast table, just the two of
them. He had smiled, even laughed, and wished her a happy birthday.
He told her however, she should have given them advanced notice. Jack
drove Wynonna into town for a special treat, and that afternoon she
made a maple syrup cake with delicious creamed vanilla frosting and
candles on top. Later in the day, Jack and Myra drove into Flintside to
drop off Wynonna then to the Wayside Inn in Desoto for dinner. Myra
felt strange being escorted by such an older man, appearing to be her
father or an uncle, but he was jovial and polite, even funny, which as-
suaged their age difference. After all, he was forty-two and she only
seventeen.

On Sunday afternoon, Jack sat on the front porch in his wicker
chair with his whiskey bottle, glass tumbler, and a Cuban cigar. Autumn
was in the air, and leaves from the poplars around the farmhouse were
falling in full color. Overhead the sky was flat and thick with cloud,
slated iron-gray in every direction. Birds by the hundreds were darting
through the trees, readying to fly south for the winter. With little left
to do, Myra walked through the fields past the cattle and the pond that
was now full from being pumped with well water. In the distance the
far tree line ran with the horizon from north to south. She thought she
would walk out and see the land for the first time. After a long way
she crossed the three-rail fence that lined the pasture. She followed
the creek and walked its banks into the shadowed woods where mushrooms and lichen covered the creek rock and steep banks. She found
a natural animal path leading in, a path made by deer and nocturnal
animals.

She twisted her way along the trail and considered all that had occurred in the recent weeks and months, how her life had changed as quickly as the wind can shift through the trees. Without warning, how could she have known what to expect? The family she had grown up with was now changed forever. Life had been, in one single word, difficult. Yet, not only difficult but cruel, too, although a silver lining had appeared that she hadn't expected.

Now she was on a different course, not necessarily one of her own choosing, yet one she judged to be of hope and promise considering her peers and their diminished lives of such paltry subsistence. The ones such as Lena living with her strange uncle and Myrtle with her family residing in the haymow of a barn; and such as others in the community facing irreconcilable endings; the Darl Smith and Mel Parrish families now homeless, and so many others leaving their lives behind to ride the rails up north in hopes of a future.

Myra walked through the forest shadows and came across an abandoned cabin deep in the woods, dilapidated with its roof fallen inward. The place looked to be a hundred years old, yet the chimney still stood reaching in through the low tree branches toward the filtered blue sky. She continued on, observing the woodland and all of its nature.

She considered herself lucky to now have a home and a place to work—otherwise under a different turn of events, she could have been homeless herself. Jack had been generous with her considering the recent events. He and Wynonna had comforted her the morning after she found her father deceased in his bed; Jack had brought beautiful white roses to her father's funeral; had had his workhands, Carter and Ben, dig the grave, too. Without hesitation, he had stood up for her, taking care of J.R. Rutledge and his band of legal advantages; had taken care of the back remunerations and was now paying her last few notes as well. He was offering her room, board, wages, and an honest way to make a living. And least of all, the new boots he had bought her at the boot shop.

On the farm, she'd been given numerous opportunities and was taking on more responsibility as the days went: planning meals, managing the grocery, buying feed and grain, procuring supplies, gathering and selling eggs to Mr. Jenkins, and even learning to drive the short bed with Jack by her side. The previous Friday, she'd driven herself to Desoto to pick-up a few things as he was busy with more pressing priorities, such as caring for a sick calf.

Jack stayed busy and left her to herself, but at times he offered just the right measure of conversation, usually in the evenings. He had done much to care for her, but of course, he had needed her as well while drilling on her land for groundwater for his thirsting herd. Yet, the course of action was nothing more than a proposition that benefitted them both. So what was wrong with doing that in a fair manner?

She was now living full time on his wide-reaching farm, attempting to do her part and make a difference. She didn't know if she felt like an adopted child, an employee, a neighbor, or a friend. They certainly seemed to prosper one other and got along just fine. Wynonna was a kind woman, actually a confidant of sorts. She had taken Myra in to work and make meals with, to plan and take care of the farmhouse. All in all, this seemed to be a natural progression while taking on its own shape for times to come. And Myra, so far, had no objections with the progress underway. Yet, with no means by which to live on her own either.

She soon returned to the farmhouse. Jack was not in his chair or anywhere to be found. She called for him but he didn't answer. After drinking water from the gourd in the wooden bucket outside, she went up to her room and withdrew the elephant box and her small suitcase from under her bed. In the suitcase she found photographs of Ila Mae and Maclin, a length of blue ribbon from her biological mother, a church bulletin given by the kind Christian women in Atlanta, pressed flowers, a report card from Mr. Burch, a story she had written as a child of a talking dog, and lastly her biological father's letter to her.

She opened the elephant box and reviewed its contents: the family's very important property deed, a bank statement from her father's banking account at The Bank of Desoto, poems by Ila Mae, her Grandmother Nancy's family journal, the old war medal, and finally The Lee County Elegy written by Ila many years prior.

She suddenly realized how sentimentally valuable and even priceless this collection was. How irreplaceable it could be. She was now lucky to still have it, she thought, considering the entirety could have been destroyed in the recent tornado. What if it had, what could she have done? She would have crumbled, as these keepsakes were all she had left. All that connected her to her past and her lost family. The thought ripped through her with fear and terror. She immediately decided the next day she would request that Jack store her collection in his safe, the fireproof steel box in his office along with his other important papers and such. Why hadn't she thought of this before?

She went through the collection slowly savoring the presence of it in her hands; the touch of the paper, the feel of the pressed flower, the softness of the blue ribbon. The Lee County Elegy was one of many simple poems that Ila Mae had written and kept. Yet by the appearance of the paper on which it was penned, it must have been her favorite. The paper was rolled and banded, made of thick-stock cotton linen. When rolled open, the words of the single-page poem were presented squarely in the center and were encompassed by a wonderfully scrolled green ivy vine that Ila Mae had inked as a decorative floral surround. The lettering of the poem was beautifully handed by Ila, as artistic as she had been.

Myra was told that Ila had written the poem in dedication of her lost son, Paul, who had apparently died suddenly in the cotton fields on an oppressively hot August afternoon, long before the three of them came along. They had run to his side in the field but it had been too late, and, from what she'd been told, Ila Mae was never the same after that. Myra rolled the paper open to read the six-verse poem for the first time in years:

Lee County Elegy

Up on the hill to a place where
Heartache and many memories bare
In my heart I know the way
And in the morning, we can see you there.

A black forever lies across the stars
The full moon's white still on high
I watched clouds moving across the sky
Forever casting themselves on our lives

Our doors have been locked with gentle care
With time and faith we shall be there
We are without our son, but our lasting call
Is with nothing left and little shared

You have left us and can't be found
Little one can you hear somehow?
In our prayers know we are side by side
Still little one, can you see us now?

You will be low and marked on stone
Without the ones you shall ever know
Take with you our heart and love
Without us all you are left below

A wonderful light shines on our land
Yet I wonder if you would rather than
I watch the morning from our home
And know somehow you are here again

Chapter 27

THE FOLLOWING MORNING Jack was up and out in the field before dawn. Myra was in the kitchen with Wynonna turning griddle cakes on the stove when Myra looked out and noticed Jack going in the barn with a young cow. One of his young heifers was at term, in the barn birthing her calf when Myra came in.

"Myra," Jack said. "Bring me those long rubber gloves." He pointed to a set of shelves on the wall. "Hurry now."

Myra could see the calf's hooves poking out of the heifer's rear end, but apparently there was a problem as the big cow was having difficulty expelling her calf.

Jack slipped on the gloves and thrust an arm inside the heifer. "It's tangled up in here," he shouted. He maneuvered to a better position and made an adjustment. When he extracted his hand while holding a leg, the young calf came out behind him, head first, birthing fluid and all.

Jack took the calf's rear legs and spread them. "It's a little bull, Myra! Look there!" He beamed.

The heifer came around to see her babe and lick him in the face. It was a well-built animal with good structure and a fine coat.

"Jack, he's so handsome."

"That's my seventh this year."

"Oh, look at his big ears, too." She laughed.

They cleaned the calf and soon it was feeding.

Not long after this, Carter and Ben arrived walking up the road with their packs on their shoulders. When they came in, Myra and Carter met eyes but quickly looked away. Jack sent Carter up into the barn loft to throw down bales of hay for feeding. Later the vet, Dr. Masters, arrived and they looked over the newly birthed calf. After this, Mr. Masters went out with Jack in the field to check over the herd. One particular calf had a swollen, pink eye and the vet applied a salve then gave the animal a supplement of goldenseal. Otherwise, the animals were in good condition.

Myra rode with Jack down to her property and they started up the pump engine to run the well. Soon the troughs and tank were full so they shut off the unit and came back up. The fodder corn was finally ready to pick, Jack told her. For the remainder of the day, Jack and Myra went with the tractor and a small trailer into the field. With machetes, they cut the stalks with their silky corn tops until the trailer was full. They threw out the corn by the water troughs along with a few bales of hay. Next they called in the cows to eat. Myra was exhausted and her hands were blistered from the machete handle. Late afternoon brought heavy rain, and the two took a break and sat on the front porch. They ate roasted peanuts out of a can until the workhands arrived while wearing their rain gear and rubber boots.

"Rainin' like hell, Jack," Carter said as he approached the porch with Benjamin trailing close behind.

"You boys go on then. Ain't much else we can do today with the rain like it is."

"Appreciate it, Mr. Waylon," Ben said as they left for the barn to retrieve their packs.

When the peanuts ran out, Jack came out with an apple he cut up while offering Myra a few slices. They were quiet for a while as they sat in the wicker chairs and watched the clouds clear away, yet it was cool so Myra went in for a jacket. Before long, Wynonna had cooked vegetable soup that she left for them on the stove. She bid them good night, but Myra insisted she drive Wynonna home because the road would be muddy, and the old woman kindly accepted.

After Myra returned, she asked Jack to store her valuable collection of family heirlooms in his office safe. She insisted that although they lived far out in the rural countryside, this certainly did not alleviate the possibly of criminals and thieves. He agreed wholeheartedly and assured her this was the purpose of the safe, not to forget the outside possibility of a house fire or a weather event such as the tornado. He obliged her, told her there was plenty of room, and he locked them in the heavy steel box inside his office.

Early the following morning, Jack woke Myra and told her he was traveling to Leesburg to attend a cattle auction. She agreed to ride along so they left in his flatbed truck just after sunrise. An hour later they arrived in Leesburg, but Jack knew his way to the auction site as he'd been many times before. The auction was lightly attended as the economy wasn't the best, but the day was clear and the weather good. Fortunately for a farmer with money to invest, the buying opportunities couldn't have been better. Jack had inherited a fair amount of property and money from his father, but he knew how to invest it and realized a good deal when he saw one. Due to the economic downturn with cattle and beef prices near rock bottom, Jack attended the AA Auction in Leesburg to get the best deal he could as he was in for buying, not selling at the current time.

Several farms were going under and many were selling their cattle for twenty cents on the dollar, this being a disadvantage for some yet an advantage to others. At the auction, Jack purchased fifteen young calves for less than one hundred dollars which included delivery to his ranch, free of charge. That evening, the transport truck hauling the trailer and the calves arrived just before sundown, so Jack was pleased. He immediately fed and watered them then set them out into the field with his herd.

Myra was exhausted. She and Wynonna heated water on the big fire pit out back and she poured a bath to soak in. Wynonna departed for the day and left Myra in a tub of suds and lavender with candles lit. The tub contained a special valve and a copper drain pipe, that when activated, drained the tub to the outside of the farm house. Such modern conveniences, Myra thought. Later she dried her hair, combed it out, and put on night flannels and new slippers. She was elated. Never had she experienced such comfort. When she returned downstairs, Jack was in his den playing solitaire as he often did at night.

She entered and he turned to ask her, "Say, would you help me find something upstairs? In the attic?"

They went up the stairs to the second floor. He revealed to her a secret set of stairs up into the attic when he opened what appeared to be a closet door at the end of the hallway. The stairs were narrow and hardly wide enough for him to use, and they were excessively steep also with high stair risers.

"Go up these stairs," he asked her, handing her a candle.

She ascended one high step and turned, looking at him questioningly.

"There are some Thanksgiving and Christmas decorations up at the top. Wynonna usually gets them down for me. See if you can find the Thanksgiving wreath for the front door, the one with the big red bow on it."

"For Thanksgiving? It's six weeks away."

"I'm going to start early this year," he told her

Holding the candle, she went up and looked into the dark attic. Momentarily she turned back and noticed him watching.

"Do you see it? It's on top of those other boxes. Right at the top, I'm sure."

She saw the wreath and leaned out to grasp it. She turned and went to step down, but instead she slipped and fell, screaming! He caught her in his arms and laughed. She was still holding the wreath, intact and unharmed, as the candle fell to the floor in splattered wax.

"My word, I could have busted my head open!" she said, laughing too, her heart racing.

"Well, you almost did! You nearly busted mine too on the way down!"

They laughed again, actually relieved. As he stepped back, with both arms he held her in her gown and their eyes met. Without warning, without pause, he bent forward and kissed her. She froze, but she gradually relaxed. For that moment her heart eased then she pulled back.

"Jack!"

He looked away. "Myra, I, I, I'm sorry—"

"—well," she stalled.

Their eyes locked, but again he quickly looked away. "I'm sorry. I don't know what got into me."

He stepped further back into the hallway, letting her slide out of his arms.

She was spellbound, speechless.

He said, "I apologize."

She searched for words, like reaching into an empty space yet not connecting with anything tangible. Finally she said, "Well, I got the wreath." She attempted a nervous smile.

She handed him the decoration, pausing. She felt as though she was suddenly lost in the dark without a light, monetarily in the middle of nowhere, alone and scared. Without a footing, adrift, suspended in mid-air. But she was able to slowly relax and look into his eyes. She was more than surprised however; she was stunned. Yet for some unknown reason, she wasn't the least bit frightened. She felt as though she was in capable hands and had nothing to fear. Nothing at least she was aware of.

The next morning he was busy in the barn when she came down for breakfast. Later he presented himself as if nothing had happened and went about his usual business. He asked her to go to the boot shop to pick up a pair of boots he'd had mended then over to the store for a few things and finally up to Desoto for a roll of steel cable—she thought just to get her off the farm for a while. The old pair of boots had been left for several weeks, and what he needed with vanilla extract and vinegar from the store was beyond her. Days later the cable still remained in the storage closet of the barn, untouched.

Before she knew it, a cold front came through and she was in the house building fires on a cold Saturday morning with Jack nowhere in sight and his truck gone out of the yard. She mulled around the farmhouse for a while, nibbling on toast and reading in the great room by the fireplace, but Jack didn't come home. She needlepointed, made a batch of chocolate chip cookies, and waited longer. The day was gray and the sky leaden. The wind moaned and colorful leaves took flight in the breeze. The fires sparked and snapped. The house was warm but quiet.

Finally he came in around supper time. She had made a beef roast with vegetables in the woodstove. He was quiet and he ate little but smelled of whiskey. He was pleasant however and retired early to his solitaire table in the small den. When she went in to check on him, he had dozed off so she went to bed early and fell asleep reading by her lamp light.

Cade was caked with coal soot as he trudged the backstreets from the steel mill. His route took him through a rough section of town where he made sure to avoid eye contact with strangers or being drawn into a conversation with a passing vagrant. The two parallel rail tracks entering into the south end of the steel mill were usually lined with cars full of coal, and the sight of them made his back ache even more. The steel mill possessed mechanized coal feeders for the main blast furnaces, but his duty was to manually shovel coal into the smaller roller mills under the flatwork presses that were extremely hot. This being November, the weather was cool, but he couldn't imagine what the peak days of summer might be.

Usually when leaving his shift, he walked the tracks up through the two track lines. He walked between the coal cars and followed them toward the aqueduct where he would scoot under a railcar and emerge onto the backstreet. The street up to the aqueduct ran behind a textile mill called Worthington that had chemical tanks erected along the back walls from one end to the other. A chain linked fence surrounded the tanks and was locked to prevent any outsiders from entering. At one end of the building a long awning had been constructed to store discarded materials and metal drums of spent chemicals the plant was hauling away. Many homeless men had made temporary lean-tos under the awning, and they often solicited Cade for spare change whenever he passed in the night after his shift.

On one such November night he was approached by a group of men who beat and mugged him for his pocket change which totaled thirty-two cents. By the time he returned to his shack under the aqueduct, he was bruised, bloodied, and penniless. Frank, his new roommate, a man he had befriended, was there in his shack.

"Holy Christ, Cade," Frank said when Cade entered and his face came under the light of their oil lamp. "What the hell happened?"

Frank Collier was a stocky man with thick shoulders and tattoos up his arms. He had worked as a longshoreman in Savannah on the port docks until the work ran out. He'd ridden the rails up to Atlanta but had been unable to find much work there.

"I was mugged over by the textile mill. They got about thirty cents off of me, and now I don't have any money for supper and some of Sam the Man's rice." He took a dirty cloth and wiped the blood from his brow. Cade had grown ragged and a thin beard lined his face.

Cade added, "If there hadn't been three, I believe I could've taken them. But one was too big. He head-locked me on the ground and the other two fleeced my pockets."

"No good bastards. Let's go back over there and give 'em what for."

"It ain't worth it. They've spent it by now. They're about as half-starved as us, anyway." Cade inspected his battered face in a small mirror that hung in the corner.

The shack Cade had constructed was sturdy. He and Frank had added shelving for storing their lamp, oil, cooking utensils, and Cade's prized alarm clock which had set him back quite a lot of money. Their beds were pallets of straw and cloth rags overlaid with canvas. And finally, they had purchased hinges and a padlock they used on the heavy wooden door. It was better than most homeless shelters but not as good as others.

The encampment had become increasingly crowded as the unemployment rate was still rising, now over thirty-five percent in the city according to the *Atlanta Constitution*. Layoffs were rampant and work was becoming more difficult to find. Over the past month, Frank had been either standing in breadlines or panhandling like many others down by the train station. However, he had recently located part-time work at the Worthington Textile Mill in the chemical treatment department where the processed chemicals were filtered and either re-used or discharged. Although the work paid enough, he mentioned that it caused him nauseas and respiratory issues from touching and breathing the chemicals.

Cade was distraught about his money being stolen.

"Look, Cade. It's no big deal. I have a little change remaining. I'll cover your meal tonight and you can catch up later."

"I appreciate that, Frank. But something has to give. There must be a better way to survive and live than staying in this shack and working seventy or eighty hours a week. I don't think I can take shoveling coal much longer. Sometimes I feel like I'm going to collapse."

"I hear that. Sometimes I sense I'm going to faint when I'm handling all the foul shit that comes out of those chemical tanks. And lately I've been feeling so sick that I'm vomiting up my supper. Maybe that rice Sam is cooking isn't good after all."

"The rice is fine with me. It doesn't cause me any problems. It's just the long, never-ending hours under those flatwork rollers that get to me. You know we're going to have to become creative and find another way out of here."

Frank said, "Don't get any stupid ideas. You know they caught Jimmy Rogers robbing the cotton exchange building over on Ellis Street. They locked him up and they say he ain't gettin' out for a long time once the court gets a hold of him. They're sending him to the Atlanta Penitentiary I bet you. And that's some place I don't want to go."

"Hell, I ain't thinking of something stupid, just something smart."

"What do you have in mind?"

"Let me wash down at the creek and let's get some supper from Sam the Man, then I'll tell you an idea I have over a bowl of meat and rice."

Chapter 28

DAYS LATER, JACK came up the long hill from town, hauling a trailer with two beautiful horses in tow. From the kitchen window, Myra saw him pulling in by the barn and unloading the animals, one a light brown palomino with a dark mane and the other a tall, red quarter horse. She wiped her hands on a towel, slipped off her apron and went out to see. Jack was tying them to the hitching rack as she came into the barnyard. Both had been well-brushed and wore nicely made leather saddles.

"Beautiful horses," she said as she stroked the back of the palomino.

"Myra, meet Honey Pot and Big Chief. These belong to Ches Kutner. He's letting me borrow them for the day, so I thought we might have a ride up the creek toward Cobb, maybe take a lunch and get off the farm for a while. There's a good trail up that way. How would that be?"

"Sounds good, boss. We don't have anything pressing here, I don't think. By the way, you know Dr. Masters came again this morning."

"How's the little female doing?"

"Her eye's better. Looks like the medicine's doing its job."

"What about Carter and Ben?"

"They rode up to Desoto in the short bed. Something about needing parts for the Massey Ferguson and more engine oil. Said they may need to go all the way to Americus if they can't get what they need at the parts store."

"Looks like we're clear then, right?"

"Fine with me."

"You want to pack a lunch?"

"Will do. I'll go back in and put something together."

Jack went in the barn and returned with two sets of saddlebags. "Here you go. We can throw our lunch into one of these."

She carried one into the kitchen and set it on the counter to prepare the food. She made chicken salad sandwiches and wrapped them in wax paper. She packed cheese, Wynonna's pickled okra, tomatoes, jars of tea, and fresh chocolate chip cookies she'd made days earlier. Soon they were ready to head out. Jack mounted Big Chief and Myra Honey Pot.

As they rode out through the north field, the sky was clear and the air cool. Myra had donned her suede leather jacket with fringed sleeves and her good boots. She placed a scarf in one of the saddlebags in case the day became too windy. Jack wore his own jacket and clipped a canteen to the D ring on his saddle. They were set for the day as they reached the gate at the far tree line and ducked under a cascade of fir branches into the shadows of the woods. They took the path that Myra had previously found and wound their way along until they reached the old dilapidated cabin.

As they rode by, Jack said, "My folks bought this two hundred and eighty acre piece of land from a man named Thomas Brewer and his wife. They leveled the Brewer's original home and built the home I have now. My understanding is that this old cabin here was originally built for his wife's mother and father—the in-law suite I guess you could say. Of course, this was many years ago. And as you can see, time has gotten the best of it."

Continuing onward they crossed Flintside Creek where a good trail followed the creek bed leading toward Cobb. The land was flatter here, and the creek flowed gently among the rocks and sandy banks of moss, the palmetto and southern oak. They crossed a multitude of deer tracks where a sandy shoal ran by the water. Minnows of silver and white darted in the shallows. The creek shimmered where the sky filtered down through the trees and refracted yellow-gold waves of sunlight against the sheer stone walls of the bank. Myra looked up and heard hawks screeching in the sky. Strata of white and blue streaked the sky overhead as an easterly wind carried from Alabama in the direction of the Carolinas. They followed the creek until reaching an outcropping of rocks that lined an abutment of a hill.

Jack said, "This is the end of my land here. Beyond this are thousands of acres owned by the Cedar Springs Paper Company. Up on the northern end of this property toward Cobb, they've been stripping out slash pine for pulpwood that they carry down to the mill in Albany to produce paper there. We're entering the backend of their land. They haven't made it back this far and won't for years to come. It's a wilderness out here. Pretty aint it?"

"Pretty. It sure is."

They rode passed a small pond of sapphire blue lined with lilies and cattails. Thick oaks hung over the still water, and tall herring with their stilt legs were gliding through on the far shoreline looking for frogs. The trail circled the water and emerged into a small glade of wire grass by the creek.

"How about lunch?" he asked.

"Okay, Jack, let's do."

They dismounted and Jack removed a large blanket from one side of his saddlebag then spread it on the ground in the shade by the creek. Myra took the lunch, knelt on the blanket and set out the food. She turned and noticed Jack removing a bottle of homemade muscadine wine from his other bag.

He turned, holding the bottle. "Been saving this. Old man Meyer grows grapes and makes this out at his place. He calls it Dixie Red. It is mighty good he says and I think so too. Would you like some?"

"Sure. Pa used to get it from him from time to time. I've had it. Pa used to get his Sweet Jenny musadine, too. I've had a sip before. It's too strong, though." She laughed and swiped her hair back from her pretty face.

She reached for the sandwiches while Jack removed the cork with a screw he'd brought along. The cork popped and he smelled the wine's aroma, smiling. He passed the bottle over. She took a sip and winced then smiled. He held the bottle and drank too.

"Wine's good for the soul you know. Eases the mind from worry and tension they say. Even Doctor Clack says that in moderation, it's good for the stomach. I just like the taste, that's all."

As time had moved on, she had grown to favor Jack though he was much older, a generation almost. Life had simply transpired in ways she hadn't expected. Given to the whims of fate, she had been placed with him actually with little options other than to accept what she could from the situation. To know she hadn't arranged this made little difference. The outcome had been beneficial considering the loss of her family and the world she had known. In ways she hadn't experienced, Jack fulfilled her with a direction and purpose, with work and a means by which to succeed. Maybe she was maturing in age. Life's circumstances had possibly required her to grown in bounds she wasn't accustomed to. Managing life on a cattle farm without being overshadowed by her older brothers had been liberating. What she had lost she had also gained in other manners. Jack let her free to make her own decisions that seemed to benefit them both, and this was proving her value in ways that before seemed too far removed. Their nights on the front porch, spending meals together, working on the farm side by side, had brought them closer. Also she had to admit he was a handsome man with brilliant blue eyes and a strong build.

They ate lunch and drank their wine. He reclined and rested on his elbows, telling her stories of life on the farm while growing up. Once years ago the barn caught on fire from a lightning strike, he informed her, and had to be rebuilt. This explained why the barn was a combination of older wood on one side and newer on the other, she thought. He told her when he was eight years of age he had been so sick with influenza that he was taken to the hospital in Albany and nearly died but gratefully recovered there. At one time, he said, it had rained so heavily, the creek and pond overflowed into the barn and the mules stood inches deep in water. Jack also told her about the successive deaths of his mother and father. And that his uncle, his mother's brother that had been blinded in both eyes in a farming accident, had traveled from Florida to attend her funeral but hadn't been heard from since. Now Jack feared he had also passed away. On a lighter note, he replayed the story of birthing a calf while standing at the rear of a large heifer. Expecting a calf to emerge he instead received a face full of manure which turned him green with nausea. She laughed heartily at this having witnessed a birthing herself in recent days. Yet she was unaccustomed to the alcohol they were drinking, so she calmed into light-headedness.

She laid back and watched the sunlight glinting through the tree branches overhead, listening to Jack describe his stories. By the end of the bottle, her head was beginning to spin, and she slipped her hand over her eyes to slow everything. Before she had removed her hand, she felt his lips on hers and she couldn't resist him, opening her mouth for his warm tongue. He wrapped his arms around her waist and pulled her closer. Quickly her blouse was up and his lips were on her breasts. She was dizzied but he tugged her denim jeans to her feet and she arched in pleasure when his tongue licked her honeyed tuft between her legs. When he slipped his trousers off, she glanced down and saw him, gasping. A sharp pain came into her and she saw stars, but she moaned with a painful pleasure, gasping for breath and digging her fingernails into his back as he thrust. Clutching the blanket in both hands, she writhed as he moved on top of her with a ravenous hunger she had never witnessed from any man. She felt as though he was inside her up into her throat, and she could hardly breathe. She cried out but he refused to cease. Their lips met but she turned her head aside from the pain and closed her eyes tightly to endure the moment, not fully sure if she was in pleasure or agony. In the final moment he cried out and fell exhausted on her, panting. He took her hair in his hands and looked into her eyes but she had turned away and was crying.

He put his head into the cruck of her neck and kissed her, but she pushed him away, now sobbing. Although pleasured, he let her cry, stroking her hair, telling her he needed her. Slowly she calmed, and he allowed her to turn so they could spoon one another on the bloodied blanket and grassy earth. He took her blouse in his hand and wiped the tears from her cheek, but she shuttered at the thoughts running through her head and sniffed her runny nose back while wiping her hand across her mouth.

Finally she looked at him and lay on her back, her small nude body against his. After few words, they cleaned themselves with fresh creek water, dressed, and rolled the blanket. Standing, he took her in his arms and assured her he was committed to seeing a relationship through, re-gardless of their differences. He explained he needed her and wanted her on his farm for good, that he had done his best to provide and express his good intentions, and that he wished she would give him a chance to see what may come. He gave her a firm embrace and told her he was well-financed for the duration of the depression and possessed consider-able savings he kept in hiding, not to mention the acreage he owned but had no mortgage against. He assured her she most likely needed him as much as he did her given to their circumstances and the means by which life often revealed little until the last moments. She agreed she did need him and his support. She even admitted she enjoyed his company and loved the farm. Where could she go otherwise? Who else could do what Jack had done? Jasper John and his wife Ella could offer no such accommodation or opportunities. Their humble home was a two room shack, for God's sake, with a slice of land hardly enough for a hen house, too. Inevitably, she was bound to Jack and knew she must make what she could, to see her new life arise. For all else would be cast away and her lot lost if she were to strike out on her own. She had now given him the ultimate sacrifice of her own virginity. Now, she was determined to see this through come what may and know she had made her best choice. Hoping God had led her here as God can do.

Shadows danced over the ceiling from the small window above. Early morning light cast gray lines about the jail cell and concrete walls. A guard had come to pile wood into the small stove at the end of the corridor by the stairs. Unfortunately, Arden's jail cell was the farthest one away, and he shivered with the cold November air. What little food was brought had made him vilely ill, and he had become dehydrated from vomiting and diarrhea. When the guard later brought more of the same watery soup as the previous days, Arden refused to eat any, instead asking for a doctor, but he was refused.

Cade and Frank drew up their coats around their shoulders as they stood in line for rice. They could feel the wind cutting down below the bridge and aqueduct. The nights were becoming cold with winter on the way. Cade's bloodied face ached from the pounding he'd taken after being mugged in the street down by the textile factory.

Sam the Man was stationed by his fire pit with his cookpot while selling bowls of rice. They could see he carried a pistol in his belt to make sure he didn't have any trouble, but everyone seemed to respect him, they knew. He'd made many friends and had become a leader of their community. Weeks prior when the police had arrived to kick them all out, Sam had negotiated with the police and talked them out of evicting the crowd. He had insisted that the encampment, which was hidden away under the bridges, would simply relocate elsewhere, and this wouldn't solve anything. He had insisted that the camp, which was like others in the city, actually served a purpose and saved the city from otherwise having to cope with the homeless in other capacities. The camps actually served as stable concentrations compared to having the homeless living on the streets, in the alleyways by the businesses, or in the backyards of local residences.

Cade and Frank took seats on logs that had been set out on the perimeter of the camp. They held their metal bowls and ate without a word until they were finished. Cade thought of his position now alone in a big city without a home. The days had passed of living on a farm and evenings with family. However, without more opportunities, he felt a rural life of farming was a life of drudgery and he simply needed more than this to sustain a fulfilling future. He thought that seeing the world would be his wish, and he suspected he had a plan to do so.

Away from the fires, sitting back in the shadows, Cade said, "Listen, there is an army recruitment office up on Spring Street."

"Yeah, I've passed it before. I've seen it, too."

"Well, I'm tired of trudging up to the steel mill and back after fourteen hours of manual labor. It's getting cold out here at night, and a man needs something more."

"Are you thinking about going up to the recruitment office?"

"I'm going tomorrow. You want to go with me?"

"They might ship you off to China or Siberia."

"Anything would be better than this shithole."

"I'd have to think about it."

"In the army you can travel, learn trades, get educated, get clothing, and get three squares a day. That's much better than what's here."

Frank looked in his empty soup bowl while still hungry, and said, "Alright. I'm in. We'll go first thing in the morning."

Ahead of time, Cade wrote a letter home to inform his family of his plans to join the army. As soon as he was signed up, he would drop the letter in the mail to Jenkins's store in Flintside.

Chapter 29

THE RAIN CAME in waves for several days until mid-November. From then it rained continuously for weeks. Carter and Ben were kept busy in the barn tearing down the short bed truck for a total overhaul with intermittent trips in to Americus for parts as needed. Wynonna and Myra were busy in the kitchen putting up jarred vegetables. Jack donned his rain gear and was busy in the field and barnyard keeping a close eye on his livestock.

Myra noticed her sickness at first in the mornings. Wynonna knew right away and they sent word to Dr. Clack who arrived days later. It was soon determined she was pregnant even a short while after she had moved into Jack's bedroom. Careless was Wynonna's first thought although she was quietly jealous as she and Hezekiah had never conceived let alone had enough money to afford more than the converted cotton shack where they lived. Jack gathered them on the front porch after the doctor's departure and swore Wynonna to silence for the time being, not desiring his workhands to know any juicy gossip.

Wynonna had known Jack since he was nineteen. He wouldn't have admitted it, but she was not only a housekeeper to him but more like a stepmother, maybe even a friend or a confidant, or at least a sounding board when needed. Naturally, coloreds were not allowed to socialize or stand in authority with whites, and Jack knew this. But he had furtively taken advice more than once from her, as she had a subtly direct way of delivering her say so whether he realized it or not.

As the doctor left in his mud-streaked car, Wynonna turned and said, "Myra, chile, I guess you have some thinking to do." She had said this to Myra but instead looked directly at Jack. "I know you've come a long way up here from down on your land but it appears things is about to change."

"I don't know what to do now, Wynonna. What is done is done, and I'll have to make whatever changes are required."

"What changes that need doing *need to be done right*, chile." Wynonna said this but her accusatory eyes remained on Jack. "I guess something will have to give lest a black mark be struck on you for good."

Myra saw her looking at Jack very intensely. Jack pursed his lips and rocked back on his heels. Wynonna turned to leave for home back in Flintside, but she said, "I guess it's going to rain again." She was still watching Jack. Myra could see she was concerned, but not about the rain.

Jack said, "Come on Wynonna, I'll take you home. Let's get in the truck."

They silently stepped across the wet yard, and Myra could hear his truck keys jingle as they climbed in. They pulled down the drive and slowly disappeared into the fold of trees on the hillside.

Later when he returned, Myra was sitting on the front porch watching the heavy clouds move across the sky. She turned when he came up the steps but she looked away in tears.

He came and sat in the wicker chair across from her, but she noticed his demeanor had change after his ride with Wynonna, a reflective look now on his face. His posture was soft, his hands folded.

"Myra. . ." He couldn't form his words and he stalled.

"Jack," she said, looking at him in the graying twilight. "After all of this has happened, me losing my family, my coming to the farm and being a part of your life. Our outing up Flintside Creek and us lying together—I don't suppose you love me, do you?"

He stood and walked away across the porch. When he turned the late daylight shown softy on his face. "I believe I do, Myra. Or at least I know I can."

"I have given you everything I have to give. Myself mostly."

"I know, Myra. I know you have. And I've offered everything I can. I've taken you from the barren land of your family—the family that has obviously abandoned you—"

She quickly looked at him. "—they haven't just yet. We don't know what occurred, but we'll eventually find out what has become of Arden and Cade. Right now I have my own issues, Jack."

"We have *our issues*, Myra. This doesn't all fall on you." He came to sit by her again.

"What can you do about it? It's not your problem."

"It is every bit mine as it is yours. And I wouldn't call it a *problem*. I would call this a blessing."

"A blessing, you think? How are we going to account for its coming? I will be marked by this. Both my child and I. You know as well as I do an unwed mother and a bastard child is a shame and a disgrace. What will I tell Jasper John after all he has done for me and my family?" She looked away, wiping more tears from her eyes, overwhelmed by where this life of tragedies might end.

"Well, I plan to make it right, Myra. I plan to take account for our doings—*my doings*."

"And how do you plan to do that?"

He came to her, knelt and took her hand. Looking into her soft green eyes he asked her, "Will you marry me, then?"

She was stunned. Her mouth slowly fell open and she felt his grip tighten as he spoke.

"I know this is sudden—everything is sudden. But, we can make it work, Myra. I really believe we can. I'm a might older at forty-two but I have what no other man can offer you, a home, a roof over your head, a successful business, and most of all, caring hands. What would you say to that?"

She was speechless. She considered her position and what might occur if her life fell apart away from Jack. Where would they go? How could she care for an infant child? What could be worse?

After much reflection to his proposal, she finally answered, "Yes, Jack, I'll marry you. I would have expected no less."

Days later on a fair and cool Saturday afternoon, a small gathering assembled on the front porch at the Waylon Farm to attend the wedding of Myra and Jack Waylon. Jasper John and Ella came bearing wrapped gifts. Jasper would conduct the ceremony and Ella would assist Myra in a white gown donated by a church member. Myra's friends, Lena and Myrtle came with Lena as her bridesmaid wearing a black silky dress of her sister's. Wynonna and Hezekiah were there. Friends of the Grayson family attended from Mt. Olive, the families of Chesley Kutner, Wilton Meyer, Daniel Bray and others. Bobby Womack and Jamie Ellis arrived with the thunderous roar of the big drilling truck that was Bobby's only form of motorized transportation. Friends of Mt. Olive brought food to serve. Elizabeth, the wife of Wilton, arranged a punch bowl decorated with a pretty table cloth. The gathering was small but warm.

The late arrival of William Tullman did not go unnoticed as he arrived in his '28 Chevrolet National, one of the few automobiles that were driven there. Most others had come by either a mule, or horse, wagon, or on foot. When William parked, he emerged wearing a nice suit that made it apparent he was well-off with his glen plaid jacket, dark overcoat, expensive dress shoes, and silver-rimmed glasses. He was tall with a lumbering gait and a gray beard. He slowly stepped up on the porch and smiled at Jack who came to greet him. Just then the Mt. Olive choir broke into song and everyone began to gather in.

William took Jack by his arm, led him through the front door and into the house. Just inside, he said, "Mr. Waylon, congratulations are in order. I suspect this is a big day for you both. I say you got a good woman it appears to me. I'm sure Mac and Ila Grayson would have been pleased."

Jack laughed and looked away to conceal his consternation. "I hope Myra would think so, too," he said, looking back at the old lawyer.

William Tullman well knew of Mac's past reservations with Waylon over their property disputes. However, Jasper John was the only man alive aware that Jack Waylon was Cade's father. William Tullman, unaware of this fact, simply considered the circumstance to be an irony of life that Myra was marrying a man that her father detested. Maclin had passed on though, and William felt Myra was indeed taking on a man of prosperity and capable means, not to mention many acres of land. And this was one reason he had come, to assure Myra of her future as it should be.

William poked his head out of the door and motioned for Jasper John to join them inside to have a quick word. He came and the three men stood in front of the great hearth that Jack's father had constructed many years earlier.

"Jack," William began. "I want you to know how pleased I am that you and Myra have chosen each other." He turned to Pastor Tucker and added, "And we couldn't have a better man than you conducting the service, Jasper John. Why, you are a pillar of this community with many respected attendees here from Mt. Olive to witness this event." He turned and motioned his hand out toward the small crowd gathering on the long porch as seen through the front windows of the large home. "So, I say we should have a toast between us three."

He withdrew a small bottle of brown bourbon from his pocket and removed the cork. He handed the bottle to Jack who smiled and took a sip. Jack handed the bottle back to William who did the same.

William said, "Pastor. Every good Baptist preacher man deserves a nip every now and then, doesn't he?"

Jasper John winked, took a small pull, and wiped his mouth. "It has been a while, but that's mighty good."

William returned the bottle to his coat pocket and said, "Jack, considering this is not only a religious ceremony, it is in essence, a legal event as well. You are taking Myra to be your 'lawfully wedded wife', and I thought we should honor her by commemorating this." He turned to the pastor and said, "I have a marriage license form here that I will file in Leesburg once the courthouse is completely rebuilt. And the reconstruction is underway as we speak."

He withdrew some paperwork from his pocket along with a pen. He looked at Jack and continued. "All marriages have a *marriage license* as a standard operating procedure. I've drawn this one up for you and Pastor Tucker to sign. Here, you can see your names on the contract, Jack and Myra Waylon. I'll have Myra sign after the fact, if that's alright with you. She's busy right now, I'm sure."

Jack said, "Well, Mr. Tullman, I didn't know I would be signing anything today. This is just an *informal* wedding ceremony here."

Jasper John and William exchanged glances.

Jasper John was jovial. He said, "I can see this is your first marriage, Jack." He and the lawyer laughed, smiling.

William said, "All weddings include the formality of a license and this one is yours." He brushed lint from his jacket and straightened his lapel. "I agree this is not a wedding that requires *formal dress,* but the license is a small, behind the scenes *formality* a part of every wedding. That's all there is to it, really. As a matter of fact, it is the law that a proper license be filed after the marriage has taken place. You are marrying Myra today, aren't you, Jack?" He smiled broadly and patted Jack's shoulder.

Just then the Mt. Olive choir broke into another song. People were seen assembling closer on the porch while holding punch glasses.

Ella came down from upstairs and said, "Come on gentlemen, let's get outside. Myra is coming down the stairs soon, and we don't want to keep our beautiful bride waiting."

William spread out two identical sets of legal papers on a nearby table and produced the ink pen. "Jack, if you would."

Jack stepped over and noticed the paper's title in large print at the top of the page: Marriage License Contract. There were paragraphs of much smaller print in the body of the paper and a section at the bottom for signatures. Jack gleaned the paper, attempting to read the language. The first few paragraphs stated the formality of the ceremony and the value of the license. Unfortunately, Jack couldn't read very well as he had only completed school through the third grade.

From behind, Jasper John said, "Jack, it's just the marriage license."

The choir sang the final verse and quieted. The gathering of friends was hushed.

Ella urged them. "Gentlemen, it is time."

Jack turned, quickly signed and the pastor did also as the witness. William folded the papers and slipped them into his jacket for safekeeping. "I'll have Myra sign as soon as the service is completed." He smiled and led the way out to the front porch.

When Myra emerged from the house, everyone smiled and a few even gasped. She was beautifully adorned in white and wore a waist-length vail. Jack was well-dressed in a pin stripe jacket, charcoal vest, trousers, and a new pair of black shoes. He came to meet her and the nuptials soon began. Jasper John gave a short sermon regarding the requirements of marriage between God, the bride, and the groom. Myra and Jack accepted each other in holy matrimony and sealed the wedding with a kiss.

Afterward, hors d'oeuvres and drinks were enjoyed along with much conversation. Many expressed to Myra their concerns for Cade and Arden yet Myra was at a loss as to their whereabouts, she explained.

She surmised they had gone seeking greener pastures, but in the same breath was surprised no letters had been sent. She confirmed she had discovered that Ila Mae had passed away, though many were already aware of this as Jasper John was the community connection to all. Daniel Bray suggested she go to Americus to the police station and file a missing person report, and she agreed she would upon her first opportunity. Everyone soon departed and Jack took Myra into the bedroom for their wedding night.

Though she cared for Jack, Myra had an ebbing sensation of being swept away without a sure footing as she was now alone and without Maclin. Maclin had been her stronghold and sure hand, but Jack had now within a short time taken his place. He had taken good care thus far, and she supposed he would simply take some getting used to. Though the marriage wasn't arranged in any way, it had grown out of a unique set of circumstances and a mutual need that the two shared. In actuality, Jack had saved her as she had lost her family and had come close to losing the land as well. If not for Jack, the mortgage couldn't have been paid. And without her consent for him to access her land, his cattle could have died off from dehydration. Although no one except for Wynonna was aware of her early pregnancy, Myra now carried his offspring, and she was committed to her unborn child for the long term.

When he took her that night upon their marriage bed, he said, "Myra, I believe I do love you. I must or I wouldn't have done this. I believe we have a promising future, just you, me, and our baby."

"I suppose I love you, too. It has all happened so quickly and we must take care of our little addition. With Christmas only a few weeks away, we'll begin decorating the house and warming it up with lots of the season's love."

That night, they embraced as a full yellow moon crested the farm of the Waylon family in Lee County. The waters of the Flint River flowed into Lake Blackshear with a lullaby of South Georgia in its heart. Not only had the tale of Lee County reached a man remiss of what his future might hold, an unborn child slept in the womb of a young mother soon to learn more of what life's secrets were to come. The year of 1931 was on the cusp of their future, although the national economic collapse was well underway. And what life had to offer was written on the slate of her future, yet as Maclin once said: Life can't always be a bed of roses.

The next day, Jack surprised Myra and took her to Warms Springs, Georgia for a nice honeymoon. The three hour drive in his truck was well worth the trip and four rainy days later, they returned to the farm. When they arrived, it was late afternoon. Carter and Benjamin were just packing up to leave for the day. Jack had them help with their luggage, and he left Myra in the house as Carter and Ben asked to have a private word with Jack outside.

Jack followed Carter and Ben to the barn. When the three entered, Jack could see Carter's sudden apprehension. Carter had previously brought in three of the new calves Jack had purchased at the recent cattle auction down in Albany.

"Jack, we may have a problem here," Carter said with an edge of concern in his voice. "You see these here calves? They all have some kind of congestion. See this 'un here?" he said pointing to the smallest one. "See, his little nose is running. And they aren't eating much either. They are sick it looks to me. These are the ones you bought at the auction in Albany a few weeks back, ain't they?"

Jack ran his hand over the coat of the little calf. "Yep, they sure are." He knelt and wiped the mucus running from the small calf's nose with a cloth. "Damn. Just my luck." He stood and looked over the others.

"It's been raining to beat the band. It's wet and damp and I don't think that's helping the situation," Benjamin added.

"I'll have Dr. Masters come in tomorrow to check them over. Say Ben, why don't you take my truck first thing in the morning to get him over here?" Jack suggested. "This may be serious."

The following afternoon, Dr. Masters confirmed that not only were the little calves infected, but a few of the mature animals were as well. He discovered some had elevated body temperatures and were dehydrated. The next day, the doctor incorporated a sack of goldenseal into the animals' feed and promised to return in a week for a follow up.

However, the additive did little good, and the herd was becoming sicker by the day. Not only were they congested and sick, but they seemed to have labored breathing as they hung their heads low to the ground while drawing deeply with their lungs. Some were panicking because of this as they became desperate for oxygen. Soon even more cattle were becoming infected. When Masters returned, he instructed Jack to separate the sick out and quarantine them in a separate field which he did. This improved the situation but within days, two of the first calves died of the pneumonia and Jack was infuriated. Apparently, the new additions had come with the infection from the auction, and this had quickly spread to the others.

As days passed, the sickness became exceedingly aggressive. More of them were becoming ill, and a few more died off during the nighttime hours. Jack could do little about it other than feed them more goldenseal that, over time, acted more as a preventative than a cure. The goldenseal was expensive too, and Jack had no other choice but to follow the doctor's recommendation. They inspected the herd every morning to find that many weren't eating well or drinking much water. Jack began losing sleep and staying in the barn until the wee hours looking after the sick. They added a higher quality feed but the sick refused to eat it. They attempted washing the cattle with brushes, soap, and water, but this didn't seem to prevent the spreading virus. Jack even added expensive vitamins to their diet but this apparently did little good, either.

Under Jack's instruction, Carter and Ben pulled out the tractor and equipment from the barn and set them in the yard. They led the newly infected animals in and made a large fire in the center of the floor while opening the haymow door in the loft to vent the smoke. This was in an attempt to get the sick ones in from the cold and rain. However, this proved useless. Soon some of the cattle were lying on the barn floor on their broadsides, panting helplessly, unable to stand. Suddenly, in one night, nine animals died. Then weeks later by Christmas, Jack had lost thirty-five cows and he became irate and out of hand.

Chapter 30

JACK PACED IN the kitchen, stood at the window, and watched the late day rain falling. Myra was standing with Wynonna close by, both nervously fidgeting.

Jack threw his hands up. "Gal damned hell. First the drought, now too much rain. The herd is sick and I'm losing a head or two a day. That goldenseal ain't doing squat, and there is no end in sight."

"Mr. Waylon, please settle down—"

"—you settle down, Wynonna!" He stepped over and pointed his finger at her nose. "I only have two hundred and twenty-five head remaining. I've now lost thirty-five and some are still sick. This virus is very aggressive. Not only that, but I'm paying to have the corpses hauled off to get the infection off my property. The sick beef is tainted and I couldn't give them away now if I wanted to. On top of everything else, I can't sell the good beef at such a loss to make up for it because the market is flat. Then eventually I could run out of money."

He paced. The smell of whisky lingered in the air between the three. He had begun to drink more heavily now that his cattle were sick, usually beginning at noon. Just days before Christmas, Myra and Wynonna had taken the mules into the woods and hauled back a glimmering spruce for a Christmas tree. As luck would have it, another calf had died in the morning and Jack was at wits end. The day had been spent with Myra and Wynonna decorating but the air in the house was tense.

"Jack, look at the big picture," Myra urged. "As Chesley said, this virus is rampant in South Georgia and it's even more widespread in Texas, according to the *Americus Gazette*. Don't feel singled-out. You did nothing wrong."

"Hell, Myra, it don't matter who's at fault. The fact is I have suffered a big loss and it will be damned hard to recover."

"*We have suffered* a big loss. Both of us," she said to clarify the circumstances.

He looked at her with a confounded expression.

"Besides we have the land mortgage-free. It could be worse." She came and stood by his side, taking his arm in her hand.

He backed away. "What do you mean we? I've worked my ass off for this land and herd, and you have shown up here in the eleventh hour."

"I know but we are still married, right?" Now she was the one confused. "Jack, I'm in this struggle with you. That's all I'm saying. If you are unhappy, I'm unhappy. And I'll do whatever I can to help out." Myra was only seventeen but she was a precociously mature young woman with a good head on her shoulders, Jack was quickly learning. She had a way with words and knew her way around a contentious discussion, too.

Wynonna turned and said, "I'm leaving this up to you two. I'm going home. Myra, would you mind giving me a lift?"

Jack said, "Wynonna, why don't you just walk? You've been walking home from work for twenty years and suddenly Myra has become your taxi service." He stood on the other side of the kitchen, leaning his hand against the doorframe. His eyes were bloodshot and his face pale from the lack of sleep.

Myra looked at Wynonna. "Don't mind him. He's having a bad day. Come on, Wynonna, I'll take you."

"To hell you will," he said, coming across the kitchen, taking Myra's arm abruptly.

She turned to see his meanness for the first time. His eyes flashed white and he looked at her determinedly.

Wynonna took her raincoat and put her hand on his arm. She said, "Jack, that's fine. I'll just walk."

He brushed her arm away. "Damned right. We're going to get things back like they use to be where you're working for me not Myra working for you."

"Jack—"

"—Myra, listen to me."

At that moment, carrying her bag, Wynonna went out the back door, closing it. She was gone.

"Jack, why do you have to be so—"

"—so what? In charge? Because this is my farm and my business, that's why."

"It's ours, isn't it? I thought it was ours." She resumed her stance in front of him, her eyes filled with hurt.

He turned but said, "I'm sorry, Myra. It's been a bad day and things are just gettin' worse." He left and took a bottle of whiskey with him to the front porch. Myra cleared away the dinnerware and went to bed early with a book and her oil lamp.

Usually Mr. Jenkins sorted the US mail in the late afternoon before he closed his store. He noticed that mail came from all over the country, even from Canada. The Meyer family received mail from as far away as California. The Bray family had relatives in Windsor, Ontario. Government mail arrived monthly from Leesburg for Mr. Burch, too. When Mr. Jenkins had grown up in Cobb just on the cusp of the Civil War's demise, mail was sporadic at best. Modern mail service had improved significantly since then, he thought.

On this day, he noted that a letter arrived from an army base in Fort Bragg, North Carolina, addressed to Myra Grayson from her brother,

Cade. He smirked, even laughed this time. He looked over his shoulder and slowly slipped the envelope under the counter with the other one. "Little vermin," was all he said.

The morning sickness grew each day beginning at sunup. She performed what chores she could but found herself soon hanging her head over a bucket. She was just beginning to reveal a newer shape, and she first noticed this while looking in their full length mirror on Christmas morning. When she descended the stairs, the Christmas tree was standing in front by the big window, unlit. She called out Jack's name but he didn't answer. Peeking out of the window, she saw his truck parked by the barn but no sight of him anywhere.

She lit the tree candles with a match she struck upon the hearth of the fireplace. There were twelve candles for the twelve days of Christmas, she had told Jack, a song she and Wynonna had sung together the previous day. She walked to the kitchen, smelling the aroma of coffee. As she poured a cup, she looked out the window and saw Jack coming from the barn with a solemn look on his face. As he entered the kitchen, the cold morning air followed him, and he threw his hat at the hat rack but it fell to the floor.

"I lost another one, Myra. It was lying on the floor of its stall this morning when I went out before sunup." He looked down at his dirty boots and took a deep breath.

"I believe this is coming to a close, Jack. Dr. Masters said so himself this week. Hopefully this will be the end of it." She held his shoulders in her hands while looking up at his sad face. "Let's try to let it go today. We can recover in time." She kissed his chest. "Can you say 'Merry Christmas'?"

He turned and poured more coffee, silent at first. Finally he said, "It is not too merry, I would say. I have suffered this devastation and it is difficult to be merry."

"Jack, come on now."

He looked at her beautifully young face. "Merry Christmas," he said reluctantly with a stern edge to his voice.

"I have a Christmas present for you."

She took him by his arm to sit by the tree. She lit kindling and logs in the fireplace then added newspaper to help the flames. She reached over and took a package from under the tree and handed it to him. He slowly tore the paper off, opening the small box. Inside revealed a pair of fine leather gloves, dark brown, well-made, with the name Hermes stitched into them.

"I found these at a store in Desoto. It looked like you needed a new pair that you could wear into town instead of that old pair you use to load your supplies and such. These are for being dressed up."

He slipped them on, turned his hands from side to side. He didn't know what to say. She had expected a 'thank you' at least. "They're real nice. This is a surprise. You didn't have to do that, Myra." He looked up and the firelight caught his blue eyes in the dim morning.

"Well, it's Christmas. I wanted to." She sat, her hands folded in her lap. Her face was filled with sleep. Her eyes were small slits and she smiled then sipped her coffee. She looked about and didn't notice another package under the tree.

"I haven't gotten you anything, Myra. I'm sorry. Been up to my knees in rattle snakes." His face was not remorseful, only blank.

"Not even for Christmas morning?" she asked.

"Well, I have never exchanged gifts, not since my parents both passed away. I haven't had anyone. Isn't this home I have provided enough?"

"Jack, I know you have provided a home. But on Christmas, don't you exchange gifts with anyone?"

"Well, I haven't had anyone, I suppose."

"What about Wynonna? She's good to you."

He rolled his eyes and looked away, but turned back and said, "Myra, she ain't nothing but a hired hand. I give her a little bonus and some of them Clementine tangerines from Jenkins he gets in this time of year. But she's just a nigger, or didn't you realize that?"

She was taken aback by this comment. She saw Wynonna as part of the family, at least nine tenths worth, anyway.

She was saddened. She was just beginning to see who this man really was. He was well-off and also a good business manager, there was no question about this. But was he that cold-hearted? Or had he not been raised properly? She had to accept he had suffered a great loss with his cattle dying off. *He was a cattle farmer,* and she realized he couldn't afford to lose that.

He said, "I have never had anyone, Myra, to tell you the truth, until now." For the first moment of the morning, he appeared contrite.

She could see he was awkward and unrefined, knew little of social graces or how to conduct one's self in a family environment. So she proposed to show him how.

She went to him and held him. "You have someone now, Jack. And I'll show you how to behave in terms of a relationship and love. And as far as this land that you have given me, I am thankful."

He looked at her with a confused expression. "The land I gave you?"

"Well, yes, when we married. We are one, now. Don't you understand that?"

"I gave you a roof to live under, I'll agree to that."

"Let me stand corrected. Yes, for the roof you have given me to keep me from the rain, this is a wonderful Christmas, Jack."

He seemed to be satisfied now with her explanation. He added, "But it hasn't been a very good year, otherwise. I've lost a lot of cattle."

"Not to worry. Dr. Masters says the herd will grow again to be strong. It just takes time."

"You're a sweet little thing, Myra. I have to say that."

He looked at her, his face still. He sipped his coffee.

"Why don't I put on some griddle cakes for breakfast? I bought some cinnamon to go on top just for this occasion."

She turned to go but her reach up and took her arm, turning her around. He saw her small nipples protruding from her cotton gown and he kissed one.

"Jack, wait."

"What's to wait for?" he said.

He grasped her by her arm and took her to the floor on the rug by the fire. He was suddenly on her, almost forcefully. His stubble scratched her face when he kissed her.

"Jack, take it easy," she requested.

He paid her little attention, and he was soon in between her legs inside her, moving slowly at first then riding her with a steady pounding as the top of her head met the leg of a nearby chair. But she let him in and took his rough handling because it was his way. She was his after all. It was apparent he didn't contain the refinement to be a gentleman, rather the hands of a rugged cattle rancher who hadn't been raised properly or taught the meaning of love, who lacked the means to be gentle or even mildly persuasive in a personal relationship. However, in time she hoped she could teach him how. As she had been raised to respect others in the home, she wished to impart upon him the meaning of compassion and personal caring.

Later in the day, he took his drink as he usually did. However, he was pleasant this time. She suggested they wrap in a blanket on the front porch and sit together to watch the first snowflakes of the season. It had never occurred to him that an intimate moment could be shared under a blanket. On one awkward occasion, she had rubbed his sore back with lotion after a long day in the field. But when in return, she asked for his aid in removing a splinter from under her foot, he had looked at her inanely and had tossed the tweezers to her before walking out.

She had begun to see that to him women were simply compensated workhands on the farm, too, needed for what required doing, including acquirements in the bedroom. Wynonna had told her of the few women he had courted, but that they themselves had been rough around the edges, too. Myra, having little experience herself, fortuitously had the natural inclination relationships needed to survive. And she planned to impart them on her husband as he possessed, on the other hand, redeeming qualities many others lacked. He was a hard worker with drive and ambition. Considering all, he worked nearly seven days a week and placed no blame on anyone else when things didn't go well. He met his financial obligations and worked well with others. He usually managed his staff respectfully, and planned for the future as he should. Myra knew he needed improvement, yet she saw his good side and knew he was a smart man. The only reservation that truly concerned her was his temper and drinking habit. This, she would need to rope-in one way or the other because when these two merged, she had learned to stand aside.

Part Four

Chapter 31

IT WAS A warm October day. Myra took Cora in her arms and set the infant on the sideboard to change her. Wynonna was preparing supper nearby in the kitchen, and she watched from the galvanized washtub on the countertop. Cora was a sweet little girl, but had been difficult to birth as Myra labored for an entire night in late July with Ruth Meyer as her midwife. Jack had left and gone to the barn with all of the crying and drama that came with having a child by natural means. He was a strong man with his arms but weak when it came to such things as child birthing and situations in the home. Nonetheless, Cora was a happy little girl with blue eyes like her daddy, and very healthy as Dr. Clack had said himself. Myra had been busy caring for their child, thankful to have Wynonna's assistance as Jack was as helpless with a child as Myra with a socket wrench.

From the kitchen, Wynonna said, "Lord, Myra, Jack has done gone back in that barn. It's like a cave he goes to, the way he clears out of the house when there are domestic chores and a baby to tend to." She was washing collards in the tub while watching Cora. "He's a funny man about being in the house too long. But he can rear a calf, sure enough." Wynonna tried to smile.

Wynonna desired to keep their conversation light. She had noticed a mark on Myra's cheek again and didn't want to bring it up as she had the previous occurrence. This would only cause Myra to lie and she didn't want that. Oh, I fell and bumped my head, Myra would say. Or, I was working in the barn with the livestock and must have hit something. But, Wynonna knew better. She had seen Jack lose his temper and throw things many times before.

Myra said, "I suppose the herd has grown a few heads. He took the losses fairly hard, though. It took months to eradicate the virus from the herd, and he stayed out there many days dealing with it. Actually, I don't believe he's gotten over it yet, Wynonna. Sometimes, he sits up in his office at night with a pencil and adds things up in a long column, mostly his money, or the losses there of, I guess. Depending on how you look at it."

"That's a man for you, though. Always adding things up. His money, his land, his head of cattle. What he likes and what he don't. Who he owes and who owes him."

Wynonna put the vegetables on. Placed the corn in a pot with water and set that on the stove. After going outside to the small wood pile, she returned with more kindling and put that in the stove, then closed the door.

She said, "Back before Carter and Ben, Mr. Waylon did his own maintenance and mechanic work. Used to be Jack had this one fellow come out to do the repairs, but whatever he repaired would soon fail. Jack had him out to repair his tractor once, but it soon broke down. When the man returned to address the problem, he insisted the tractor hadn't been maintained properly, and that it wasn't any o' his fault. So Jack paid him again. The next time, he came out to work on Jack's truck, but whatever he did done broke again. Then there was the incident with the roof of the barn over the hay door that wouldn't stop leaking, All along, Jack's keeping a long list of these problems—actually wrote them down, he did. Finally Jack fixed the roof himself and went out looking for that man. When he found him, he beat the ever loving stew out a him and demanded his money back. Jack's a big man, you know. So, we ain't seen that man around here no more." She shook her head, looking down at the supper she was preparing.

"He has redeeming qualities, though, I know."

Wynonna looked directly at her and the bruise on her face. "When it comes to his farm and land, he does, I'll agree."

Myra held her hand over her bruised cheek and turned away in the shadow of the doorway toward the dining room. Wynonna slid the ham into the oven to cook, took some plates out and put them aside for later.

Wynonna said, "Speaking of Carter, it is kind of quiet around here without him. He used to stir up a ruckus sometimes. You know he worked for Mr. Waylon over ten years."

"I don't think he and Jack were getting along. It was apparent their time had run its course and he moved on, I suppose."

"Whereabouts did he go, anyway?"

"Ben said he moved down to Albany to work for a big commercial outfit down that way. As hard as work is to find, he found another job at an ag-equipment factory on an assembly line, Ben said. Something about Carter's uncle working there is what I heard. I believe Carter was a good mechanic, good with tools and such."

"Things is tight with Jack taking up the slack, though. I guess he'll eventually hire another hand to replace Carter. But girl, he needs to get his drinkin' under control, that's what I say."

"I wish he would."

"He's different when he's been drinkin'."

"More different than night and day."

That moment, Jack stumbled into the kitchen. Wynonna and Myra looked up, startled and quickly hushed. Myra went to set the table while Jack washed up. But he wondered why his ears were burning and it was so quiet in the house as Myra and Wynonna usually kept a conversation going. Myra set Cora in a baby seat on the supper table and gave her a bottle. When Myra and Jack sat to eat, Wynonna took her coat and walked out the back door. She had to get home to prepare another meal for her husband, Hezekiah.

Right away, Myra smelled the strong scent of whiskey in the room. Obviously, Jack was now taking his drink while working in the barn. Over time, his habit had become worse. A few days earlier, he had drunkenly dropped a heavy work tool on his foot and was now limping.

"What you and Wynonna been talking about?" he asked after they ate and she was clearing the dinnerware off the table. "I could see you two talkin' up a storm through the kitchen window when I came up. But as soon as I walked in, you two hushed up quiet as little church mice."

"Nothing too much. Just about Cora and her sleeping habits," she said, thinking quickly.

"Did she say anything to you 'bout that bruise on your face? Did you tell her how clumsy you are with doing your work?"

"No, she didn't say anything to me about it."

She tensed as she passed him in the doorway to put the dinner plates in the washtub. Cora was crying again and no matter what Myra did, she wouldn't stop. Dr. Clack had suggested colic, but it had not passed though Myra had tried his recommendations. With Jack's demeanor, Myra was so nervous that when she entered the kitchen, she accidently stumbled on the threshold and the ceramic plates in her hands went flying, crashing to the floor in pieces.

"Gal damned, Myra! Don't be tearing up my property!"

He grabbed her arm and jerked her up. "And don't you commiserate with Wynonna about all that goes on around here. What happens between you and me stays that way, understood? No one has to know you are having problems dealing with Cora and your little issues. That you are depressed."

"I told you, I'm not depressed. Becoming a mother is trying, I'll admit."

She slipped her arm free of his grasp and stood back, but he pulled her closer until they were nose to nose. "You listen to me! You better get straightened out! I don't need any lollygaggers on my farm! I have enough to deal with and breeding my cattle, too!"

That night, she left their bed and went into another room to sleep. He asked what the matter seemed to be, dismissing their earlier confrontation. She told him of her trouble sleeping when he snored loudly as she knew his drinking seemed to exacerbate the problem. Soon he was asleep, and she went to bring Cora and her crib in with her.

Driving his Chevrolet National, William Tullman returned to Americus to meet with his stock broker, a trip he took at least once per quarter. With the slide of the stock market, his broker recommended buying gold bullion because spot gold prices were increasing daily. After his meeting, William went to the First National Bank to do just that, then to speak with J.R. Rutledge at Americus First Trust Bank to check on Myra's situation, not wanting to bring it up with her as she was now married to Jack Waylon.

After their cordial introduction in the banker's office, William said, "What has happened to the Grayson property? I know Jack Waylon is paying the last of the mortgage payments. But are you aware that Myra Grayson and Jack Waylon have wed?" He couldn't help but throw a little salt in the banker's wound along with some general conversation.

J.R. had not heard this, but he could have cared less as William explained the events. Rutledge had gravely disappointed his daughter, Bethany, having promised her the land instead. Now she hardly spoke to him.

William went on, saying, "Her brothers apparently have departed and left the problem with her, anyway. But it doesn't matter now as Jack Waylon has plenty of money. He put a well in at her property and was pumping water up to his land. Do you know Jack Waylon?"

J.R. ignored the question, avoiding the recollection of his punishing defeat by Waylon on the Grayson property. Instead, he rose from his desk and went to the window to look out. He said, "You obviously don't know what happened in Americus, do you?"

"Know what?" the attorney asked.

He returned to his desk to pour a glass of water from a pitcher on his credenza. He sat and said, "Mac Grayson's son, Arden, is in the city jail at this moment."

"Arden is in jail? For what?"

"You know that my brother-in-law is the sheriff here in Americus, didn't you? Sherriff Dale Blackburn? He informed me a few months ago about the situation. Last I heard, Grayson was in for aggravated assault with a deadly weapon, but he has now been charged with attempted murder."

"Assault with a deadly weapon? Attempted murder? What exactly happened?"

Rutledge explained that Arden was witnessed committing the act by several known businessmen. That he had run down a local man into an alleyway in an attempt to either apprehend or rob him, which they weren't sure.

The banker said, "Apparently the police hauled him in months ago. I heard he was tried. Now he's awaiting sentencing and transportation to the Atlanta Penitentiary."

This created an entirely different situation, William suddenly realized. He said, "Surely he has attempted writing home, but Myra hasn't heard from him."

"I don't know all the details, truthfully."

"Well, who was his legal counsel? Surely he had representation."

"I'll make a phone call to see, but around here the wheels of justice move as slowly as blackstrap molasses, you well realize. I know for a fact my brother-in-law is in his office right now. Let me make a call."

He phoned the operator. "Police department, please."

Rutledge didn't mind. He relished the fact that Grayson's son had fallen into tragic circumstances. And he wanted Tullman out of his office anyway as the lawyer was beginning to leave a sour taste in his mouth.

The sheriff sat at his desk across from the old lawyer. He said, "We're sorry, Mr. Tullman, but bail wasn't granted. I'm sure no one had the cash to do so, anyway. No one that I know has much cash anymore. It will be a while however before Mr. Grayson is sentenced and taken to the penitentiary because we are shorthanded around here. The whole county is. Seeing how this town is rife with criminal activity during this poor economic climate, we have our hands full."

Sherriff Dale Blackburn leaned back in his chair to reveal his rotund gut, his shirt stretching out and the buttons straining. He wore a neatly pressed uniform, however, and William could see his pistol and holster hanging on a hook behind his desk. The badge pinned to his thick chest sparkled from the overhead electric lighting in the police station.

"I prefer to take no more of your time but would rather speak with the public defender's office as soon as possible. Or the judge handling the case would be even better. Can you arrange that? I'm a locally retired attorney and know some of the judges in this county, as a matter of fact."

"My brother-in-law asked me to meet with you, and I'm busy as you can imagine, but seeing the judge would be more difficult. He has a full schedule, too, I'm sure. As for a public defender, I don't think Mr. Grayson had one."

"No representation? He should have had the right to a counselor. Otherwise, it's not fair to try a man, sentence him, and lock him up without one."

"I am not aware of what happens in every court case, Mr. Tullman. I have my own responsibilities. But I'll see what I can do."

"Can I see Mr. Grayson in the meanwhile? To have a talk with him?
"As his attorney?"

"No, I'm retired. Just as a family friend."

"Sorry, but visiting hours are only on Mondays."

"Alright then, as his attorney. I'll take the case."

Sheriff Blackburn rocked back in his chair to observe the old man in front of him, gray-haired and arthritic, but knowledgeable, too, the sheriff assumed. Running his hand across his desk, he slid a note pad aside as if to stand, but instead he hesitated and questioningly eyed the old lawyer.

William added, "Years back, I was a practicing attorney around Albany and Americus, practicing in Lee, Sumter, and Dougherty Counties for over thirty-five years. But I still hold my license. Here in Americus and Sumter County, I recall Judge Stanford and Aldridge. Do those ring a bell with you? Are they still on the bench?"

The sheriff said, "Yeah, I know them. Okay, I can see you've been around."

"I do know my way through a court hearing, Sheriff Blackburn, and I know what rights Mr. Grayson has and which ones he doesn't."

Blackburn considered his options and said, "You'll have to wait a while, Mr. Tullman. Come out and sit in the lobby. We'll let you know."

Several hours later he was led to a room inside a secure section of the jail where steel bars and a wide table separated the room's attendees. Arden had already been brought in when William came. Arden looked gaunt, eyes dark and his expression void of emotion.

"Arden?" William said as he sat at the table and looked through the steel bars at his new client.

"Mr Tullman! How did you find me?"

"Son, I was here in Americus on unrelated business, but I heard you'd been arrested and were in the Americus Jail. Tell me what happened."

Arden explained what Cotter Rye had stated concerning Jack Waylon's employee, Ben Dollar, and his knowledge of the attempted murder of his father. He further explained his doings with his pistol and how he had landed in jail.

"Before I proceed with your case, I need to tell you something very important, Arden." The attorney paused to gauge his client's reaction. "Your father died months ago, Arden. I'm sorry."

Arden starred for a long silence. "Died? He has died? Why has no one come to tell me? And to get me out of this shithole? I wrote home several times but no one has come."

"No one has received any letters. No one knew you were here, son."

Arden turned and cried softly. He knew his father had been ill and he wasn't surprised, only saddened he hadn't been informed and was unable to make the funeral.

The lawyer asked, "What have they been doing with you here?"

"They hardly feed us, and I've been sick without the availability of a doctor. They put us on a chain gang, and they've put us to work on the farm of Judge Henry Lucas, tending his crop, hauling his rubbish, and digging his ditches."

"You have been working on a government employee's land? The judge's land to benefit the judge?"

"Well, yes sir. They come, chain us, and take the six of us out most days of the week depending on the weather. Once we were taken to Sherriff Blackburn's home to build a new chicken coop. I believe the building materials were supplied by the city as well, according to the truck delivery man." He asked, "Where are Cade and Myra?"

Willian frowned and explained all that Arden had missed in the recent year. That Cade had disappeared, and Myra had married Jack Waylon for the reason she had been close to destitution after their cabin was destroyed by a tornado. Arden was stunned more than furious. Cade? Myra and Jack Waylon? In all of eternity, he couldn't have imagined the outcome as it was. Also, considering he had been isolated in a time capsule of concrete and steel though no one had found him there.

"I'm attempting to meet with Judge Lucas this afternoon, as a matter of fact. I understand he's busy at the moment, but I'll return soon enough. You'll have to wait a little longer until I can get you back in front of the judge."

The new courthouse was made of granite and the courtroom of custom millwork. Modern lighting had been installed, and the room was filled with plush leather seating and long oak benches. Unfortunately for Arden, renovations to the police station and jail had not been done as the failing economy had prevented it. Tullman and Lucas actually knew one another, so before the court appearance they spoke in his chamber. It had taken Tullman hours to get an appointment, and the clock on the wall displayed the time: 4:30 PM.

Tullman told the judge, "Judge Lucas, I assure you he isn't the type of man to rob anyone. I personally know him and his family. There must have been some mistake."

The judge was a short, bald man with tired eyes and much to do. Because Mr. Tullman was a known attorney, he had allowed him the appointment otherwise it would have taken weeks if not a month.

The judge said, "Mr. Tullman, for whatever reason, one can't go out and settle any dispute they please with a firearm. That's certain. We can't allow locals to go about firing their weapons anytime they choose, anytime they have disagreements."

"What did the witness say? Are you sure it wasn't self-defense?"

"Not when the man who got shot was shot in his backside while in the process of running away. I doubt it."

"I'm sure we can work something out. As you've said, apparently the other man involved wasn't hurt. He's fine. Furthermore, it isn't legally just to try and convict a man without the presence of a defense attorney unless he waived his right to one, which he did not. There was no attorney present with Mr. Grayson, no assigned jury, and no formal trail."

"Mr. Tullman, we have only a few public attorneys and literally hundreds of cases. All of the other attorney's left after their pay was cut in half. Unfortunately, mine has been cut too. There was not much I could do about it."

Officer Crandall, now having returned from his medical leave, led Arden up the stairs into the courtroom. Arden was not handcuffed or shackled. Yet he was worn and wind-burned from fieldwork on the judge's farmland. He was thin and dirty from lack of proper hygiene, and his clothing stunk, too, not to mention his unshaven face.

Crandall led him to sit beside Tullman at a table that faced the judge's bench. They exchanged glances then turned to face the court.

"Judge Lucas," Mr. Tullman began. "In light of the event that there was no public defender or a proper jury trial for Mr. Grayson, I call for you to strike the charges against my client. Also would you consider the time he has already served as being sufficient reparation for any crimes he may have committed?" The lawyer clasped his hands together and added, "Considering the city confiscated his wagon, mules, and firearm, too, would you also consider this payment as a fine?"

Judge Lucas said, "I would as a partial payment. Yet it has cost the city considerably more to house and feed him in the year's period."

"Has he not been working at your farm in the interim, Judge Lucas? Doesn't that count for anything?"

"Who says he has been doing work on my behalf?"

"The defendant did, your Honor. That is who." He turned briefly to look at Arden.

"That would be hogwash, Mr. Tullman, simply hogwash, even accounting for my cut in salary here in Sumter County," the judge stated. He then added, "Mr. Tullman, would you kindly escort your client to the bench?"

William and Arden stood and went in front of the judge. He asked, "Son, what ring are you wearing on your small finger?"

They all looked, the judge, the attorney, the bailiff, Officer Crandall, and Arden. The ring Arden wore was his mother's gold wedding band with the striking diamond setting, the ring Maclin had given him for the wagon ride to Americus to place on Ila Mae's hand for the return trip. Arden had kept it hidden behind a piece of broken mortar in his cell wall during his incarceration, as a keepsake of his mother, or to return home to his father.

"This was my mother's wedding band," he said, looking up at the seated judge.

Judge Lucas replied, "That's a mighty fine ring. What's a grown man doing wearing his momma's wedding ring?" he said, chuckling. "How about handing that over to me so I can have a look?"

Arden removed the ring and placed it in the judge's hand.

"Mighty nice, yes sir," the judge said while holding it between his thumb and index finger, admiring the sparkle and shine as he turned it in the bright lights. "How about this ring in exchange for your fine? I'll take this, I believe." He slipped the ring into his front trouser pocket and smiled.

All present exchanged glances. The bailiff and Officer Crandall looked away, studying the floor and their boots.

"Consider it accepted, Judge Lucas," Tullman said.

"All charges are then dropped as this case is closed. I'll have this recorded with the county. Son, you are free to go."

Later that evening, Judge Lucas presented the ring to his wife, and she was pleased at the fine gift he had purchased for her. He told her to consider the gift an early anniversary present although their anniversary wasn't for another six months. The beautiful ring fit perfectly, too, so Mrs. Lucas was elated, and she called her sister in Atlanta to brag right away.

Chapter 32

UPSTAIRS, MYRA HID with Cora in the narrow stairwell of the attic. She stood behind the solid wooden door and listened. When Cora began to cry again, she attempted muffling the sound with her hand. She could hear Jack downstairs going through the house, opening and closing doors. He was drunk again and had lost his temper over a minor problem, something about his wash not being done on time and still hanging damp on the clothesline. Although Wynonna had left earlier with what she had claimed to be a stomach ache, Jack had forgotten this. It was now 5:00 in the afternoon.

Myra heard him exit the kitchen door and call her name again.

"Myra! Myra!" he called as he walked toward the barn.

She knew this was her chance. She took Cora in her arms and quietly went down the stairs and stepped out the front door leading to the porch. From the end by the railing, she observed him in pursuit, entering the barn. She ran off down the hill to her property and passed her demolished house on the rise. She took the path to the lakeshore where it was quiet and safe until Jack could sober up.

Myra stepped down the embankment and sat on a large flat rock that was known as the 'Family Rock'. Maclin and Ila Mae had rested here many afternoons while sipping tea and enjoying the sunshine. From the rock, they had all fished in the lake. Arden and Cade had both cleaned bass and dressed deer too on the rock. The rock was the size of a farmhouse table and almost as rectangular, although Mother Nature had naturally shaped it over a hundred thousand years with the hands of time and eternity.

She cried, now seeing her inclement circumstances for what they had become, having lost her family to the grips of fate and now living with an abusive man in the middle of nowhere. From the beginning it had seemed right, but she had been naïve in the final analysis. Having had no other options she accepted his home, the roof over her head, good food on the table, a farm of many acres, and the security it held. This had ultimately drawn her to him. She had indeed been hungry, almost starving when the horrid tornado hit and she went to live there. Desperate people do desperate things, she realized. And that past life now appeared to be so far away. It seemed to have been a different existence, a different planet, a different place in time. In honest retrospect, she had had no other option.

The depression had taken the country down by its girders, and jobs were few and far between. People had become irrational and reckless. There was nowhere else to go, nowhere to turn. But *marrying* Jack Waylon had been foolish, she finally decided, even if she was pregnant. In the beginning he had seemed secure and stable, even accommodating and nice. However, the stress of losing such a portion of his herd along with the poor economy and the plummeting value of all land had done him in.

He recently explained to her that he had added it up.

All in all, he had lost *over three-quarters of his value.* He was for all intents and purposes, a half-broken man who had lost his mind, too, and didn't realize what value he still possessed—a good wife and a daughter, a property without mortgage, and food on the table. Many others were so much worse off, couldn't he understand that?

Wrapped in a blanket, little Cora sat in Myra's lap in the cool daylight by the water. She was a sweet girl with mild, milky skin and thin hair the tint of amber. Her big blues eyes seemed to take in the world with wonder and fascination although she was only a few months old. Myra thought she would be so smart judging by her wondrous expressions and her observing eyes watching the sights around her.

When Myra returned home that evening, she quietly crept up the stairs. She went to put Cora in her cradle for the night but noticed Jack in his office going through the cash box he kept in his bottom drawer.

Myra stepped softly into their bedroom but Jack heard her come up.

"Myra? Come in here a minute."

With hesitation, she went into his office with Cora in her arms, but she saw a glass of whiskey beside him on the desk. She observed the glare in his eyes that usually accompanied more drinking and a bad mood. She tensed and said, "What is it Jack?"

"Where the hell have you been? I've been looking all over for you two. I'm hungry and it's late."

"I took Cora down to the lake. I thought you were busy. The last I saw, you were out in the barn."

"Next time, don't disappear like that without first telling me."

"Alright, I won't. No problem, then." She held her baby and stroked her sleepy face.

"Myra, something else. My cash box is missing money. Did you come take any out?"

"No, I don't think so." She paused and had to think quickly, knowing where this conversation might lead. "Well, on second thought, I may have because I needed cash for Cora's stomach medicine when Dr. Clack came earlier this week."

He looked confused. Lately his eyes were always red with dark circles. His hands sometimes had tremors in the morning until he took a drink. On one occasion when he returned from Desoto to buy his whiskey, he was distraught because none was to be had, and he'd had to return days later when it became available. Myra was not only beginning to worry about his health but for her and Cora's as well.

"No, I paid Clack when he left. For his visit and the medicine, so couldn't have been that." He looked up from his box and stood. "You sure you haven't been in here for something else?" He took a step toward her and placed his hand against the doorframe, looking down at them.

"Maybe last week when I went up to the store for a few things. I didn't know I had to keep a log."

He didn't like that comment and he grabbed her arm.

"Ouch! That hurts, Jack."

"Well, why don't you tell me where my money disappeared to?"

"I don't know. I tell you most of the time when I take any out."

Days before, he had misplaced his truck key and claimed to have left it on the kitchen table. As it transpired Myra had found it in his dirty laundry, but he had refused to admit his mistake. On other occasions, he had lost various items such as paperwork or correspondences, but he soon determined this was her responsibility to locate whatever had gone missing. On this night, he was again confused, inebriated, and in a foul mood.

"Seems to me money is hard to keep track of anymore. I use to have little problem before the two of you came along." He looked down at Cora. The oil lamp on his desk cast a tall, dark shadow against the wall. Myra was becoming concerned. "And why is my desk in such a mess? Who could have been in here besides you? Wynonna maybe?"

"No one, Jack. Wynonna wouldn't come in here for just no reason, and she certainly wouldn't steal anything from you. If that is what you are implying."

"You three are just a big mess, Myra. You always need this and that. Cora always needs the doctor. Wynona's getting uppity needing you to drive her here and there. Now, she's probably been in here going through my desk."

"That's not true. She's honest and would never consider doing that. How can you say that? She's been working here for over twenty years."

"She may not be here much longer, now that I have you to do her work for me."

"And what, leave her with no job? Her husband can't support them both. You know that."

Cora began to cry and Myra attempted rocking her in her arms.

"This damned baby! I thought Dr. Clack had her straightened out with this colic business. You give her anymore of that medicine yet?"

"Yes, she's had her dose for the night."

"That medicine cost me ten dollars! It ain't cheap! And it don't work worth a damn!"

Cora continued crying and wouldn't cease.

Suddenly Jack yanked her out of Myra's arms and headed for the stairs.

"Jack! What are you doing? Come back here!" She followed him down the stairs and grasped his shirt collar as he rounded the corner into the kitchen.

"Jack! What's going on? Put Cora down!"

He turned while holding the infant. He raised his hand and brought it across her face with a hard smack. Stumbling, she slipped back and tripped on the threshold, falling onto her back. When she stood, Jack had exited the kitchen toward the barn. She ran after him, but he shooed her away with his arm while holding the baby.

"Jack! Come back!"

He went into the barn and closed the barn doors, latching them.

Myra yelled, pounding on the tall wooden doors. "Jack! Open up!"

He hollered back, "What's the problem? You don't like someone taking something what is yours when you don't expect it?"

"Jack, don't be like this! Let me in. Don't you harm Cora!"

The night was suddenly silent. The sky was clear and the stars shone in the heavens. Myra looked up to the hay door leading into the loft far above her head, and she knew there was no other way into the barn.

"Jack!"

Moments later, he flung opened the barn doors and the barn was lit by an oil lamp.

She sped in and looked about. "Where is Cora, Jack?"

He nodded toward the storage room.

She looked to see a padlock on the door.

"What have you done with her?" She raced to the storage room and pulled at the latch, yet the door was securely locked with the heavy steel padlock.

"Jack, you bastard! What have you done to her?"

"Well Myra, who knows. But I believe I'll just keep her in there until you can explain where my missing money went. Let you see how it feels."

"There is no missing money! I have stolen nothing! Now open this door!"

He walked out and strode off toward the house, abandoning them.

Myra ran to the mechanic's toolbox against the wall and found a crowbar. She went to the door and desperately wedged the bar behind the lock. With all of her strength, she placed her foot against the old wooden door and pulled as mightily as she could. Rocking back and forth, she pried at the lock and began to work it loose. With a final yank, the lock broke off pulling the hinge out with all the screws. She took the lamp and entered the storage room but Cora was nowhere to be seen. She tossed boxes aside, moved things along the shelves, pulled farm implements out of the corner and let them fall to the ground. Then she heard a cry.

"Cora!" Myra quickly guided the lamp around the room and finally found her baby on the ground, under the bottom shelf while still swaddled in her blanket.

"Cora, thank God!" She took her and left the barn with the baby in her arms.

Jack was standing at the back door of the kitchen, watching. Myra came in the house, tightly holding her child. She had nowhere else to go.

"You see, I thought I should teach you a lesson!" He placed his hand on the edge of the countertop, but he slipped off which caused him to keel forward, almost falling.

"Jack, you are drunk. You've had too much to drink. Go to bed and sleep it off."

He followed her up the stairs toward their bedroom as he bumped along the walls. He sat on the bed, but she forcefully pushed him backward and he laid out on the bedcover, his boots still on the floor. After a few moments, his eyes shuttered closed and he passed out.

Myra thought to take the truck but she had nowhere to go. She certainly didn't want Jasper John and Ella to know of their problems. Then the word might spread around the community. With no other option, she took Cora into the other bedroom and locked the door for the night.

In the morning, Jack was up early and out in the pasture with some emergency. How he was able to keep this up, Myra couldn't understand. Sober but hungover, he came back into the house to apologize before Wynonna arrived. He agreed he had been out of control the previous night, but he would not admit to having a drinking problem. He insisted his drink helped him through the tough times, but she had seen him transform from being a fairly decent man into a raging alcoholic in a short period of time. He had always taken whiskey but now the habit had escalated out of control. Due to his financial problems and having lost so many cattle, apparently he was unable to cope; this was all she could surmise. She had heard many stories of other families in the community falling apart, after their losses, due to the Great Depression. The entire country was falling apart. She had attempted to garner Jack's empathy. But Jack threatening Cora had gone too far.

Their conversation elevated into another argument just as Wynonna walked in for the day. She could see the look on their faces, and she frowned deeply. Myra told them she was going for a walk to cool off, so she went out the door.

She took Cora and went down to her land, to the gravesite of her family to sit in the shade and look on her family names. They were all lined up, their names cut into the hard stone. She wept for her father, knowing she needed him now more than ever. What would he have to say? What advice could he have offered? Nearby her father's grave was Paul's. Paul was the brother she'd never known, the brother that had swept the family's soul away in a sad undercurrent from which her father could never free himself. Paul's headstone was the smallest of the group and this caused her to cry even more.

She held her daughter and stepped around the destroyed cabin. She sobbed for the loss of her family's home, not knowing how to take it. The structure was a hulk of a shell, the stark roof beams black against the sky, the walls caved in, the tin roof thrown into the nearby woods. She returned to the Family Rock to think things through and to watch the smooth water across to the other shore. She was at a loss as to what could come next. She had no clue and couldn't predict her future. She could only hope for an alternative plan to protect her child.

Myra heard something and turned. She thought she heard her name being called, but it wasn't the voice of her husband. Hindered by the lake's embankment, she couldn't see up to the house or the hillside beyond it.

She heard it again. Was that Arden?

She took Cora and raced to the top of the embankment. She noticed William's tan Chevrolet parked by the fence in the morning light. She saw Mr. Tullman walking in her direction, waving. Then Arden came around from behind the house, also waving. She burst into tears and laughter, and ran up the path to meet them with Cora bouncing in her arms.

By chance just outside of Flintside, they had passed Wynonna trudging her way back home. She had warned them that Mr. Waylon was in a foul mood and had just fired her. Tears on her face, she was distressed, now out of work after twenty years of service to the Waylon family. She suggested they look for Myra and Cora where they often hid when Jack grew irate and out of hand. Down by the lake, she had suggested.

Myra ran into Arden's arms and he hugged them both as William stood by, smiling.

"Arden! What on earth happened? Where have you been all of this time?"

"It's a long story, Myra, but the short version is that I was illegally detained in the Americus jail. I was forced into slave labor on the properties of a local judge and sheriff." He smiled nonetheless.

She stood by him holding his arm, tears still in her eyes. He was thinner with black sunken eyes. His complexion was red from working in the fields with a look of utter exhaustion crossing his face.

He said, "Who is this? She's beautiful, Myra."

"This is Cora, my little girl. Cora, meet Arden."

They looked at one another for a long moment. Cora was satisfied sucking her pacifier.

She said, "Arden, so much has happened. Really it's been terrible. I just don't know where to begin. I've missed you so much and have needed you more than ever."

He said, "William explained everything. That Pa has died, Cade has left, and that you married Jack Waylon but also exchanged groundwater for mortgage payments. I'm so glad you worked something out, Myra. You were smart to make that decision. We could have lost everything."

He winced. "But now, you've married Waylon. Is that right?" A look of pain flushed his face

"Yes I'm afraid so. But, you should know that I was nearly starved, Arden. I had nowhere to go. After the tornado, he let me in his home and he treated me so well in the beginning. He offered me security because I was being evicted by the bank. But more importantly, I don't know what has become of Cade. He's disappeared without a trace. It's not like him to do such a thing."

William said, "Myra, you must appreciate that *many people* have abandoned their homes and have left during this horrible depression. Many Lee County farms have foreclosed, and people don't want to face the circumstances. Times are hard. Cade has done what many did and left."

"But, he hasn't written to let us know where he has gone."

William just frowned.

Arden said, "Listen to me Myra, let me tell you what I've learned. When I went to Americus to get Ma, I inadvertently ran into a fellow up there, a man named Cotter Rye. He said his uncle happens to be Ben Dollar, and he claims that Ben Dollar told his family that Jack Waylon is the one that was responsible for driving the truck that knocked over the woodpile. The woodpile that crushed Pa up at the Big River Lumberyard! Dollar witnessed the whole event! It was Jack Waylon because he wanted to get rid of Pa to access our land—to come down and pump out the groundwater. That is how I ended up in jail, by chasing down Cotter Rye after he realized I coincidently knew Ben Dollar and Jack Waylon! *It is a small world*, don't you know?"

"What? Are you absolutely positive? That can't be."

"Yes. Because Cotter Rye knew the details of what happened at Big River Lumber. Otherwise how could he have known that? Why would he know that and tell it to a complete stranger? He knew Ben Dollar and Jack Waylon's names. He detailed the entire story before he realized, by chance, I was somehow connected to the man that was assaulted, *being our father!*"

"That explains a lot," she said. "How could he have done that?"

"I don't believe you even know who Jack Waylon really is."

"Obviously not. But now I've gotten myself into an abusive situation. Part of Jack's herd died off with pneumonia, and apparently his finances aren't well, either. He's lost a lot of money, and he's taking it out on me and Cora." She looked down at her baby in her arms.

William asked, "Has he beaten you, Myra?" He looked pained as he noticed a light bruise on her cheek.

"Yes, and I don't know what to do about it. I'm so glad you two are here."

William said, "You're going to have to get out of there. You can't stay in that house."

"I must for the time being. I'll have to stay temporarily until we can figure something out. We'll have to outsmart him. If I leave him, he will discontinue paying the remaining mortgage payments. There are only seven or eight left, but if he refuses to pay, the bank could still reclaim the property, isn't that right?"

"I could pay them," William offered.

Arden and Myra met eyes and they looked at their old friend. Myra placed her hand on his arm.

Arden added, "It's just not safe for you, Myra. He could hurt you and Cora in the meanwhile."

"But also there are other *very important* items we have in there. Our father's prized elephant box with *our property deed*—it is the only one that exists. Also don't forget Nancy's Journal of our family history, the old war medal, Ila Mae's writings, and the Lee County Elegy, too. Also I have my little suitcase in there with my father's letter to me from Atlanta when I was so young. I have to retrieve those things, I must! They are irreplaceable and priceless! And the problem is that he has them locked away with his own valuables and papers inside a steel safe in his office. I asked him to put my valuables in there myself. I insisted this. But now I have no key. He has the key."

William said, "I have an idea to keep you out of harm's way in the meantime, until we can get you out safely and figure out how to bring Waylon to justice. For that we'll have to get Ben Dollar to talk."

"What do you have in mind?" she asked.

▲ DELTA

BOARDING PASS

ROSE/JAMES G

TSA PRECHK
3 006 2384238384 1
JO8BZA

DLXXXXXX3028

QAWQAOMP

FLIGHT	DATE	CLASS	ORIGIN		SEAT
DL2667	20SEP	Q	BOSTON	DEPARTS 1249P	**28A**

OPERATED BY

DELTA AIR LINES INC | MAIN | DESTINATION DETROIT | BRD TIME 1209P | MAIN 2

DEPARTURE GATE A15 *~SUBJECT TO CHANGE*~

ROS30FD24/AP

BOARDING PASS

ROSE/JAMES G

DLXXXXXX3028

FLIGHT	DATE		SEAT
DL2667	20SEP		**28A**

ORIGIN
BOSTON | MAIN 2

DESTINATION
DETROIT | EQP01

OPERATED BY DELTA AIR LINES INC

Chapter 33

WHEN THEY PULLED up to Jack's house in William's Chevrolet, he was sitting in a wicker chair on the front porch. He turned his head when the car doors closed and they approached him on the porch.

"Jack! Look who is home! It is Arden, isn't this wonderful!" She could see he was unconcerned, but she wanted to ignore this and portray the moment as a happy homecoming.

Jack slowly rose and ran his hand over his head. His was hungover and his eyes were bloodshot. "Arden, what the hell, boy, where on God's earth have you been?"

"Been locked up in the Americus jail." He instead looked at Myra holding her baby.

"Jail?"

Arden explained his charges. "I had a fight with a man that robbed me, Mr. Waylon, and I was charged although I was protecting myself in self-defense. My assailant happened to be acquainted with the judge and I was jailed unjustly then wrongly convicted, too. I served a year doing slave labor for the judge and a local sheriff, but I was finally released yesterday with Mr. Tullman's help."

"That don't sound worth a damn, boy. You got waylaid sounds like to me."

Myra cut in, "But Jack, now that Arden is home, do you think it is alright if he stays here with us? You wouldn't mind would you?"

Jack glared at them and scratched his belly. "Well, I don't know." He looked to Mr. Tullman and said, "How about you, Mr. Tullman? You were the one who got him out of jail. What do you say?"

"I can't help any further, I'm afraid. I'm leaving for Birmingham in a few days to visit my daughter and grandchildren. I'll be gone for quite a while, maybe a month."

"Jack," Myra put in. "Since Carter is out of the picture and has gone on to Albany for work, why don't you hire Arden to take his place? Arden is one heck of a worker. I know because I've seen him myself."

Arden said, "Mr. Waylon, I'd be happy to do whatever work needs doing."

"He has a back as strong as a bull, Jack. He may be a little thin at the moment but he'll beef-up in no time."

"Well, Myra, I'm not too sure considering—"

"—Jack, he has nowhere to go, don't you understand?" She glanced at Arden while still holding his arm. "Jack, think about this. You're over-loaded as it is. What about all that lumber you just purchased? You've been talking about rebuilding the haymow. That's a three man job, isn't it? You, Ben, and Arden could do it. Sometimes three men can do twice the work of two, like you say. You've said that yourself. Or, Arden could be in the pasture tomorrow morning first thing if need be. I can run him up to Jenkins's for a dress of clothes and new shoes. He'll be in good shape before you know it."

Jack pondered.

William said, "Mr. Waylon, this is your wife speaking to you."

Jack and William exchanged stern glances. William was old with age, but he stood as tall as Jack.

Jack looked Arden over. "Alright then, Myra, if you think it's best," he said, capitulating.

"I'll get inside and put lunch on. Arden, you go clean up in the wash closet inside the house. I'll get you soap and help you load buckets of water into the basin. Tomorrow, we can make you a hot bath to soak in. For now, you can wear some of Jack's clothes with a belt and roll the pants up until we can get you into town."

"Alright, sounds good," he said, rubbing his hands on his thighs, ready to get started.

"You must be hungry still," she said.

"I haven't eaten anything decent in a year, except for once the judge's wife gave me some cold bacon and eggs. That was until last night. Mr. Tullman kindly took me for a good meal."

"Well, let's get you inside and cleaned up. There is plenty of bread until lunch can be ready. Jack can show you around this afternoon and introduce you to Ben, his workhand. There's enough lunch for everyone too. Mr. Tullman, how is that?"

Indifferent, Jack remained silent. His head ached and his mouth was dry. He stood observing everyone and their happy expressions. But he wasn't too sure. There was going to be another person in his house and at the dinner table from now on. A stranger as far as he was concerned. And he wasn't absolutely sure he liked that idea.

Myra was glad they had pulled it off. She knew having Arden close by served as security, too. Her immediate concern was locating the key to the steel safe. As soon as she could obtain their valuables, she would be ready to leave. She knew she must tread carefully and keep up the show until the key could be found. As soon as Jack left the house for work, she would begin searching.

The following morning after breakfast, Arden was ready for work. He ate five scrambled eggs, eight pieces of bacon, a large bowl of grits, four pieces of buttered toast, an apple, drank coffee and three glasses of milk.

The house was quiet without Wynonna, and Myra was already beginning to miss her.

Jack stared silently and ate his eggs, watching both Myra and her brother eat heartily. Before long, Ben came up from town with his pack, so Jack and Arden went out to meet him in the barn. Without delay, Jack immediately put them to work.

Beforehand, Jack had purchased supplies at the lumberyard, and a stack of rough-sawn wood rested inside the barn. He had planned this project ahead of time, and after second thought, he considered it fortunate that Arden had come when he had.

"I need to replace flooring in the barn loft and rebuild the haymow frame. This here barn is at least sixty years old, and one day I'll have to replace the whole barn. But for now, I'd rather rebuilt what is in place, and the fall season is a good time for this kind of work."

The three went up a ladder into the loft to examine the haymow. Jack pointed out the dilapidated flooring in the loft and the structural pieces of the haymow frame that needed replacing or reinforcing. The haymow was essentially a stud-framed partition without wall boards. Bailed hay was lifted in and stored inside one end while the other faced the hay door of the loft just under the roof's ridge pole. Outside through the hay door, a lifting block was mounted to a thick beam. This was a mechanical system of pulleys and ropes for lifting bailed hay off the ground below to be stored up in the haymow. Stacked hay lined the exterior wall of the barn down on the ground, and it needed to be lifted up to the loft.

Jack suggested they first replace the necessary floorboards. Before long Arden was on the barn floor with a handsaw cutting lengths of thick board as Jack called down the measurements from the loft above. Ben was busy pulling the old boards and throwing them out of the hay door onto the ground thirty-five feet below. After several hours, they were sweating profusely in the cool morning air, shirts damp and their hair wet.

"Hey, Jack, how about those guns," Ben commented while Arden was below quickly cutting through the wide planks. Jack and Ben were now driving long nails into the pieces needed for reinforcing the haymow.

Below, Arden overheard their comments. "I've sawed some thick trees in my time." He smiled while holding the handsaw, looking up through the large center opening in the loft floor above.

When they completed their task, the three men left the barn and loaded the refuse wood into Jack's truck.

"Ben, you and Arden carry this load out to the back field and dump it in the woods for it to rot out there. I'll go in and check on lunch." Jack turned and walked toward the house.

Out at the far tree line, Ben pulled alongside a cluster of thick oaks, and the two men went about throwing the discarded lumber over the fence. After half the wood was unloaded, they stopped to take a break in the shade of the trees. They sat in the grass and took a drink of water from Ben's canteen. Arden glanced over and noticed Ben observantly watching him. But Ben glanced away. Arden thought he saw contemplation in his face although Ben remained silent for a long while. In the meantime, Arden was considering how he might compel Ben into a revealing conversation about the lumberyard accident, to discover what he knew about it. He was biting his thumbnail, pondering an angle of pursuit when Ben suddenly spoke.

Ben leaned his way and said, "Arden, I'm sorry to hear about your pa passing away last year, and your house being demolished by the tornado."

Ben studied Arden for a moment longer.

Ben wondered if Arden and Myra might ever discover the truth about Jack Waylon and his attempt to murder their father. Initially, Ben hadn't wanted to divulge anything. He feared Waylon and his authority. He feared losing his job most of all, and if he lost that, it would be difficult finding a replacement. He well knew this. He realized that Carter had found a job through his uncle, but he had no such connections.

Arden said, "First the weevil, then the drought, and the loss of our cotton crop, now the economy going south." He looked into the sky and rested his arms on top of his knees. "Now, Ma and Pa have left us. Not to mention the loss of our home and my stint in prison. We've had a bad run the last few years. There's nowhere to go but up from here. I hope somehow something good can come from it." Arden looked down and ran his hand over his jeans to brush off the wood splinters.

Ben had thought over this for months. He had harbored Jack Waylon's secret for far too long, and he couldn't hold it in any longer. He felt for Myra and what her family had been through, both collectively and apart. He'd had nothing to do with the lumberyard incident other than to withhold a testimony.

He turned toward Arden. "Listen man, I need to level with you about a few things. I may be severely jeopardizing myself by doing this, but I must tell you what I know about your father's injury at the lumberyard."

After their candid discussion, they quickly finished their task and returned to the farmhouse for lunch. Myra and Jack were in the kitchen, serving up plates of food. Ben and Arden came in, and Myra could immediately read Arden's demeanor, his tone, and the intense look on his face expressing that something was awry. She hadn't seen him in a whole year, but she knew him as well as the day he left. He winked at her then followed Ben outside to the plank table to eat and further their discussion among themselves. On the other hand, Jack didn't notice anything different. Myra ate with Jack and Cora in the house.

After lunch, work resumed and the three returned to complete their job in the barn. Jack slipped a set of wrenches into his back pocket and led the men up into the loft for further instructions. He took a heavy wooden box and set it on the floor, opening it. Inside was a newly purchased lifting block.

"I want to replace the old lifting block because it's rusted and doesn't work very well. We have a load of hay stacked against the barn, and we need to get it lifted up here." He stood. "Arden, take this over to the hay door, would you?"

The lifting block and ropes were fairly heavy, about forty pounds. Arden carried it and set it on the floor by the hay door. Jack unlatched the door and let it swing inward, revealing a beautiful view of the farm and the fields in the distance.

Arden and Ben exchanged glances. Ben watched Arden as his eyes darted about, studying the situation. Jack turned to speak and the men quickly looked away with composed faces.

Jack had the tallest frame and longest arms. He said, "I'll get the old block off the support beam."

He took a wrench from his pocket. He stepped to the edge of the hay door and leaned, reaching out of the barn to grasp the block. Behind Jack's back, Arden nodded toward Jack while looking at Ben. Ben also motioned out toward the barnyard and quietly mimicked pushing Jack outward. Without hesitation, they nodded silently in agreement.

When Jack held the edge of the doorframe and stretched outward, he placed the wrench on the rusted lifting block to turn the nuts. Ben peeked around the side of Jack and could see the ground far below. For a quick second, Ben and Arden locked eyes. A moment later, without delay, Arden stepped forward and thrust Jack out of the hay door. Jack screamed, arms flailing, and he plummeted thirty-five feet to the ground below where he landed squarely on his head with a heavy thud.

"Shit! Arden!"

They both stood in the doorway, looking down at the motionless body of Jack Waylon splayed over the barnyard.

"He sure as hell ain't moving," Ben said.

"Hell no, Ben. He can't. He's probably dead."

They raced down the ladder by the stalls and out of the barn at the other end. Arden rolled Jack over onto his back. His eyes were wide open but deathly still. His neck was bent at an odd angle, and blood ran from his mouth. Arden leaned forward to hold his wrist, but Jack had no pulse. He was gone.

"We better go get Myra and tell her Jack slipped out of the hay door." Arden couldn't help but smile. "One hell of a bad accident, wouldn't you agree?"

"Yeah, just like at the lumberyard," Ben replied, finally relieved.

Just then, however, Myra ran out of the farmhouse as she had heard Jack screaming.

"Oh, my God!" she cried.

"He's dead, Myra," Arden said. "No use in pining over him, now. He just wasn't worth it."

Chapter 34

BEYOND THE TRAIN station, Myra stood on the street corner and rain began pelting the pavement. Thunder broke in the distance, and she quickly opened her parasol. The spire of the steeple jutted up beyond the tall oaks, and she saw the First Methodist Church of Atlanta only blocks away. She hurried along the sidewalk to keep from getting soaked as she dodged other pedestrians on the way. The large suitcase was heavy, and she strained to carry it along the street by the oncoming traffic of cars and buses. When she approached the church, she noticed an elderly woman standing under the brick inset of the front door.

"Myra, is that you?" the woman asked as Myra came up the front steps, out of the rain.

The woman was a thin, gray-haired woman wearing a wool shift, a pale scarf over her head, and beads around her neck. She reached out to hug Myra, and the fresh scent of lavender soap came with her. Myra looked into her soft gray eyes and thought she might recognize her, but Myra had been only three years of age at the time, now twenty years in the past. The woman held her shoulders and pulled back to have a closer look.

"Myra Burns," she said.

"You are Sharon Ross, aren't you?"

"Your father would be so proud. I understand you have a little girl now named Cora."

Myra swiped a tear from her eye. She was so emotional and couldn't control her feelings. "Yes, she's two. She's growing up so quickly, but I left her behind at my farm in Flintside because she's too young to make a trip this far."

"Just think, you were only three when you made the trip down. And you were alone, weren't you?"

Myra had to think back. "Well I guess you are right, but I suppose I had to. Maybe for that reason I'm a little overprotective now."

"I can understand, Myra."

She said, "Let's get inside out of the weather for a minute." The woman took her and led her into the church vestibule where it was dry and quiet.

Inside, she paused, holding Myra's hand. "Yes, the last moment I saw you, you were getting on the train that morning for Americus to meet Jasper John Tucker."

"That was a lifetime ago. It's hard to believe so much time has gone by."

"But, it's a shame Jasper's older brother, Lester, passed away not long after you left Atlanta. He was a good man and found many homes for the indigent and orphaned at the Methodist Home for Children. We would have cherished a letter from you, but somehow the lines of communication were lost after Lester's death, until Jasper John located me. Lester was greatly loved, you know, by the church family."

"It is an honor though to come and meet with you. I look forward to what's in store. I've thought about this day for years."

She smiled. "I see you have your overnight bag."

"Yes, and I have some things to share with everyone."

They looked out of the clerestory windows to the street.

Sharon said, "The rain has slacked. Let's go. It is only a five minute walk. Hopefully the rain will hold off."

They departed the church and walked along the street. Traffic was congested and many people were lining the sidewalks in every direction. Glass-windowed storefronts were filled with groceries and clothing goods. Myra could smell the scent of cooking food from several restaurants along the way. Gas streetlights ran along the sidewalks, and streetcars came and went.

Soon they entered a side street among a row of small houses, some with nice plantings and trees, others having small fences against the road with gates leading up the stairs to their front doors. At one nicely maintained home, Sharon led Myra up the steps and knocked on the door, waiting patiently. An attractive middle-aged woman of fifty came and greeted them. She was a short brunette with stark blue eyes and a clear white complexion. Her hair was peppered gray and lines of age crossed her face.

"Myra?" the woman said. "It is good to finally see you again. My name is Carolina Shackelford. I knew and worked with your mother, Clara McCarter Burns, years ago at the Worthington Textile Mill here in Atlanta."

"Thank you for having me." She smiled.

"Why don't you have a seat so we can talk? I'll get some cake and coffee, how would that be?"

She soon returned and sat across a small table from them. While enjoying their refreshments, she said, "My husband, Martin, travels a good bit and he's out of town right now. So we have the place to ourselves."

Myra said, "Tell me about you."

"Well, I started working at the Worthington mill many years ago. I worked in the yarn and fabric spinning mill for about five years until Mr. Johnson promoted me to the position of purchasing agent under the mill vice-president. Of course Clara, your mother, worked in the dye processing mill with all of the chemicals, and that is when the sickness began. Your father, Willis, was a maintenance supervisor, so the textile factory is where the two met and began their courtship. Clara and I remained friends until her death. But she didn't become seriously ill until a few years after leaving the mill for other work —actually just a year or two after having you. Many of the other employees in the dye mill were becoming sick, too. I was fortunate. I was on the other side in the finished spinning department, and I soon transferred up into the front office. Now there are unprecedented legal cases being brought against Worthington for what is being termed as 'industrial toxic waste'. I'm so sorry you lost both of your parents to that. Since then, your sisters have both married and moved out of state. Marsha has moved to Illinois and Carla to California. I'll give you their addresses so you can write them."

When Myra had contacted Sharon Ross through Jasper John, she discovered more of her past and that she indeed had had two older sisters. This she had discovered before her trip to Atlanta. But she was elated having been told of a photograph that remained of her family.

"Would you show me the photograph? I've dreamed of this for months."

Sharon said, "We were very lucky to have found it in Pastor Lester's memoirs and things. It took a while but here it is."

Carolina stepped away to a cabinet and returned by Myra with a blurred black and white photo dated 1912 of the Willis Burns family: Willis, mother Clara, Marsha, Carla, and Myra. The composition of the photo portrayed the five sitting on the stoop of a small, dilapidated house. Myra was in her mother's lap, a ribbon tied in her hair. The family was side by side, closely tucked together. Her father sat in the center, and his long arms embraced the whole family. Willis had such a genuine smile on his face. So, Myra smiled, too, feeling hot tears streaming down her face. Myra was taken and entranced by this moment, and she couldn't restrain herself. Sharon softly patted her back when she sobbed.

Myra saw the resemblances between her, her sisters, and her mother, their graceful, slender lines with high cheek bones and striking eyes. In the picture her mother appeared to be laughing and Myra laughed too, wiping more tears away.

Carolina said, "Your mother originally came from a place in north Georgia. A place called Fort Mountain outside of Chatsworth. You also have an uncle, her younger brother, a man by the name of Silas McCarter that was a bestselling author and an award winning novelist. One of his novels was named *Down from the Mountain*. That was his autobiography of their lives on Fort Mountain."

Carolina took the dishes to the kitchen. Myra and Sharon exchanged smiles.

When Carolina returned from the kitchen, Sharon said, "Of course, your father stayed with me until his death after your mother died. He was vilely sick and had lost his job, but he had nowhere else to live after he was evicted from his rental house. As it happened, I was your parent's neighbor, and I was also a member of the Methodist church where Lester was the preacher. Your father loved your mother and you three. He was a good man. But he died slowly and he finally passed away the day after Easter Sunday. Marsha and Carla went to live with a family in Birmingham, Alabama, but they only had room enough for two. So, we found a home for you with Jasper John and then Mr. Grayson. Not long after you left, Lester died unexpectedly. Then a few years ago, I miraculously received a letter from Jasper John. I was elated. He had located me through the Methodist church. And that is how it came to be we have met today."

Carolina asked Myra, "I understand that you recently lost your husband. That is so tragic, Myra. Tell us about your life in south Georgia."

"Of course, I was orphaned seventeen years ago. Maclin and Ila Mae adopted me informally. In other words there were never any legal papers drawn up or agreements signed. I just became one of theirs and

I loved them both dearly. A few years ago, Mac suffered an accident in the lumberyard while loading wood beams and was nearly paralyzed. Since then he has passed away." She looked off momentarily, thinking of it, how unfortunate it had been, not desiring to reveal the ugly truth to them, the realization that her late husband had attempted murdering her father out of greed.

Myra continued. "It seems my life is one disaster after another. After Maclin and Ila Mae died, I married a man named Jack Waylon, our close neighbor. He was an older man and we had little Cora. But following Cora's birth, Jack had a fatal farm accident and slipped out of the hayloft of our barn while doing maintenance work. My brother and a co-worker witnessed it. It was horrid. He broke his neck and I had to take over the farm."

She smiled. "My brother lives there now, with his wife too. Her name is Natalie. Her family was originally from Lee County. They moved away years ago so her father could take a job up north. But fortunately, they recently returned—luckily for Arden. Her father lost his job because they shut down the newspaper in Illinois where he was hired. My brother is happy though, and they plan to start a family soon."

Myra took out some old photographs to share with them. She showed them an old war medal they had inherited, a war medal given to her great grandfather following the War of 1812. She also withdrew from her case Nancy's Journal and a few poems written by Ila Mae including the Lee County Elegy. The two women were warmed by the memorabilia and looked over the photos of her family. They read a few of the poems and found them to be simply written yet with a soulful heart. Myra showed them her daughter's crucifix which she had brought on the trip for good luck, the one given to her by Ella Tucker at Cora's christening.

They went in Carolina's car and drove through the marshy slums of east Atlanta. Myra's childhood home was uninhabited and falling apart.

The streets were lined with silt from the earlier rain, and coloreds had overrun the neighborhood. As they drove, they watched in silence and saw the demise and destitution in the faces.

The Negro women were sitting on their front porches, living in lean-to shanties of patched slat board and peeling paint. They were smoking stover tobacco and boiling collard greens in large cast iron pots in their side yards; their pickaninnies like front porch monkeys swinging from the wooden railings and the arms of their chairs; little children barefoot and brown-eyed with milky smiles and timid faces. Endless clotheslines were strung from house to house and seemed to draw up the construct of their togetherness, bailing wire holding doors to their frames, and warped plank board undergirding their way of life. These homes certainly had no running water or electricity, and daylight could be seen glinting into one side and through the other.

The rutted road splashed with mud while the colored women watched as they drove past in silent stares; a world of desecration drifting by in a manner that can't be described with pen and paper as poverty can't simply be explained away in the chronicled bindings of history books. Poverty was written in their still eyes and grief was drawn on their weary faces.

As they went, Mrs. Ross pointed out her old home, too, where Myra's father had suffered such pain and had died. The place was vacant, the doors boarded up, and wild kudzu vine crawled across the roof and in through the broken windows. As Carolina turned the car out toward the city, they remained quiet. Black smoke bellowed from the stack of an industrial plant located next to the slash-rent housing district of post-enslaved Atlanta. And they could smell the foul stench as it wafted through the air.

Later that night, Myra took Sharon and Carolina out for dinner to a nice restaurant in the Hillary Hotel on Peachtree Street. After the meal, they perused the streets and window shopped, strolled through a women's boutique, passed a bar called The Commodity, and stepped into a jewelry store by the name of Wilson's to have a look around.

On the return trip to Carolina's, Myra asked, "So what else about my mother can you tell me? I know she came down from Fort Mountain to live in the city, but what more can you share?"

Carolina had to think back thirty years. She said, "Your mother ran away from Fort Mountain as a poor, pregnant teen. She traveled to a place called Stilesboro, Georgia to live with a woman named Bodeania Gilmore to raise her fatherless child there. But the child arrived stillborn, unable to endure the long trip from Fort Mountain. Unfortunately, Bodeania died of a sickness too, and Clara remained there for a while with her husband, Charles Gilmore, on their tremendously large and beautiful ranch until she came to Atlanta to attend Mercer University. She was actually one of the first women to attend the school, which certainly raised the hackles of some stodgy old men here in town, let me tell you that." She laughed.

Myra thought that in similar ways, she had experienced life much as her mother. Their circumstances were eerily comparable, both having had unplanned pregnancies then taking up residencies with older men on large stretches of land before finding themselves where they should be. Both being torn with their own circumstances to find a loving family in the end; like mother like daughter, she thought. Time comes full circle in the closing chapters of a storybook, and she was encouraged with her mother's life as it was much like her own. However she could hardly remember her, though at times she felt her presence and voice inside leading her by the light of day.

Chapter 35

SHE DROVE UP the hill to her farmhouse in a new 1934 Packard Twelve Victoria. It was a real gem, silver-white, with long graceful lines, a convertible top, and a stunning fabric interior. According to the salesman in Atlanta, this beauty held a twelve cylinder masterpiece with one hundred seventy-five monstrous horsepower and even more torque to boot. The supple ride of this car, he had informed her, was like taking a cruise up Lake Huron out of Detroit in a deep hull yacht a hundred feet long. The handling and suspension was deemed unprecedented in the industry along with the new adjustable shocks, synchro-mesh transmission, and hydraulic-assist brakes. Carolina Shackelford and Sharon Ross had been impressed when Myra pulled out of the dealer's showroom in this glorious beauty. When she drove home from Atlanta and came through Americus, people turned and stared in amazement. With a map in hand, she had negotiated the highways and backroads home to Flintside during the eight hour trip. But she was glad to get there to see her husband and baby.

As she pulled in, Bobby heard the rumble of the powerful engine and he came out of the house holding Cora. He was smiling from ear to ear when he saw the Packard. He couldn't believe his eyes.

"Mrs. Womack, you look well put together in that fine car."

She stepped out and took Cora, holding her tightly.

"Not too bad for a country girl," she replied, kissing him.

Bobby Womack was from modest means however he was a good man with his heart in the right places. He stood well over six foot and had the build of an athlete though he had honed his chops working construction, handling a rig and drilling for groundwater deep in the earth. He had sold his outfit to his partner Jamie Ellis and came to marry Myra on her land. Slowly but surely he was learning the cattle trade. They had had a few setbacks, had made some costly mistakes along the way, but they were working hard to put their lives together.

"This Packard set us back $1,250.00. You think I spent too much?" she asked.

"Good grace, Myra. I thought you were talking a Ford Coupe before you left on the train for Atlanta." He rounded the car and ran his hand along the sleek fenders. His dark hair blew in the breeze. He was so handsome she thought she might burst.

She added, "But it was my estimation that automobiles are difficult to sell in this economy. They were asking $2,500.00. I believe we got a good deal at the price I bargained for."

"Take us for a ride. I'm sure Cora here would love to fall asleep in that cushy backseat."

At that moment, they heard another car coming up the hill. A tan '28 Chevy National came into view, and Mr. Tullman waved out of the window as he parked behind the Packard.

"Myra. Nice car you're driving. Top of the line, she's a real glamour." He grinned, looking into the windows at the sumptuous interior and full instrument panel. He turned, holding a large thick envelope. "I have a few things for you two."

"What are they?"

"Your records," he said. "The reconstruction of the Lee County Courthouse has been completed. I have filed your property titles and new marriage certificate, as well."

Bobby took the envelope and looked inside.

"As the surveys stand, you now own the two hundred and eighty acres of Waylon's land, and you share fifty more with Cade and Arden. That totals three hundred and thirty acres. Because Jasper and I coerced Waylon into signing a nuptial contract before your wedding ceremony, getting the land into your name at the new courthouse after his accident was effortless. I don't believe Waylon even knew what he had signed because he was so anxious to get his hands on you. We implied the paper was a mere wedding license. But it was actually a marriage contract involving his assets. Signing under duress and without proper legal counsel? Maybe, but it doesn't matter now because he isn't here to contest.

"As for the McCarver property, when Cade relocated the boundary markers up the hill toward the old barn, that essentially became part of the Grayson property as there were no other records in the courthouse available to contradict the original acreage. So, the apple orchard is yours. The McCarvers had no children with claims. Now the probate court has accepted the new survey, and the county has assigned the remaining land to be sold at auction."

Bobby asked, "What, it must be another ten acres, right?"

"You could probably buy it and get a good deal as land is still cheap. But bide your time because when this economy recovers, property values will escalate quickly and you'll be sitting on a gold mine."

"You're suggesting that we buy the remaining ten acres? Maybe so, but we would have to talk about that." Myra looked at Bobby and he shrugged.

Bobby said, "Also the tree line this side of the orchard narrows down by the lakeshore. A little work with some extra hands and we could open the site line for a long view up the lake valley. That would be a premium vista up through there. It's beautiful."

"Beautiful. You're right," Mr. Tullman agreed.

Bobby slipped his hand around Myra's back.

She said, "I appreciate all you've done, Mr. Tullman. You have gone above and beyond. What do I owe you for your services?"

"Why nothing except some of your sweet molasses cookies, a cup of coffee, and a little conversation every now and then." He smiled.

"Come on in, Mister," she said teasingly. "I think we can set you up."

"Don't mind if I do," he replied jovially.

Myra walked Cora by her hand into the farmhouse, followed by Bobby and Mr. Tullman. The four went straight for the kitchen where Wynonna brewed a pot of coffee and took out the cookie jar. Wynonna was glad to have returned to the farm as she and Myra were not only workmates but good buddies. Myra couldn't decide if Wynonna was a sister, a mother, or a friend. Just good 'ol Wynonna was good enough, she figured and left it at that.

Myra told everyone about her trip and what she had discovered concerning her mother and father and their histories there. She told Bobby that the two women, Sharon Ross and Carolina Shackelford, had been very accommodating, and that she planned to return one day in the future with him.

Later a tap came at the door. Myra went and there stood Darlene Jenkins, the wife of Mr. Jenkins. Myra was surprised to see the estranged woman standing at her doorstep, one she hadn't passed ten words between in all of the years. Darlene was meekly dressed in a threadbare coat although it was warm out. Her canvas shoes were tatters of cloth with holes in them. She possessed an ashen complexion and brown age spots with a permanently applied expression of sadness crossing her face, apparently having led an unhappy life with such a foul man.

"May I come in, Myra?" she asked.

She held three letters in her hand as she entered. She said, "I saw you driving through town in that fine car out there, and I thought it was time I came out and had a word with you." She looked pained and she hesitated, but instead she reached out and handed Myra the letters.

Rather timidly, she said, "I have felt dreadful for a long time over this, but my husband is a vindictive man who hasn't a friend in the world. I thought you deserved an explanation."

Myra looked to see Cade's handwriting on the envelopes. It was his unmistakable block-style handwriting in all caps. The letters were made out to Myra Grayson.

"Myra, I'm sorry. These came on the mail truck a long piece back, but my husband hid them and refused to deliver them into your mailbox at the store. They've been under the checkout counter there for a while. I'm sorry if this has caused any pain. I'm real sorry."

Mr. Tullman stepped over and took one of the letters to study the postmark. He said, "Did you know that was illegal, a federal offense? You can't retain posted US mail from its recipient. That's a punishable crime, Mrs. Jenkins." He frowned which drew long wrinkles on his face.

She replied, "Well, I'm not sure about that. I just knowed it was wrong, either way and although late, I'm delivering 'em now. Without my husband's consent I must say. I'm likely to take a beating when he discovers this, what I done." She appeared to have missing teeth, a few incisors up front most likely from the backhand of her husband. She chewed her rubbery lips and smelled of chaw and a coal fire.

Darlene pointed to one particular letter Myra held. "This 'un here arrived just a few days ago." She added, "I didn't read any of it. I mean, *I can't read*, anyway."

Myra looked at the return address which stated Fort Bragg Army Base, Fayetteville, North Carolina.

"Oh my God! He's joined the army!"

She ripped open the envelope and gleaned it silently. She placed the letters on a side table for reading later, and she clasped her hands together. At that moment, she heard Arden and Natalie coming in from a horseback ride out on the property. She ran out on the front porch and yelled, "You two, get in here! I have some wonderful news!"

Arden and his wife quickly lashed their palominos to a hitching rack and came to the house. Other than cattle, they were also experimenting with horse breeding while enjoying an equestrian lifestyle. Myra had built a new barn with a modern design and all of the new conveniences. Arden especially liked dealing in horses and spent day and night caring for them.

When they came into the house, Arden asked, "Where did that limousine come from? Did you take that all the way from Atlanta? Where's the limo driver?" he asked, chiding her, a big grin on his face.

His wife, Natalie, was a petite woman of twenty-two with a studious appearance and a librarian's eyewear. She read book after book and had been educated in a college in Illinois. She asked Myra, "Beautiful car. How was Atlanta? I hope you had a nice visit."

"Natalie, it was wonderful. I'll tell you two about it later. For now, I have this."

She handed Arden the letter. He instantly noticed the return address. "Fort Bragg Army Base? He joined the army? That boy doesn't have enough discipline to tie his own shoe laces much less join the army!" he said, laughing vociferously. "He can't even get out of bed in the morning before noon!" They all laughed, Arden smiling the brightest.

"I bet he will now," Myra said.

"No later than four-thirty am, I bet you," Mr. Tullman added.

"That's not for me," Bobby said. "I'd have trouble eating the food, not after Myra's good cooking around here. I'm spoiled rotten."

Myra gave Bobby a shy smile and nudged his shoulder.

Bobby added, "No telling where they might ship him off to. Wherever, it will probably be far away from here."

Myra said, "Well, that's what trains and planes are for."

He laughed. "I'm game. Just tell me when and where."

They all laughed, Bobby laughing the loudest.

"Hey, let's cook up some supper. I've been on the road for eight hours since the break of dawn," Myra said to the group at large and gave Wynonna a wide smile.

Mrs. Jenkins stood sheepishly in the corner. She hung her head and went for the door but Myra tugged her arm. "Darlene, how do you like your sirloin steak? Medium-rare or well done?" Darlene lit up. "Medium is fine, please."

Just as Wynonna was putting the steaks onto fry, William took Myra out to the back porch for a personal chat. She was tired from her trip to Atlanta. First, the long drive to Americus, then the difficult train ride through all the stops and finally to the station in Atlanta. That in and of itself, had been tiring. Then there was the visit, driving through east Atlanta, eating out, shopping for her car, and the stressful drive back home.

They sat alone, across from one another at the plank board table. She looked at him wearily.

Mr. Tullman said, "Maclin would be proud of you, Myra."

He looked out over the rolling pastures and the fences that ran forever into the distance. Hundreds of cattle covered the landscape for as far as he could see. The new barn had been painted wine-red, and the yard fencing had been built tall with two gates, one at each end. The garden was flush with fresh vegetables and the pole beans were flourishing. Ripe tomatoes were ready for picking off the vine. Sunflowers stood six feet against the rail fence. White cotton lay over the rolling hills down by the lake, and the sun was setting to the west in colors of gold and yellow.

Myra turned to the old lawyer and said, "Life is good on the Womack Farm. Bobby's a good man, and he's going to take care of me and Cora. As a matter of fact, we discovered I'm pregnant."

"Congratulations, Myra, keep up the good work. I'd say you deserve it."

"Most of all, thank you for all you have done for my family." She clasped his hands. "We turned this house upside down, didn't we?"

"It wasn't easy locating that big brass key. I agree with you there."

"Finding that key was crucial, because I don't believe we could have blown opened that steel safe with ten sticks of dynamite."

"How he got that heavy safe up the stairs and into his office is beyond me. It must have taken eight men and a heavy wooden gurney-frame to support it."

"It still remains there, and we use it now to store our important papers, too."

"How much cash and gold coin did you find?"

"A lot, Mr. Tullman. We haven't even counted it all. One thing is for sure, Jack's father left him a great deal of money and property."

"No worries now because it is all yours, well you and Bobby both."

She patted his big hand, and he nodded his thanks also with a look of pride she seldom saw on his face because he was so modest.

Over the course of that year, Mr. Tullman appeared to have aged with his arthritic gait and slowing movements, his swollen hands and his tired face. Unexpectedly, the following month, he passed away in the comfort of his own bed. Myra and her family traveled to Birmingham in her Packard Victoria to meet his daughter and family for the first time where they lived in Mountain Brook. They all put him to rest on a lovely hillside next to his late wife, and Myra left red roses on his gravestone.

Weeks later, another letter arrived from Cade stating he was being shipped overseas to England, yet with the country once again expecting more difficulties in Europe. Myra prayed for Cade and wished him well, hoping to see him one day in the near future. However, the secret of his paternity was buried with Maclin and sealed on the lips of Jasper John, so Myra and Arden never discovered Jack was Cade's father.

She and Bobby watched the day end on most evenings from their farm on the hilltop. The sky was lined with cotton clouds cast by pink rays of the setting sun. Birds flew overhead and threw their winged-shadows on the days of their lives as they hoped they would always be free. The flatland of Lee County would forever be home, albeit she was from another family in a distant life she hardly understood.

When her second child was born, she took him and bathed him in the back porch trough in the pristine rainwater that had fallen the night before. She also promised herself to visit Fort Mountain one day to know of her mother's beginnings and where her kin had come from. From her newborn child, to a distant past called Fort Mountain, she could feel them in her bones. Myra was a southern girl with fire in her blood, and she took no prisoners when it came to dealing in terms of her heart. And this, she bred into her own children. She had gone through the world, and it had left marks on her. But she had traveled through life also and had left her own mark there too. Life was life and Myra had known both the benevolence and the iniquity of it all.

The day she and Bobby left Lee County to return to Atlanta for the burial of Sharon Ross, Cora was five and Robert, two. They had kept in touch over the years as Sharon was instrumental in locating Mac Grayson for Myra's placement as well as caring for her father in Atlanta when he had died of chemical poisoning.

The morning was fresh as Bobby drove up the highway toward Americus and Forsyth in the direction of the big city lights. Later in the day, the setting sun was just falling off the horizon when Myra saw it in the wisp of a cloud. It was the soul of Sharon Ross going to heaven to meet Ila Mae, Maclin, William Tullman, and Jasper John's brother, Lester. Myra was pleased, and she said a prayer for the departed just as Atlanta came into view through her glass windshield.

Made in the USA
Lexington, KY
09 August 2019